Praise for *Catch the Moments as They Fly*

Woven through *Catch the Moments as They Fly* is an almost Fitzgerald-like preoccupation with the corruptions and compromises of the culture of 'self-improvement' and social aspiration. Glasgow and Kilmarnock are much more than mere backdrops to the delicate web of human voices and fates in the novel: their own civic destinies, spanning two world wars and decades of aftermath, play a powerful and evocative part in this wonderfully vivid and moving portrait of the past.

Wayne Price,
author of *Mercy Seat*

Catch the Moments as They Fly is, simultaneously, an engrossing and affecting love story, a family saga, and a deft portrait of Scottish urban life in the wake of two world wars. Subtle, layered, and full of captivating historical detail as well as vividly drawn characters, this is a novel to get lost in. Absolutely compelling.

Jane McKie,
author of *Carnation Lily Lily Rose*

Praise for Zoë Strachan

Negative Space

A perfect eye for the small detail... Intimate and real.
Scarlett Thomas, *Independent on Sunday*

A powerful portrayal of grief.

The Scotsman

Spin Cycle

Pitch-perfect, intelligent construction, unrelenting tension and a redemptive flourish of an ending.

The Big Issue

The tension never dips, the dialogue is perfect. A must read.

Daily Record

Strachan breathes life into her characters and settings, and there's a warmth to her prose which suffuses reading about them with a sense of intimacy.

Glasgow Herald

Ever Fallen in Love

The novel excels at evoking the mind games, the vile but subtly plotted erosion which one driven friend can exert on another... astute, intelligent, almost entirely convincing.

Tom Adair, *The Scotsman*

Strachan sustains strong undercurrents of menace and regret... The fug of student common rooms and bars is expertly conveyed, alongside the clean-washed emptiness of the coast.

Chris Ross, *Guardian*

Ever Fallen in Love doesn't disappoint. Unafraid of the unspoken and the unresolved, the story gets under your skin and lingers there uncomfortably.

Lucy Scholes, *Sunday Times*

There is no doubt this is a hard-boiled book and it pulls no punches. Strachan writes in great detail about the psychology of her protagonists with objectivity and perception. The incredible trick she pulls off is that we do end up identifying with her introverted hero Richard, mainly because his journey is so complex and constantly blighted by his hopeless sexual obsession with the straight, taunting, malignant Luke.

Alice Thompson, *Scottish Review of Books*

Catch the Moments as They Fly

ZOË STRACHAN

A Blackwater Press book

First published in the United States of America by
Blackwater Press, LLC

Copyright © Zoë Strachan, 2023

All rights reserved. No part of this publication may be reproduced, stored in a retrieval system, or transmitted, in any form or by any means, electronic, mechanical, photocopying, recording or otherwise, without the prior permission of the publishers.

Library of Congress Control Number: 2023940691

ISBN: 9781963614220

Cover design by Eilidh Muldoon

Blackwater Press
120 Capitol Street
Charleston, WV 25301
United States

blackwaterpress.com

For David Miller

VIRTUTE ET INDUSTRIA

motto of the Burgh of Kilmarnock

Here's a bottle and an honest friend!
What wad ye wish for mair, man?
Wha kens, before his life may end,
What his share may be of care, man.

Then catch the moments as they fly,
And use them as ye ought, man:
Believe me, happiness is shy,
And comes not ay when sought, man.

        Robert Burns

The 1930s

Rena, 1936

Today Rena is going to change her life. The thought lights something inside her and for a second she imagines a future in which she'll recall this day like a scene from a motion picture: bags being packed, doors slamming, cold words spoken clear and hard. Usually when she wakes up her anger has faded and she starts her day resigned, more than a little resentful, but not today. This morning she clings to that flutter in her tummy that tells her *this is it, I've had it up to here, this is it*.

With the fiery pulse of rage spurring every footstep, every movement of her hands, Rena looks in on her mother, who shrinks under the covers and mumbles that she's going to have a long lie on account of a headache. Little wonder, after last night. Rena's father is not home, thank the Lord. He stormed out, temper and all, and usually when that happens he's gone until teatime the next day. Rena assumes he stays up in town, although she has no inkling of where. She gets Jamie up and dressed and takes him downstairs for his breakfast. Once his egg is in front of him, chopped up with butter in the little blue bowl, she makes tea for her mother, checking around as she does so to make sure there's nothing at Jamie's height for him to get into mischief with. He's a good quiet child, but the last thing she needs is for him to wrap his chubby paw around the bread knife, or a box of matches.

'Finish your breakfast,' she tells him. 'And don't move from there.'

She summons as much authority into her voice as she can and it works: her little brother looks at her wide-eyed and fearful. She stands for a moment and slowly, still watching her, he spoons some egg into his mouth. A fleck of yolk falls onto the handkerchief she has tied round his neck.

'Good,' she says.

After delivering the tea she marches along to Thomas's room, bangs on the door and walks in without waiting. He sits up in bed, bleary, dark hair falling in a cow's lick over his forehead.

'You'll need to look after Jamie today,' she tells him. 'And check those cuts on ma's head. I combed the glass out of her hair and there's only scratches, but have a look at that lump. If she feels bad we'll need to do something.'

'But I'm playing in the match this afternoon.' He rubs his eyes. 'What's happening anyway? Are you not going to school?'

'No, I am not.' Rena lowers her voice. 'I was lying awake all night thinking and I'm putting an end to it.'

'To school?' he says, a smile creeping across his face.

'Don't be a dafty.' She takes a deep breath. 'Thomas, I'm going to do what I said.'

He pulls his blanket up to his chin. 'Last night was bad.'

'And if it gets worse?'

Thomas looks towards the open door of his bedroom.

'Oh don't bother, she can't hear us. What will Bandy Sanderson do if you aren't there?'

'Come and get me,' Thomas says. 'Probably. He went round and dragged Wullie McGee out of his scratcher for the semi-finals. That's how we all ended up with the German measles.' He scratches behind his ear, as if at the memory.

'All right then, you'd better go. But wake her when you go out.' *Just do something*, Rena is thinking; *You're the oldest and I'm the one making all the decisions, all you have to do is mind your wee brother*. 'Or leave him with Mrs Skilling next door. Write a note and Ma can collect him later.'

Thomas looks pained. 'Can't you do it? I don't like Mrs Skilling.'

'Nobody likes Mrs Skilling. Just ignore her when she starts prying. Curiosity killed the cat.'

'Aye and imagine the look on her face if I said that to her,' Thomas says, and they both smile. 'Seriously though, what about the window?'

'Oh, bugger the window,' she says, and then claps her hand over her mouth, astonished that one of her father's words has escaped her lips.

Thomas grins and swings his legs out of bed. 'All right then,' he says, standing up. 'Good luck.'

Rena goes to her room where she finishes dressing in her smart, sober clothes: her skirt with the large pleats, her good blouse, the black wool belted jacket. She pins her cameo brooch at the neck, as if she's going to church or visiting. Tucked away at the back of her drawer, under her handkerchiefs and scarves, is a manicure set in a leather case. She unfastens it and looks inside. Money, slowly and carefully pilfered from her father's wallet, ever since she overheard her aunts telling her mother that she didn't have to put up with it, that she could leave. Hetty flustered, stuttering. *But, but he...* until finally she got her words out: *No. The children*. So, a penny here and there, Rena took, nothing he'd notice. Needs must, she told herself, and she's been proven right. If the devil wasn't driving before, he is now.

She counts it, then counts it again as she puts it into her own coin purse, even though she has known for a fortnight that there's enough to get her to town. She made her decision last night. Not when the dining room window shattered, not when her father grabbed his hat and slammed the front door behind him, not even while she dabbed peroxide on the cuts on her mother's scalp. No, Rena made up her mind when she was crawling around the floor with dustpan and brush, picking up every last shard of glass so that Jamie couldn't hurt himself on it. She ties the laces on her shoes and surveys herself in the mirror one last time to check she's respectable. The set of her eyes looks older than her fifteen years and her skin is as pale as an invalid's, but respectable she is, for now.

As the train crawls across the bridge and into the station Rena looks at the river stretching out below her. The air is sooty and grey but she can see motor cars and buses crossing the Clyde, and beyond that people on the suspension bridge, a man and woman pausing halfway across, to look up at the train perhaps, while working folk pass them by, running errands and marching to appointments in the vast warehouses and terraces that edge the water. She pictures herself for a moment, living amidst all that bustle, and tries not to think of her father's laugh as he said that he would never let her mother take his children from him. In the distance, beyond the flatness of the Green, she can see factory chimneys, tall and tireless. At last the train slows to a halt. As she alights on to the platform the ticket collector says something she doesn't quite pick up. His smile has a cast to it that she doesn't like and she walks by, hurrying ahead in case anyone from the village got on without her noticing. She isn't sure if her pilfered cash will allow her a tram – she doesn't know what tram rides cost – but it can't be more than a couple of miles to Nell's, if she can find her way. She pulls her satchel closer to her side and crosses the main concourse. The glass roof is murky overhead and the light spills through in uneven rays, hitting the gilded lettering of signs that point towards the coffee lounges and bars of the Central Hotel, the entrance to Lewis's department store. A flicker of memory stirs at that, but she bats it away and walks on, through the main exit and past a man in a sandwich board advertising a sale of railway lost property, *Including Furs*. Then she is out into the city. A new world in which there are people careless, or carefree, enough to leave furs on trains.

As it happens the walk is unnecessary. Rena has enough money for the tram that will take her within spitting distance of Nell's flat. A uniformed nursemaid with a huge Silver Cross pram offers advice on routes without being asked. Rena is conveyed – standing at first, and then perched on a single seat by the window – past cinemas and theatres and stores. Policemen stop the traffic and usher the tram through intersections, as if the law is on her side for once. At Charing Cross she sees the soar of the Grand Hotel, imagines for a split second her aunts taking her and her mother and brothers there to check in. A refuge, a place to be looked after. The terraces of the west end are black with soot but the tearooms and tobacconists play host to streams of ladies with short hemlines and gentlemen (and less gentlemanly types) in smart suits. By the time they reach Nell's neighbourhood the streets are more subdued, the pedestrians fewer. The driver turns to call out her stop, and she hurries after the other few passengers disembarking at Clarence Drive. She stands at the side of the pavement and checks Nell's address for the fifth time that day. She's been driven by anger and the momentum of the journey, but now uncertainty creeps in. Her plan didn't extend beyond getting to her Aunt Nell, the nearest of her mother's three sisters, and now she can only be five minutes away. A whisper at the back of her head reminds her that Nell lives in a bedsitter. She takes in sewing, and Margaret still nurses, and Min works in her antique shop. If money is the way out of this, Rena can't see where it will be found.

Nell's building is grand, the end of a terrace of townhouses with parapeted windows and steps leading up to the front door. But the gardens are tangled, the stucco grimy and peeling, and when, cautiously, Rena climbs the steps to the columned front door she realises that although Nell lives at 20A, nothing says A. She goes back down to the pavement and looks again at the building, notices flagstones leading to a smaller door and the basement flat. Here are A and B, and a bell pull which creaks painfully. Rena waits, then rings again. Nell isn't in. Why had Rena not thought of that? Her money won't extend to a cup of tea and a bun in the bakery she walked past earlier, not if she's to get home again, and loitering in the church across the road doesn't appeal. There's nothing for it but to lay out her handkerchief on Nell's narrow step and sit down, praying she won't get piles from the cold stone. Thank heavens it is the basement, tucked out of sight. Someone would move Rena on, surely, if she was sitting on the front steps between those stone balustrades. Bells ring faintly from somewhere and a passer-by checks his watch. Rena's stomach grumbles in recognition of lunchtime. Her father might decide to come home from work tonight, remorseful or otherwise, and if he does she'll need to be there. By five fifteen at the latest, in case he leaves early. She can wait another two and half hours for Nell. She has to speak to her in person, privately; who knows how long it would take to chore the money for a telegram, and the village postmistress would see every word. Her stomach rumbles again and she takes a deep breath. *What in God's name were you thinking of, Irene Lennox?* But no. She can't afford to let doubt in, not for an instant. Nell will come home, and she will sort everything out.

And so she does. Like a tweed-clad whirlwind. All Rena's prepared speeches go out the window and all she says, all she needs to say, when Nell finds her niece sitting on her doorstep like a tyke is:

'If we don't do something he's going to kill her.'

Within minutes tea has been made, sewing work put away, soup heated on the hotplate, and Nell is prising the lid from a tin moneybox and hurrying upstairs to the telephone cabinet to call the other aunts, Min and Margaret. Rena eats her soup slowly, revelling in the sensation of being looked after while recognising that those few words – *if we don't do something he's going to kill her* – can never be taken back. Whatever she has done is irreversible, not just for her but for Thomas and Jamie too.

By the time Nell returns a plan has been set in motion, to which Rena must acquiesce, although that voice in her head is shouting at her now for her stupidity, for not realising the way things are between men and women, for not accepting that perhaps her mother has brought some of this on herself. And then at last, when a car door slamming outside heralds the arrival of Min, Nell lays her hand on Rena's shoulder and says, 'You did the right thing, pet. It's time to put a stop to it.'

Rena, 1937

They couldn't stay in the village. Rena supposes she knew that's how it would pan out, but ever since she arrived on Nell's doorstep that day she had been imagining the city, the big and bustling city through which she'd ridden on a tram and walked alone. But the city is expensive and it's where her father works so here she is, lying awake in the same bed as her mother in a rented flat in a red sandstone terrace in a town miles away. Miles from the family who have drawn together and got her mother out of that house and that marriage, and miles from the shame of divorce. 'If it's good enough for Mrs Simpson it's good enough for our Henrietta,' Nell said, but even her sisters thought it bad taste, what with bunting everywhere for the coronation of the new, and presumably better, king. Min and Margaret must have been formidable in the war because they had no trouble driving to evacuate a woman and her three children while her husband was at his office. Rena had their belongings packed and ready to go, the aunts arrived at two on the dot, and the entire operation lasted no more than a quarter of an hour. 'No ifs and no buts, Hetty.' No time to glance backwards at the big stone house sitting back from the road, nor to wave at old Skilling looking out from her doorstep. 'Neb bothering you, is it?' Nell called over, much to Rena's delight.

Hetty begins to snore, and Rena screws up her eyes and tells herself that she did the right thing. *Remember Irene, whatever it takes.* That's what Nell had said, and that's what Rena did. A lie in the place of a truth, tit for tat. Adultery trumps battery. The judge had perked up then, seeing a chance to be finished in time for lunch. And Rena had been good, she knew that, standing there in front of all these people and agreeing that yes, she had seen her father with other women, and when her mother confronted him, that's when he hit her. Her lip trembled as she spoke, and she hoped it looked like upset rather than rage.

Min's husband Donald spotted the For Sale sign going up on the shop when he was on his way back from the auction house at Ayr, and after sticking his head around the door, shaking hands, and handing over all his auction cash as a deposit up front, the sign came straight back down. A newsagent and tobacconist, it sits on the main road and does a trade in confectionery and drinks as well. Hetty has never worked before, but it'll keep her from brooding and she'll have Rena and Thomas to help her. They're young and adaptable, and there's no point in him going to a new school now, at his age. As for Rena, well, she got them into this so no leaving certificate for her either. Her father's lawyer and accountant prevaricated over the settlement but it has paid off the shop, more or less. A mortgage or a tenancy in one of the new council houses they're building is out of the question; too much prying into background and circumstances, and Thomas isn't old enough to sign for anything.

At least the flat is only a few minutes from the shop, which will make the early starts easier. It isn't so bad; Min has come up trumps with furniture from auction houses, Nell got hold of bedlinen, and Margaret's covering the hire purchase of a new gas cooker. 'Enjoy it Irene, because that'll be your inheritance spent.' Rena stares up at the ceiling, the plain cornice so different from the plasterwork foliage that crowned the rooms in her father's villa. They'll be glad of that cooker; she has plans. If people come to the shop for morning rolls, then surely they might be tempted to a pancake or crumpet too? And her mother can bake; it was never her scones that set Rena's father off.

Lying there awake Rena wonders if he's sad that he won't see them again. He let his temper show in the courtroom, and for once it did them more good than harm. She knows he'll be too proud to come and look for them. 'Good riddance to bad rubbish,' he was heard to mutter. Even Uncle Donald said that showed what kind of a man he was, and Donald is not given to venturing opinions when faced by the full phalanx of Jarvie sisters. What would Rena have done, without her aunts? Thomas wasn't big enough to stand up to his father, and the only time he tried he got a broken rib and a black eye for his trouble. Rena shifts herself gradually onto her side, trying not to wake her mother. Let bygones be bygones, they say, but the past isn't meekly left behind. It pops into your head when you could do without it, and Rena knows already that all its ignominies are better folded up and tucked in a box, to be buried somewhere with no X to mark the spot. The future is what counts, and even as she lies awake she feels it rushing up to her. A future that will begin in just a couple of hours when she and Thomas will go to open up their new business.

'So what've you to remember, Ma?' Thomas says, as he and Rena gulp down cups of tea and get ready to leave. Neither of them say it, but they're both aware that this is likely the first time Hetty has been left alone since she was removed from the marital home.

'Your husband's dead,' Rena chips in. 'You're a widow. It was the flu. Very sad.'

'My husband's dead,' Hetty echoes. 'I'm a widow.'

'And what name do you go by?' Thomas prompts her again.

'Mrs Jarvie.'

'That's it,' Rena says. 'Forget your married name. We're all Jarvies again now. Remember that when you register Jamie at the school.'

Hetty puts an egg on to boil for Jamie, going to the wrong cupboard for the pan at first. It's only September but she's swathed in a burgundy belted cardigan-jacket that Nell knitted for her, as if insulating herself from the flat, from her new life in Kilmarnock. 'Five years old already,' she says, with a sniff. 'And fatherless…'

'Still my baby brother,' Rena says, taking a deep breath and chucking him under the chin. It's been months of planning and sleeping on couches and in spare rooms, of seeing solicitors and attending court hearings. Her mother could be grateful. 'And there's still some unpacking to do, you know, if you feel like keeping busy.'

'And then come straight to the shop and we'll show you how well we're doing,' Thomas says, and wraps Hetty in a big embrace that brings a smile to her worried face.

'You're such a good boy, Thomas,' she says. 'I don't know what I'd do without you.' There's just enough time for Rena to feel hurt before Hetty adds, 'And you too Rena, of course. My big girl.'

They pause outside the flat while Thomas fumbles in his pockets and brings out a packet of cigarettes. Across the road there's a dead end, leading to the gate of a big house that overlooks the park. Much larger than the house they left behind. It must have some view, Rena thinks. She can hear the squabbling of rooks in the trees nearby.

'Since when do you smoke?' she says.

'Since Donald kept offering me when we were out moving furniture together. Though I'd tried before at school, mind.'

'Had you now?' Rena says. 'Donald did well to put up with us all, didn't he?'

'Min has him under the thumb,' Thomas says, puffing away and speaking as though he's an expert on marriage.

Rena suppresses a smile. Her brother is trying to grow up too, thank the Lord. 'Don't be mean,' she says. 'He was quick enough to help us, wasn't he?'

'Aye, he was.'

'Aren't you going to give me one?'

'I didn't think…'

'Oh go on, there's no one to see.'

Thomas lights the cigarette for her and she coughs, sticks out her tongue in disgust.

'It'll get better,' he says. 'You just need to keep trying.'

She nods, tries another puff. 'Mum blames me, doesn't she?'

'What do you mean?'

'For us ending up here. I did what I had to, didn't I,

Thomas? Even if she won't forgive me for it.'

Thomas puts his arm around her shoulders. He's had a growth spurt and is head and shoulders above her now. 'Course you did, sis. Don't get worked up about it. The old bastard would've killed her one day, and then how would you feel?'

Rena nods. 'Look,' she says. They're almost at the shop and sure enough, there's a sack of morning rolls looped over the door handle as promised, and newspapers tied up in bundles outside.

Thomas stops, although she has the keys in her hand. 'If I could have been more, well, maybe…'

'No,' she says. 'No, I won't hear it. He might have killed her, but he would have killed you. So don't ever say that.'

They take the grilles off the windows and unlock the door. They've been in before to check the stock but it seems pokier now. Two of the walls are shelved for dry goods and tins and there's a wooden counter and a glass cabinet for dairy and meat, not that they've any meat to sell yet. Rena sweeps the linoleum floor (she did it the day before, yet somehow it's dusty again) and Thomas unparcels the papers and puts them in the rack. It's dull, and grim, and early, but neither of them complains. It'll be worse in winter.

'I make it one minute to the hour,' Thomas says after a while. He goes to the door and draws back the bolt. 'Come on, we should do it together, for luck.'

Rena looks at her watch. 'Shall we make a wish?' she says, joining him.

'I'll tell you what I wish…'

'No don't, then it won't come true.'

They count down from three and with one hand each

turn the sign on the door from *Closed* to *Open*. As they do so Rena's wish is that that this won't be forever, that things will get better and that they won't have to pay all their lives for their temerity in not putting up with the way things were. That she'll have a bed of her own once again, and new clothes to wear. Her father liked them well turned out; if it was his intention to spoil them for what the future held, it worked.

Their first customer comes in at two minutes past, and they soon discover that the newspapers that should have been kept aside haven't been. Rena smiles and smiles and apologises and makes a list of who takes *The Bulletin*, *The Glasgow Herald*, *The Times*. She's still getting to grips with all the local papers. By eight they're both searching for Pall Mall, Black Cat, Craven A and rolling papers, in between climbing the small step ladder for tins of ham and evaporated milk.

'Bit young for it, aren't you?' a man says to Rena as Thomas makes his third attempt at weighing out two and fourpence of tea.

'It's our mother who'll be running it,' Rena says, smiling blandly towards the flour and sugar.

'She's just taking our younger brother to school,' Thomas adds.

Once the man has gone Rena whispers, 'No need for everyone to know our business,' but before Thomas can reply two women come in for newspapers and barley sugars and there's no avoiding their questions.

'And where is it you're from?' one asks. 'The city, is it?'

'That's right,' Thomas says. 'The other side of the city.'

'I always thought the Boyles would sell to someone local.' She glances at her friend. 'That'll be them gone back to Dalmellington now he's retired.'

'Aye.' The other woman draws out her vowels, as if going back to Dalmellington is no more than the previous proprietor deserves. 'I heard a woman was taking it on.'

'Our mother.' Rena tries to keep her smile pinned in place.

'Our father's dead,' Thomas chimes in.

'And you've come all the way here,' the first woman says, leaning over the counter to squint at the price labels that are pinned to the shelves. They're the same ones that Mr Boyle left behind him; Rena and Thomas know better than to put anything up when they're just through the door. The woman purses her lips. 'Do you ken folk in the town then?'

'Not really,' Rena says. 'But we're settling here. A change for our mother, you know.' The women look unconvinced, somehow, and she adds, quickly, 'Do you take a newspaper? Do you need it put aside? We're still working things out.'

'Aye, well. We'll look forward to seeing your mother when she's here. Jarvie, is that a Catholic name?'

'Not that I'm aware.' Rena sees that Thomas is trying not to laugh and it cheers her up enough to stay bright and breezy until the women have paid and gone.

'Might as well have taken out an advertisement on those billboards next door,' Thomas says. 'Because I'm guessing that pair are the bush telegraph.'

'They did rather put us through it, didn't they? Reminds me of old Skilling in West Kilbride.'

They fall into silence for a second, then she reaches out and takes Thomas's arm. 'We're going to be all right here, Thomas, aren't we?'

'Course we are, sis. We're some team.'

By nine o'clock the news has travelled. *I hear you've come from the city. I hear your mother has moved in to Beansburn. I hear…*

'Why do folk have to be so nosy?' Rena hisses, when the tinkle of the bell fades behind three park-keepers after rolling tobacco and the shop is empty. 'Why can't they just say hello, or I hope you're settling in, or isn't it mild for this time of year, and get on with it?'

'Good thing we were here first,' Thomas says. 'Get the third degree now and then Ma will never have to answer a question about where she's from or why she's here.'

'I hope so,' Rena says. 'And I hope to God she's keeping up the widow story for the school. Now, open the till and let's have a look.'

'Not so dusty,' Thomas says, as they peer in the cash drawer.

'We've got to keep buying all this though,' Rena sweeps her hand towards the shelves behind them. 'The sitting stock will only last us so long and we'll need to keep on top of things.'

They manage the weights and the till well enough, and although Thomas messes up the change once, he's apologetic and charming enough for the woman to laugh and wait until he counts it out again.

'I'm just pleased you still have rolls,' she says. 'Sometimes I'm too late and they've all gone.'

'Really?' Rena says, her mind working fast. 'Well, we can deliver, if you like. It would only be a small extra charge.'

She makes a careful note of the woman's address and how many rolls she'd like each morning. When the customer has gone Thomas says, 'What are you thinking Rena? How will we do that?'

Rena sighs and leans on the counter for a second. Her legs are tired already from standing and there's flour all down her front. She hadn't wanted to wear an apron but she'll have to. Thomas is already in a blue overall coat, presumably left by Mr Boyle.

'There are four of us who need a living from this place,' she says. 'So you're going to have to check your bike for punctures, because one of us will be out on it tomorrow morning.'

Bobby, 1939

Bobby feels as if the cobbles are listing under his feet but he's on dry land now, it's just his body hasn't caught up with his brain. Usually it's the other way around. The sky and the river are grey, as grey as the belly of a ship, and a fine mist blurs the buildings. The air smells like home, and the accents that ring through it are broad and familiar. *Well, Bobby Young, you did it.* He was cocky, sure, thinking the city couldn't hold him, but he did it, didn't he? Went all the way across the Atlantic and back. Liverpool, Labrador, Boston. Further than his mother and sister and anybody else in his miserable excuse for a family thought he could, further than any of them ever have, and he has his steward's wages to prove it. He'll be damned if he's heading straight back to them in Uddingston, no matter what promises he made when he was so seasick he thought he'd rather die than suffer another minute of it. No, he'll go to the Broomielaw and the Seaman's Home, and he'll think on his life and what he wants to do with it. The world's a bigger place than his family would have him imagine.

A commotion near the Lascar conveniences at the Queen's Dock draws him over, and he puts his kitbag between his feet. Down on the deck of a steamer two men have set terriers after a rat. There's a chorus of cheers and groans when it's caught, according to who's been lucky and who has lost their money. A man nudges Bobby in the ribs, 'I could kiss that Bessie-dug,' he says. 'She's just won me ten bob.'

'Last one, last one.' A third Lascar is taking bets and Bobby elbows his way forward, just for the fun of it, and puts a few pennies on Bessie to do it again. Her tawny face is smeared with blood and she's wriggling against her collar, which is held tight by one of the men on deck, while the white and brown dog to his left is still.

'Three, two, one,' shouts the man running the book, and one of his friends on deck shakes a sack and a rat springs free. Less than a second later his companion releases Bessie and the other dog, who hare after it to cheers from the spectators on the wharf. For a second Bobby thinks Bessie's going to do it, but the white and brown terrier beats her, seizing the rat by the throat and giving it two sharp, efficient shakes. Ah well, that'll teach him to gamble his hard-won money.

'Could have used a dog like that on the *Euryades*,' says a voice behind him. Big Jens, one of the Norwegian boys, in mufti in a heavy knit sweater and donkey jacket.

'Aye, you're not wrong there,' Bobby says. 'Headed to the Home?'

Jens nods. There's a splash as one of the Lascars throws the dead rat over the side, and the crowd disperses. 'But I have been out long enough to get thirsty.'

As soon as Jens says it Bobby feels it. A surge of excitement – he made it back! – and yes, a raging thirst. So what if the sun isn't over the yardarm. So what if it had taken him weeks to get used to his ration and nothing more. Jens isn't a bad sort, and in his own gruff way he was kind to Bobby when they hit the big swells and he started vomiting and praying to a God he was fairly sure didn't exist. Fetched him a pail, a wet cloth and a tot of rum, never joined in with the jibes. 'We were all there once, Bobby, and some don't like to remember it.' It turned out there was a difference between the Firth of Clyde and the middle of the fucking ocean. As they walk along to the Broomielaw and the Double Six, the stench of manure mingles with something frying in one of the quayside restaurants. Bobby feels the cobbles getting firmer underfoot. The rain might be pelting down but he's on dry land again. Jens mutters something about being more likely to drown in Glasgow than at sea.

'You should come to Norway, Bobby,' he says. 'Less rain. Better money.'

'Love to, but I don't speak the lingo.'

'You don't have to speak at all. Isn't that why we go to sea? To do as we are told. Like a marriage.'

'To a different ship each time?'

Jens laughs and pats him on the back, pushing him towards the doors of the Double Six. 'That's my kind of marriage. Tire of one, get on board another.'

And if she goes down, you go with her. Bobby doesn't say it out loud though, because Jens has the barman pouring them whisky and a chaser, and he's telling a story about somewhere on the other side of the world where you have to marry the girls to sleep with them, but it's all right because it's only temporary and they've got a fellow right there, sort of a priest, who makes sure it's all kosher. And before long Bobby is buying another round and telling Jens in all seriousness that the *Euryades* saved his life, and she's the only woman for him. He deserves to kick back a bit, doesn't he? He thought the sickness would kill him and he survived. That's a sign.

There's a ripple around the bar room, a lot of wheeshting and shushing, as the barman brings a radio up on to the counter. He turns up the volume until a familiar voice can be heard. At first Bobby doesn't get it... *the maintenance of the life of the people – in factories, in transport, in public utility concerns, or in the supply of other necessaries of life. If so, it is of vital importance that you should carry on with your jobs...* and then it becomes as clear as day: *It is the evil things that we shall be fighting against – brute force, bad faith, injustice, oppression and persecution – and against them I am certain that the right will prevail.*

Bloody Hell. There he was congratulating himself when he's only gone and joined the Merchant Navy in time for a war.

Anyone who has a home in the city leaves and goes back to it, and the mood dips but only temporarily. The Chinese chaps in the corner are soon engrossed in their game of mahjong again. Bobby spots two of the cooks from the *Euryades*, placing their bets. Other than that, those left in the Double Six have nothing better to do than keep drinking, because who knows what tomorrow will hold. Apart from Jens, who has his plan worked out, and how's Bobby to tell if it's a good one?

'I will be outside the pool when it opens in the morning, and I am signing for the longest trip as is possible, as far from Europe as is possible. Panama. The Cape. New Zealand. If you are a wise man, Bobby, you will do the same.'

'I don't know,' Bobby says, because he has no idea if

he's a wise man and at the same time he can hear other voices, loud-mouthed lads who're going to get themselves onto a battleship toot suite to fight for King and country. Better not make any decisions tonight, better to leave Jens behind and tag along with Paddy the donkeyman and his new pal Conor as they wind their way between the warehouses and past the melting ice and shiny scales sluiced from the fishmarket, to a dank cobbled lane and Betty's Bar, with its promise of softer company.

'D'you have to marry them first?' Bobby hears himself slur.

'Ah you're some man, Bobby Young, so you are,' says Paddy, and it seems like a compliment, an acknowledgement that Bobby can reinvent himself. There might be a war on, but he's still standing, and that's the way it's going to stay.

Rena, 1939

At last, Rena thinks. The news they've been waiting for, these past few years in this town that's become home. Nobody knowing them, them knowing nobody, and always the threat of a bad penny turning up and souring their hard-won life with scandal. Bigger news than the war, in the small world of their family.

'Mother,' she says, looking up from the newspaper. 'All your troubles are over.'

Hetty is intent on learning to work the slicing machine they have recently hired for the shop, as Rena has figured out that there's a scrap more profit in cooking a ham themselves in that new gas oven. She doesn't respond. One, two slivers of meat fall onto the plate, too thin to be sold. Thomas pops them in his mouth and swallows. Rena sighs – why must he be so greedy? – and shifts along so that he can lean over the counter beside her. She picks up a newspaper and runs her finger down the Deaths column, the type blurring before her eyes. Words and phrases spring out – *dearly beloved, untimely, at sea, peacefully at home* – but then she loses them again. Did she imagine it? She blinks and starts at the top of the list again, the newsprint blackening her finger as it goes.

'There.'

Lennox, George Bartholomew. July 21st. At home, after a long illness. It doesn't mention Hetty, nor does it say that George is survived by his three children, Irene, Thomas, and James. Rena should be pleased by this, she knows. She doesn't want anything that connects them with that man, anything that taints them with divorce. And yet, there's something about their absence from the black and white of his existence.

'So the bastard's finally popped his clogs,' Thomas says.

This gets Hetty's attention and she fumbles for the reading glasses she wears on a chain around her neck. Rena and Thomas stay quiet, giving her time to work her way down the list of names until she finds the one they have been looking for, in both marriages and deaths, every day since they left the village behind them. Hetty remains still, and Rena waits until she has read the notice once, then again, before laying her hand on her mother's shoulder and repeating:

'All your troubles are over.'

Hetty jerks upright, awkward because of her bad back, and removes her glasses. She dips her head slightly and walks into the back shop, their name for the small, chilly room with the sink and table in it, and the back door that leads to the outside WC they share with next door. A moment later they hear the quiet sound of crying.

'You'd think she'd be pleased,' Thomas says. 'After all she had to put up with.'

'I'd better get her some tea,' Rena says.

'Leave her a minute.'

Rena shrugs and removes the ham from the slicing machine and places it back in the cabinet. 'Well, close that door. We don't want anybody who comes in to hear her.'

Thomas does so, and then as she wipes over the surfaces of the machine she says, 'I want to go to the funeral.'

'What for?'

Thoughts jumble through Rena's mind but what she says is, 'To see him buried, once and for all.'

Thomas nods. That was the right answer, she thinks. The real reason is more complicated; something to do with bearing witness, yes, but also not being cut out. They were his flesh and blood. He owed them more than the divorce settlement. A settlement that didn't stretch through that first, hard winter once they'd stocked the shop. The neighbour across the entry, old Mr Reid, noticed their bunker was always empty and left a basket of coal at their door. Rena ignored it the first day, and the second. They weren't there to be beholden to anybody. But Hetty's fingertips got whiter and more numb, and Jamie's cough worsened, and in the end Rena brought it in and set the fire. Since then they've accepted his tatties and rhubarb, and left baking in return, and it's true what they say: a fair exchange is no robbery.

'Let's see if we can borrow the motor from Min and Donald,' Thomas says. 'We want to look swank.'

Rena knows he wants a car of his own, has done ever since Donald taught him to drive. It would help them with the shop and oh goodness, how it would ease those winter deliveries. Thomas takes his turn, and at least she has a lady's bicycle now, but the minute Jamie is old enough, she'll be sending him instead.

'You know we'll get a car, just as soon as…'

'Aye, I know, but that's not it.' He looks towards the back shop. The sound of sobbing has ceased. 'She'll want to come as well.'

'Well she isn't,' Rena says. 'People might recognise her.'

'They might recognise you, more like. Carrot Top.'

Rena shoves him. 'How many times do I have to tell you? It's strawberry blonde.'

The bell on the shop door rings as a customer comes in. Rena smiles and closes the newspaper, greets Mrs Watson and listens to her order. She puts four morning rolls in a paper bag, uses the cheese wire to estimate a quarter pound of the Dunlop cheddar.

'Just a little over. Shall I trim it for you?'

'Och no, it'll get used just the same,' Mrs Watson says, as if she's above such things as extra ounces. Rena feels a twinge of envy. The day will come when she can say the same – it doesn't matter, what's another tuppence ha'penny here and there?

'Anything else for you today?'

Hetty emerges from the back shop, moves into position behind the till. As she polishes her glasses on her apron, Rena makes a quick assessment; does she need to refer to a vague bereavement to cover her mother's tears, or will Hetty rally to the cause?

'Oh hello, Hetty,' says Mrs Watson. 'I was just wondering where you were. Some weather we're having, isn't it?'

Oh yes, the damp goes for Hetty's backache, but you have to make the best of things, don't you? After all, there's a war on and if it's anything like last time… Rena relaxes. If Hetty has ever regretted the change in life that obliges her to serve behind a counter, she's never said. Nor has she ever expressed relief at being rescued from having six bells knocked out of her every time the meat was tough or the tatties soft, or her husband had the notion to beat her with a frying pan. She gets up at five and bakes regardless. She chats to the customer as if nothing has happened, as if today is just like any other day. And if Rena is blamed, or forgiven, her mother doesn't say. 'Did you hear about old Mrs Dalziel, well, if that isn't enough to make you count your blessings!'

When the Thursday of the funeral comes they leave Hetty in charge. Without discussing it, they don't tell her where they are going. Rena says something about a meeting with a new wholesaler. They tell the truth to Min, when they ask if they can meet in the town and take the car for an hour, but Min's on their side. She's the most worldly of the aunts, with her husband and their business and her cropped Marcel wave, and she's made no bones about the fact that she never liked their father. She agrees that taking Hetty to the funeral would be a disaster. Jamie is in high spirits; it's a treat for him to be in the shop proper, running up and down the ladder to pick up anything Hetty can't reach, and always the promise of a sweetie from one of the jars if he gets bored. Thank heavens it's a Saturday. Rena's strict about school. He hasn't been told about his father's death; why bother him, when he's absorbed all those stories of Hetty as a widow so well. Or at least he's never mentioned otherwise. He was only small when they left anyway, a tiny figure sitting on Auntie Nell's knee in the front row of the public gallery in the courtroom.

And now George Lennox is dead and gone. Rena tries to remember the big house, tries to imagine not sharing a bed with her mother, not hearing the boys arguing through the wall. They'll move somewhere bigger one day, just as they'll get a car and she'll have new shoes before she polishes the leather of her old ones clean away. She gets changed quickly then checks herself in the mirror in the hall, pinning her hat in place and fixing her enamel lily of the valley brooch to her lapel. Thomas emerges from his room, straightening his black tie. Although the hat covers most of her hair the rest stands out brighter against the black, but he doesn't seem to notice.

'Don't know why I'm bothering,' he says. 'It's not as if I'm grieving.'

Rena wonders, but doesn't mention it, whether the will has been read.

There is a service in the memorial chapel before the interment, but they wait it out in the car park. It's a fine day for it; clouds scud across the sky, birds are singing, and the rose border is alive with the drone of bees. On the other side of the cemetery, a man is pushing a mower up and down the grass borders of the path in a slow and easy rhythm.

'Thomas, give me one of your cigarettes would you?' Rena says.

'You obviously don't remember the last time,' he says, but extends the packet to her anyway. Today she makes a better stab at it, leaning against Donald's Austin and managing not to cough at all. When the doors of the chapel open she crunches the butt into the gravel with her foot.

Together they watch the mourners file out, more than

a dozen of them, more than twenty. A gust of wind carries over the faint scent of mothballs. Who are they all? But then Rena begins to recognise faces. There's Mr Williamson from the bank, who stood as a character witness for her father. Thomas straightens his shoulders, spoiling for a fight perhaps, and Rena is glad he's there with her. He has grown into himself and is tall and broad-shouldered, and if he's his father's son he's shown no sign of it, doing the heavy work at the shop without a grumble and always thanking Hetty for his dinner (even when it's tough or not enough, which is the case more often than not). His suit is such that if anyone casts them a second glance they'll see that the Jarvies are managing just fine on their own. She catches sight of a familiar pinched face under a shapeless hat just as Thomas whispers, 'There's auld Skilling from next door.'

Is that your mother taken another fall? She is awful clumsy, isn't she? There are other people Rena has never seen or cannot remember. At least her father wasn't much of a churchgoer, she thinks, thankful that the funeral is at the large cemetery on the outskirts of the city rather than back in the village. It's only looking back that she can see that she always wanted to get out of that place, ever since the eleven plus when boys started trying to put their hands up her skirt and girls wouldn't talk to her because they thought she was stuck up. The crowd proceeds through the cemetery and she and Thomas follow behind them. As the incline of the path increases they pass box trees trimmed in bulbous shapes, and Rena has a flash of memory.

'We were here once before, weren't we?'

'Granny Lennox,' Thomas says. 'Maybe?'

'It rained. I hate to see a burial in the rain. But you

were only little.'

'And Jamie wasn't even born.'

They pass a shrouded urn, an obelisk and varying shades of stone and marble. There isn't a family lair, it seems: the brand new Lennox headstone is flanked by three generations of Dippies and the unfortunate two-week-old Isabella Louden. Granny Lennox is nowhere to be seen, although she and Thomas were so sure they'd been to this cemetery before. The gravediggers keep their distance, caps tucked in their pockets but otherwise unperturbed, smoking and talking in low voices. Rena is about to nudge Thomas and suggest they leave before anyone turns and notices them when she sees the woman. Standing to the right of the minister, a little bit blowsy, even under her smart black suit; is she older than Hetty? A black veil on her hat, feathers as well, flashy. Handkerchief raised to her eyes and even from here Rena can see that the woman has a coral manicure – at a funeral! – and the sparkle of a ring on her right hand. Paste, she hopes.

Rena hears the minister reiterate that George Lennox died after a long illness. She imagines him in his bed, how angry that must have made him. The way his face would darken so that he was purple with rage. Nobody else seems to be looking at the woman. It is as if she isn't there, or is present only in Rena's imagination. A surprisingly deep voice, Rena recalls. *And you must be Irene, I've heard so much about you.* Yes, it's coming back now. How could she have forgotten an afternoon out with her father, just the two of them? The two of them plus the woman they bumped into by chance. *Fancy meeting you here! Let's have afternoon tea, George, shall we?* Rena isn't imagining it. The woman is there and it is her, recognisable under the veil and the extra weight. She must have been the one that nursed him. Who else was there? He hadn't remarried, or at least the death notice didn't mention it. Rena's mother was his only wife, and Rena his only daughter. But the woman is there at the front, in the place for family.

Rena taps Thomas on the arm. He is glaring at the minister. The words of the 23rd Psalm drift towards them and the pallbearers (and who are they when they're at home? Not Thomas, of course, so who?) sink the coffin slowly into the ground. Rena hears the brittle scatter of the soil the woman throws in to the grave.

'Well, that's him planted,' Thomas mutters. 'Time to go.'

Rena nods, and just as she's turning to follow him she catches the woman's eye and sees a sudden flash of recognition. Auntie Ruby, yes, that was it, and Rena was young enough to buy it, naïve enough to forget about it. She didn't commit perjury after all, and George Lennox is six feet under. The box she's kept locked inside her need never be opened; the past is past and she can stretch into her future. Irene Jarvie. The woman's hand jerks, her handkerchief flaps. She isn't surprised, Rena realises. It's as though she was expecting to see Rena and wants her to wait. But the minister is only at *my cup runneth over*, and Rena walks away. Her father will have left his money to that tart then, and Hetty and the family won't see a penny of it.

Rena, 1939

Rena ties the handles of the bag containing her last delivery of the morning together and hooks it onto the gatepost of Low Borland, making sure it's secure enough to foil the sparrows that are hopping around the prize bull's trough. Thankfully the beast is standing still in the left field, swishing its tail every so often. She doesn't quite like when it comes closer, and scratches its behind against the fence beside her. All present and correct: a dozen morning rolls, one *Standard*. Rena looks up and sees Mrs Templeton striding along the driveway towards her, one hand open in a wave.

'Braw morn, isn't it?'

'Can you believe it, there's heat in that sun already,' Rena calls, wiping her hand across her forehead. 'The perspiration's dripping off me.' Ladies don't sweat, after all; Hetty tells her that even when the pair of them emerge from the wash-house they share with the other flats with scarlet faces and chapped hands. She checks her watch. Six thirty. Ahead of time.

'Idyllic when it's like this. You'd never ken there was

a war on,' Mrs Templeton says. 'How's it going in the town?'

Rena pauses, one foot on the right pedal of her bike. Spuggies, that's what Jamie calls them. He's picked up the way they speak around here. They're in the hedgerow now, still chirruping. When she goes over Assloss Road in the morning she sees rabbits and voles and all sorts. 'They took our front railings,' she says. 'Left the gateposts at least, but it looks a state.'

'Armaments,' nods Mrs Templeton.

'It's the least we can do,' Rena says, and regrets it. It was compulsory, not like joining up when you're too young to be conscripted.

'And I hear it's Mauchline they're sending the Tallies to.'

Rena doesn't really know, but tries to join in, 'Jamie saw them moving folk out of the Grand Hall just yesterday.'

Mrs Templeton nods. It isn't hard to imagine her with a gun, nudging POWs along. 'Aye, mind when I first came in the shop I just assumed he was your son? He's lost that ginger now though, you'll be glad of that.'

'I was only twelve when he was born.' *And I'm not ginger*, she wants to add, *I'm strawberry blonde*. Instead she imagines what it would feel like to nudge Mrs Templeton along with a gun.

'Aye well, you're old and wise enough now to ken that some folk are no better than they ought to be.' Mrs Templeton pauses. 'We got a letter from our Billy yesterday.'

'How is he?' Rena asks, with as little enthusiasm as manners will allow.

'Asking after you.'

Billy Templeton has asked her out twice; once when

he came into the shop and once when he came to catch her at the delivery. The first time Thomas was there and gave him a look, even though poor Billy had made the effort and changed out of his work clothes and combed his hair for the occasion. The second time he flustered her, surprising her in the dark on a spring morning, his hands a mess from a calving. She told him her ma won't let her, and when she heard he'd joined up she was pleased to get him out of her hair, God forgive her. It is not easy to avoid courting a boy, unless you have one already.

'Oh. And is he… all right?'

'They don't let them say much, and he was never one for writing letters.'

'Ah well,' Rena says. 'I'd better get on.'

'Aye, no rest for the wicked.'

Rena wonders if this is another dig. Her rejection of Billy, which wasn't snootiness even if that's how it came across. 'You'll be missing him on the farm,' she tries.

'Boys. Tell them what you want, but you'll never convince them there's as much effort in feeding the country as there is in fighting for it.' Mrs Templeton's voice catches. 'He didn't have to go. He could have stayed at home, with us.'

Rena bites her lip. 'It was Thomas's birthday on Sunday,' she says.

'Oh aye.' Mrs Templeton nods, unhooking the bag from the gatepost. 'Ah well, my cousin down at Newmains got two POWs, but the Ministry's prioritising arable, apparently. As if kye milk themselves. But maybe we'll be lucky.'

'I hope so.'

'And Billy would like to hear from you if you were

minded to write. I'll leave a note of his details.'

Rena stands up on her pedals to struggle up the brae to the Glasgow Road, calls a cheery hello as she passes old man Wilson with his sharp-looking collie dog and his shotgun slung over his shoulder. He holds out his hand and she stops.

'For your mither,' he says, pulling a dead rabbit from his bag by the hind feet.

Hastily she pulls her cardigan from the bicycle basket, lets him put the rabbit in there. Realising she should hide it, she tucks her cardigan back over the rabbit, hoping there's no blood to stain it. Her fingers sink into the soft fur for a second. It's warm, as if it was still alive. Maybe Jimmy Wilson has an arrangement with the gamekeepers from the estates. Maybe not.

'Thank you,' she says. She has a spare roll for her own breakfast, but she can't exactly give him one morning roll in return for good meat. 'Thank you very much.'

He nods and walks on. She'll carry something extra tomorrow. Maybe he has a sweet tooth, and they're still managing to turn out cakes and pastries thanks to a decent supply of eggs and a fair stock of saccharine.

When she's on the main road she freewheels almost all the way down from the primary school past the creamery to the shop, the breeze cooling her cheeks as she goes. Checking there's nobody around, she stretches her legs out for a moment for the end of the hill, suppressing a whoop of exhilaration. She whizzes past a group of young men on their way to work at the quarry and hears a rough shout. It sounds like *torte*, and she thinks of the Chantilly baskets and blancmanges in their recipe book before she realises that the man meant something less complimentary. And then she sees her mother standing outside the shop waiting for her, and when Jamie runs up to the bike and puts his hands on the handlebars he speaks so fast his words jumble. Rena catches the one that counts though: 'burgled'.

The first thing to go through Rena's head is a phrase of her mother's: *pride comes before a fall.* Freewheeling down the hill in the sunshine as if she hadn't a care in the world, as if they were ahead of themselves for once. And almost at the same time another feeling comes, not in her head this time but in her stomach, like bile. How dare they? How dare that man shout, how dare someone steal from their premises?

'When did this happen?' Rena says. 'I was here to collect the deliveries at five fifteen. Where are the police?'

Hetty has rolled the belt of her coat around her hands. She tugs at it. 'I was waiting for you to…'

'Do I have to do everything myself?' Rena storms into the shop – cash register forced open, tipped on its side in the thief's haste to get at the money, yesterday's takings and no more, as they do the banking on a Tuesday first thing – and ducks under the counter to get to the telephone.

'Jamie,' she calls, finger poised over the dial. 'Go into my bicycle basket. There's a rabbit there.' She grabs a dishcloth and throws it to him. 'Wrap it in this and run home with it before the police get here. And don't get sentimental.'

'Can I see their guns?' he says, 'They've got them now for when the Germans come.'

'The Germans aren't…' Rena starts, but he's already running off with the rabbit. She wants to put her head in her hands. Hetty is hovering by the doorway, still fiddling with the belt of her coat, as if the burglar might be lurking through the back. 'Oh Rena, what are we going to do? A burglary. A burglar in our shop.'

'We'll deal with it. The police will deal with it.'

'The police,' Hetty says, as if she's never heard of them before. 'Oh, I wish your father was here. He'd…'

Rena stops dead. 'He'd be worse than useless.'

'Don't say that, Rena. Sometimes you need a man to sort things out and now Thomas will be going,' she hiccups over a sob, 'and we'll be here on our own. How will we manage?'

For a moment Rena can't breathe. It feels like the rage she used to feel at her father. Maybe that's what he felt too, when he looked at her mother, maybe that's why he did those awful things. But she has to swallow it, bury it deep down before the police come. She has to take charge. As she has since she was fifteen years old. As she has since they came to this town. As she does every bloody day of her life.

'We'll manage, Mum,' she says at last, forcing herself to reach out and touch Hetty lightly on the arm. 'We always do.'

When the police car draws up Rena is standing outside waiting. Reserve constables, she supposes: an older man and one with a pronounced limp. The buttons of the older one's uniform are stretched over his barrel chest, and the younger one seems to be having trouble keeping his bobby helmet straight. Perhaps they've just had to choose as best they could from uniforms left behind. 'Are you Mrs Jarvie?' the older one asks.

'No, it's my mother,' Rena says, waving towards Hetty. She tries to gauge his response. The police were no use when they were in the village, when that busybody Skilling sent for them. 'Oh dear, Irene, I thought there had been an intruder, when I saw the state of the door.' Either they couldn't read between the lines or they didn't care to.

'And your father, does he own the shop?'

'We lost him to the flu before the war.' Rena tries to look saddened, and then realises that the old lie has now become truth. Maybe that's the way it works: if you keep saying something, it turns into the real story. If only he had died sooner, while he and her mother were still married. Then they'd have inherited the house and his money. But at least there's no danger of Hetty getting muddled and giving the game away now.

Jamie runs up, and she puts her arm around his shoulders. 'My wee brother. He was first through the door. I dread to think what might have happened had the burglar still been there.'

This is the right tone, she decides: respectable, aggrieved, vulnerable. This should make the police's role as protectors and law upholders clear. While Hetty makes tea the policemen note down what's missing: money from the cash register of course, and it'll now need repairing, as well as a good quantity of tobacco and the few remaining bottles of ginger beer.

'About as much as a man could carry in his pockets,' the older man says, before determining that the door was forced – as if none of them had thought of that – and more disturbingly, opining that the thief might have been watching as Rena collected her deliveries. Rena doesn't have to pretend to be shaken by the notion of a man watching her going through her morning routine, planning for the moment when he would have a chance to spoil something that she's worked hard for.

'Anyone else help you out here, or is it just your mother

and yourself?'

'My other brother, Thomas. But he's...' her voice catches. 'He's just signed up.'

The policemen nod gravely. 'Well Miss Jarvie, it looks like an opportunistic crime rather than what we'd cry a habitual offender. There's more of it about these days, sad to say.'

'You'd think people would pull together,' Hetty says, pouring them more tea and hesitating over replenishing the rock buns. Rena nods at her. 'We pulled together before,' Hetty says, placing three more buns on the plate. 'All my sisters were nurses, and we lost our three brothers in the Great War.'

Rena stays quiet. She told Thomas not to go, to wait until he was called, thinking maybe it would all be over before then. But that seems to be the way of war, Mrs Templeton is right. It makes men stupid and leaves women to manage on their own. And women are never really on their own, they always have other people to see to first. Rena has heard about the wages in the munitions factories at Bowhouse and Ardeer, but she has her mother, and Jamie. And the shop, even if it says *Mrs & Mr T Jarvie* above the door.

'These cakes are the business. You two could run a tearoom, once the war's over.' The policeman closes his notebook and tucks it into his breast pocket where it spoils the line of his jacket even more. 'We'll ask around, see which of our, ahem, regulars, have money in their pockets. Of course there are other priorities, as you'll understand.'

Rena has no idea what might be more important than retrieving their hard-earned cash, but tries to look grateful. They're playing, she thinks, playing at being big polismen when they don't know much more than she does.

'I just can't believe that someone would…' She was going to say 'dare to' but the younger of the two men, the one with the limp, interrupts with, 'We see all sorts in our job, Miss, I'm sorry to say.' He smiles at her but she doesn't want his sympathy; she just wants him to do his job, if he's capable of it.

Thomas is almost as angry as Rena when he's told what has happened. By that time she and Hetty have cleared up the mess, the shop is open as usual, and Rena has warned her mother not to say anything to customers. She doesn't want the family to be seen as victims; any hint of charity is the death knell for business, they've seen it happening already since the war started.

'What a time for me to be leaving,' he says when he's calmed down a bit. 'You and Ma'll need to take care of everything.'

'I wish you weren't going,' Rena says. 'Thomas…' Her voice breaks a little and she feels tears prickle behind her eyes.

'Buck up, sis,' he says, putting his arm around her. She can't help feeling that he's playing a role too. 'You know I'll be careful.'

She nods, determined not to give in to the tears because if they start, she might not be able to stop them. 'Make sure you are. Because if you come home wounded, I'll kill you myself.'

After two days, and no news, Rena is still sick as a dog about the money they've lost but finds herself agreeing with Hetty that there's nothing for it but to put the burglary behind them. Then as she is taking in the newspaper boards in the evening she sees a police van drawing up. She recognises the older of the two policemen who spoke to her on Tuesday. He winds down the window and beckons her over.

'Is your brother still around?' he asks.

'Yes. He's just done cashing up.'

'Good. And your mother?'

Rena shakes her head. 'She's gone home to start the dinner.'

Thomas comes out carrying one of the window grilles, followed by Jamie with the key for the padlock. 'Hello son,' the policeman calls over as he gets out the van. 'I'm Constable Beattie and this is Constable Scobie. You'll have a wee half hour to spare?'

Rena realises that they didn't offer their names to her or Hetty when they came before, and she didn't think to ask. Thomas hands the grille to Jamie and walks over. 'Have you caught him?' he asks.

The policeman nods towards the back of the van. 'We apprehended him earlier today in Townholm.'

'So will it go to court?'

Rena hadn't thought of court, of official documents and fact-checking, people prying into their business. Into their past. How could she be so stupid?

'He just needs to learn his lesson,' the policeman says. 'Nip it in the bud, as it were.'

Thomas doesn't say anything.

'There's people who seem to think war's an excuse for all sorts. Sickening, really, when you think on what's going on overseas.' The policeman pauses. 'Your sister was saying you've joined up.'

Thomas nods.

'Good lad, good lad. Give the boy a nip out the flask, Scobie, and we'll drink to his health and to giving the Krauts what for.'

They each take a swig from a hipflask and Rena sees Thomas turn to one side to try and hide his grimace. It feels strange, all of a sudden, to be standing there on the pavement next to the police van. The bus trundles past and Rena thinks of Jamie, checking on the shop clock to see how long it takes to go round the turning circle at Castle Drive and drive back down towards the town. He loves going on the bus but rarely gets the chance, given that Shanks's pony is free.

'All right then,' Beattie says, 'We'll escort him in. Once your kind sister here's brought us a brew and maybe a couple more of those fine cakes for while we're waiting.'

'What in the blazes am I meant to do?' Thomas hisses, as Rena makes the tea.

'I don't know. But if this goes to court the divorce will come out, and everything we've been working for will be spoilt.' She adds sugar to each cup and stirs. 'So just…'

'Just what?' Thomas says, pulling at the lapels of his overall.

Their eyes meet, and then she looks away to place two empire biscuits into a bag. The icing is thin and the jam has been replaced by carrot marmalade, but even so they're better than you'd get at Gardner's in the town. 'Just do whatever has to be done.'

Thomas helps her carry the tea out and they watch Jamie painstakingly locking the grilles. When he's finished he hands the key to Rena. 'Go tell Mum that we'll be late for tea,' she says quickly, putting her hand on his back.

'No,' Thomas says. 'He's staying with me. Get back in

that shop, James.'

Jamie looks to Rena again. He's been chewing at his lip again; there's a speck of blood on it. She digs her fingers into his shirt until she feels his flesh yield underneath. 'He's only young, Thomas.'

'Old enough to learn,' Thomas snaps. 'Get in there.'

Just because you're wanting to be the big soldier man, Rena is about to say, but she sees Beattie looking at his watch and pushes Jamie towards the shop.

'I'll tell her myself,' she says. 'And you,' she spits at Thomas. 'You'd better look out for him. One hair on his head, do you hear me?'

Thomas nods and follows his brother into the shop. He's scared, Rena realises. Halfway along the road, she hears one of the policemen say, 'Shift yourself, ya Fenian bastard, we don't have all day,' and she turns to look back at the miscreant, the man who has caused them so much trouble. His hands are cuffed behind his back and he's hunched over, slighter and older than the nightmare figure she imagined watching her stuff her bicycle basket and panniers with rolls and newspapers for the delivery run. She isn't close enough to smell it but she can tell he's a drinker; the strawberry nose on otherwise greying skin. The policemen close over the awkward second door Thomas had to fit for the blackout and return to their van.

Almost exactly half an hour later Thomas and Jamie arrive home. She sees them from the window, walking with a two-foot gap between them. Thomas is red-faced, Jamie pale. Thomas washes his hands immediately, Jamie goes to his room. They don't speak over dinner, not even to praise Hetty for eking out the last of the rabbit casserole with Mr Reid's potatoes and two hard boiled eggs.

'I wonder what's wrong with them,' Hetty says, as she

dries the dishes Rena has washed.

'It's nothing. I never did ask you, how did you manage with cleaning the rabbit?'

'Oh, I had to call on Mr Reid to help me, I couldn't tell which bits were for throwing out and which for keeping.'

'You'll need to be careful, he'll think you're leading him on.' Rena isn't entirely serious, given the age of the man, but once she's said it she wonders.

'Don't be ridiculous, Irene.' Hetty pauses. 'And I don't like to say, but we'll not be having that rhubarb again.'

'Why on earth not?'

Hetty leans towards Rena. 'I saw him emptying his po over the plants this morning.'

Rena gets the giggles. 'What on earth do you mean, his po? Does he not use the lavatory in the entry like everyone else?'

'Apparently not at night,' Hetty says. 'Oh dear, to think of the crumbles I've made.'

Rena pats her mother on the hand. 'Well, you did wash it first.'

'Even so, Rena, it isn't nice.'

'It is not. But we might be glad of stewed rhubarb as time goes on. They're never done telling us that food is a munition of war.'

She's in better spirits when she goes through to wipe the table, but her mood shifts when Thomas announces that he's going out.

'Where?' she says.

'Nowhere,' he says, and again she bites her tongue rather than ask if he's going to the pub down at Dean Street. It opens on a Thursday, doesn't it, with its fresh ration of beer. Please God don't let him get like our father, she thinks. Please God don't let me lose him.

The 1940s

Rena, 1943

Rena came of age a long time ago. Maybe when she was fifteen, and they came to Kilmarnock, maybe before that. But today, the eleventh of February, it's official. She is twenty-one years old, and her mother has gathered her three sisters together in Glasgow to buy Rena a fur coat. Clothes are Aunt Nell's territory, and she's the one who said she couldn't think of a better time to buy fur than during a war. Min backed her up: better to put your money into something you can sell if you have to. Being in their company, away from the shop and the flat and the small town where she still feels like a stranger, even after almost six years, is like a present in itself. The thought of the shop with just Jamie and Alma niggles at her. He's still a child after all, though Alma has helped them out twice since Thomas went away and seems sensible and trustworthy. So far.

They meet in the station and begin what feels like a long walk. The trams and buses are full of passengers, and there are people in motor cars, all of them believing – just like Rena and her mother and aunts – that their journey really is necessary. It's under a year since the bad bombing but the buildings are intact and imposing, here in the town centre at least. Rena sees uniforms and gas mask cases, street preachers insisting the end times have come and a man in a sandwich board advertising Sylvia the Scientific Palmist. Her thoughts turn to Thomas, and for a moment she's tempted. How else are you meant to find out what's really happening? Margaret pauses to feed a coin or two into the Salvation Army tin and Min makes a comment about charity beginning at home.

'For the wounded,' Margaret says. Min falls silent, and Rena realises that they are outside the YMCA, which is acting as a hostel for soldiers and sailors. Rena never met her uncles. She has seen the photograph, of handsome boys smothering their nerves and innocence with excitement and smart uniforms, the day before they shipped out to fight in the Great War. Thomas looked just the same when he went; playing up the bravado, with only his sister noticing the tremble in his hands. Margaret was a widow at the age Rena is now. All the sisters apart from Hetty volunteered as nurses or auxiliaries. Rena's father hadn't married so that his wife could work, no matter what was going on in the world. Margaret went first, her duty as the eldest, and Nell was next in line, eager for adventure. Min didn't want to miss out, and so Hetty was left behind. At least Thomas is somewhere warm, according to his last letter.

Sensing the dip in mood, Rena suggests a cup of tea after the journey and Nell leads them to James Craig's, where the usual fare has been replaced (somewhat ostentatiously, Rena can't help but think) by victory sponge and ersatz coffee. Rena could have made better herself, but they can get things that city folk struggle to find.

Good things, like butter and eggs.

'God only knows what they'll make when we do win the war,' Min says, poking at her slice of cake with her fork. Hetty says it isn't so bad, but that's what Hetty always says. Rena's mother is in her element though, surrounded by her older sisters, with nobody likely to call on her to make a decision, not even about what kind of cake to choose. Now the dust has settled and she's actually a widow, Hetty has resumed her position as the baby of the family.

They walk past the Picture House and La Scala, both advertising newsreels, although La Scala is still doing a high tea with the four o'clock showing. There are more women than men, and many of the men are older, or injured, or in uniform. In her imagination Rena has visited Copland's, Daly's, Tréron's, mink and chinchilla rippling around her ankles as she twirls on plush carpets in front of huge gilt mirrors. Nell leads them past the department stores, further along the street. The buildings grow taller, the new hotel soaring above them, pale and modern amidst the soot-blackened sandstone. A group of American servicemen emerge from the revolving doors, tall and smart and smiling, a far cry from the souls scuttling in and out of the Y along the road.

'I don't think they've been out yet,' Min mutters. She prides herself as a judge of character, says it's vital in the buying and selling business. For a second Rena wants to defend them. This is a different war, and these men have come from further than any of them have ever been (although cousin Belle writes as if Vermont is paradise on Earth, and sometimes sends parcels of cotton semmits and maple candies to prove it). One of the men tips his hat to Rena. She ignores him, and as they walk on she hears a wolf whistle and laughter, though whether it's directed at her or the next woman to pass by she doesn't know. Hell mend them.

'It's just up ahead,' Nell says, and tidily Rena sweeps away her movie star fantasies. The window displays are modest but then window displays are, four years into the war. The big stores promised Utility Wear – Coming Soon! 'Well, we'll wait and see what kind of quality that is,' Min had said. Here there's an emphasis on sheepskin – gloves, hats and collars – and the mannequin is wearing something labelled as 'New! Sable-look!' And yet behind the window, towards the back of the shop, Rena glimpses rails of coats hanging silkily to the floor.

'Nell! How are you?' the proprietress says, emerging from behind the counter as soon as the shop bell rings. They kiss each other on the cheek, to Rena's surprise, as if they're continentals. There's a round of how-do-you-dos and nice-to-meet-you-Miss-Jacobson, and Nell explains that she's often called upon to reline furs, not that anyone's asked how they know each other. Remodelling takes a heavier sewing machine than hers. Rena's heart sinks a little. She knows she should appreciate that they've pooled their money to treat her, but she doesn't want second hand, second best. She wants something new, fashionable, luxurious, for once. Hasn't she worked for it? Hasn't she kept everything going? Furs aren't on voucher but the prices are fixed. That's why they've come here, somewhere Nell knows. So that she can negotiate. Make an arrangement. But if they suggest 'sable-look', which Rena sees is also available in seal, beaver and mink-look, she'll have to make up an excuse. She would rather wear good wool than dyed rabbit.

Hetty, Margaret, and Min sit on the sofa while Nell

and the shopkeeper hold an unintelligible conversation about weights and qualities. There's a giggle and Rena turns to see Nell holding Miss Jacobson's arm and laughing. They must be friends, she realises. She knows that Min and Donald have luncheon parties for neighbours and customers that drop in for drinks, but she hasn't really thought of a spinster like Nell as having friends. She wonders what they do together. Heading to one of the rails she runs her hands along the rows of coats. Ankle length, ballerina length, right up to jackets and capes. The scent of the lavender bags on the rail doesn't quite cover the camphor reek of mothballs. Amongst the cool, smooth fur there is tough leather. Rena's hand catches on claws and glassy eyes, and she sees tails hanging in fringes. So fine and feminine on the surface, but underneath there's an armoury.

'Just below the knee?' The question echoes along the sofa and Rena concurs. Yes, that would be practical. Her legs are one of her good points, after all that cycling she used to do.

'Of course shorter lengths are very much the style now,' Miss Jacobson says. 'But that's the thing about fur. It will never go out of vogue.'

She guides Rena towards a rail of suitable coats, the colours graded from pale tan up to jet black. As if checking something she knows already she pulls one of the darker coats out and holds it up to Rena's face.

'A bit harsh, with your colouring.'

Rena nods. Over by the sofa Hetty has draped a fox stole around her own shoulders. It looks as if it's whispering in her ear.

'George bought me one of these, after we were married,' she's telling Margaret. 'I wonder whatever happened to it.'

Maybe Rena's father had burnt it, to prevent it whispering any cunning words of wisdom. Rena remembers a silk dress stuffed in the grate, the flames licking up round the fireplace while he shouted something about Hetty's sisters dressing her up like a whore. She had to press her hand over Jamie's mouth to make sure he didn't cry.

'Musquash,' Miss Jacobson says, removing another coat from the rail. 'Beautiful colour, this one. There's almost a chestnut tone, hang on…' She unbuttons it and spreads it over the counter where the weak winter daylight is stronger, smooths the pile. 'Rather special, really.'

Rena sees an ivory lining, decorated with gold fleur de lys. She takes off her own coat and hands it to Nell, slips one arm and then the other into cool silky sleeves. 'They're the right length,' she says. Her hands are pale against the fur.

When Rena looks at herself in the mirror she is surprised. She can hear noises of assent behind her but sees only herself in the mirror. A grown woman, glamorous and unassailable in her coat.

She turns to them and catches Nell's eye. 'Beautiful,' Nell says. 'That's the one.'

Miss Jacobson, Hetty, Margaret and Min are standing in a semi-circle around her. She can hear Nell and Miss Jacobson whispering, working out the price, and this being passed on to the others for approval. As Rena turns back to the mirror for a last glance, she notices a man outside the window of the shop. He's looking through the glass, quite intently. Looking at her as if he too has been bewitched by the fur. He meets her eye and Rena stares back, catching him in her gaze, and then Mrs Jacobson notices and steps towards the window. He turns, nonchalantly, as if he's waiting for someone.

Rena feels naked when she takes off the coat. She pats it one last time before it is folded and packed.

'Oh look,' says Min. 'Why don't you just wear it? It's February and you're in town after all. We can wrap your other coat and put it in a bag.'

Rena nods. She can feel her heart beat faster, she's so pleased with her present.

'And have you always been in the fur business, Mrs Jacobson?' Margaret asks.

'Miss,' Nell says. 'It was her father's business.'

'Yes, I inherited it. And now I run it alone.' Miss Jacobson finishes writing up the receipt and reaches under the counter for a large bag.

'Must be hard,' Min says. 'I'm so fortunate to have my Donald.'

'You are,' Margaret says. 'Two wars in a row means that plenty more of us are going to have to manage without a man by our side.'

'No shame in that,' Nell says, 'the bother they seem to cause at times.' Miss Jacobson issues a little snort of laughter. Margaret frowns.

'Thank you so much for your help, Miss Jacobson,' Hetty says.

'A pleasure to meet any family of Nellie's. Enjoy the coat, Irene.'

When they step back out into the street, the rush of noise surprises Rena. She draws her new coat closer around her. Wan February sunshine is breaking through the clouds and touching the livery of the trams, the buckles on people's shoes and bags, the windows of shops. Almost as if everything is normal.

Margaret looks at her watch and says, 'We should

think about getting back. It gets dark so early.'

'I suppose, but it's so nice to see the town, isn't it?' Hetty murmurs.

'Not so nice in the pitch black. Do you know that woman well?' Min turns to ask Nell, who replies, 'Oh well, I've done some work for her. Folk don't wear opera capes or fur down to their ankles now, do they?'

Rena stops listening. The man she saw before is standing by a lamppost, smoking a cigarette. He smiles at her, and as he does so something dawns on her. He isn't smiling at the Rena who cycled so far in the early mornings to make deliveries that the palms of her hands blistered, the Rena that the boys called a tart and the girls thought was above herself, the Rena who cowered in the corner with her brothers while her father advanced on her mother with murder in his fists. All those Renas of the past and more can be excised, cut out of the story of her life. Reflected in his eyes is Rena in the future, Rena in a fur coat.

Bobby, 1943

Bobby Young is out and about, strolling along from the Y towards the Grand, a lightness in his step in spite of the cold, after a successful game of cards with a few Yanks the night before. Even if he says so himself, he does know how to make his own luck at cards. One of the few skills the Merchant Navy will teach a man. Money in his pocket lends a sense of opportunity to the day, and his eyes are open, seeing what they can see. He's near Charing Cross when he spots the girl, through the window of the Jewish furrier, her hair the brightest thing on the busiest street in Glasgow this dreich, smoggy lunchtime. Turning this way, then that, appraising the glossy coat that hangs from her shoulders. The shop woman adjusting the sleeves, checking the length of the hem. Well, well. He pauses for a moment, wanting to catch a glimpse of the girl's face when she turns back to the mirror. When she does turn she sees him straight away, fixes his eye with a cool stare that knocks him for six. Pale skin, a strong face, good-looking rather than made-up pretty, and she's smart into the bargain.

The shop woman steps forward as if to chase him and he pretends he was straightening his tie in the window and turns away, looks at his watch. Whoever said *meet you outside the Jewish fur shop*, he wonders, but it's the best ruse he can think of. He reaches in his pocket and pulls out a coin, tosses it and slaps it on the back of his hand. Heads she buys the coat, tails she doesn't. Heads. He isn't in a hurry, he'll wait and see. Quite the investment, for the middle of wartime, but some people do all right out of it all. Mind you, he has two bob to rub together and all of his limbs, and you can't say fairer than that. A lot of the other men in the Y have been wounded, or they've gone a bit doolally, especially the poor blighters who fought first time around as well. Bobby has been to some bad places, and met some bad people too, but they haven't all been trying to kill him, and he's kept his wits intact. His last ship, the *Hester*, survived so many torpedoes that she's become almost legendary. Bobby doesn't think the old girl's luck will hold though, and he doesn't fancy her next voyage one little bit. Another Atlantic convoy no doubt, alarm bells ringing all damn night and waiting, waiting for the crashing and buckling of metal that no tin hat will survive.

The girl doesn't just buy the coat, she walks out wearing it. Flashy, he thinks, then looks again. Four women flanking her, the way the corvettes cluster round the *Hester* until she's out in open water. The girl glances round, sees him standing by the lamppost, doesn't crack a smile or tip a wink. He got it wrong. She isn't out treating herself on some man's money, she is unquestionable in her respectability, chaperoned by her mother and what? A coven of witches? As if on cue, flakes of snow start drifting down, dissolving almost before they hit the pavement. Pure as.

He imagines the tiny flakes settling on her coat, melting against the fur. She isn't immature though, there's something else there, in the way she holds herself. Head up, setting off with a long stride so that the shortest of her companions has to trot to keep pace. Everything about the girl is confident, firm – he takes a peek at her ankles, just to be sure that there's the promise of good legs – apart from that softly curled hair, quivering as she walks, still the brightest thing this drab, blackout-ready street has to offer. He tosses the coin from hand to hand, slaps it down again. Heads he'll follow her, find a way to ask her out.

Tails. Best of three then. Heads and heads again. There you are, Bobby Young, it's fated.

She's way ahead now, and he has to run a few yards to get within proper sight of her, up at the Beresford Hotel where two floozies with dye jobs and painted lips are laughing with a group of Yanks. Fair game, he supposes, for all parties concerned. The girl he's following though, she's above all that. He can see it from here. She was born to that fur coat, square across her shoulders, swinging by her calves as she walks. How to speak to her though, that's the problem. He imagines she'll be capable of scorn, all women are, and he doesn't want to see that kind of expression sour her alabaster face. But he has to take his chance soon, or else she'll know he's been following them. One of her companions gets in a fankle trying to put her umbrella up against the increasing flurry of snowflakes, and he seizes the moment along with the brolly.

'Allow me!'

'Oh, thank you son, thank you. So kind.'

His luck is in, she's the soft touch. And the blether, it turns out, as she launches into chitchat about the weather.

'Given it's so bad, Hetty,' says one of the others, drily,

'don't you think we should get indoors? I'm sure this gentleman has somewhere to be.'

She's not charmed by him, not a jot. He lets himself look downcast. 'Unfortunately not. I've been stood up by a friend.' Then, as if noticing the girl with the red hair for the first time. 'In fact, didn't I just see you along the road, outside Jacobson's? That's a beautiful coat. You couldn't have chosen better with your colouring.'

He takes care to smile at the guardians, as though their superior taste is responsible. And is he imagining it, the hint of a flush creeping up those pale cheeks? The blether says, 'Well, it's our Irene's birthday, and even though there's a war on, we wanted to mark it.'

'Many happy returns,' he says. 'Oh look, this is a bit forward, but you don't have a birthday every day and I'm not home much, as you can imagine,' he casts his eyes downwards, 'What with… well, you know. Would you ladies take pity on me, and let me stand you a cup of tea? The weather's taken a turn for the worse and, foolishly, I'm out without my overcoat.'

He can afford to liberate his coat from the pawn in the afternoon, he thinks, just as he can afford to stand five complete strangers five cups of tea. He knew today was a day of opportunity and sure enough, the women exchange glances and the one with the bob and pencilled brows says, 'Well, all right then. But don't let's go back to Craig's. Their tea was rotten this morning. I'm certain they didn't boil the water fresh.'

The spring in Bobby's step continues into the evening. The temperature drops too low for snow, and he's glad to have his coat back. Glad to think back over his day.

Rena, they call her. Irene is the Sunday name, her father's choice, he heard someone mutter, but the father's dead. The blether, Hetty, is the mother, and the others are Rena's aunts. Clubbing together to buy her the fur coat, but still. There was some mention of getting back for a shop, which he gathered Rena helps out in. That's just fine. He's been with women who expect to be kept and frankly, it's a pain in the arse. Whatever you do, it's never enough. Rena isn't like that, he can tell. Twenty-one and unwooed, can that really be so? He's been compared to other men before – unfavourably, of course – and he doesn't like it much. But she's different. It's clear she's no pushover. He played it well, grateful for the company over tea and keen not to intrude. All above board. Left them almost without asking Rena out on a date, then hesitated – just for an instant, as though dinner was out of the question. And sure enough:

'That's very kind of you but I live out of town.'

'How far out of town?'

'Twenty miles.'

No problem, he said, no problem at all.

'Och, whyever not Rena? Nothing wrong with a nice evening out.' That from the one with the eyebrows, Min, he thinks she was called, though it's hard to tell one from another.

'It'll give you a chance to wear your coat.' The dry one might not have been taken in by charm but she helped him out there. Nell, he remembers her name all right.

'All right then. Dinner on Saturday.'

'Six o'clock?'

'Six o'clock is fine.'

He will need to get hold of a car, and petrol, but it feels right that there are some obstacles in his way. Enough to prove that she's worth it, and nothing's insurmountable. Tucked into the breast of his jacket is Rena's address written on the back of the tearoom's card. Six o'clock on Saturday. He'll see her again then. And now, well, now he has money in his pocket and something to celebrate.

He eschews the Grand, keen to avoid the Yanks from the night before. It's cocktail hour for them and their thoughts will be turning to recouping their losses. One winning streak is lucky, two in a row looks suspicious, and refusal may offend. He knocks into the Wee Hoose for a sharpener, runs into two island boys fresh out of training. They're seventeen if they're a day, and more scared of the city than of the Hun. Not enough time to go home to their families and sweethearts, turns out they're staying the night in the Y before packing out tomorrow at 0800.

'We're neighbours then. Bobby Young. Merchant Navy. Let me get you a drink.'

There's still beer available but it's limited to two per customer, and boy, it turns out these lads have a thirst on them. One has sandy blond hair and a sweet face that looks younger than his blue eyes. A sailor's eyes, Bobby recognises, weather-faded and always staring towards a far horizon. Turns out the boy has other lands in his sights as he asks, 'Is there anywhere around here we could meet a couple of girls?'

Avuncular, Bobby offers cigarettes, which are gratefully received. 'Well,' he says, 'That depends. Are you talking about finding someone to wine and dine and start a correspondence with?'

'We've only the one night, eh?' The dark haired one has an accent that he must be tormented for in his battalion. Jock will be the least of it.

'How about the dancing then?'

The blond one perks up. 'That sounds more like the thing, Donal?'

Bobby smiles. 'No problem at all. Take your pick. The Locarno, the Empire, the Grand. How are your boots?'

'Eh?' Donal looks at his feet, perhaps trying to see them through the eyes of a girl at the dancing.

'I mean, do they fit you? Because you'll end up walking any girl you meet five miles home at least, before you even get the chance of a peck on the cheek.'

The blond one stares into the bottom of his glass as though he'll find the right words down there amongst the dregs of his beer. 'No but, it's a city, isn't it? There's… or the other lads say there's…'

Bobby slaps them both on the back and laughs. 'I think I understand you now boys. I know just the place that'll serve us some drink, though maybe not the finest cognac mind, and that's frequented by exactly the kind of ladies you're hoping to meet. Drink up and follow me.'

He takes them to a club he knows, a well-run place not far away, in a quiet Georgian crescent. Membership available on the door. Grateful, they buy him a skinful of ersatz gin before disappearing into the night with their chosen girls. And good luck to them, Bobby thinks, because don't we all want a little companionship in this world? Someone to hold us, just for a moment or two? Though to be honest, there won't be much affection for poor Donal, who for some unfathomable reason has copped on with Carmel, a nippy forty-year-old notorious for a rough-handed contempt that must be an acquired taste. There will be none of that for Bobby though. He's happy to drink himself tired and stroll back to the Y without getting into mischief, to dream of Rena and how the Hell he'll get hold of a car and enough petrol to run it twenty miles out of town and back on Saturday night.

'Bobby Young.' The voice is shrill, and inches from his ear, and he knows he should be able to put a name to it but can't, not until it says, 'The nerve of you showing your face in here.'

Oh God, he has it now. 'Mabel,' he says, sitting up on his bar stool and looking towards her.

'Don't you Mabel me. Don't you speak to me.'

You spoke to me, he wants to say, but reason doesn't work on an angry woman. On any woman. He can feel his mood slipping away, his evening slipping away, because he knows what's coming next, fast as a torpedo out a U-boat and bound to strike true.

'After what you did to Anne.'

He sits up straight now, tries to meet her eyes. 'She…' he begins but Mabel cuts him off.

'Aye, and would she have if she hadn't been mixed up with you, eh? You're spineless, Bobby Young, you won't even admit it…'

She keeps talking, but Bobby hardly hears. He's back trying to unlock the front door of that grimy flat. A key on the inside, jiggling it with his own until it fell with a clang on the floor beyond. He wishes he'd turned and walked away.

'What do you want me to say?' he says to her, 'Don't you think I…' His voice is too loud, and he tries to clasp her arms for emphasis but it goes wrong, somehow, because she's screaming at him to get his hands off her and then she shoves him, square in the chest, and he falls backwards, taking the bar stool down with him.

Turns out Mabel has a friend with something to prove, because he lays in to Bobby while he's still sprawled there on the dusty floorboards. And all Bobby can do is try to cover his face, and think of that day, think of opening the door and walking towards the kitchen, think of Anne and their miserable excuse for a life together. Mabel might be a drunk and very likely a tart as well, but she's right, he deserves this. It's been in the post and now it's being delivered upon him, one kick at a time.

Hands pull him up and drag him out, bundle him down the steps. He collapses on the pavement, frost against his cheek, and waits to see which parts of his body will start hurting. Most of them, it seems. He twitches his hands, his feet. Nothing's broken. Stupid bastard couldn't even give him a proper kicking. He coughs, and his ribs scream in pain. The awful thing is, one of the awful things is, that it's no worse than has happened to him before. And it's a whole lot better than what will happen to those two poor infantry boys if they get sent across the Channel. He feels in his jacket. Nobody has robbed him, that's a start. And there, in his breast pocket, over his heart still, that little card with Rena's address on it. If ever he needed to do something, it's this. A man can't change his life on his own, not for the better anyway. That's a fact. And if Bobby doesn't change, well, it's downhill all the way. Slowly, he presses his palms to the icy ground, pushes himself to his feet. They've thrown his coat out after him, he sees. That's something else. Awkwardly, he eases his arms into the sleeves, looks up at the sky. The new moon shines in a bright sliver, and the stars pop out the dark sky like diamonds. He hears Anne's voice in his head: 'One day I'm gonnae jump right up and grab those sparklers and put them in a necklace.' But Anne stopped reaching for the stars a long time ago, and now she has gone and Bobby is all alone. That's why he needs a change. That's why he needs Rena.

Rena, 1943

Hetty is still up when Rena gets home. Well, half up; she's dozing in the chair in front of the embers of the fire, something indeterminate that she's knitting for the war effort unravelling on her lap. Bobby has insisted on coming in to pay his respects, which makes it sound more like a funeral than a date, and so the least Rena can do is offer him a cup of tea. She started to feel queasy on the drive back – maybe it was the wine, which she'd never had before – and the darkness over the moor road was disorientating, what with the ARP masks over the headlights. Now she would rather that Bobby left her to recall their conversations and marshal her thoughts. The flat is pokily familiar after the glitz of the evening; the curtains drab against the Anaglypta, the brass teapot with the amber glass handle the only thing that catches the light.

'And did you have a nice time then?' Hetty asks, standing up to shake hands with Bobby.

'We did. We had a lovely meal at the Grosvenor restaurant in town.' Rena feels quite sophisticated referring to the city as 'town'.

'The Grosvenor, oh yes, I believe my husband took me there once.'

Bobby looks serious. Rena has told him that her mother is a widow, no need to mention ancient history now. 'I'm sorry for your loss, Mrs Jarvie,' he says. 'War is a terrible thing.'

Rena sees the confusion on Hetty's face and shakes her head slightly. 'It was before the war,' she says briskly. 'That's why we moved here. A new life away from the memories.'

'I understand,' Bobby says, and although he doesn't know the half of it, Rena feels as if he does understand, in some way. All evening, he's listened to her when she's been speaking.

Hetty busies herself adding a coal or two to the fire, which is an extravagance as Bobby won't be staying that long. She likes to have a man to fuss over, with Thomas still away and Jamie just a boy. Rena puts her coat away, buttoning it up carefully and smoothing the fur as she places it in its protective cover. Moths would be a tragedy. She makes the tea, with an ear open for the conversation in the next room, in case her mother says anything out of turn. Images flash through her mind; of the maître d' in a dinner suit, the candles on the table, the crystal glasses of white wine. Bobby made some joke about Riesling and when they'd be able to drink it again, and the maître d' brought something he said was more patriotic (*maître d'*, *Riesling*, Rena has stored up each new term). The menu discreetly noted the food order on restrictions on meals in establishments – *only one dish of fish, meat, poultry, game or egg may be served or consumed at a meal* – but it was a banquet nonetheless, presented on gilt-rimmed plates by deferential staff. Half-grapefruit, roast duckling with apple sauce, peach Melba. Coffee rather than tea, and no washing up to do, nothing to intrude on the illusion. She tried to memorise the menu so that she could describe the food in detail to her mother but that will have to wait until tomorrow, so that she doesn't appear gauche in front of Bobby. A piano player in the corner, palms in pots. Rena supposes that she did know such places existed, but they lay in the murk of the past, her father's shadow cast long over them, or were invented for the pictures she and Hetty go to at the Regal or the Plaza. Now she knows that there are people who go to restaurants, who eat peach Melba, who laugh and drink wine in amongst the palms. For years it seems she has been working every day (including Sunday, when she's baking) without getting any closer. Her mother and her brother keep telling her to put her feet up, but there's too much to do. She puts out several cubes of their precious sugar, planning to take two herself to sweeten her stomach and help it settle, and carries the tea tray through.

'Look Rena, Mr Young has brought us some chocolate!' Hetty holds the bar aloft. 'Blended chocolate as well. The other stuff has gone downhill, don't you think?'

'Oh, it's nothing. I don't have a sweet tooth myself so it's much better going to someone who'll appreciate it. But please, call me Bobby, Mrs Jarvie.'

'Well, it's very kind of you. And are you driving all the way back to Glasgow tonight? That's an awful long road in the dark, isn't it?'

'Well, I may stay in an hotel,' he says casually. 'If there's one you could recommend.'

'I'm not sure the George would let you in at this hour,' Rena says. 'Nor whether you'd want to stay there. Bit of a fleapit, by all accounts.'

Bobby laughs, offering round cigarettes. Hetty goes to refuse but then takes one, as she sometimes does in company. These small acts of daring are the closest thing Rena has seen to rebellion against her dead father. More to the point, it's a sign that Hetty has taken to Bobby. And why not? He's smart, not a hair out of place, and he has manners. Rena appreciates the ease with which he chats to her mother, the way he lights her cigarette – with matches from the restaurant, she notices – without breaking conversation. 'You must remember I've been at sea,' he says, now lighting Rena's, then his own. 'I've slept in some pretty unsavoury places.'

Hetty laughs. She sounds almost girlish. 'And petrol, is that hard to come by in the city?'

Bobby shrugs. 'Well, it all depends on where you go and who you know.'

Hetty smiles. It's the same kind of answer they give in the shop, when customers marvel over their scones and traybakes or wish out loud that they could manage a wedding or birthday cake. Rena is careful though. Shortages make people spiteful, sometimes, and it doesn't do to draw too much attention to their connections with the dairy farms.

'We read about the bombing in Clydebank,' Hetty says. 'And saw it in the newsreel. We had a bomb too. In Maple Drive.'

'Just the one,' Rena says. 'Nothing like Clydebank.'

'Still a tragedy for those two families,' Hetty says, and a gloomy silence threatens to fall.

'The war won't last much longer,' Bobby says with confidence. He talks about fronts and retreats and America and newer, better bombs. Hetty laps it up. As far as Rena is concerned, one of her mother's failings is that she has always believed every word a man tells her. Rena knows she's worried about Thomas, of course she is, but she takes his letters at face value and turns the wireless up for the songs and skits and off for the news from overseas. Rena listens to as many of the bulletins as she can and is less convinced by Bobby's analysis – why would the Merchant Navy know so much? – but she does believe the war will end. It must, because Thomas must come home, and in one piece.

The clock on the mantelpiece strikes eleven and Hetty struggles to suppress a yawn. 'Another cup of tea?' she offers.

'No, no thank you, I'm keeping you from your bed,' Bobby says. 'I should be going.'

'Will you be going out again?' Hetty asks, and it takes Rena a moment to realise she means to sea, rather than for dinner.

'I report to Greenock at the end of the week,' he says. 'No idea where I'll be headed yet, of course.'

'Oh,' Hetty says, 'Such a shame you couldn't be stationed at Largs. My sisters took me for an afternoon out and there were ever so many people there.'

'Well, we all do what's needed, don't we? And our boats must get through, or the country starves.' He grins and Rena feels a bristle of energy in response.

The dinner was more than she's eaten in a long time, and when she walks him out to the front steps and thanks him for the evening her head feels as full as her stomach. She wants to go to bed now, to take off her shoes and her corselette and stretch out. He hesitates, and she looks at the low sandstone walls that border the sloping front gardens, imagining their railings smelted into battleships and tanks.

'Rena,' he says, and suddenly it seems as if her heartbeat must be audible.

'Yes?'

'I would like to see you again, before I go back to sea. Could I take you out again?'

She nods. 'I'd like that.'

'Who'd have thought it,' he says, his breath condensing in the cold air. 'The girl in the fur coat.'

For a moment Rena thinks again that he's going to kiss her. Isn't that what men are after, for all their politeness and fancy gestures? Billy Templeton certainly looked as if he was going to try it that winter's morning, and she was glad to have a five-bar gate between them.

'How about Thursday?' Bobby says.

'Yes, that would be fine.'

'Maybe we could have lunch, and you could show me the sights of Kilmarnock. If you can take the afternoon off.'

'I'm sure I can. But I don't know if we've anything that would impress you when you've been to all these places.'

He looks past her, towards the shadowy outlines of the trees where the park borders the road. 'That's the thing,' he says. 'When I'm away, all I think of is coming home.' He makes an odd gesture, a kind of shiver like a dog shaking itself free of water. 'I'll write and let you know what train I'll be on. Number six,' he says, looking at the painted number on the sandstone beside them. 'Let me just write the address down again to be sure.'

He rummages in his pocket and pulls out a stub of pencil and the Grosvenor Restaurant matchbox.

If he didn't try to kiss her, does that mean that he doesn't want to, that he doesn't like her? Or that he does?

Rena worries suddenly that there was some kind of test involved in the dinner that she failed to spot at the time. He starts the engine of the car and pulls away, waving as he makes a wide U-turn. He must have decided to drive back to Glasgow after all. Even in the dim light of the moon the frost glistens on the road. It might not be as dangerous as submarines and planes, but it is still a long road in the dark.

As she turns to go back into the entry she sees that Jamie is there at the window in his pyjamas, his pale face serious. Probably not the only one looking out to see what a car is doing here at this time of night. Did Bobby see her brother, she wonders, with a horrid recollection of sly allusions to the age gap between them. Thomas always tells her not to be silly about things like that but Thomas isn't there now, by her side in the shop, and she knows that makes her more vulnerable to wagging tongues. For all he told Jamie to look after her, to be the man of the family, she's the one who does all the looking after. She'll need to talk to Jamie, now he's seen Bobby, but that can wait until the morning. Tonight has been fun, and it's a long time since Rena had fun. Not only that but an education: now she knows what Riesling and peach Melba are, and she's heard stories of Italy and America. So many new things to file away, and so many more still to discover. 'I want to make something of my life,' Bobby told her. 'Getting by is all very well but there's more out there for me.' It was as if he was giving voice to her own thoughts, thoughts she's barely ever acknowledged before. Because Rena knows there's more out there for her too, she can feel it. More than early rises, deliveries and shop work. She has changed her life once before. Maybe she can do it again.

Rena, 1943

'It isn't surprising,' Hetty supposes, as she and Rena prepare breakfast together on Thomas's second morning at home. They have the kitchen window open and already they can hear the slow creaking roll of Mr Reid pushing the mower back and forth over the drying green. Rena would have thought there would still be dew, but she's glad of his efforts.

'What isn't?' she asks.

'Oh, you know.' Hetty gestures around the kitchen. For all the treats scrimped and bargained for, Thomas has hardly stopped to drink the real coffee they've been saving for him, though he managed to stuff a square of his favourite flies' cemetery into his mouth on his way out the door the evening before. He only has a two-day pass, but there he was, off out with people Rena didn't know. Who is this Ralph, she asked, and Thomas's reply was full of condescension. These alliances he's made in the RAF seem, for the moment, to trump family.

'And what do you know about it?' Rena snaps. When Thomas joined up she'd been pleased that there were stations nearby enough at Ayr and Turnberry, but now that he's running around catching up with all his pals from training, it's a blessing well disguised.

When Thomas is in the house, Jamie follows him about like a puppy dog. Has he flown a plane, has he shot a gun, has he killed anyone, has he seen Hitler? *No, yes, that's an official secret, and all I can say is that it's true that he's only got one...* Rena is thankful that Jamie is eleven, far too young to join up himself. She prays the war will be over well before he turns eighteen. Prays the war will be over anyway. She hasn't even had a chance to say to Thomas what she's never admitted in her carefully breezy letters; that every morning when she's drinking her tea she can feel a scream surging up from her stomach at the thought that one day the knock on the door might come, the black-edged telegram.

But at least he's here and getting up and washed for breakfast today, she thinks, spreading a fresh starched cloth over the table. Here and in one piece, not like these poor fellows you see on the newsreels, lying on stretchers, cigarettes wedged in their mouths, dirty faces smiling for the cameras, limbs bandaged up. No, if she didn't suspect he was putting a brave face on some of it, she'd say the war was good for Thomas. He's brown as a Spaniard, and more at ease in his skin than she's ever known him. Even now she can hear him singing to himself, one of these silly wartime songs. Hetty bustles in with the pot of tea.

'That's the eggs almost done,' she whispers to Rena. 'Shall I put the bacon on?'

'Yes.' Rena nods to Jamie. 'Go and tell your brother that breakfast is ready when he is.'

Jamie's eyes grow wide at the tray Hetty carries in.

Crumpets, a pat of butter, two boiled eggs, a slice of bacon each and a tiny bowl of sugar for the tea. And all to be shared; Rena isn't a martyr, saving all their points so that only Thomas can fill his belly.

He comes in wearing his uniform, dark hair combed back. 'Very swish,' she says. 'What's the occasion?'

'Och, who needs an occasion? Being back home with you, and Mum, and Jamie. Sitting down to a feast like this.'

He adds three sugars to his tea and spreads half the butter on his crumpet in one go, with a flourish of entitlement. 'Lovely grub. You don't get this in the mess hall, I can tell you that.'

Hetty tuts. 'How can they expect you to fight on an empty stomach?'

Rena nudges her under the table. Thomas doesn't like any mention of fighting. It must be too awful out there, she thinks, although the newsreels haven't mentioned Malta that she can recall. Hetty slips half of her own crumpet on to his plate as if in apology, but Rena notes that she holds on to her bacon. Last time Thomas was home on leave he ended up eating most of Hetty's share as well as his own, but her mother does like her food and it seems maternal indulgence only goes so far. Jamie opens his mouth, ready to ask something else about jumping out of planes probably, but Thomas speaks first.

'As it happens,' he says, 'I do have a bit of news to share.'

Rena pours herself a cup of tea, eyes the cigarettes he gave her from his allocation, sitting on the sideboard. 'Oh yes?'

'Yes.' He puffs out his chest. 'I am pleased to tell you that I am engaged to be married. I'll be meeting my fiancée's parents this morning, and I'll bring her back to meet you at tea time. So I hope there's still some cake left.'

Rena's head swims. Hetty is looking to her for a response, hands twitching in excitement. Jamie is nonplussed, and seizes the opportunity to edge the last crumpet from the plate.

'Engaged,' Rena says. 'Who is it? What's her name?'

'Her name's Evie,' Thomas says. 'Short for Evangeline. You don't know her. She's from up Fenwick way.'

'Congratulations!' The word bursts out of Hetty. 'Oh son, a wedding! A wedding at last.'

'Where's she from? Where did you meet her? When?' Rena is still trying to piece it together. She should be so pleased, but all she can think is can they afford it, what they'll do without Thomas, and who is this woman who's snared him? Rena has worked so hard to make them a new life, worked her fingers to the bone for years, and then the war came, and now this.

'She's in the WAAF. We met at a shindig in Prestwick when I was training. Ralph knows her family.'

We've never even met this Ralph, Rena wants to shout. 'You can hardly know her,' she says.

'We've been writing,' he says. 'You'll like her.'

Rena imagines Thomas in a trench somewhere looking at a letter addressed in Rena's handwriting and a letter addressed in this woman's. Which would he open first? Oh, it's stupid. She knows so little about his life now, after knowing everything for years. There might not even be trenches in Malta, given that his recent letters to her have mentioned warm weather and swimming. Just him trying to put a brave face on things, probably, now that the siege is over.

'Anyway,' Thomas says. 'You're a dark horse, Irene Jarvie.' He glances at their mother. 'A little bird tells me that you've been courting as well. And I want to meet the chap that's stealing my sister's affections.'

'Oh Thomas, don't change the subject.' She can feel her tell-tale blush mottling up her neck and onto her face. 'I am happy for you, of course I am. It's just, there's no need to be hasty, you know.'

'There's every need,' Thomas says grandly. His voice seems deeper, more authoritative than it ever did before. 'There's a war on. We have to take our happiness today, because we don't know what'll happen tomorrow.'

He's parroting someone else's words, Rena thinks, and then she hears him say that the banns are posted, the date is set, and he has been granted another forty-eight hour leave for it. 'A wartime romance,' Hetty murmurs. 'Wait until I tell my sisters.'

For a second Rena recalls her aunts surging into the room, taking charge, just as they did back when she got her mother away from her father. But this is different. This is a happy occasion. A celebration.

Bobby, 1943

There are a lot of superstitious men at sea, and Bobby has tried hard not to become one of them. But now, heading back from Newfoundland on yet another of these damn convoys, he's thinking about whether luck has its limits and that you never know when your transgressions will come back to bite you on the arse. He hesitated, didn't he, before he signed the articles for this voyage, and if he'd known they were carrying bloody steel ingots at five ton apiece he'd have absconded before they weighed anchor. As it is he's on his hands and knees scrubbing under the sinks, and it doesn't seem to matter how many cockroaches and slugs he scoops up because there are always more to take their place. He can't abide the smell of the bleach that chaps his cold hands as he scours, and it only makes a momentary dent in the stench of stagnant water. Shipshape and Bristol fashion, that's a laugh. No matter what he does, the fo'c'sle stays filthy. And if the *Annapolis* gets hit she'll sink like a stone.

He keeps his life vest in his hand when he goes up on deck to throw the scummy water overboard. The rain is beating down and the ship is pitching heavily. Once he's done he stops by the fore hatch for a smoke. Posh Roly is already there.

'You ever wonder how you ended up here, Young?'

'Not half as much as I wonder how you did,' Bobby says, cupping his hand around his match to no avail. Before Bobby met Roly, he'd have said that breeding was what they did to dugs and horses to make them run faster. The man looks like a cross between Phil the Greek and a brick shithouse, and sounds like Lord Haw-Haw. 'Bloody thing.'

'Ought to get yourself one of these,' Roly says, pulling out a flashy silver lighter. 'Works in all conditions.'

Bobby takes a grateful draw of his cigarette. 'Ta. Seriously Roly, why the fuck are you here, doing this? Chap like you could be an officer somewhere cushy.'

Water sweeps over the deck, swilling around their shoes.

'One thing about this life, Young, it's unpredictable. And another, it's short. Scouse lad on the lookout told me he saw a torpedo cut across the bows.'

'What the fuck…'

'Oh, he reported it. And who knows, boy's barely off the teat. Might've imagined it.'

'When?'

Roly shrugs.

'Did he see the other ships? The corvettes?'

'Can't see a fucking thing out there, never mind under the surface. *Alone, alone, all, all alone, alone on a wide wide sea.* That's us Young. *And ne'er a saint took pity on, our souls in agony.*'

Bobby feels panic rising in his breast. 'We've got to tell folk. The engine room boys…'

'The many men, the beautiful...'

'For Christ's sake Roly, have you been at the morphine again?'

But Roly doesn't reply, just stays propped against the wall, staring out at the swell and puffing on the cigarette held firmly between his lips. Bobby thinks of slapping him but he knows Roly boxed at school and is just as happy using his fists as his RP.

'You get to the mess and I'll go to the engine room,' Bobby says, more gently, but Roly's in a dwam and there's nothing for it but to take his hand to the man's cheek, hard as he can. Sure enough the fists are up but he recognises Bobby, recognises where he is and what might happen.

'Sorry about that, old chap...' he begins to say and then they both see the next torpedo shooting through the darkness, hear the explosion as it hits something – hits another ship in the convoy – over to their port side. The flames outline it for a second, and the clanging of the bells blows over on the wind. 'Christ, was that the *Creekirk*?' Roly cries. 'The purser owes me money.'

'Where the fuck are the corvettes?' Bobby says, and then he's running, scrambling down the ladder, not even thinking it might be suicidal but that the lads in the engine room are already in a bloody metal grave.

'Pramesh, Pramesh, get your boys out of here,' Bobby shouts as he bursts into the engine room. It's hot as Hell and noisy too.

'Scatter signal. She needs as much coal as we can shovel.'

Bobby grabs Pramesh's arms, looks him in the eye. 'They're right next to us Pramesh, and the convoy's all over the bloody shop. No fucking way we're going to outrun them.'

Pramesh starts shouting to the firemen in their own language, and Bobby guesses he's convinced. As he starts to climb back up to deck there's a tremendous bang and he's thrown clean off the companionway. He picks himself up. The ship isn't moving and he sees Pramesh running towards him but can't hear what he's shouting. The engineer grabs his hand and hauls him to his feet, shoves him at the steps again, and they haul themselves up as fast as they can, running and sliding across the deck as the short and long blasts sound. Clumps of wet ash fall on them from the funnel.

'Where's the fucking lifeboat?' Bobby hears a man shout, and when they reach the starboard side they see it's been cut free and is bobbing in the water below. The ship is listing towards it and Pramesh makes as if to jump down but Bobby sticks his arm out and stops him, grabs hold of the Jacob's ladder instead.

It's moments later that the *Annapolis* drops under the surface, pulled down by those steel ingots. Bobby shivers to see it, and their lifeboat makes a horrid surge towards the spot where she was before it's buffeted up on the next wave. After some shouting it becomes clear that the port lifeboat is across the water from them. The Master is on board, last man off the ship apparently. So Roly must be there too, surely. Beyond that they can see a fiery glow that means another ship has been hit, but whether it's from the convoy or one of His Majesty's nobody can tell.

'Where's the compass?' Bobby hears someone say. There's nothing in the lifeboat, it turns out, no sea anchor, and certainly no alcohol, which Bobby isn't alone in wishing for. It's freezing and he's soaked to the skin already, but at least they're afloat, that's something. They hear another explosion behind them, every man craning his neck to see that another ship has been hit. The boy next to Bobby crosses himself, muttering what sounds like a prayer under his breath. Bobby leans in, the boy is shivering so, and hears that he is trying to make a deal with God. *If you get me out of this I swear I'll go to mass every day, if you get me out of this I swear I'll never…* Bobby would promise his right eye and both bollocks to the Devil if it would get him home safe from this one.

A shout comes from the bow of the lifeboat. Someone's in the water, clinging to a spar of wood. A survivor from one of the other boats.

'Stay where you are man,' Bobby hears, and then: 'Oh Christ, he's swimming for it.'

The man manages the three hundred yards to them and they haul him over the side and clear a space for him to cough the water from his lungs, but he lies still. Bobby sees the purser check his pulse and pull back his eyelids, turns away when they find a tarp to pull over the body. For the first time in years he feels the slosh of seasickness in his belly and he scrambles over to the side, leans out and vomits into the chopping water below. It catches in the wind and spatters along the side of the lifeboat, only to be washed off a second later. The explosions sound further away now, but they're still coming.

'This is Hell,' the praying boy says when Bobby makes his way back to his space. His eyes are wide with terror and there's a trickle of blood on his temple that Bobby didn't notice before.

'You don't get there unless you're deid, son,' Bobby says, although he's not so sure that's the case. 'And unlike that poor bastard there, we're still breathing.'

Even in desperate circumstances, when you're more afraid than you've been in your life, it turns out that your head can nod on your shoulders and you can fall into a fitful sleep. When Bobby opens his eyes the rain has dropped to a smirr and the waves are a little calmer. His watch has stopped, and when he shakes it he sees water inside the case. He takes it off and throws it behind him, right over the side. One of the deckhands takes out a mouth organ and starts playing.

'Shut up you cunt, this isn't the fucking *Titanic*,' a voice shouts.

The first light of the dawn seems to be trying to fight its way through the dense fog that surrounds them. Every two minutes one of the ABs calls over to the *Annapolis*'s second lifeboat to make sure they're sticking together. Bobby listens for the echo from the other lookout, needing to know there's someone else out there. No compass, no sea anchor. A quick death is surely better than a long, slow one, drifting in the middle of the ocean. His clothes are sodden and clammy against his skin but his mouth is parched. He sooks on his cuff, just to wet his lips and tongue, then spits the salt from his mouth. And so it goes. *Port ahoy, starboard here. Starboard ahoy, port here.* The only way of marking time is by counting the minutes between the calls, and after ten calls, twenty minutes, Bobby realises that's a shortcut to madness. If there's more than a second's delay before the response from the second lifeboat he feels the panic rise in his breast. And yet he's grateful for the fog that swaddles them. He doesn't want to see what's out there, not really. Occasionally a bit of debris hits the side of the lifeboat and that's enough to set up a chorus of whimpers from those whose nerves are keeping them conscious. His tongue is glued to the inside of his mouth and he dreads to think what will happen when the thirst really sets in.

Then suddenly the wind is picking up again, and there's a chop in the waves that doesn't bode well.

'Port ahoy,' the lookout bellows, as if sensing the change in the weather too, but this time there's a shout from over to their right, a new voice. Almost as posh as Roly's, which makes Bobby's lips crack into a smile. The dense outline of a ship looms beside them in the mist.

'*Bluebell* here. Can't stop, there's still a U-boat about. I've nets over the side so you'll need to jump for it and climb aboard when we pull alongside.'

Rescue happens quickly, after all the waiting. There have been times that Bobby hasn't cared whether he lived or died, but this isn't one of them. All that's beating in his heart is the need to catch hold of the net and scurry up the side of the *Bluebell*. He knows the rope must be stripping the skin from his hands, but they're too numb to feel it.

And then it's a case of lying on the deck alongside the other survivors from the convoy, two hundred if there's a man, packed in like a game of sardines, all hoping that they can outrun the U-boat and get back home. Pramesh is beside Bobby, his back turned as he sleeps. From time to time Bobby stares at the engineer's shoulder until he sees the rise of his breath. Across the deck, if he cranes his neck, Bobby thinks he can see the top of Posh Roly's head. And if he's not mistaken he sees the shuffle of cards. Lucky bastard. Once twelve hours have passed without incident, and with scarcely three mouthfuls of water apiece, fear of death gives way to grumbling about their wages being stopped when the *Annapolis* went down and speculation about where they'll be taken.

'Loch Ewe, it'll be,' one man says.

'Nah, it's Greenock. Got it from the First Mate.'

Greenock. A hop, skip and a jump from Glasgow, and which way then? Bobby concentrates on the place as if by the power of his mind he can ensure that they get there in one piece. He can feel the raw growl of hunger in his belly, and his bones ache like they've never ached before, but he's alive, and he's going home.

When they sight land Bobby feels exhilarated, as though he's the one who has guided the *Bluebell* into the Firth.

'Well praise the Lord,' he says, sharing one dried out smoke from Roly's tin as they draw near Millport. 'Did you ever see anything so beautiful?'

'Not a patch on Alexandria. But at least no fucker is trying to blow us up.'

'I'd drink to that, if I had the price of a dram in my pocket.'

Roly pats him on the back. 'Never fear, Roly always has a bob or two squirrelled away. And besides, I owe you one.'

Roly holds good on his promise. They line up in a scout hall behind the town and a roll call of ships is made before they're assigned their rail vouchers.

'Blasted Southampton,' Roly says. 'Ah well, Doc prescribes that I get blotto before they put me on the train. Care to?'

Bobby's lips twitch at the thought. 'Not this time. I'm on the three o'clock to Glasgow and I'm turning over a new leaf. Going to ask a girl to make an honest man of me.'

Roly shakes his hand. 'Best of luck to you then, Young. And do it proper. Ask the father's permission, if the poor bastard isn't being shot at by Gerry.'

Bobby embraces him. It seems all right, given what they've been through. 'Give me an address and I'll pay you back the loan.'

'One thing I've learned from this debacle. Never lend a man money unless you don't give a fuck about losing it.'

'No, but I swear I'll…'

Roly shakes his head. 'We could both be at the bottom of the Atlantic, Young. On the subject of which, there's a pub here called the Dead Man's. So if you'll excuse me…'

Bobby salutes him as he goes, and then walks towards the train station. The sky is overcast but it seems to Bobby as if everything is glowing, from the sugar sheds to the grubby tenement blocks to the sandstone of the station itself. He looks at the station clock. A pint of beer, maybe two, and that'll do him. The Horseshoe looks a pleasant enough howff, and he's just crossing the road to get to it when a voice behind him calls out, 'Well, if it isn't Bobby Young from the Broomielaw.'

'Paddy,' Bobby says. 'You'll not believe the shaky do I've had.'

Paddy looks rough, and he's been drinking. 'What I do believe is that you still owe me a favour.'

'I don't owe you anything, Paddy.'

'Ah but you do, Bobby my lad, because if you'll remember you borrowed a car from my old mate Declan.'

'And I paid him for it in points and cash.'

Paddy shakes his head as if there's water in his ears. 'Naw. You didn't pay me for setting it up.'

Bobby stops and looks at him. He wants to say that he's seen a fellow die in front of him and that he's been lying on a deck for days, not knowing if his feet would touch dry land again. He wants to try to explain that there are men like Roly in the world, and men like Paddy, and he knows which kind he'd lay himself on the line for. But Bobby doesn't say any of this, because now that all the fear has gone what he finds in himself is rage, and it's rage that drives his fist into that smug Irish coup. Did he survive being torpedoed in the middle of the fucking Atlantic just to have the screws put on him by this son of a bitch? Anger surges through him and he doesn't stop, not even when Paddy is bleeding on the ground and has had enough.

The MPs lock him up overnight but they're sympathetic enough when he tells them the story, which he does with some embellishment, even showing them the crumpled, dampened picture of Rena that has survived against the odds in his breast pocket, much to their approval. 'Aye, you wid borrow a car to take a lassie like that out.' He's allowed one misdemeanour, after what he's been through, especially seeing as all he did was take a swing at a Mick. His card is marked though, nothing they can do about that, so he might have trouble getting on another ship unless they're desperate. But that's no problem at all to Bobby Young, because the longer it is until he sets sail again, the better.

Rena, 1943

Rena tries one more time, on the morning of the wedding. Truth is, Thomas was wrong. She doesn't like Evie, not really. She's another one having a good war; a flirt, carried away with all the excitement. As they are getting ready to go to the registry office in the town Rena asks her older brother, are you sure? He clasps her hands and she feels his certainty in his grip, and also the cusp of his temper. She can't push it any further than this, she realises. This is new for Rena, new for the family, and she understands that if she tries to make Thomas choose, he'll choose Evie. Even Hetty's enthusiasm for the wedding has waned now that she has met the bride to be; Rena overheard her confess to Nell that she isn't quite sure Evie is good enough for her boy. She has no such reservations about Bobby, who'll be arriving soon to escort her only daughter. Rena chooses not to ponder on whether that means Bobby is a better catch, or whether she herself is worth less. Thomas is happy though, she can see that.

'I'm so pleased for you,' she tells him. The hint of sadness in her voice is to be expected. They've been through a lot together, after all. He loosens his hold on her slightly.

'Oh sis, I'm glad. I knew you'd like her. I knew you'd understand.'

She smiles, frees her hands to brush imaginary oose from his uniform. The buttons are gleaming; whatever Thomas has been trained to do, looking after his clothes is a part of it.

'Do I look all right?' he asks. 'You know me. Never was the man about town.'

'You look perfect,' she says, appraising his face. His skin still has a hint of a tan, and he has grown a neat little moustache for the occasion. 'Never seen you more handsome.'

'Don't want to let her down.' He checks himself in the mirror again, pulls out his comb and runs it through his hair once more. 'I need more Bryl on it, don't you think?'

'You don't. You're fine.'

'Last minute nerves,' he says, replacing his cap at just the right angle, buttons to the front. For a moment her heart leaps. 'Anyway, when will this man of yours be arriving? I want to get a look at him.'

'Any time now.' Rena glances at the clock on the mantelpiece. It's one of Min's rejects from the antique shop, painted in the oriental style with ladies in kimonos at the bottom left and a crane on the right, the dial under glass. A touch gaudy perhaps, but Rena has always liked it, and all it has is a chip in the lacquer at the back. Some of Min's gifts are less desirable, like the pokerwork table pocked with woodworm that they sit the ashtray on.

'Well you look great, Renie.'

'Thanks,' she says, checking her own reflection in the glass. New shoes at last, and Evie gave her a pair of nylons. Least said about that the better, Rena thinks, her mind a flurry of American servicemen. They have so many things, and they're so generous, Evie told her. *I'll bet they are*, Rena thought, unkindly. Still, she's glad of the nylons.

Evie wears her uniform for the ceremony too, augmented by a bouquet; 'lilies at a wedding,' Aunt Min mutters, and Rena's minded to agree. The bride is a tiny thing next to Thomas, five foot if she's an inch, though the heels help. Her hair is done in curls and pins, her lips and cheeks rouged, and she smiles all day. People in the street as well as the waitresses at the wedding breakfast cast approving glances. A handsome man and a pretty girl, in love and dedicated to serving their country. A good news story. They've driven to a hotel at Alloway, not so far from where Thomas and Evie met, and the couple will stay there for their night's honeymoon before he goes back to Malta. They're going to the RAF dance later on, once the families have left. Evie's parents aren't smart but they're farmers and they've coughed up for the wedding. There's an older spinster sister, Jean, and Rena wonders if maybe now Thomas will inherit the farm. That'd be a living, she supposes, although she can't imagine him up with the lark and milking cows. Later she is introduced to a great lump of a cousin, a Godsend according to Evie's father, and revises her opinion. Was there a hint of disappointment there, that neither of his girls has managed to marry a farmer's son?

'Lost in them?' Bobby sits down beside her. He has a glass of beer in his hand and he's brought her a lemonade. She's so glad to have him by her side again. The last few months have felt like an eternity, going through the motions in the shop, feeling as if her life was consumed by waiting.

'It all went off well,' Rena says. 'Didn't it? I'm so glad the cake worked out. I was on tenterhooks holding it in the car.'

Hetty dug up a fancy two tier stand with a vase that stuck into the top layer of cake, and Rena has been up to high doh zigzagging sugar ferns to add to the real anemone blooms that crown the royal icing.

'It was perfect, Rena,' Bobby says. 'I'm glad I could be here.'

'Me too,' she says. 'Though I wish it hadn't taken such dreadful circumstances to bring you home.'

'Survivor's leave is better than the alternative.'

Rena nods. Bobby is alive, and she is happy for Thomas, she is. And for Evie too.

'Do you ever think of tying the knot?'

She sits up straight. 'One day, I suppose,' she says. It's the last thing on her mind. It has always been the last thing on her mind; look where it got her mother. Evie will stay with her parents while Thomas is away, but after the war he'll need a house, and a job. If the farm's no go, he'll be back in the shop. If it's a push to support the four of them, what will it be like for five, for more?

'You're right about weddings,' Bobby's saying. 'They make you think about the future.'

'God willing this war will end soon, and we'll have a future,' Rena says.

'If it does, and if we do, I'd like to spend it with you, Irene.'

Under the table, he reaches for her hand, his fingers questing between hers so that he can hold it tight. 'What I'm trying to say is, would you consider being my wife?'

Rena can see her mother sitting amid her sisters.

Hetty's cheeks are pink and she's chattering to Donald. Someone's given her a sherry, clearly.

'Oh, Bobby, what happened was awful but it doesn't mean…'

'No, I'm serious,' Bobby says. 'Never been more serious about anything in my life. That last time, Rena, well, I don't mind saying it shook me up. But what it did was make me realise that I don't want to go on alone. Without you. Your brother's already given his blessing, I took the liberty of asking. And if may be so bold, I think your mother will approve.'

What does Hetty know about marriage, Rena wonders, staying with that brute until he came close to killing her? What does Thomas know, proposing to the first pretty girl to catch his eye at a dance? And what does she know, really? How is she supposed to know about making these decisions?

'This isn't how I imagined it,' Bobby says. The pressure of his hand on hers weakens, but he doesn't let go. 'Is it that boy from the farm, Templeton? Had you planned to wait on him?'

'No,' she says quickly. 'No, it's not that. I just wasn't expecting…'

Billy Templeton is the only thing close to a suitor she's had, and even if he does come home in one piece, what would that mean? Moving up the road to a cottage by the farm, becoming more like Mrs Templeton every day? She glances over to where Thomas and Evie are still laughing together, and then she looks at Bobby. He's come back from being shipwrecked thinner than before, not to mention the chapped skin and bruises, but he still has good strong features and always stands up straight. Her family like him, he doesn't need mothering and she has never seen him drunk. More than that, he knows about the world. He's seen places she can't fathom and he talks about the future as though it's theirs for the taking, war or no war.

'If it's no,' Bobby says, and this time she can feel that he is going to let go of her hand, let go of her, 'Just tell me. Please, Rena.'

She grips his hand firmly in her own. 'It's yes,' she says. 'Yes, Robert Young, I will marry you.'

Bobby, 1944

He shouldn't have waited until the day before the wedding, Bobby knows that, but he wanted the weight of family expectation on his side, of the registrar booked and invitations sent out. He's not really a coward, just in love. Unwilling to risk anything getting in the way of his life with Rena. A proper life, without the constant nauseous swell of the ocean below you. There's the possibility of a business too; she has her heart set on a tearoom, if Thomas is taking over the shop. Doesn't want to work for anyone else, and he can see that. Work, and a wife. A home.

When Rena asks why he didn't tell her before, he has no answer other than the truth: he was scared he'd lose her. (There's an untruth behind it, of course; when he protests that the past means nothing to him and he doesn't think about it ever, he is lying.) Rena's face is clamped shut, and she's looking over the bridge and down to the river surging over the stones below. He thought it better to go for a walk, rather than have the conversation in the house, although Hetty might have been an ally. Hetty's all right. It'd be water off a duck's back to her, he thinks, looking down to where two mallards are dabbling where the river pools before the cascade. Hetty knows that nobody's perfect; nobody except her dead brothers. *Age shall not weary them, nor the years condemn.* Other folk are allowed to be fallible. And he's good enough at that, isn't he?

'I'm sorry, Rena,' he says. 'But believe me when I say it doesn't matter. A chapter of my life I wish had never happened, yes, but no more than that.'

Rena's face is pale but her hair glows, even on this dull autumn day. Behind her the grey stone of the castle keep rises above the trees. Rena led him here first, to walk on the quarry trails that used to be open to the public (and, yes, he did steal a kiss or two under the trees but no more than that, no more) and then to stand at a distance and point towards the new gatehouse that had been built on to the castle. She told him she used to drop off papers and milk at the Dower House on her morning run. He could feel her pride, her entitlement by association. Now her brother Jamie does the deliveries, when called upon, to the lodge on the main road.

'We were too young,' he says. 'And she wasn't… well.'

Rena's eyes are fixed on the spume below as she says, 'What do you mean, wasn't well?'

Bobby sighs. He wants to tell her the truth, but he doesn't want her to know the whole story. 'I found her one day, when I came home. She was lying on the kitchen floor. She…' No, he still can't go there, not even in his mind's eye. Rena is looking at him now and he has to keep going, has to tell her. 'She'd been dead for hours, the doctor said.'

He feels Rena stiffen at his side. 'Dead,' she says.

'How?'

'It was under the counter. I thought it had been put in the wrong bottle but they said not.' He wants to reach out and squeeze Rena's arm, burrow his hand under her sleeve and touch warm flesh, because what's coming still strikes ice into the marrow of his bones. 'She'd drunk bleach.'

There. He's said it. Now it's his turn to gaze into the distance, and the trees sagging low over a rock that extends into the river. There's a man and his son there. The boy has a stick with a fishing line tied to it, and he's swinging it back and into the water, again and again without success. Probably a hanging offence, and isn't that where they used to do it, just to the right there on Judas Hill? But Dalgleish the forester only patrols with his dogs on the weekends, and the war has made people braver about some things. The man takes the boy's arm, slows his cast. Eventually Rena speaks.

'I didn't want any more secrets,' she says.

Ah Rena, he wants to say, all our lives are secrets. We're the sum of them. 'I'm sorry,' he tells her again. 'My sister Eleanor, she's the only one who knows, and she hated Anne, always said I was a fool for marrying her.'

But I wanted to do the honourable thing, be a man for once. Anne was so happy when he slipped his mother's garnet ring on her finger. It was going to save her, save the both of them, if she hadn't drunk her way to a miscarriage, then drunk her way much further than that. Once, in the heat of a row, she'd told him the truth too; she didn't know whether it was his child. And even that didn't bother him, not compared to the threat of losing Anne. Well, he'd lost her in the end, hadn't he. She told him he'd be sorry, and she was right.

'Shh,' Rena says, and for a second he worries that he's voiced some of these dark thoughts from long ago. 'I don't want to know her name. I don't want to hear her name spoken ever again.'

He looks into Rena's eyes. Clear and green and guileless, under her pale lashes, but can he still see beyond them, into her pure soul?

'All right,' he says. 'That's it.'

Rena fixes him with her gaze. She looks very young but sounds deathly serious when she says, 'I don't want anyone to think I'm second best.'

'No one could ever think that,' Bobby says, and means it. 'There's nobody but you, Rena. There hasn't been since you looked at me through the window of that shop on Sauchiehall Street, since I saw you walking out, your hair outshining that beautiful fur coat. No one could hold a candle.'

The man and his son have given up on the fishing lesson and walked up the path by the river. The brambles are coming out, and every so often the boy stops and picks one and pops it in his mouth. They'll still be sour, Bobby thinks. It's only September but he can feel autumn gathering on the blustery wind.

'What did you mean about secrets?' he asks, keeping his voice gentle while his mind shuffles the deck: is she Jamie's mother, did Hetty poison the father? Nothing would surprise him, and as he runs through the options, he finds nothing that would bother him either. For the first time since he met her Rena opens up. She tells him about her mother's divorce, starting with the day she woke up and decided to trade in their miserable life for something better.

'Rena, you amaze me,' he says, imagining her sitting alone on the train into Glasgow, hands folded on her lap, worrying more about the tram fare to Nell's flat than the scandal of divorce. His heart swells with love, and just a touch of relief.

She shrugs. 'Something had to be done.'

He takes out his cigarettes, offers her one and lights it for her. His own father hadn't passed on much in the way of advice, unless it was showing by example that working in a mine will destroy your lungs sooner or later, but at sea there had been a few men who liked to tell the younger ones what they knew. Always light a lady's cigarette, Posh Roly had told him. Always open the door, always help her into her coat. Don't pull out her chair though, you aren't the bloody waiter. And it's worked so far, hasn't it? Unless Bobby falls at the final hurdle.

The wind is whipping the trees overhead now, and the first of the russet leaves scatter into the puddle by their feet. The smoke from their cigarettes is snatched away as soon as it's exhaled. Bobby reaches towards the low keystone of the bridge, feels the soft dampness of moss rather than the hard stone he expected. 'I'm sorry I didn't tell you that I'd been married before. Before I proposed.'

Rena flicks her cigarette end over the bridge and into the river below. Bobby follows it with his eyes but it disappears in an instant in the foamy water.

'The banns. They were posted here. What address did you give?'

'The Broomielaw. The Home for Seamen.'

'Good. If anyone ever recognises your name, if anyone ever asks if you were married before, you lie to them, do you understand? You lie.'

'Yes. But nobody will recognise me, Rena, not here. And,' he reaches for her hand and she lets him take it, 'I'm nothing without you. You know that, don't you?'

'We're equal,' she says. 'Now I've told you about the divorce. We know each other's secrets, so let's never mention them again. When we go to that registry office tomorrow… it's a new day. We're not lugging the past around behind us.'

Yes, Bobby thinks, yes. 'All right,' he says.

She lays her hand on his arm. 'From now on, there's only the future.'

You're a lucky man, Bobby Young, he tells himself, as he leans in and kisses her chastely on the lips. And don't you ever forget it. He silences that cocky little voice in his head that reminds him that you make your own luck. Didn't he know Rena was the one, as soon as he saw her, even though he was shivering in the snow with his coat in the pawn? He knew it enough to follow her along the street, to play it all above board, to do things properly. To borrow the car, to drive Rena home afterwards, never overplaying his hand. Just as he's doing things properly now, asking permission of her brother and ordering a posy and corsage of real lily of the valley, her favourite, at the florist to surprise her.

As he goes to meet his sister from the train the next morning, he imagines Hetty answering the door to the florist, cooing over the flowers. A corsage for her as well, and for Evie who is matron of honour. And then he thinks of Rena, pinning the flowers to her lapel, as self-possessed as ever. In a couple of hours she'll be his, or he'll be hers. He tries to swallow his nerves, tries not to glance across the platform to the station bar. Not a drop will pass his lips before this wedding, not a drop. When Eleanor walks up to him the first thing she does is sniff his breath. There never was any subtlety to Eleanor. Her husband was killed in North Africa, poor chap, and bitterness has seeped into her since. A nippy sister and a lumpy niece of fourteen who's too shy to speak; not much of a family for his side of the registry office. Rena had asked about Merchant Navy mates, but he didn't want them as part of his new life, not really. Men he'd been stuck on a ship with, that he'd seen the worst of in between rare glimpses of the best. He's found a best man, at least; Gerald who sat at the desk next to him in the clerk's office, dull but a respectable Baptist. Said the others were still at sea. Rena wasn't bothered; Evie and Thomas are the bridal party, her mother as matron of honour. She hasn't had much of a chance to make friends. It's all been about work and family for the Jarvies, since they moved to this town.

'You will never cease to surprise me, Robert,' his sister says when he takes her across the road to the Temperance Coffee House. 'I mean, we all ken what happened last…'

'We do, and that's behind us.' It's a waste of a grand building, not to serve drink, but he's glad he decided to make the point and take Eleanor somewhere so emphatically respectable.

The niece – Peggy after their mother, though she doesn't look as if she has half that woman's wit – is engrossed in a scone as leaden as her countenance and doesn't seem to be listening. He tries to feel sorry for Peggy. She's not a pretty girl and she was young when his brother-in-law died. Charity fails Bobby here though; he can't help but think being caught in a roof-fall a week before the pit closed was a desperate attempt to avoid spending more time with Eleanor.

'Oh I get it, keeping secrets already are we?' she goes on, waving the empty milk jug at the dour waitress. The waitress's sigh is audible as she ambles over with a replacement and slops it down, spilling some on the table and neglecting to wipe it up.

'As a matter of fact, no,' Bobby says, keeping his voice low and waiting until the waitress is gone before adding: 'Rena knows all there is to know.' So put that in your pipe and smoke it, he thinks, noting with satisfaction the look of surprise on Eleanor's face. 'But not a word, do you hear me? This is a happy occasion.'

God knows what his sister expected, but he's sure it wasn't someone like Rena. When he turns and sees her walking towards him as he waits in front of the registrar, his nerves abate. She is wearing a green dress coat and white gloves, with mink trim on her collar and at the hem, her pillbox hat set at a stylish angle. Her hair blazes against the green, as if it's drawing all the light in the room. The scent of lily of the valley reaches him before she does and he feels his mouth twitch in a smile. She meets his eye then glances down at her little bouquet. The florist has added a silver horseshoe to the corsage, for luck. Bobby can't remember agreeing to that, but maybe it's no bad thing. Cost him a fortune, as did the gold wedding band in Thomas's breast pocket, and that long, lonely night he's just spent in the George Hotel, hoping not to get bitten by bedbugs, resolutely not going downstairs to bribe the night porter to slip him a bottle from the bar. But isn't it all worth it, for Rena?

Time slows down as he repeats the vows. Anne's there for a split second – *in sickness and in health* – but he shoves her from his mind. There's nobody but Rena, *for richer, for poorer* (but let it be richer), *forsaking all others. I do*. Once the words are out, and the ring is on her finger, minutes feel like seconds and the clock's whirling ahead. He's smelling her face powder, her touch of cologne, as they kiss, he's shaking hands with Thomas, he's hearing Eleanor put on her la-di-da voice to speak to his wife – his wife, there are second chances after all – and before he knows it they're round the corner in the photographer's studio, flanked by Thomas and Evie, and he's blinking again and again as the flash goes off in his face.

'Just once more, eyes open this time everyone!'

The whirl of time stops for a moment, as they all freeze for the wedding portrait.

And then they're in his new uncle-in-law Donald's car being driven to the hotel by Troon – Rena's choice again – and he can see the heave of the sea ahead of them but he's safe on dry land.

'You're so daring, Rena, wearing green to your wedding!' her Aunt Margaret exclaims, climbing out of the car that Thomas has borrowed for the day.

'That's old wives' nonsense,' Nell says. 'Our Irene's always loved green.'

Yes, he thinks, and Eleanor can put that in her pipe and all. She and Peggy, having seen the deed done, are on the train back to Glasgow. He takes a deep breath and catches the salt in the air. He's safe. They're two miles from the sea and high above it, and he can see Arran in the distance, snow still clinging to its peaks.

At last, at long last, he's holding a glass of champagne by its stem, a wedding treat from Min and Donald who like things fancy, waiting for Thomas to propose a toast to their good health so that he can reply and take a drink.

Rena smiles as the bubbles fizz up her nose, and he reaches for her hand and squeezes it and takes one sip, then a larger one, and thinks he's never been so happy in all his life before. And if, at the back of his mind, a little voice is saying *you've got away with it for now, Bobby Young, but you never know what's in the offing*, it's easy to silence it with just another sip. And here's Thomas, to buy Bobby a whisky and offer more congratulations. Evie is over with her family, her back to her husband. What was Thomas thinking, getting married rather than getting laid? And to Evie of all people, pert enough to mean you'd never rest easy, if you were a man like Thomas.

'Trust you to look after my sister,' Thomas is saying, with enough of a slur in his voice to earn him a row from Rena, and Bobby's nodding, nodding, shaking his hand again, submitting to his clumsy embrace. He hasn't got married to get laid, it's the furthest thing from his mind, although tonight they'll be in the same bed, the one Rena's been sharing with Hetty all these years. Preparations have been made: Hetty will stay with Nell in Glasgow, Jamie's to go to Thomas and Evie in their new Corporation villa. It will be Bobby and Rena alone in the flat, alone with the tick-tock of that funny oriental clock, him alone with Rena and her pale skin and perfect lipstick and tailored green wedding suit. Married, he tells himself, for as long as we both shall live. The nerves are back, jangling enough to make him order another double when nobody's looking, knock it back at the bar. But Rena isn't Anne, and it wasn't him that made Anne the way she was. That swell under his feet is whisky and excitement, that's all. Nobody's going to be swept out to sea today.

When he wakes up in the morning it takes him a while to understand where he is. He imagines the dorm at the hostel first of all, then the George Hotel the night before the wedding. The panic brings everything into focus. No, he didn't drink before the wedding. He is married, the register is signed and Rena never looked so beautiful, so pristine. He cranks open one eye, sees striped wallpaper. He's in the double bed at Rena's house. Except he can't remember going to bed, can't remember climbing the front steps to the red sandstone flat, can't remember saying goodbye to their guests although he can picture his cow of a sister with a triumphant expression, as though all her expectations have been met. But that needn't have been yesterday, Eleanor has worn that expression before. He'll prove her wrong. He's proved her wrong already. He's married Rena. He stretches his arm across the bed, but the linen sheets are cool and all that's there of his wife is the lingering scent of lily of the valley.

Rena, 1945

It's meant to be a celebration, and Rena is pleased, of course she is. The end of the war in Europe at last, what they've all been praying for. Jamie is out on the drying greens setting up the trestle tables with his friend from around the corner, and she and Hetty have been baking like mad. It looks like it's going to stay dry for them. She decides to use the last of their dried fruit in some rock buns; they're catering the party, they have to make an impression. Especially as Thomas has already written to the Food Committee, for a license to sell rationed and other goods once he gets home. There's no way the shop will support them all without it, but she just wishes that he was here to enjoy it, and that Bobby hadn't had to go to sea again. She hadn't realised how awful it had been last time, how close he must have come to being killed. He told it like an adventure story – the man with the harmonica, the boat creeping up alongside, the captain's voice coming out of the mist and startling them all – and Hetty and Jamie were all ears. It was only in the morning after their wedding night that he confided in Rena, when she'd got up off the couch and sorted her hair, put on her lipstick, and gone back into the bedroom. Steeling herself even more than she had the night before, wondering why he still hadn't wanted to do what men are supposed to. In the end his snoring had been too much and she'd taken herself off to get some sleep. But he was the one who apologised, said he was an idiot who didn't deserve her, told her how badly he'd been scared. She should have known, Rena realises. A ship torpedoed in the dark in the middle of the ocean. *And the worst of it was, I didn't want to die with nobody to miss me, I didn't want to be alone ever again. To be without you.* He held her close, and she held him back, although he was trembling and smelled of alcohol. Silly to think that Hetty might've told her what to expect; Rena still recalls being thirteen years old and running to her mother screaming that she was bleeding to death.

Once the rock buns are on the cooling rack she goes to freshen up. She has to sponge herself down, she's so warm from all the work she's put in already, and she doesn't want to spoil her new frock. Nell ran it up for her, in a nice striped cotton, to look just like the ones in the advertisements for Horrockses. Thank heavens it's sunny. Her summer shoes are still good, but her winter ones need replacing. And why not lipstick? It's meant to be a party, after all, and she is a married woman. She adds a shortie cardigan (Margaret's work, this time, from one of her own that she unravelled), before taking the baking tray from the oven and laying the buns out on the rack.

'Oh, you look a picture,' Hetty says. 'So nice to see you out of those shop aprons for a change.'

Old Mr Reid is out with the rusting bayonet that Jamie always wants a shot at, using the blade to weed between the bricks that pave the area outside their entry. Rena assumes the thing is decommissioned, though goodness only knows how former Lance Corporal Reid managed to hold on to it.

'This is a happy day right enough,' he says, flicking a dandelion into a bucket.

'It is,' Hetty replies. 'There were times when I wondered if I'd live to see it.'

'Don't be so morbid, Mum,' Rena rolls her eyes. 'We're meant to be celebrating.'

'That's as might be,' Mr Reid says, 'but between you and me, I wouldnae recommend that elderflower wine of Mrs Gemmell's. She gied me a bottle for trimming the hedge and it ran right through me.'

Thankfully Jamie runs over to ask for string to tie the bunting to the washing poles now that they've taken the lines down.

'There's some in my tool box, just inside the entry door,' Mr Reid says.

'Ta, Mr Reid,' Jamie runs off.

'I mind when you arrived here and he was just a bairn. And now here he is, almost done with the school.'

'I know,' Hetty says. 'He's daft on cars and the like. We're hoping for an apprenticeship.'

'Aye well, tell him to give the Forces a wide berth,' Mr Reid says, running his fingers along the deep V-shaped scar that puckers his right cheek. 'Where's your brother now?'

Jamie's her brother too, and Mr Reid knows Thomas's name fine well. Rena feels a sting of irritation.

'The Mediterranean, somewhere. He's due to be demobbed in a month or so. Now, let's start getting that food out, Mum. We need everything to be just so before the councillor arrives, although I suppose this'll be slumming it for him.'

'Well girls, it looks spot on to me,' Mr Reid says, saluting them both and slinging his bayonet over his shoulder. Hetty beams at his chivalry, and Rena relaxes. The sun is bright now, catching the red sandstone of the terraced flats, and although the tops of the trees are swaying the tablecloths and starched bedsheets are staying put. Most of the garden plots have been turned to vegetables, but the honesty is just coming into flower along the hedges, and the last of the tulips combine with the first of the purple alliums to make a bit of a show.

'We didn't make such a bad home here, did we?' Rena says, moved by the occasion to put her arm around her mother. She isn't expecting approval, and she doesn't get it, but Hetty too is in her best frock, and she's been fussing over the sandwiches all morning, making sure everything is perfect. Her gold locket catches the light. Inside there is a picture of Rena's father looking stern, and on the other side Hetty's three brothers, all in uniform, just before they went to France.

'I wish Thomas was here,' Hetty says.

'Me too. It won't be long.'

'I thought Evie might have arrived by now.'

'She said she'd bring down cream from the farm.'

A small cheer goes up over by the wash-house. Jamie and another boy are up on the low roof. In the absence of a flagpole they've managed to string a Union Jack to the chimney, where it's fluttering in the breeze. Rena watches for second to make sure Jamie lowers himself off down without injury.

'And did I tell you that Mrs Gibson said yesterday in the shop that the Provost might come by,' Hetty says.

'Fancy that,' Rena says. 'Well, I hope he'll take an empire biscuit. You hardly notice the dried egg in those.'

Together they begin to carry out the plates of scones, and the crumpets, and the jam they've put up from the raspberry canes on their plot. Easiest thing to look after and they grow like a weed, Mr Reid promised, and they've been glad of his advice. Jamie has managed their little garden all on his own. If he's so good at growing things, maybe a nursery would take him on and train him up? Somewhere decent.

Evie arrives off the bus from Fenwick carrying two small churns of cream, and quickly sets to whipping it for the scones and the sponge. She's wearing her uniform from the WAAF, which momentarily makes Rena feel as if she's dressed flippantly. But it's so nice to be in a full skirt for a change, something that swishes as she walks, and the war's over now, isn't it? She couldn't join an auxiliary force; she had to keep the shop going. Hetty did her bit for the WVS. All those socks and shawls, and tying up surprise parcels for the troops. Hoping that Thomas would receive one from somebody as well.

When Councillor and Mrs Gibson turn up she's wearing a summer hat, which reassures Rena. In fact, if she was honest, she'd say it was over the top, what with the colour and all those fake flowers. It's more like an Easter bonnet, and she looks forward to asking her mother what she thought of it later on. In his speech Councillor Gibson makes particular mention of their vegetable gardens, and the contribution made to the war effort. He is particularly grateful, being on the Food Committee. Between that and the railings, Beansburn might well have provisioned a whole ship! Everyone laughs. Some beer has been taken, and in spite of Mr Reid's warnings, some elderflower wine as well. The Provost won't be able to make it, due to all his other commitments, but he has asked Mr Gibson to pass on his appreciation. They have done the town proud. The councillor finishes by offering a special vote of gratitude to the Bungalow Stores for such a fine spread, and Rena can feel herself blushing in pride. She's sitting between Hetty and Jamie, and she smiles at them before dipping her head in acknowledgement of the compliment.

'That was smashing, Rena,' Evie leans over and says, between mouthfuls of scone. 'You did such a fine job.'

'It's the least we could do, really.' Rena smiles at her sister-in-law. 'And thank you, for bringing the cream.'

Hetty goes off to make sure they've brought out all the sandwiches, and Evie shifts along to sit next to Rena. 'It's nothing at all. After all, I'm part of the family now, amn't I?'

Rena nods and picks up the teapot. 'Yes, of course.'

'And I'm bursting with excitement, although it might be too soon to say, so I don't want to write to Thomas yet, but I just have to tell someone.' She reaches for Rena's arm and drops her voice. Rena stops mid-pour. 'That's twice now, with no monthlies. And usually I'm regular as clockwork, even when the rations were low.'

'Oh,' Rena says. 'Oh my goodness. So soon! That's wonderful news.'

'I know,' Evie smiles, proudly.

'Mother will be so pleased. May I tell her?'

'Would you mind hanging on? Just another few weeks, until I'm absolutely certain. Then I'll write to Thomas as well. But I just couldn't keep it to myself, Rena.'

'No,' Rena says, squeezing Evie's arm in return for the confidence. 'How are you feeling?'

'Fit as a fiddle,' Evie says, glancing at her watch. 'In fact, I must dash. My friend Izzy is coming to collect me. There's a dance at the base tonight.'

'But are you up to it?' Rena says. 'And without Thomas…'

'Oh, I know. I can't wait for him to come home again. You must be the same about Bobby.'

Rena nods. 'He's on his way, but of course they can't write from the ship.'

'Poor boys, missing all the fun!' Evie takes out her compact and powders her nose, then adds another thick layer of lipstick.

Rena walks her to the entry door and sure enough, a motor car is already idling at the kerb, driven by a young man who waves at Evie enthusiastically.

'Izzy's new fellow,' Evie says, by way of explanation. She pecks Rena on the cheek and runs down the steps. There's a girl in the passenger seat right enough, and another in the back who leans across and throws open the door for Evie. Rena can't imagine being so carefree, heading off to a dance as though it's the most natural thing in the world, while they have all the clearing up to do. And Thomas not yet home.

Still, when she goes back to the drying greens the sun has stayed out and somebody has rigged up their radio by an open window so that they can hear the music playing. When an eightsome reel begins to form, the couples lining up on the grass, Mr Johnstone's wife calls off, red-faced and wheezing, and he grabs Rena by the hand and draws her into the dance instead. The steps come back to her from school, and soon she's whirling with the rest of them. She hears someone yell, 'The war's over!' and joins in when everyone shouts out *hooray!* in response. Maybe

Evie has the right idea after all. Everyone deserves some fun after the hard work, a moment in the here and now without worrying about what's to come.

Once she's stripped the willow a few times she too is ready for a breather. As she pours some lemonade from a pitcher into her glass, Councillor Gibson comes over to speak.

'Mrs Young, may I thank you again for a lovely spread. You and your mother.'

She's out of breath from all the dancing and has to take a sip from her drink. 'Forgive me,' she says. 'The dancing… It's nothing really. The least we could do, when we've the shop.'

He leans closer towards her. She catches a hint of alcohol on his breath even though he has a teacup in his hand. 'Now, I shouldn't say, but your brother will be hearing favourable news from the committee, about extending the range of goods on sale.'

'Oh,' Rena says. 'Thank you.'

Gibson puts his finger to his lips. 'Shhh! You didn't hear it from me. Though I must say, I've always been partial to your cakes.'

At least the heat in her face will disguise any blushing this time. 'Thank you. That's such a relief. And my husband and I, well, with Thomas married we're thinking of a business in catering.'

'Well, you certainly have the talent for it,' Gibson says, and if she isn't mistaken he's looking at her bust. Damn Nell's sewing, her top button has popped off and the edge of her slip is showing. Better to pretend she hasn't noticed. Gibson looks thoughtful. 'I don't think I've met your husband, have I? At church, or whatnot?'

'He's from outside of Glasgow, you see, and he's

hardly had a chance to live here, since we were married. Merchant Navy. We'll need to move, when he comes home.'

'Ah, that explains it,' Gibson says, as if this has reassured him in some way. 'A tearoom, you said?'

Rena smiles. 'Well, if you really think our baking is good enough…'

'Never had better, but don't tell Mrs Gibson's mother that. Well, I can give you a little tip there, I think. With the army camp closed at Annanhill, the Corporation is looking to return the park to recreational use by next summer. Plans include a refreshment facility.'

'Goodness,' Rena says. 'Well. That could be an excellent spot.'

'It'll come back to the committee for approval.' Gibson taps his nose. 'Husband and wife team's exactly what's needed. Can't have that house sitting empty much longer. How long did you say Mr Young would be away for?'

'Another six weeks at least.'

'Ah, really? Well, that's a pity, when you're only recently married…'

The Union Jack has dislodged from the wash-house chimney and is being chased across the drying green by the Johnson children. Rena keeps smiling as she watches, unsure if Gibson is expecting her to say something.

'If you need anything, anything at all my dear, you just let me know.'

As Rena is thanking him again for his kindness she can see Mrs Gibson looking over intently. He turns and waves to her. 'Better go. My wife doesn't like me talking to pretty girls like you, Mrs Young. Or may I call you Irene?'

Rena agrees, and shakes his hand rather awkwardly, sure now that her cheeks are quite scarlet. As she helps clear the tables, making sure to get all their dishes back, Rena thinks about what Gibson said. She wishes, even more than she has before, that Bobby was home with her.

'Heavens,' Hetty observes. 'Your cheeks are rosy. All that fresh air and dancing.'

'I suppose so,' Rena says, fanning her face with her hands.

Hetty looks around and then leans towards her, an empty cake stand in her hands. 'I didn't like to say earlier, but did you see Mrs Gibson's hat?'

Rena, 1946

Rena walks along the Irvine Road, past handsome sandstone bungalows and semi-detached houses, set back above steep front gardens. There's a skim of frost at the edge of the pavement and the icy air catches in her chest, but spring is well advanced. The stunted rose bushes and bare hydrangeas are alleviated by clumps of purple and white crocuses. Some of the houses have names etched in the glass above the front door: Belleview, Kildonan, The Acorns. She would like to name a house one day. Her father's family had, that grey house in West Kilbride, but she can't for the life of her remember what it was called. Hetty would know, but Hetty rarely talks about those times now and Rena doesn't want to send her off down memory lane, rose-tinted spectacles firmly in place. Now it's only the slam of the front door and Bobby's heavy steps in the entry that jar her from sleep and remind her of her father coming home drunk. 'Got to take the work when I can get it,' Bobby says, and while she's glad of the extra money he brings home from the bits of buying and selling he does after his clerking job she wishes he didn't always have to drink afterwards, even if he does bring home food and cigarettes. 'It's just what men do,' Hetty says, and maybe she has more sense than Rena's credited her with.

When Rena crosses the road the red sandstone gives way to white-painted Corporation four-to-a-block villas like the one Thomas lives in. His has two bedrooms; just as well, with Evie so far gone now. The tree-lined driveway that leads to Annahill House is right at the edge of town. The grass harbours drifts of snowdrops; sparkling clean, with tiny zigzags of green around the inner petals. Daffodils are pushing up too, edges of yellow showing in the buds, almost ready to burst open. If it wasn't for the rhythm of two sets of hammer blows, falling slightly out of sync – or is it an echo? – she'd think the place was deserted. There must be men at work in the walled garden or the greenhouses, now appropriated as parks department nurseries.

The house rises before her, four Ionic columns supporting the portico, four splayed steps up to that grand front door. A mansion once, until it was bequeathed to the town after the Great War. Still a mansion, really, even if the state of it since the army camp was dismantled has sparked letters to the paper. Now that the war is over people are turning their attention closer to home, and Councillor Gibson's committee has finally met and decided that the building must be occupied as soon as possible. He came into the shop for cigarettes one morning and reached right over the counter to squeeze her hand, with other customers waiting behind him, watching. 'About that little opportunity I was talking about.' Now the windows look blank, and Rena realises that the shutters behind them are closed. There is a car parked outside, so MacPherson from the council must be here already. She checks her hat, smooths her skirt, and walks up the wide steps to the front door. The bell is so stiff she can hardly pull it, and the noise it makes is more of a tortured creak than a ring.

'Mrs Young?' a voice calls behind her. She turns and nods. 'Come this way please,' the man says. Presumably he's MacPherson, though he doesn't introduce himself. 'We'll be using the side entrance.'

There's a moment of pleasantry about the weather – initiated by Rena – before he asks the question: 'And Mr Young?'

She's all prepared. 'Family illness called him back to Glasgow, I'm afraid.'

Mr MacPherson makes a noise akin to a tsk. 'Well,' he says. 'That's a pity.' He looks at his watch.

'But,' Rena says smoothly, 'my husband is perfectly happy for me to view the premises and make any decisions necessary.'

'The papers,' Mr MacPherson taps his briefcase.

Rena forces her lips into a smile. 'If we agree that everything is satisfactory, then I can assure you that Mr Young will be in your office tomorrow morning first thing to sign the paperwork.' Even, she thinks, if I have to tie him to the bed tonight to stop him going out drinking. She should have brought Thomas with her. These things always work better with a man. But Thomas has applied to the committee to expand the range of goods in the shop yet again, and they can't muddy the waters.

'Very well,' MacPherson says, looking at his watch again as though somehow she is wasting his time. She's on the verge of setting him straight, telling him that Bobby will be behind her all the way, but instead she follows him round the driveway to the side door.

'So this would form the entrance to both the business premises and the dwelling house,' he says, sorting through a bunch of keys until he finds the correct one to fit in the lock. Inside, a poky hallway opens onto darkness. MacPherson feels for a light switch and clicks it, but nothing happens. He sighs and edges forward. After some fiddling and what sounds like a muffled curse, one set of shutters creak open. The room is big, and high ceilinged, the floor covered with a mess of newspapers and – Rena manages not to squeal – a dead pigeon near her feet. She edges backwards. The Lord only knows how it got in. The air is fusty, and it's icy cold.

'The original kitchen downstairs was removed at some point,' MacPherson says. 'That level is all storage now and you won't have the use of it. But if you'll follow me there are facilities through here that were put in more recently.'

Recently? Rena reaches out and tries one of the big brass taps, which screeches into life before releasing a sputter of brown water into the Belfast sink. It takes both hands to turn it off, and she turns to MacPherson, eyebrows raised.

'The tenant will be responsible for any upgrading,' he says.

'Hmm,' she says. 'And there's a flat, I hear. How is that accessed?'

'There's another door at the back of the house.'

She waits, and then says, 'Well, shall we go and look at it then?'

'Would it not be better to wait until Mr Young is available?'

'Mr Young has full confidence in me,' she says, as

cheerfully as she can. 'And when I saw Mr Gibson this morning he did emphasise that the Corporation wanted a quick decision.'

'Did he now?' MacPherson smirks.

The flat is a dingy caretaker's conversion, with thin walls and bisected cornicing. In what MacPherson laughably calls the master bedroom, the previous tenant has left a metal-framed single bed that looks as if it has come from an asylum. The bathroom is cold as ice and the enamel of the bath stained, but there is a WC at least. And the address is Annanhill House, isn't it, whether you have the entire building or not. It won't be so bad in summer time, she thinks. MacPherson is quiet, and she can't tell if he pities her – looking for employment, her husband nowhere in sight – or thinks she's a timewaster. He would never guess at all those early starts on the bike, those Sundays baking and Mondays in the wash-house with Hetty. But the war is over now, and all kinds of people's lives are changing.

'With a new venture like this, it's better to be as near to the premises as possible,' she says. 'You need to keep an eye on everything.' One day, she'd like to move into a new house, she decides, one which has nothing left over from the past, one which will be all her own.

'A tearoom, is it?'

Rena nods. 'The committee thinks it's too far to go into the town from here for refreshments.'

MacPherson has a nose that looks as if once upon a time somebody punched it. When he exhales it comes out as a snort. 'Do they indeed?'

'So my husband says,' she adds, quickly. It was her that Gibson told, not Bobby, but she doesn't like MacPherson's tone.

'Well,' MacPherson says. 'I don't envy you the work. It's going to take a lot of elbow grease to get it all fit for purpose, and all for a year's lease.'

'Where there's a will there's a way,' Rena says. 'I can assure you.'

MacPherson indicates that she should precede him, and they descend the narrow wooden stairs. He must think she's mad, even considering it. But what can she do? Thomas will be happy enough in the shop, but she is ready for a change. They can't live the way they are, with Hetty in Jamie's room and her in that same bed she's been sharing since she came to the town. If everything works out, in summer the place will be busier than the Howard Park. And if they make a success of it, well, Gibson as good as promised that the Corporation would extend the lease. In the distance smoke billows from the tall red chimneys of the brick works. There's a risk, yes, but it is outweighed by opportunity. Bobby understood that as soon as she told him, and he was willing to take the chance. He might not be here by her side, but he's with her all the way.

'Is nine convenient for Mr Young to come in and sign?' she asks.

'Are you quite sure he would not like to see the premises himself before committing? I don't want to take the time to draw up the papers if there's any doubt.'

'Quite sure. He will be there to sign the lease, so I would be grateful if you would prepare it this afternoon as planned.'

MacPherson doesn't offer her a lift, not that she would have accepted if he had. A smarmy type, and just as well if he does think this is a fool's venture. If he saw the future that she can see, the hard work certainly, but the money it will bring, he'd be clamouring to raise the rent and bring in more viewers. Instead he thinks he's passed it off on a silly woman. Oh, this will be the start that she and Bobby need, a chance to work together, to begin to make their mark. As she walks along the drive she sees two men in blue overalls standing under a tree smoking, a wheelbarrow and discarded tools beside them. One of them looks her up and down and calls out, 'Hello, how are you today?'

His accent is German and Rena realises they must be prisoners of war, and is about to hurry past when the other man tips his cap to her and says to his companion. 'Otto, leave the Fraulein to make her walk in peace.'

Otto shrugs. 'She is smiling so I am saying hello.'

'Hello,' Rena says, standing straight and making sure her wedding ring is visible, if either of them cares to look. She's never met a German before and her curiosity is getting the better of her. The other man stubs out his cigarette, wipes his hands on his overall and comes over. 'My name is Paul. And my rude companion is Otto.'

'I'm Mrs Young. Irene.'

'See Otto, the Fraulein is a Frau. No chance for you.'

Otto makes a dismissive noise, whether of Rena's marital status or of his chances she can't tell.

'And you work here, on the grounds?' she says, hastily. They don't look like devils incarnate. They're wearing dark blue work trousers and matching shirts, sleeves rolled up over their elbows. One has sandy blonde hair combed into place, the other, dark hair with a middle parting. His shirt zips up the front; Rena hasn't seen anything quite like it before.

'Yes…'

Otto interrupts, 'Don't tell our boss. We are not

allowed to fraternise, and he is an angry man.'

Rena laughs in spite of herself. 'I won't. Is it, do you… like it here?'

Paul nods seriously. 'Better than being in a camp.'

Images from the newsreels flash through Rena's mind, but of course that isn't what he means.

'But the weather is very bad,' Otto says. 'That is why we must stop work when the sun shines.'

She laughs. 'Well, Paul and Otto. It was nice to meet you. And perhaps I'll see you again.' She wants to share her good news, even with strangers. German strangers. 'My husband and I, we'll be coming to work here too. To start a tearoom. We'll be living here, in the house.'

'When?' Otto asks.

'Well, as soon as we can. As soon as we're allowed to.'

'In that case, we will be here,' Paul says. 'And if you are in the house, you will need work done, and we are here to work.'

'I would rather work for a nice lady than an angry man.'

'Maybe her husband is angry,' Paul says.

'Why would he be angry? He has a pretty wife.'

Rena says goodbye and hurries along the drive before they can see her blush. She can hear them speaking in German and laughing. At her? She doesn't know. Wouldn't some help be useful though, she thinks. Anything is possible, after all, in this new life she's going to build. All she has to do is make sure that she gets Bobby in to the office on time in the morning to sign the papers.

Bobby, 1946

Two minutes past nine isn't bad, Bobby thinks, looking up at the clock on the corner of the council buildings. Rena would have liked to come with him, he knows, but Thomas needs the help in the shop and Evie can't manage. It might be twins, they're saying, given the size of her. Hetty is up visiting Min and Donald, and her sister Margaret who has moved in with them now her sight is failing. He feels – Rena made him feel – that he let her down by not being at the viewing, but what was there to do? She doesn't want him to go back to sea, which is just fine by him, and so if he can make a few bob here and there, dropping things off and picking them up, well, that's how it has to be. Thomas gave them the motor as a wedding present, and to buy Rena out of the shop, and it deserves to be driven. Better an errand boy in the city than here in the town, where people's noses bother them.

The woman on reception is stern, a battleaxe with pince nez and curls set solid enough to withstand a hurricane, ostentatiously glancing towards the clock when he tells her that Mr MacPherson is expecting him. Bobby gives her the full dose of charm, and even though he's just going through the motions he's gratified when she simpers as she directs him to MacPherson's office. He checks his watch again as he walks along the tiled corridor, checking the plates on the doors as he goes. Seven minutes past nine. Oh well, seven's a lucky number, isn't it?

The office is just like the one he clerked in before he went to sea. Men sitting in rows like secretaries in a typing pool, everything the colour of over-brewed tea. There is going to be no more of that for him, no more *sir, yes sir*. Rena is right. Why work for someone else? Just to end up like Mr MacPherson here, in his early twenties and old before his time. Perk up, Bobby wants to say. You've got the rest of your life ahead of you. Anything that's happened to you before now is just teething trouble. MacPherson gets to his feet as though it's an effort and shakes hands. He doesn't have a strong grip, but Bobby feels the faintest pressure where his second and third fingers meet his palm. So it's like that, is it.

'It's quite irregular for someone to take on a property without seeing it first,' MacPherson says, shuffling through the documents with the slow hand of someone whose working days linger too long.

'Ah, but my wife saw it, didn't she? And she's a sensible lady.'

'Hmm,' MacPherson says, making it sound like an accusation. Bobby bristles. He's in a good mood, and cheek from this glaikit item is not part of his script for the day. MacPherson glances up from the lease, notices Bobby's expression, quickly regroups. 'There's a clause here, I mean, about the condition of the place. You need to agree it, see, and if you haven't inspected the property yourself, well, you've only got what your wife's said to go on.'

Spineless too, Bobby thinks. How did he get on in the war, or did he stay cosy at home, his Corporation job protected? He recalls Rena's description of the ground floor of the house, the debris in what's to be the tearoom and the failings of the flat. He rattles off a list of faults, beginning with the plumbing in the kitchen and ending up with, 'And it goes without saying, doesn't it, that the whole place could do with a lick of paint. It's been very poorly maintained by the previous owners and as far as we can make out, the Corporation hasn't lifted a finger.'

MacPherson's mouth goldfishes and Bobby wants to snap at him to breathe through that crooked nose of his. Instead he says, mildly, 'I told you that my wife was a sensible lady.'

'I didn't –' MacPherson begins, then thinks better of it and rotates the lease so that it's facing Bobby on the table. The man at the desk nearest to them pretends he hasn't been staring, waiting to see if an argument is about to begin. 'Page one and page four for your signature.'

'I'll read it through first, if you don't mind,' Bobby says, making a show of looking around for a chair. MacPherson gets up and fetches one from behind an empty desk. He works his way through the document carefully. Not much schooling, but he can read just fine, and he knows to check anything he's putting his name to. Learned that in retrospect, really, after he signed on the line to sail under the Red Duster. The initial term is one year, application for renewal to be made in writing on or before the date of payment of the twelfth month's rent.

'What's this?' he asks, stabbing his finger towards clause eleven on page three.

MacPherson sits up straight, as if sensing a power shift in his favour, wee plook that he is. 'Standard Corporation clause.'

'And what's that when it's at home?'

'In every commercial lease the Corporation issues.' MacPherson is quick to get superior, when he has the chance. 'If the tenant doesn't leave when served a notice of eviction, they may be prosecuted and or forcibly evicted. And in twelve, here, as the property includes a dwelling house, the Proprietor may give special consideration for a Corporation house on termination of the lease.'

'All right,' Bobby says. He ignores the pen that MacPherson has used to indicate where to sign and takes his own from his breast pocket. A wedding present from Rena, silver plated and ready to bring him luck. He unscrews the cap and there, in two flourishes it's done. Entry date 13th September, and they will have a house, and a business. 'Is that in order?'

MacPherson examines the document as if he'd like nothing more than to find it null and void. 'Yes,' he says, at last.

'Well, here's a wee lesson for you for free.' Bobby leans over the table and drops his voice to a whisper. The man at the next desk has his head down now, as if scrutinizing figures on the ledger in front of him, but Bobby knows his ears are wagging. 'It's not on to express doubts about another man's wife, whether you're talking about her business sense, her steak and kidney pie, or the size of her arse. Because when you do, you're likely to cause offence. Do you understand me?'

MacPherson nods. His face is scarlet with humiliation.

'I said, do you understand me?'

'Yes.' MacPherson meets Bobby's eyes and there's hatred in his expression. He has a bit of spirit in him after all.

'Is there a problem?' enquires the earwigging clerk at the next desk. He looks like a tougher nut. Older, with receding ginger hair, and big, capable hands.

'Everything's in order,' Bobby says with a smile, and pushes his chair back. 'Just shooting the breeze with young MacPherson here. Thank you very much for your assistance.' He extends his hand to MacPherson, who has no option but to shake it, and leaves the tea-brown office with a spring in his step that carries him along the tiled corridor, past all those other offices full of clerks, past the battleaxe at reception to whom he tips his hat and says, 'Thank you very much, and you have a nice day!' almost like he's one of those dupes from the Midwest he used to sidle up to at the Grand. Well, he's won a different kind of card game today, and the thrill is beating through him. Nine forty-five. That's fifteen minutes until the Station Bar opens, not that Bobby needs to think about that, oh no, he has other fish to fry.

He carries on past the cinema and stops in at the florist by the viaduct that carries the trains south, to Carlisle and London. A bouquet for Rena, that's the ticket.

'What colours does she like?' the woman asks, and he says, 'Green,' then laughs, because none of the flowers in the shop are green.

'How about blue?' she says, and points to irises and some tall pointy things that look a bit like lupins to his untrained eye.

'White,' he says, seeing a metal pail full of creamy white roses. 'Roses, some leaves and plenty of that frothy stuff. How about that?'

'Grand,' she says. 'How much do you want to spend?'

There's the rub. Has he money in his pocket? He can't quite recall. He came home early last night, just like Rena said, but of course he did have just the one with Roy and the Italian boy he knows who might be able to get hold of this or that, if the price is right. His fingers sift through the coins, judge their size. It's fine. Everything's fine. 'Just make it look good,' he says, and the woman does, hand nimble in fingerless gloves as she ties up a bouquet fit for Rena.

He hides it behind his back as he enters the shop, the bell announcing his presence. Thomas is nowhere to be seen, but Rena hurries out from the back shop, wiping her hands on a dishcloth. Her hair is tied back in a scarf and she's wearing a pinny, so she looks like one of the girls in the war effort posters you used to see, although Bobby never saw a poster girl who'd come close to Rena.

'Is it all right?' she says. 'Did you sign?'

He hesitates for a moment, until the fear shows in her eyes, then whisks out the bouquet. 'Congratulations, Mrs Young,' he says. 'We are going into business for ourselves.'

She kisses him on the lips then tells him off for buying the flowers, but he knows she's pleased. She puts them in a vase in the middle of the table in the flat, and keeps coming back to them, touching a petal or leaf as she passes, letting her palm hover over the cloud of baby's breath. As they go to bed that night, together for the first time in a long time, as Bobby isn't working that night, he says to her, 'This is just the beginning for us, Rena, you know that, don't you?'

She nods, and he reaches out to touch her arm. He'll try again, to make her happy in the right way, in the way he hasn't managed before.

Rena 1946

Another bottle. The toilet wouldn't flush properly in the new flat at Annanhill although Rena thought Donald had fixed it, and now she knows why. Standing on a ladder, managing to shift the lid of the cistern, and here it is. There's no label so she pulls out the cork and sniffs it. Whisky. Bobby has become partial to whisky and he seems to have a never-ending supply of it. She suspects, knows, that some of his errands to Glasgow have been to deliver 'wastage' from Johnnie Walker to his acquaintances there. Nothing to be said or done about it; they need the money and she can't do it alone if he goes back to sea. She pours the whisky down the toilet, takes pleasure in washing it all away. The flush seems fine now. A visit to the doctor is an extravagance, but what else is she to do to help Bobby?

As she pushes the window open to get rid of the stench of alcohol she sees a van coming along the drive. Donald delivering the not-so-good tables and chairs he and Min have squirrelled away from house clearances and yes, there's Nell in the passenger seat so she'll have brought all the tablecloths and doilies she's managed to get her hands on. Rena checks herself in the mirror – her curls are going limp and goodness, she looks tired. No wonder. It's been twelve hours a day getting the place half-habitable, and that's with all hands on deck. She insisted on Jamie's help and Thomas comes after work sometimes. Now Evie has given birth to twins he seems glad of the change of scene, even if it's spent painting walls. Once the rooms were cleared of junk Rena paid Alma to come in and help her with the cleaning. Alma's good, and cheap, and she works as hard as Rena. If this all comes off, she's told Bobby they should think of taking her on as a kitchen help or waitress. Best of all, as it turned out, the Parks foreman was happy enough for them to use Otto and Paul, and Bobby has charmed them into extra effort with his reminiscences of Hamburg port and the promise of an illicit bonus when it's all done. Having said that, the Youngs don't have a penny to their name right now so they need the doors open and some customers coming in. She looks at her watch. Time to go.

'I'm here about my husband,' Rena says, once she has been called through to see Dr Meikle. She arranges herself in the chair and thrusts her handbag towards the floor. Dr Meikle coughs, hacking until something rattles unpleasantly in his lungs, and as he glares at her handbag she guesses that she isn't the first woman to utter these words in his consulting room.

'What seems to be the trouble, hmm?'

She wonders why he doesn't write himself a script for the phlegm. Meikle has been the family physician since Jamie got scarlet fever, and she's fairly sure that he does write himself scripts for other things. But doctors know best, that's the thing. Jamie recuperated with no lasting effects, didn't he? She takes a deep breath, invoking her reverence of the Hippocratic oath and praying for a marvellous new medicine that'll sort Bobby out.

'He drinks too much.'

Shorter than she'd planned, but to the point and nothing Meikle couldn't have guessed if he turned his mind to it. The doctor scratches his chin. His nails rasp against skin and hair, and she imagines flakes falling to the collar of his shirt. He clears his throat.

'I know your husband, Mrs Young, and he's hardly a down and out.'

Rena is taken aback for a moment. 'Well,' she says. 'We're trying to open a business, and all my family are rallying round and we're working, I'm working, every hour God sends, and I need Robert to be there too. I mean of course he must go to his work, but if he would just come back and help out.' She takes a deep breath. She can't quite say about the bottle in the cistern. It seems too sordid, Hippocratic oath or not.

Meikle nods. 'I see. And you are tired, are you?'

For a second she worries she's going to cry. 'Yes, Dr Meikle, I am tired. I'm exhausted, to tell you the truth.'

'I can see that. And from what you're saying, there's no chance of taking it easy at the moment, feet up, concentrating on domestic life?'

She shakes her head. 'We've moved into the flat, but there's still too much to do.'

'All right,' he scribbles on a pad in front of him. 'I suggest we focus on your health first of all, Mrs Young, because a tired wife, a complaining wife, does not inspire a man to come home.'

'I never do…'

'Here. Take as directed, for the tiredness.'

I never do complain, she was going to say, but she accepts the prescription. 'Thank you. Now what about Bobby? I really am concerned about him.'

'Mrs Young. I see many things in my profession. People confide in me. I'm sure you can imagine, hmm?'

She leans forward in her chair. He leans back in his. He is expecting her to simper; she does. 'Oh yes.'

'You're an intelligent woman, after all.'

She can't help swelling slightly in his praise, the implied sharing of confidentiality.

'One of the things I have observed in my years as a family general practitioner, is that we men are fragile creatures.'

He bares his yellowing teeth. It takes Rena a second to realise that this is a smile.

'Mrs Young, listen to me when I tell you that it can be difficult for a man to be married to a busy woman, an ambitious woman. I am speaking frankly.'

'I appreciate it.'

'I have your records here.' He indicates a substantial brown paper folder. 'You've been married a couple of years now, and still no children.'

Her expression must have slipped into impatience because Meikle raises himself in his seat and says more firmly, 'I bring this up because a normal family life is a stabilising influence on any man.'

She sighs. 'I wondered, I mean, my Aunt Margaret was a nurse, a matron, and she mentioned that there are places people can go for help. Sanatoria, I mean.'

'I don't quite follow. For yourself, you mean?'

'No, I mean for Bobby. To give him time…'

'You're his wife, Mrs Young. If it's anyone's job to help your husband, it's yours.' Meikle chuckles. 'Look.

Nurses are almost always good intentioned, but they aren't doctors. Let's not think of such drastic measures as convalescent homes when the simplest solution might be the most natural one. Are there' – his catarrh bubbles into a swift bark – 'any problems?'

For a second her mind fills with favours and figures, tea and coffee hoarded and creditors unpaid. Then she realises Meikle is alluding to problems in the bedroom.

'Everything's fine,' she says quickly. The way things are just now, it's a miracle if Bobby manages to get his shoes off before coming to bed, and she's not bothered about anything else. She feels a bit queasy. Meikle isn't buying it, she can tell. 'Of course we've been very busy, with the business…'

He softens. 'Hard work may be necessary and even desirable, hmm, but it's no substitute for healthy marital relations. But to put your mind at ease…'

Within five minutes she's staring at the ceiling while he prods and grunts away between her legs. Her thoughts turn in the direction of Alma, who has nine children. That many mouths to feed makes her a good worker, for a Catholic, and she seems to have the sense to keep her husband off her now. The last one was born four years ago, or was it five? Rena concentrates on keeping still and wonders what on earth Meikle is doing down there. She's grateful to have Alma to help with some of the rough work, the floor scrubbing and dish washing that will need to be done every day from now on.

'Everything appears to be in order, Mrs Young,' Meikle tells her when he's done. While she sorts her clothing she hears him light a cigarette and scrawl some addition to her notes. She pulls the curtain back and he looks up, disinterested.

'I suggest that if you want to curtail your husband's drinking, you make every effort to conceive a child as soon as possible.'

Rena feels tearful again, and hopes the plumbing will muster enough hot water for a soak. She nods and hardly manages to say goodbye. When she goes out to the receptionist the woman consults her notes and says, 'No need, Mrs Young. Doctor says there's nothing to pay today.'

Bobby, 1946

Bobby holds his hands gently over Rena's eyes as he walks her down the steps and onto the driveway. 'How are you feeling, my love?'

'Better.' She'd been sick as a dog earlier, which isn't like her; apparently all the Jarvies have cast-iron stomachs. Nerves, he reckoned. It's a big night for them. Their biggest so far.

'That's my girl. Shame if you missed all the fun and games.'

'I'm fine. Just anxious about getting everything done in time, I expect. If we make a good go at this, well, they'd be fools not to renew our lease, wouldn't they?'

'They would.' It's true. They've transformed the place, with elbow grease and borrowed money. 'Now, no peeking.'

'I'm not. What is it you're going to show me?' He can hear trepidation in her voice, as if she thinks he's bought something they can't afford; a new car, a racehorse.

'Wait and see. You'll love it, I promise you.'

He nods to Otto, who's poised next to the electricity connection. No switch as such, but Otto has a talent for electrics, and swears it's safe as houses. 'But not like houses back home, Bobby, you understand. Because some of them were not safe at all.' Jamie's standing by too, waiting to see her reaction. Otto fiddles with the wires and whoomph! All along the driveway, red, blue and yellow bulbs are strung between the trees, lighting a path towards the house. Towards their tearoom, and their Hogmanay tea dance. He releases his hands.

'Oh!' Rena says. 'Oh.' She turns and clutches both his arms, turns back to look. 'It's beautiful! How on earth…'

Jamie comes running over, followed by Otto and Paul. 'Do you like it? We've been at it all day.'

Her brother's a big lad now but still young for his age, as far as Bobby's concerned. She snuggles him in close to her, closer than Bobby, and says, 'I love it. I can't believe how clever you all are.'

'Otto's the clever one,' Bobby says. 'He's the one that knows his electrics. All I did was collect a few bulbs and make the council an offer on some cable that was left in one of the old stables.'

'You weren't writing to them again about keeping the car there?'

'Those pigeons crap all over the paintwork. But the council's made itself clear that we're presumptuous to ask for a garage. Us giving them money is another matter.'

'Well, it is magnificent. Well done, all of you.'

'It was Bobby's idea,' Otto says, with a shrug. 'But your brother here, he has the makings of an electrician. We couldn't have done it without him.'

'Well, I'm just pleased you didn't electrocute him,' Rena says.

Bobby has to admit, it does look magical. It's going

to draw people from Bonnyton and beyond to see in the new year with them. 'Right, what's to be done inside? With those lanterns lit folk are going to be beating a path to our door.'

Rena takes his arm. 'We've done it all. Me, Mum, and Alma. We're all set.'

Good, Bobby thinks, good. If we're all set there might be time for a stiffener.

'And here's Thomas in the car,' Rena says, waving.

Thomas is to help Bobby keep an eye on the clientele, along with Otto and Paul, in case anyone gets rowdy. They've done four tea dances so far, but this is the biggest. And it's Hogmanay. The end of the year makes some people unpredictable. Bobby gestures over to the side of the house where there's space for guests to park.

'Good to see you, Thomas. All ready for tonight?'

'I am indeed. And Evie'll be here in five minutes,' Thomas says. 'Insisted on walking with the pram. Concerned about her figure, although I keep telling her there's no need. At least there's a chance of the wee devils being asleep.'

'Notice anything different?' Rena says.

Jamie points to the driveway. 'Look what we did. How do you like our light show, eh?'

'My God,' Thomas exclaims. 'How the Hell did you manage that?'

'Bobby and Otto and Jamie did it,' Rena says. 'There was cable in one of the sheds. Bobby wrote to the council and asked if he could buy it.'

'At a knock down price, of course,' Bobby adds.

Thomas laughs and slaps him on the back. 'You've an eye for a bargain, Bobby Young, I'll say that for you. And you Jamie, maybe you'll pluck up the courage to ask a girl to dance tonight.'

They're still standing outside talking when Evie trundles the pram along the driveway. 'Come and see my babies,' she calls. Two bunneted heads are just visible over a crochet blanket.

'Forgive me Evie, but I can't tell which is which,' Rena says.

'This is Malcolm,' Evie says, running a finger along the pink cheek of the baby on the left. 'And this is Evelyn. And they're going to be good little angels for their Granny Jarvie, aren't you my petals?'

'You're a lucky man, Thomas,' Bobby says. He can see Rena trying to hide a look of disdain at Evie's baby talk, and perhaps Evie senses it too because she says, 'And you'll be pleased with me, Rena. I've been chatting up the Young Farmers and a gang of them are coming down here instead of staying in the village hall.'

'That's grand, Evie, thank you,' Bobby says and Rena nods, more interested in the prospect of customers than in her niece and nephew. Customers who'll be paying for teas and coffees and light refreshments, but who might just be tempted to something a little stronger if they're people he knows, or might invite into the back storeroom where there happens to be enough drink laid up to knock out a battalion. Rena knows – he assumes – but she'll turn a blind eye as long as there's no trouble and it puts money in their pockets. She's pragmatic that way. One of the qualities that sets her above any other woman he's known. Besides, she was pleased to have a few new packets of nylons, and those came from the same place as the sauce: the master's cabin of the *Opalia*, stuffed with whisky, rum, and cigars by the Chinese second steward, a man Bobby bunked with on the *Hester*.

He waits until the band arrives before he takes one himself. A discipline, just to prove he can. The musicians are glad to accept a libation and the promise of more when they take a break. Bobby sets aside a bottle for himself in the back store room and has a nip whenever his business takes him there. By the time the dancing begins – and who'd have thought it, it's Evie that starts it, dragging Thomas unwilling to the floor but making him smile nonetheless – Bobby has a quiet buzz on. Evie can dance, and you'd never guess to look at her that she'd recently given birth to twins. The band is encouraged by her enthusiasm, and soon the floor fills up. His eyes meet Rena's across the room and she nods before stooping back under the serving hatch they've assembled across the kitchen doorway. It's going to be a success. Not even nine o'clock and they have a crowd in.

An hour later and they have a queue, one person out, one person in. Minto, the councillor from Bonnyton, is there and has been availing himself of Bobby's store room stash. On the house, Bobby insists, because it's as well to keep him sweet given that he's seen to it personally that they can stay open until the bells.

'Best thing that could have happened in my area, a fine local amenity for community gatherings. And that's exactly what I'll tell them when the lease comes up for renewal, you just leave it with me. I want you and Mrs Young staying right where you are…'

He emphasises this by prodding Bobby's lapel. Bobby's thanking him when Jamie pokes his head around the door and whispers, 'The farmers are outside. Otto and Paul are trying to get them to hang on but they're all het up.'

'Excuse me, Councillor, a few more guests!'

'Of course, of course.' Glowing and beneficent, Councillor Minto lets himself be ushered from the room. Bobby turns the key in the lock and mutters to Jamie, 'Oh Christ, how many?'

'A dozen. Maybe more.'

Rena is weaving between chairs, clearing tables and stopping to chat and joke. She isn't a natural at having a good time herself, but she does have a talent for helping other folk enjoy themselves. She can smile all night and never let on that her feet are killing her. Sometimes she'll lay her legs over his knees, let him massage her calves. He waves and she sweeps over, tray of cups ready to be delivered to Alma and Hetty, who are taking turns with the washing up.

'The farmers have arrived and there's no room in here. And we'll be expecting more, I daresay. It's only the back of ten.'

He can see Rena thinking. 'It's not about tonight. It's about everyone telling their friends and coming back to the next dance. The driveway, is it clear?'

'All the cars are round the side and on the grass.'

'Well, can we move the party outside? It's a clear night and it's hotter than Hell in here.'

'Charge entry just the same? Close the gate and Otto and Paul can let people in.'

'Yes. The band's due its last break. Let's get them outside for the final hour. We've gallons of milk. I'll have Hetty make a vat of cocoa.'

'Jamie,' Bobby shouts. 'I need your help. Give the Young Farmers drink, a bottle to pass around, but stick it under your jacket and make sure nobody sees. Here's the key to the store. Then come back and help me shift the band. Rena, have Evie and Thomas ready to start dancing in the driveway. Then go and charm Minto. Anyone who lives near enough to be bothered by the noise is here anyway.'

Rena's right, it is hotter than Hell indoors, hotter than the engine room of a ship, even with the windows flung open. Bobby pats his breast pocket, but he's left his flask in the store room with the rest of the booze. No time to get it now. 'Extra cash for the lot of you if you can be set up and ready to play outside in ten minutes,' he tells the band, waving a handful of notes to prove it. They spring into action, a wee bit of military training still left in them.

'This is such fun, Bobby,' Evie squeals as she heads out after them, Thomas in tow. 'Come on girls, next one's lady's choice!'

It works. He looks for Rena, wants to go and put his arm around her and survey what they've done, but she's either stuck in the kitchen or he can't see her in the crowd. He has a quarter bottle to replace the missing hip flask and it won't last him. People are laughing and dancing and the steam is rising from their hot breath in the chill winter air. The band is building up to a frenzy and yes, with the fairy lights still shining yellow and blue and red, the world looks to Bobby the way it's meant to, the way it always should. Sparkling and bright, and just a little fuzzy around the edges. He moves away to drain the bottle unseen. Just as he's tucking it under his car to move tomorrow, he hears a couple getting into their own motor.

'Did you ever see the like?' the man is saying, but just as Bobby lets a smile spread across his face the wife chips in, 'Coloured lanterns and dancing outside! And half of those folk were fou. I don't know who they think they are, putting on a show like that here.'

The car door slams and the engine sputters into life. Bobby unlocks the passenger door of his own car and feels around in the glove compartment. It's his lucky night. An emergency half bottle. 'And a happy fucking new year to you too,' he says, raising it to the departing car. Who do they think they are? They're Bobby and Rena Young, and they're shaking some fun into this staid wee town with a Hogmanay dance it won't forget in a hurry. He glances at his watch. Quarter to twelve. Time to find Rena, and put his arm round her, so they can watch together while Paul sets off the fireworks.

Rena, 1947

Rena slings the glass cloth over her arm. There. All the cups, all the saucers, ready to go. She goes out into the tearoom, walks around the tables straightening the starched linen and adjusting the milk jugs and ashtrays. Little vases on each table, each one with a flower and a sprig of green courtesy of Paul, who used to have what he calls a *Kleine Garten* and is enjoying working in the walled garden now that the weather is warm enough to yield some blooms. Veg too, from the allotments that were dug when the war started and still supply runner beans and – useful this – onions. No sugar bowls on the tables as yet; nobody knows when it'll be off ration. Small touches mean class, and everyone says what a good cup of tea you get here. The evening dances have been mobbed since word got around about Hogmanay, and how much fun it was with the lights and the band and people spilling out on the driveway. Quite continental, Rena thinks. She likes the sense of the word on her tongue, though the closest she's been to abroad is Millport. Paul says Annanhill reminds him of a place back home, a dancehall with lights just like theirs, and tables outside, and a crowd of people every night. 'You need big mirrors on the walls,' he told her, 'and candlelight.' She glances at her watch. One thing at a time. The scones will be ready to come out the oven and the flies' cemetery will be cool enough to slice. On her way to the kitchen she stops and leans on a table for a moment. She hates not being nimble on her feet. She's so heavy, and big, and she can't believe that the baby is actually due in just a fortnight. Or is this her forevermore, all bloated ankles and running to the lav every ten minutes?

'Sit down, rest your legs,' Hetty says when Rena gets to the kitchen at last.

Rena shakes her head. 'The scones…'

'I'll get them,' Hetty says, taking the glass cloth from her. The wireless is on and the heat from the oven has made the big room hot, which doesn't augur well for the pastry that Hetty has been trimming around the tart tins. They have to use up last year's apples, but Rena decides not to think about that and sinks gratefully onto a hard chair. Hetty pushes another over for her feet.

'Oh dear,' Rena groans. 'Thanks. That does feel better.'

As she lifts the trays of scones out the oven Hetty says, 'You should take some time off, dear. Rest up for this last little while.'

'Oh what's the point?' Rena says. 'If I'm next door in the flat all I'm thinking of is what needs to be done through here, and it's not as if…' She sighs. 'Well, you know.'

Hetty transfers the last two scones to the wire cooling rack and wipes her hands on her apron before rummaging in her handbag. 'While I remember, a letter came to

Beansburn for you. From Glasgow. Here you go.'

Rena takes the letter and closes her eyes. A moment later she hears Hetty pad out of the kitchen, and call out a greeting to Alma, who has just arrived. It'll be ten to nine then; Alma likes to get there in time to have a cigarette and a chat before they open up for the day. Grudgingly Rena opens her eyes. The letter is official looking, the address typewritten on thick white paper, and some kind of embossing on the seal. She has no idea what it might be; business letters go to Bobby, and her aunts favour flimsy blue envelopes when they write. Stranger still, it's addressed to Irene Jarvie Lennox, so it comes from someone who doesn't know she's married. She reaches across the table for a butter knife that's lying there, then slits the envelope and pulls out the letter and another sealed envelope, thinner this time. The letter is from a solicitor in Glasgow. After reading it, Rena sits up and eases her feet off the chair.

'Mum,' she calls towards the tearoom doorway. 'You're right, I am going to have a lie down. Alma, you can open up, can't you?'

'Course I can.' Alma pokes her head around the frame. 'Oh, would you look at the size of you. I swear that belly gets bigger every day. Not long now, is it?'

'Not long at all,' Hetty echoes.

'Another grandchild for you, Mrs Jarvie.'

Hetty appears beside her and beams. Rena knows how much she enjoys seeing Malcolm and Evelyn but Evie has her own mother and is always pushing the pram up to Fenwick. With Rena's child it will be different.

'Are you all right, dear? What was that letter?'

'Just an old supplier from the shop.'

Hetty frowns. 'You do look pale.'

'I'm just tired. I'll be fine if I can have a nap. I'll be through again for the morning rush.'

As she walks slowly back she hears Alma say, 'You just don't know where to put yourself at that stage, do you? But it's a good big baby. A boy, I'd put money on it.'

'Oh, I hope so,' Hetty says, but to be honest, Rena doesn't really care what it is, as long as it comes out in one piece and lets her get back to normal.

When she reaches the bedroom she wonders whether to risk taking off her shoes but decides against it. She might never get them back on again. Instead, she stacks up the pillows and lies back against them, closing her eyes to conjure the memory that the solicitor's covering letter has nudged towards the front of her consciousness.

It might have been the first time she'd been in a department store, and it was even more unusual for Rena's father to take her somewhere on her own. He drove, and Rena felt very grown up in the front seat of the car. What age could she have been, eight? George Lennox had some family money from his mother, whose people had been in the shipyards, and he'd made more through his business concerns. Even now, Rena wasn't sure what the business concerns were. Import was mentioned, and he went to an office in Glasgow most days of the week. She remembers once leaning her head on Bobby's shoulder, back in the early days, slapping him playfully when he whispered: *sounds like your old man was a crook*. In the store there was a big hall with staircases running up each side to galleries above, chandeliers overhead. They took the elevator, and Rena was a little scared at the rattle of the gate as the attendant, smart in his Commissionaire uniform, closed and secured it. He winked and said, 'Second floor, Miss,' just as if she was a big girl rather than a child. Flashing through the cage she could see perfume bottles giving way to hats and thrillingly, a mannequin twirling round, showing off the astrakhan cuffs on her velvet coat while women sat on chairs and watched.

'You've never met your Auntie Ruby,' her father said.

Rena shook her head. When they got out of the lift he put his hand on her shoulder, looked behind him. The attendant smiled and winked again as the doors closed.

'Don't tell your mother. She and Ruby, well, they don't get on.'

'Is she one of the sisters?' Rena wouldn't usually ask her father a question, but everything about the day was already so funny. Funny peculiar, not funny ha ha.

'No.' Her father laughed; a rarity which made him seem younger, all of a sudden. 'And not a peep to them either, do you hear me? Let's say she's my side of the family.'

Rena remembers walking around a balcony gallery, stocked with dozens upon dozens of hats, perched on display stands like birds of paradise. Then they turned into a coffee salon, where they were shown to a small round table with a starched cloth. Rena reached out to touch the carnation in the vase, felt the tickle of the leaves beside it. Everything seemed shiny and modern; the glass light-fittings overhead, the wall panels. After a moment Auntie Ruby arrived, wearing a cloche hat not unlike the one the mannequin downstairs had been modelling. She unpinned it and placed it on the empty seat beside her.

'Found something nice?' Rena's father said, indicating the large cardboard shopping bag on her arm. The name of the store, what was it? It was written in script on the side, gold on black.

'Just the necessaries,' Ruby said, and smiled at him. 'Thank you.' She turned to Rena. 'And you must be Irene. I've been dying to meet you.'

Auntie Ruby was wearing makeup, Rena realised, like an actress. Except hers was in colour, of course: blush cheeks, red lips, pencilled brows. That should have been a giveaway, really.

Imagine taking your daughter to meet your fancy woman. And to think that she'd forgotten it, that she'd been so sure she was lying in the courtroom that day, when it became clear that battering your wife was hardly grounds for divorce. And at the time she'd been bought off with a new pair of shoes, nice lace ups with a little heel that had taken some getting used to. Ruby had sat and watched her try them on, clapping her hands at how smart they looked and beckoning the salesgirl to bring them in a less drab colour. She'd been fun, Rena recalls. When they drove back to the village she was still full of it enough to ask her father, 'When will we see Auntie Ruby again?' But by then his mood had changed, and all he did was mutter to her to put it from her mind or he'd throw her new shoes out the car window. Even at eight Rena knew not to cross him, and then that night it was business as usual. Thomas cowering in beside her and worrying, worrying because Mother had grown so fat and slow – and now Rena knows what that was only too well, doesn't she? – and mightn't be able to get out of Father's way. And by the morning, she was so used to pretending it was all a bad dream that she must have done as her father told her and forgotten all about Auntie Ruby.

Our late client Mrs R Fitzsimmons, according to the solicitor who managed to trace Rena to her mother's flat. As if Rena would want charity from her father's fancy woman, as if she would lower herself. And yet, the sum is noted on the letter and it's substantial. £100. Enough to pay back Min and Donald and then some. But what's the point, with Bobby drinking every penny he can get his hands on? There's money missing out the till every night, she's sure there is. She can't tell her mother, that's for sure, and Thomas is doing all right now, with the shop. No need to tell him, he'd only say to write back with a sternly worded refusal. But isn't she owed something?

She fingers the edges of the smaller, hand-addressed envelope, tempted to tear it in half. What could that woman have had to say to her, that she left this with her will? Rena hesitates, then opens it. She skims over the shaky copperplate writing: *Dear Irene… wished you would have stayed after the funeral so that I could speak to you… I know George missed you even if… accept a token…* Rena looks away and then she does tear the letter in half, and in half again. She'll take the money, because beggars can't be choosers, but she'll be blasted if she'll take the pity alongside it.

Back in the tearoom Rena feels the heat straight away and takes herself outside to sit on a bench. The Parks Supervisor is driving past, the windows of the van rolled down. Rena nods and gives him a bright smile and he stops opposite her. Alma always says that he fancies himself something rotten.

'Lovely day, Mr Harvey,' she calls.

'Indeed it is, Mrs Young. Indeed it is. We've just redone the floral clock by the station, the plants had got that withered.' He gestures to the mess in the bed of the van.

'I'll need to take myself along to see it,' she says, then

laughs and gestures helplessly at her bulk. 'If I can!' Another car comes down the drive, and yes, it's Bobby in the Austin. Here to do some work, she hopes. 'Here's my husband coming to cause trouble as usual!'

'Aye, well I think I could be tempted to pop in for my coffee later on.'

'Why don't I just have Alma bring it across to the walled garden at eleven? And today's scones are particularly good, even if I say so myself. You'd take a scone?'

Bobby takes off his jacket and lays it neatly in the boot before he picks up a box of supplies. 'Hello Fred,' he calls as he passes.

'Aye aye, Bobby,' Fred shouts, then continues round to the garden.

'That man's got his eye on you,' Bobby whispers, settling himself next to Rena on the bench. She can feel the heat coming off him, after the exertion of unloading the car. 'And no wonder, the way you flirt with him.'

'Don't be ridiculous,' Rena says, 'It's just he's been so helpful, and with Otto and Paul…' Bobby is smiling at her and she realises he's joking. Before she can shoo him he kisses her on the cheek. She's never been good at being teased, even with two brothers, but she's glad to see Bobby like this, in high spirits but sober. She lays her head on his shoulder and he rests one hand lightly on her bump.

'Not long now,' he says, and she repeats it after him like an invocation. 'Not long now.'

The day is busy, and at one point she has to leave Alma to hold the fort while she whips up another batch of pancakes. Plenty of visitors to the park. If they could get a freezer they could do ices. Bobby, having run his errands, is playing at being a customer. He's sitting with a pot of tea and Rena sees Alma bring him a slice of Battenberg.

'You should let him serve himself,' she says.

'Ocht, it's no trouble,' Alma says. 'And he got his own tea.'

'I'll take these plates,' Rena says. 'I could do with keeping moving.'

'It's the best thing for it,' Alma agrees. 'Take it from me.'

As Rena walks past Bobby to deliver two scones with jam and cream she sniffs. She can't tell if it's whisky or not, at that distance, and he's sly enough to add it to the pot so that steam still rises from the cup.

By the time Hetty leaves to get back in time for Jamie coming in from school it has quietened considerably. The sky has clouded over and the warm spring temperature dropped. The few remaining customers are finishing their cups of tea and asking for their bill. Rena empties the ashtrays and ascertains which tablecloths won't do another day. The door creaks open – she'll need to get Bobby to do something about that – and a man and a woman enter.

'Are you still serving?' the man asks. His suit makes him look as if he's come straight from business, and he has ginger freckles to match his hair. She's in a dull blue Utility-style dress and if Rena's Auntie Nell was there she'd have it off her to redo the shoulders to fit.

'Oh yes, we're open until five,' Rena answers cheerfully, waving towards the nearest table.

'Two pots of tea,' the woman says as she sits. 'And what cakes do you have?' It sounds slightly aggressive, but sometimes the accent can do that. Rena's was always softer, coming from the village by the sea, and she's taken pains to mute it, make it harder to place.

She smiles at her customers, always professional. 'Scones, pancakes, Battenberg, Empire biscuits,' she turns to check what's left in the chiller, 'or we've still got a couple of meringues with strawberries and cream, and an angel cake.'

The man, who is on the paunchy side, asks for a meringue. 'Still a rare treat,' he says. Rena nods. Every grain of sugar is hoarded to make them, and she's just lucky she's kept up with the farms for the cream. He looks at the woman.

'Have you not got any sponge?' she says.

Rena shakes her head. 'Just the angel cake left, I'm afraid. We sold out of Victoria sponge earlier on.'

'Oh well, I suppose I'll have to make do with that then,' the woman says.

Rena goes to prepare the tea, casting glances back at them. She puts doilies on the plates, takes the cakes out of the cabinet. Stupid woman, she thinks, placing the angel cake carefully in the middle of the plate. Making do with angel cake indeed; she looks as if she's had to make do with a lot less than that.

Rena delivers the order with a smile which the woman doesn't return. Does she think she's being patronised, Rena wonders, but she dismisses the thought when she brings the bill to Mrs Cunninghame and her sister and exchanges some small talk about the new flood defences by the river. She just wants things to be nice, for the tearoom to be as good as it can be. Mr Harvey comes in to return his cup and plate. The man calls him over and they shake hands, start chatting, but in low voices, so that Rena can't catch a word. Mr Harvey leaves without calling over to Rena and Alma, as he usually might. The woman whispers something to the man beside her. He nods. She catches Rena's eye and looks away. Yes, there's definitely something strange about the pair. The way they are looking around the place, as if they've never been in a tearoom before. The woman picks at the cake, examining the filling as though there might be something nasty lurking in it. Rena doesn't skimp with baking. Better to have a few good ones, and when they've gone, they've gone. No whipped-up lard for her. If it says buttercream, that's what it is. She hurries back into the kitchen. Bobby is still there, washing dishes quite the thing, cup of tea by his side.

'Once a steward, always a steward,' he says with a grin.

'Find a reason to go out there,' she says. 'Tell me who that man is, the one with the red hair, with the hard-faced woman.'

Bobby returns a moment later. 'He works at the council. Property, I'd guess. I saw him when I went in to see MacPherson and sign the lease for this place. Don't know his name.'

'I wonder if he's here to check up on us?' she says. 'I mean, we haven't heard back about the lease yet…'

'He was a clerk then,' Bobby says, shrugging his sleeves back down and buttoning his cuffs. 'Not much above MacPherson.' He hesitates, takes a mouthful of tea. 'I don't think he'd have the say-so. Our case was going straight before the board, and with Minto and Gibson both behind us, I don't see what could go awry. Not when they've already agreed to a license for baking on the premises.'

Rena nods. 'Tell me again what Minto said.'

'At Hogmanay he said to leave it with him, and when

I saw him the other week he told me not to worry. And he winked.'

'A wink isn't a promise. There's no guarantee he'll get back in. The paper said Labour losses were predicted for Bonnyton.'

'Nobody'll get rid of a civic restaurant, especially one that's doing so well.'

Rena nods. It is doing well. Lunches and high teas by arrangement, and plenty of compliments from their customers. Money is coming in faster than it's going out, for once.

'No news is good news,' Bobby says, putting his arm around her. She won't try to smell his breath, she won't. 'If they weren't going to extend beyond the year we'd know about it by now.'

Rena is nice as pie as she clears their plates and asks if everything was all right. The man nods and says it was, and she sees him taking in her bump, trying to pretend he's not looking. She's used to that by now, the size of her (please God let it not be twins like Evie), but there's something else in his eyes. Embarrassment, certainly. Taking the saucer with their money on it back to the counter she hears them muttering to each other and then the woman says, 'It's perfect, Archie, so it is.'

She has a coarse voice, Rena thinks. It's nothing to do with the accent, it's all in the upbringing. Suddenly she's exhausted again. Let Bobby manage on his own, she needs to lie down. Her feet are overspilling her shoes and she has to steel herself to drag her weight up the stairs to the bedroom. Tomorrow she'll write to the solicitor, and she'll accept Ruby's money, but she won't tell anyone – not even her husband – what she has done.

Bobby, 1947

The ground beneath Bobby is washing to and fro, to and fro. Is he on the *Annapolis*, waiting to be struck, or in a lifeboat, drifting to his death? Dread seeps through him and he flexes his left hand, feels the rough material of a blanket on top of him. He lets the hand pad further afield, and hits the gritty wood of a floor. A floor he is lying on. Nothing's moving but his throbbing brain, which feels too big for his skull, as if it's swollen with… He prises his dry tongue free, tries to moisten his mouth with saliva. Whisky, yes, and something cheaper and rougher than that. He doesn't know where he is, but he can't shift himself quite yet. Opening his eyes is unlikely to improve matters, so he scrunches them tighter, holding on to a few more moments of ignorance.

Get him out of here, I don't want him near me…

Bobby remembers the Station Bar. The closest pub to the hospital after he'd dropped Rena off. Another chap there in the same boat. A pint or two, a companion. After a while they went out and telephoned together, one holding the line while the other stood on the platform listening to the roll and boom of the barrels from Johnnie Walker being loaded on to a train on one of the sidings. Trying not to look over to Mount Pleasant, and the infirmary looming there, black with soot. The man got the good news while Bobby was told it could be hours yet. 'Better go home and rest, Mr Young.' What to do? Well, if waiting's a game, it's one better played with a drink in your hand.

It was a grey day but there was a glare behind the clouds, that flashes back to him as he lies there, moving his toes to feel if his shoes are still on. They are. That's a good sign. If you still have the shoes on your feet you probably haven't been robbed and you've almost (if not quite) certainly refrained from getting up to no good with a woman. Bobby sees himself striding down John Finnie Street, anxiety dogging every footstep because whose fault is it that Rena is where she is if not his? The Portland Arms, yes, and from there a brisk walk to the Clansman. Staying within a quarter hour radius of the infirmary, just about. What then? He'd like to think he telephoned again, but all that fills his mind is Hetty herding him out the door, Hetty more forceful than he'd ever seen her. 'Best just leave her be for now, Bobby dear, just for now.'

He hadn't turned up empty handed, oh no. Rena likes things for the house, and God knows that place needs brightening up. He would swing for MacPherson, for the Corporation, for the whole fucking lot of them. *A success to the tenant but not a success to the town*. That's their excuse and they're sticking to it. In the meantime, a gift for Rena. He saw it in the window of that shop she likes, swanned in and bought it just like that. Left it in the ward for her, he assumes.

Bobby creaks one eyelid open, but it's dim, almost dark wherever he is. He makes a gentle investigation of his pockets and finds a cigarette carton, and his wallet. That'll be empty now, likely enough. Why did he have to stop before he went back to the hospital, in that manky howff by the cattle market of all places? To celebrate, he thinks weakly, to buy drinks for all the men in the bar and have them raise their glasses to him, and to Rena, and to their new baby girl. Well, he made a fine job of that. He isn't on the *Annapolis*, and there's no excuse for the state he's in. For a second he wishes he was back at sea, afloat, with a ration of rum to see him through and no chance of temptation outside of port. Because it seems to Bobby that everything has changed, apart from himself.

Rena, 1948

There's a steady dripping noise in the corner of the bedroom. Water oozes from the wall and plinks into a glass mixing bowl placed against the skirting board. Rena should replace the newspaper that it's sitting on, it must be soaked through by now, but she can't muster the energy. The baby is asleep, and all Rena can think to do is lie on the bed in this miserable hovel of a place. In the corner of the room is a new standard lamp with a pleated silk shade. The base is turned wood, good quality, and gold braid runs around above the fringe. Rena hates the thing. What kind of a man gives his wife a standard lamp to celebrate the birth of their child? And what kind of landlord serves an eviction notice to a woman about to give birth? Two days later Rena's waters broke. Probably all the heavy lifting that did it. She shudders at the thought of the infirmary. It took another day for Janet to be born, a full twenty-three hours of agonies and indignities before she had a healthy ten-and-a-half-pound girl to hold in her arms. And then Bobby staggered up, tie loose and suit rumpled, having wet the baby's head long before he saw it.

'I brought you this.'

'Just get him out,' she whispered to her mother, who was sitting by the bedside knitting a matinee jacket for the baby; the baby that Bobby didn't even seem to notice, asleep in the cot by the bed. 'I don't want to see him. I don't want him near me.'

Hetty managed to coax Bobby out into the hallway and away, aided by the husband of the woman in the next bed. A final mortification. 'My Joe was just the same when I had our first,' the woman said, as one of the sisters came to open the windows so that the icy blast of air would chase the stench of drink out. Meant kindly, but all Rena wanted was to be away from her and back home. With or without the bloody standard lamp. And looking at the four silent children ranged by her neighbour's bed, the oldest a sombre girl of about ten holding the new baby, Rena vowed that she'd never end up in that place again. One child is enough, no matter what. God rot Dr Meikle.

One step forwards, two steps back. Is this how it's always going to be? Rehoused, they said. The place is a slum, at the lower end of the town and due for demolition. Not fit for having a baby sleep there. Rena can feel the damp in her own chest and she's strong as an ox. Was. Now she's just tired, and it's all so dark and dull. She closes her eyes and tries to conjure that Hogmanay party, when everything seemed so bright and possible. The war was over, Thomas was home safe, and Bobby came to find her before the bells to kiss her and pull her out into the driveway to dance the new year in, under the twinkling lights he'd rigged up as a surprise to please her. She'd been sure she was pregnant, another new beginning, but hadn't said. She wanted the night to be theirs, just the two of them. It feels like a very long time ago. She doesn't know where Bobby is now. And that bloody lamp standing there as a reminder of it all. The grime on the windows means the room is in a perpetual half-light but she won't even plug the thing in because she's too worried about the wet oozing so near the socket.

On the bed beside her is a pencil drawing on thick paper. A sketch Otto did of Annanhill house, the stucco façade, the two columns of the portico, the trees at each side. Tiny figures strolling past. *VJ Day*, it says, in slanting letters. Rena runs her finger lightly over the paper. He'd pressed it into her hand, through the window of the car as Bobby drove her to the hospital. Blew her a kiss as well, though Bobby didn't see that. It hardly seems real now. She'd imagined everything going on as before, her and Bobby together, with a baby sleeping in a pram in the shade of the big cherry tree. She clasps the drawing to herself, avoiding her sore and swollen breasts, not mindful of smudging it now, or of crumpling the paper. With her eyes closed it seems more vivid, the life she should be living.

Tap tap tap. Waking groggily, Rena assumes it's more water coming in. Tap, tap tap tap, tap tap. No, it's someone at the door. She rolls onto her side and ignores it. The taps become louder and then, of course, she hears Janet snuffle and waken. Once she's awake she decides she's hungry, and then she begins to cry. Whoever is at the door will know that Rena is in, so she gets to her feet and goes to answer it.

'Rena, whatever's happened? You don't look yourself at all.'

Rena doesn't have the strength to ask what her mother is doing there. One fat tear rolls down her face, followed by another, and before she can even try to stop herself she's bawling almost as loudly as the baby. Hetty pushes in and closes the door behind her, takes Janet in her arms, and ushers Rena through to the nasty little kitchen with its one remaining pulley lath swaying at an angle overhead. Once there, she takes charge. Prepares a bottle for Janet to stop her crying, and gives Rena a cup of sweet tea and her cigarettes. Rena perches on the edge of a chair, smoking, while Hetty holds Janet up and sniffs. Janet flails her arms, opening and closing her hands and smiling a dribbly smile at her grandmother.

'I'll need to change her.'

Rena nods.

'And when did you last bathe her?'

'Yesterday. I don't know.'

Hetty looks as if she's going to question this but she thinks the better of it, pours some water from the kettle into the big sink and tempers it with cold, rolls up her sleeve to test it with her elbow. She moves smoothly around the baby, Rena notices, every gesture assured, still second nature even though streaks of silver are appearing in the long hair that she wears plaited and twisted into a bun, a style from her youth that she has never changed. Eventually, as if having Janet cradled in her arms gives her confidence, Hetty says, 'This won't do, Irene.'

Rena sighs. 'I was just tired. The baby was asleep and I dozed off.'

'I mean this place won't do. It isn't fit for a child. It isn't fit for you.'

That familiar pulse of rage sparks then dies in Rena's chest. 'Well, given that we were turfed out our flat and lost our business into the bargain, I'd say that I don't have much choice in the matter.'

'Thomas and Evie...'

'I know,' Rena says sharply. Her brother is in a Corporation house in a good area, with two bedrooms, and the last time she saw Evie she was full of the joys. And she has two children; how does she cope? Janet starts girning and Rena watches as Hetty swaddles the baby tightly and pokes the bottle into her mouth again. Janet closes her eyes and focuses on the warm milk, her long lashes pressed against her pale cheeks, while Hetty coos down at her.

'You could come back to me. Jamie can sleep on the settee, you and Bobby can have the box bed.'

The heaviness Rena feels inside sinks lower than her chest, into her stomach. She can feel it there like nerves. 'I'm not going back. I can't.'

Hetty shrugs. 'Min and Nell are coming to see the baby,' she says. 'Margaret isn't well enough to travel. I don't know what they'll make of this.'

Rena cradles her cup. She wishes her mother would leave, so that she could lie down again with a blanket over her and try to get back to sleep. 'It's where I live now.'

Janet has fallen asleep again now, in Hetty's arms. Why doesn't she go down so easily for Rena? Hetty gets up and places her in her Moses basket, then picks it up and puts it on the table as if she thinks rats will crawl out and start nibbling at the child. And well they might, Rena thinks, bitterly.

'Once Bobby has a job again you'll be able to move.'

'I worked my fingers to the bone for that business. You saw me.'

'I know you did, dear. But it's harder, becoming a mother at your age. You just need to settle into it.'

Rena wants to say that she's only twenty-seven, but it's true, she feels older.

'There will be no need for you to work like that again.' Hetty looks around, almost as if she thinks this has all come as a consequence of Rena working rather than being satisfied with being a wife. 'Oh, I dread to think what your father would have said if he'd seen you living here. A grandchild of his being raised in a place like this.'

And that's it. The anger that flickered and died a few moments before catches and burns. A grandchild of his? Janet has nothing to do with him. She belongs to Rena and Bobby, and they can provide for her. In a glaring flash she sees the flat through her mother's eyes, in all its poverty, and imagines the expressions on the faces of her aunts if they were ever to cross the threshold.

Within half an hour, Rena is properly dressed, with her face powdered and her lipstick painted on. Her hair could be better – she hasn't had it done since before the birth and it hangs forward over her forehead – but she finds a few Kirbigrips and shores it into half-curls. She hasn't washed it, so it stays. Hetty doesn't say a word, just gets Janet ready as instructed and then begins to footer about in the kitchen.

'What are you doing?' Rena asks, as she runs through to look for her hat.

'Trying to get this sink clean.'

'Waste of time. You'll never notice the difference and we're not going to be here for much longer.'

She opens the small suitcase she's carrying and stuffs in some necessities for Janet next to her own clean underwear and nightshirt.

'What on earth are you doing, Rena?'

Rena takes a deep breath and looks at herself in the

cracked mirror above the kitchen sink. She's taken a high colour from the exertion and looks faintly hysterical, it's true, but that's just fine. She runs her index fingers along her eyebrows to coax them into shape; she used to use pencil and a little mascara because of her pale brows and lashes, but today a smudge of lipstick will have to do.

'Does Janet need changed again?'

Hetty leans over and sniffs under the blanket in the Moses basket. 'No, she's fine.'

'One minute then.'

Rena hurries out into the grimy hallway and then into the even more grimy communal bathroom, where she passes water and changes her sanitary dressing. Things haven't quite settled since the birth but she'll just have to manage. For a second she thinks again of her sister-in-law, dancing around the place only weeks after having twins. Rena wasn't cut out for this, not at all. It was meant to settle Bobby down and it only seems to have driven him away. But she can take care of things on her own, can't she? She's done it before. She goes back up the stairs and into the flat, takes the suitcase and scoops Janet out of the Moses basket. The pram is downstairs in the entry. She's amazed nobody's stolen it, with them the only tenants at that end of the terrace.

'Right, Mother, I need you to pack up anything that's worth keeping and then go out and telephone Thomas and have him come and move it over to his in the car. I'm not spending another night in this place.'

Rena thinks of Councillor Minto, reciting his Burns when he came by Annanhill to drink 'tea' with Bobby. Well, she's the one nursing her wrath to keep it warm now. There are two people in this town that can help them, and Minto is one. Bobby can deal with him, and she has an inkling of where to find Bobby.

The nearest pub is the Bickering Bush, and the road under the bridge is awash. The pram runs through the deep puddle easily, but the water slops over Rena's shoes and her feet are submerged. Lounge or bar? What's the difference? She checks Janet is tucked up under her blanket and pushes the pram to the walk, then takes a deep breath. Lounge sounds nicer. She pushes open the door but the wooden tables are devoid of customers. It looks bleak, only a couple of brewery mirrors on the walls and the lamps not even on in spite of the dinginess. There's nobody behind the bar but it connects to another room; she can hear a low chatter. So she retreats and goes through the door to the right marked public bar instead. Everyone falls silent, just like in a cowboy film. Bobby isn't there, and she hurries out, hearing a rough comment behind her and then the barman saying something about 'another yin lookin for her man,' a chorus of laughter without a scrap of humour in it. Well, what's she supposed to do? Sit there rotting in that horrible flat?

Next she tries Glencairn Square, with no luck in either of the bars there. Walking along Titchfield Street she's furious that Bobby is putting her through this. Something will have to be done, but one thing at a time. She feels a warm surge of blood in her dressing and stops for a moment, giddy, leans on the handle of the pram. She should never have listened to Meikle. Calls himself a doctor but the problem wasn't her, was it? Another deep breath and she keeps going. She has another two miles to walk before she's done, no use in stopping now. The next pub is the Auld Hoose, and sure enough there Bobby is, standing at the bar, one of only two customers at this time of day.

'Rena! What are you doing…'

'Come on outside, I need to speak to you.'

He gestures helplessly at his unfinished glass of beer. 'A drink, so we can talk indoors?'

'I left the baby,' Rena whispers, nodding towards the door.

The barman looks up from his newspaper. He's wearing a white shirt with grimy cuffs and a black waistcoat. 'Don't serve women,' he says, folding his paper and pushing it aside.

'Believe me, I have no desire…' Rena begins, but the man has riled Bobby, who has stood up straight and pushed his glass away.

'This is not a woman,' he says. 'This is my wife. And if you know what's good for you…'

Rena puts her hand on his arm and he swallows his words and leaves with her. His walk is steady, thank heavens. He looks down into the pram, reaches towards Janet's sleeping face then draws his hand back as if he might be scalded, or scald her.

'A daughter,' he says. 'I can't believe we have a daughter.'

He's picked some time to get misty eyed and paternal. 'I want you to go to the Empire Bar,' Rena says.

'What?' He looks befuddled.

'We'll walk around the park with Janet until you're stone cold sober,' she says, 'then you'll go to the Empire Bar and you'll find Councillor Minto, because I know that's where he goes, and you'll do whatever it is you need to do to make sure that he demands that we're to be rehoused immediately. Tell him it's an emergency. They must have some provision for emergencies.'

Bobby shakes his head, like a dog coming out of

water. 'It won't be enough. Emergency rehousing is what we got.'

'I know it won't be enough. That's why I'm going to see Gibson.'

'He won't be in the Sun Inn. It isn't his night.' They wait to cross the street. Around them are shoppers, messengers, people with normal lives. Where does Bobby go, she wonders, when the pubs close in the afternoon?

'I'm not going near another stinking pub. I'm going to his house. I'm going to shame him into helping us get moved.'

Bobby nods. 'Minto'll be after cash.'

'What?'

'Well. Didn't you wonder, at Annanhill?'

Looking down, Rena notices tide marks of puddle water around the ankles of her stockings. This is the furthest she's walked in days. Weeks. 'But he said...'

'Oh aye, he liked it all well enough. A short stagger from his house and always a skinful to drink. But the Hogmanay late opening, even getting Sutherland to let Paul and Otto work for us.' Bobby rubs his thumb and middle finger together.

'Paul and Otto liked us.'

'I know they did, Rena love. We'd never have got moved out in time without them. Those bastards wouldn't even give us an extra month.'

Everything's feeling shaky, but she has to see it through now. 'How much?'

'Doesn't matter. We don't have it.'

Rena sighs. 'I can get something. If we go by the bank.'

She's already dipped into Ruby's money but there's still something left for a rainy day. Well, it's raining now, isn't it? Scarcely enough for a deposit if they were to find somewhere else, but it's the principle of the thing. The Corporation owes her.

She sends Bobby off with a spring in his step and a handful of notes that might or might not convince who they need to convince. He calls her darling, worries that she's wearing herself out, and she's glad of this – she hopes against hope that this will get through to him, shake him up. The whistle goes in the Glen and for a while she feels as if she's being carried along on the swell of workers who flow out into the street. By the time she reaches the Cross they've dispersed, and she only has her own two feet to rely on as she keeps walking in the rain, pushing the pram up Portland Road and Wellington Street, past the shop which is now closed – hopefully Hetty got hold of Thomas, and he's moving their things right now – and past the flat where she shared a bed with her mother. She keeps going until she reaches the big sandstone villas on the very edge of the town, finds one with a sweeping front lawn and perfectly trimmed hedge. Up the driveway she goes, the pram sticking in the gravel, right up to the tiled steps. She squeezes her eyes shut and then opens them again, seizes hold of the shiny brass bell pull. Maybe it's the noise, or maybe just that Rena has stopped walking, but Janet wakes, scrunches up her face, and screams. When Mrs Gibson comes to the door Rena doesn't even get to utter a word of the speech she's prepared before she sinks to her knees and passes out on the bottom step.

Rena, 1948

Rena locks the bathroom door behind her but this new flat is still small enough for her to hear Thomas explaining the situation – notice served at Annanhill, that first awful flat, Rena's resourcefulness – to Nell and Min. When he utters a loud expletive to emphasise his feelings about the council, Janet begins to cry. At least Hetty is there to deal with the noise. And Bobby, well, Bobby is nowhere to be seen. There's a surprise. Rena has told them that he's gone to sound someone out about work. On a Saturday? Nell asked, resisting raising her eyebrows. She's right; the truth is Rena can't be confident about where he is, other than it'll be somewhere with a license to serve quarter gill measures. She splashes some cold water on her face, feels her skin tighten. Can old dogs learn new tricks? Because here is her family, Bobby's family, waiting for him in a flat that might be small, but that's clean and watertight, with an indoor toilet and a cooker rather than a range thick with decades of grease.

Part of her flinches when she goes back through to the living room and sees Hetty dandling the baby. The standard lamp is not only plugged in but switched on, and Rena doesn't even curse it any more. The pinkish glow of the silk shade is the prettiest thing in the bare white room, with its dark dining table (too watermarked for Min to sell) and two horsehair settees that don't quite accommodate everyone so Rena and Evie have to sit on the hard dining chairs. Janet is quiet now, apart from occasional gentle belches coaxed from her by her grandmother. She's a novelty, an unknown quantity in the family. Min reaches out her arms, and then Nell, and a strange game of pass the parcel ensues, punctuated by murmurs about her crop of reddish hair, her wee fingers, her Jarvie nose. Even Thomas lays his cigarette in the ashtray and takes a turn, and she'd have thought he'd have had enough of babies to last him a lifetime.

'What a pity Margaret wasn't able to come and see her,' Hetty says.

Rena recognises the quality of the silence. Margaret has contracted pneumonia on top of her shingles and it's serious enough for her to be kept in the hospital for now. But Min and Nell are concentrating on the baby today, and on Rena, and they won't put a dampener on their first visit with their great niece. Janet was meant to be the prize, wasn't she? It doesn't feel the way Rena thought it would. These tablets that Meikle has given her make things worse, but what can she do? She completed the form for the new National Health and he's her GP from now on, for good or ill. When she woke up, still on Gibson's doorstep with Janet screaming her head off, she insisted on seeing her own doctor. He might be useless at some things, but at least Meikle was suitably dismayed by news of her domestic circumstances. Now she's still drinking a foul bottle of stout every day to build up her iron, and sure enough, the memory of the pain has faded and the bleeding has stopped. In a way it couldn't have worked out better: Mrs Gibson, mortified when a nosy neighbour came out to see what the fuss was about, and Councillor Gibson when he arrived home to find an impromptu sickbed on his settee, well. They had a new set of keys within forty-eight hours. Two councillors on the Youngs' side was enough to sway it. But now, when she's alone in this bloody flat it feels as if she's outgrowing it, like Alice after she'd eaten the mushroom. The memory of a childhood book, of herself as a child, gives her a shiver. At least the tablets stop the tiredness, although sometimes it seems that when they wear off she's more tired than ever. Nell turns to Evie, as if to pass Janet on to her in turn, but Thomas says they'll need to go. He finds the aunts too much, Rena knows, when they're all together like this.

'Does it put you in the mind for another one?' Hetty says, nodding at Evie. There's an embarrassed silence, and everyone tries not to look at Thomas, as though it's nothing to do with him. Evie smiles.

'Och no, I've got my hands full with the twins. Although they're no trouble at all really. My sister was glad to take them today.'

'They'd be fine if you didn't spoil them,' Thomas says. He's put on weight since the war finished and the shop trade picked up. Evie's still slender, and she'd need to be for her new dress in green and white with a neat little pussy bow at the neck. It has a fancy bias detail over the hips that Nell looks about ready to unpick there and then to make a pattern. Rena wouldn't manage stripes going in all those directions. Thomas looks at his watch and she goes to fetch their coats from the bedroom.

'The flat's more than sufficient, isn't it,' she hears Min say. 'The kitchenette is very swish.'

'It's better than that one they had above the tearoom,' Hetty says, and Rena could slap her. 'I never liked it. Too cold, and always the feeling that you were rattling around inside a big building.'

'We've a couple of wee occasional tables in the shop that would fit well in this room,' Min says. 'I'm just saying, Rena,' she raises her voice although Rena is only standing in the doorway, a couple of feet away. 'I'll keep back a couple of wee occasional tables for you.'

Thomas holds Evie's coat for her to get into and says to the room in general, 'I mean, it's not as if that bugger's the only one who was in the bloody war.'

He's referring to the new tenant of Annanhill House, Rena realises, whose war wound prompted his wife to persuade her brother in the council property department to make sure they got the lease of a nice wee business in their home town, the place where they were all born and bred. Nell and Min exchange the glance they always do. Their war was bigger than this one; they lost more.

After Thomas and Evie have gone Rena steels herself to make another pot of tea and put out more shortbread. This family runs on sweets, and when there's only saccharine they eat twice as much to compensate. Evie's the same, though you'd never know to look at her. For a second Rena isn't sure if she hears whispering or not from the sitting room. She stays still and listens. Yes, there's a question about *bearing up*. She can't hear Hetty's answer.

'You might have told her about it, Hetty,' Nell says. 'For goodness sake, even I know that giving birth isn't always a walk in a park.'

Hetty mumbles something and Min chokes on her tea. 'You always were the naïve one,' she says between coughs.

'Don't we know that,' Nell mutters, as Rena comes back in with the tray.

Min takes charge of the pot and Hetty puts Janet down in her Moses basket.

'Well,' Nell says brightly. 'If there's one thing about the Jarvies, they never give up.'

'My name's Young now,' Rena says, but she accepts the arm that Nell rests around her shoulders and lets herself sink into the now-vacant settee and lean against her aunt.

'Aye,' Min says. 'It is. But we all know that blood is thicker than water.' She looks askance at Hetty, fussing with Janet's blanket, as though wondering how she made the grade. 'So what are you planning to do next?'

Rena feels something stirring inside her, breathes into it. Pure rage. 'That bloody man,' she says. 'That bloody crooked excuse for a man and his tart of a sister. This'll do nicely, she said. It was our bloody tearoom, we did it up and we got it going, working our fingers to the bloody bone because we thought they'd let us stay. Do you have any idea,' she fixes Min with her gaze, 'the shame of it? Evicted from our home, and that, that cow of a woman, there before we were even out the door. And all because her husband has bloody shrapnel in his brain and her brother works for the council.'

She pauses for breath. Nell hands her a cup of tea and she sips it. It's even sweeter than usual. After a second she says, 'I don't understand it, Nell. We had a lease. We were running the business well. It was an asset.' Janet burps again, as if on cue. 'We've a baby, for God's sake.'

Nell sighs. 'There's always someone who wants what you've got.'

Rena reaches for a piece of shortbread, eats it in two bites. 'I wish we'd never come to this bloody town. Our faces have never bloody fitted here.'

'It's the way of the world,' Min begins.

'A piece of nonsense is what it is,' Nell says. 'But Minny's right. It isn't what you know, it's who you know. You got moved here, didn't you?'

'We shouldn't have had to,' Rena says.

'Nevertheless, Rena,' Min says. 'If I were you, I'd start making friends in the right places.'

Late in the afternoon the sky darkens and the aunts start thinking about getting home. Min has borrowed Donald's car and she'll drop off Hetty and then Nell, before returning to Balmaha.

'Such a long way,' Hetty says. 'What did Donald say?'

'I reminded him that I'd driven a bleeding ambulance, pardon my French. Nobody'll be shooting at me on the Eaglesham moor.'

Hetty insists on bathing the baby and putting her down, with Min and Nell pretending to be interested in every last detail. Neither of them have children and Rena knows it's a kindness. One less thing for her to worry about, with Bobby still not back. She wishes Margaret was there. She was a nurse more recently than the others, and she might know how you get someone to dry out.

When everyone has gone, Rena sits at the table and takes a teaspoon from the tray. Min brought potted heid, and Rena, suddenly ravenous, begins to eat it straight from the dish, letting the jelly dissolve in her mouth. The flat is very quiet. She switches on the wireless to try and give it a bit of life. She knows she should be pleased that they got out of that hellish damp flat – and everyone has said so at some point this afternoon, even Thomas, whose anger rivals her own – but she hates these squat, white four-to-a-blocks, the drying greens exposed between them so that she dreads hanging a washing.

How can she explain what she used to feel, walking up the drive to Annanhill and knowing that she lived there, that in some small way the drifts of daffodils were hers, along with the raft of cherry blossom on the tree by the front door. Those were the prizes, after all those years in the shop. But Nell and Min bolster her. They're robust. Sympathy's no use unless it comes with a good kick up the behind as well. She wouldn't have got her mother away from her father without them. She misses Margaret though, the oldest and wisest, the best at taking charge. She might be in the hospital but she still has her wits, Min and Nell are agreed on that. Rena decides that she'll telephone as soon as her aunt is discharged. She wants to hear her voice, know she's still there. Maybe this town isn't for her after all, maybe Min could look out for premises near Balmaha. Maybe Donald would come in as a partner. But no, her brothers are there with her and she will make a go of it in this town, whatever it takes. She realises that she's eaten the entire dish of meat and feels a bit ashamed. Blood might be thicker than water, but if she and Bobby can pull together, the two of them could set things right.

The 1950s

Bobby, 1950

Here he is, in dry dock. Even he couldn't outflank Rena and those bloody women who stand behind her in their widow's tweeds. Well, only one's a widow but they rise up towards you in an indistinguishable mass. Rena needed a rest, he can see that. The shadows under her eyes, the fraught nights with Janet crying and crying, kicking around the Corporation flat all day. Rena isn't made for leisure, although that's how he imagined her when he saw her first, and he's not sure she's made for motherhood either. So yes, he understands that some time at Min's will do her good. A bit of company and help with the baby, fresh air and the view of the loch. A distraction from losing the tearoom to that bastard. Bobby knows what nepotism means. And if a wee voice ever questions whether there's an element of revenge, for showing up MacPherson that day he went into the council offices to sign the lease, Bobby silences it.

And there's the rub. Because now he's stuck here, signed into this convalescent home by that quack Meikle – at Rena's insistence, and thanks to her Aunt Margaret having worked with the matron – even though there's no real need that he can see (or not now, in the morning, with the sun still climbing towards the yard arm). They've actually gone through his things. 'No alcohol on the premises, Mr Young.' The nurses have learned a trick or two from the SS, it seems. Even so. Bobby bounces on his bed. The mattress is better than the ones at the Y, that's for sure, and there's more space between the beds. Red brick buildings, high ceilings, big windows; built as a fever hospital, if he recalls, and now it's not a loony bin but a convalescent home. Somewhere to dry out, although that isn't the story he or Rena will tell. Didn't he end up with pleurisy when he was on the Indian Ocean? Don't his lungs still flare up from time to time?

The man in the last bed on the left wakes and sits bolt upright, eyes staring, face a sheen of sweat. His mouth opens wide and he points at the ceiling although there's nothing there but cool white paintwork. Almost before he's started raving there's a shout of 'Bed Four!' and two nurses are there, one on each side of him. Bobby jumps to his feet, grabs his cigarettes and heads for the door.

'What's up with him?' he asks, on his way past.

'Convulsions,' the younger nurse says, and just as Bobby's thinking she might be the soft touch she produces a big metal syringe and drives it into the man's arm. His mouth closes abruptly and he stares unseeing at Bobby before falling back against his pillow. Bobby leaves the nurses tucking the sheets round him like a straitjacket and goes out to the grounds to ponder how he's going to get through this. He lights a cigarette and begins to walk the perimeter, but there's a wall all around the place, apart from the gate and gatehouse. They are miles from the town, far enough for the air to be better, surrounded by countryside. Birds are whirring back and forth, none of them pigeons or sparrows. Bobby mistrusts nature. He didn't see a lot of it when he was growing up and what he's experienced since hasn't changed his mind.

'Can you spare a cigarette?'

Bobby turns and sees a man a bit older than himself, in modish paisley-patterned flannel pyjamas and a striped dressing gown, balancing on crutches. 'Sure,' he says, and holds out the pack then flicks his silver lighter. A present from Rena, after he signed that ill-fated lease on Annanhill, their initials engraved on it. *IJ & RY*.

'Bert Coscarelli,' the man says, wedging the cigarette between his lips and hirpling into step beside Bobby. 'So, what are you in for?'

'Lung trouble,' Bobby says. 'Souvenir of my time at sea. Bobby Young, pleased to meet you.'

Bert nods. 'Leg injury. As you can tell.'

'Bad luck.'

'Maybe.'

There's an inflection of some kind in Bert's voice; not Italian, that's for sure, but not local either. They keep walking, over raked gravel paths. The grass is cut, and the small trees that punctuate the grounds look as if they too are kept in check. There must be a groundsman. Not that Bobby is pondering who comes in and out, who might have a wee sideline, not at all. Presently they reach the small brick gatehouse, where a milk float is stopped at the barrier. The porter is talking to the driver.

'You'd think it was a prisoner of war camp,' Bobby says. 'Sorry. I didn't mean…'

Bert stops and swaps both crutches to one hand to remove the cigarette from his mouth. 'Doesn't matter,' he says, waving it away then taking one last drag before discarding it. 'Papa Coscarelli died before the war so it was no odds to me. Mother's from Bantry Bay by way of Galston.'

The porter pushes the barrier aside and the milk float rattles forward. 'What do they think he's going to smuggle in?' Bobby mutters.

Bert sighs. 'If there's anything you want from out there,' he points his crutch awkwardly towards the gate, 'you're going to have to get your wife to bring it in or learn to live without it.'

If any part of Bobby was dreading going to bed early, with lights out enforced, it was needless. Tea wasn't so bad, light on the meat and heavy on the tatties but there was enough, and apple crumble to follow. A read at the newspaper, and a last stroll and cigarette, and he was pleased to get between crisp sheets in a bed that wasn't either shaking with Rena's frustration at the crying baby or seething with her disapproval at him coming in late.

'Slept like a log,' he said to Bert the next morning at breakfast, chipper as anything, and who wouldn't be with good Ayrshire bacon on their plate? It's another matter that evening, after a rainy day that felt like eternity. Worse things happen at sea; his usual refrain, and indeed at two in the morning it feels almost as if the bed is swaying like a bunk on ship. He can feel his thoughts spiralling in a way he's not accustomed to, in a way he tries to avoid. This is going to be harder than he thought. He tries to think of Rena, and Janet, why he's doing this, why he can't let himself be untethered. But it's a tearful Rena he sees. Not the one he married, the one who glows and is full of fight, but the one who finally cracked and said it: 'No wonder your first wife killed herself.' A broken doze brings a dream memory of Anne, getting up out the bed and pulling her dress back on, taunting him. 'You're a useless kind of a man Robert Young, aren't you?' Then he's back at sea, and there are U-boats all around.

He must have yelled out, because when he opens his eyes the nurse is looming over him. *Ship's sinking*, he tries to tell her. *Torpedo.* What's a woman doing on board anyway? Bad luck at sea. He can feel the water around him already but it's hot, it's helluva hot. He must have imagined a woman, and is there a better or worse thing to imagine than that? Ah Christ. Someone mops the sweat off his brow and when he opens his eyes the nurse is back, with that big metal syringe in her hand. He sits up and grabs the water from his nightstand, gulps it down.

'It's all right,' he says. 'Just a dream. I'm sorry. I'm all right.'

The six o'clock ward round comes as a blessed relief, even with the accompanying reek of disinfectant, and a cold shower banishes a few of his night demons. He's no invalid, in amongst the war-wounded and the syphilitic and the cancerous, so he dresses properly in his shirt and jacket before taking his tea outside. Smartness shows respect for oneself and for others. There's a pecking order, he's sensed it already, and those who have brought their illness on themselves are on the lowest rung. He stands by the rowan tree at the edge of the drive, breathing deeply. The dew is still thick on the ground, and the hazy sun hasn't yet burned off the mist that he can see drifting down the hills. Soon he hears the sound of crutches on the gravel, and Bert appears at his side. When he turns to say good morning Bert laughs as he replies. He's still in pyjama trousers, has to be for the leg Bobby assumes, but he's topped it with a shirt and sleeveless pullover. It looks off, somehow; Bert has the air of a chap more used to a well-cut suit that flatters his bulk.

'Sweet dreams?'

Bobby raises his hand to his face, as if he'll be able to feel the bags under his eyes. 'That obvious?'

'When you stop for a moment things creep up on you, especially in a place like this. You wouldn't be human if they didn't.'

Bobby shrugs. 'Not much chance of a kip when *Lost Weekend* over there's ranting through the wee small hours.' The man with convulsions is now parked in a wheelchair on the sun terrace, tucked in a tartan blanket and sound asleep.

'Ah yes. *Bed Four*.' Bert mimics the nurses' call and then taps the side of his head, as if to impart a secret. 'The night sister will give you a powder. Just ask.'

'I don't need anything,' Bobby says, though it's always good to have a last resort. He shudders, thinking of Anne. She had a last resort all right. And where would he be now if she hadn't?

'Feeling the cold?' Bert asks, and Bobby realises that he's shivering in spite of his jacket.

'Are you up to a walk?' he says, accepting one of Bert's cigarettes.

They form a routine of morning walks and evening chess games. Bobby hasn't played since he was on the *Hester* and he discovers a talent for it. Some of the other men play cards, but cards and boredom are a bad combination. Sharping only works when you hit the mark once and move on, not when you're in close quarters. He remembers Posh Roly and Taffy dangling a midshipman over the side once, holding a leg apiece. 'But I've given him his money back,' the man whined. 'Nobody gives a fuck about the money,' Roly said. 'The point is that there's enough sharks in that water down there.' Lesson learned about a square game, and for Bobby too. And besides, cards go with drinking, and desperation, and he isn't desperate. So what if he and Rena have hit a rough patch. Other opportunities will come their way – the more he thinks about her uncle Donald the more he wonders if one shed full of junk and antiques can be enough for the man. But Bobby still has a roof over his head and he still has Rena. That's what this is all about, after all. And if on the fourth night he sees Anne sitting at the end of his bed, well, every man has his limit. No shame in admitting that. He pads up to the night nurse and she sighs, scornful and shrewd, and fetches a cup of water and two small blue tablets. Bobby knocks them back and pads back to bed. He knew what kind of woman Anne was when he married her. When he met her, for Christ's sake. That isn't what worries him. What worries him is that she had the measure of him, and that everything she said was true. He thinks of Janet in her crib, tries to imagine a baby in that old, cold single end with Anne. It would never have worked, would it?

When Rena visits there's a pause in the tea service which Bobby can only describe as cinematic. She's wearing trousers – long, wide-legged trousers with a high waist, topped by a sharp little short-sleeved blouse – and she looks a foot taller than he remembers.

She smiles, almost shyly, and swishes her hips so that he can admire the buttons at each side. 'Nell ran them up for me. What do you think?'

It isn't the buttons that he's admiring. 'You look… sensational.'

Seeing her with her hair properly curled, the colour back in her cheeks and her lips painted in, he understands that when he grabbed his hat and coat and felt in his pockets for money to drink, he was running away from another woman going to pieces in another hellhole of a room and kitchen. He can't tell Rena that, not ever, can't even mention Anne's name, so all there is to do is make amends.

He smiles and takes her hand and listens as she tells him how calm Janet is with Margaret, how much Margaret loves to hold her niece now her sight has gone.

'How's the business?' Bobby asks, and Rena tells him of American customers and a chair sold from under her while she was eating her lunch. 'Wouldn't they do better in a town?' he muses, waiting to see if she'll pick up the cue.

'Where they are suits them,' Rena says. 'People take holiday houses and day trips, and there's no competition.'

'Min's canny,' he agrees. Rena clasps his hand, and for a second he feels elated. She knows he's thinking ahead again, that he's making a go of this for her.

'They've been a good help to me. To us.'

He nods. 'And we'll pay them back every penny we owe them, I swear.'

They have tea, and he introduces her to Bert, who hasn't had any visitors since Bobby arrived, and then he takes her on a stroll around the grounds, giving Bed Four a wide berth. It's a fine day, the sun bright enough to send the shadows of the white clouds scudding across the bleak heather-clad hills beyond the wall.

'We'll get through all this,' Bobby says. 'You know that, don't you?'

She holds her hand up to shade her eyes and looks towards the car park where Donald is waiting, giving them some time alone. 'I don't want to keep Donald back,' she says. 'Do you want to say hello to him?'

'It's fine,' Bobby says. 'Give him my best. Good of him to bring you out here.'

'Yes.' She hesitates. 'Everyone has been very kind.'

'You look swell,' he tells her again, but her smile is only half there. He can feel the urge to do something melodramatic, grab her by the shoulders or prostrate himself in front of her, shouting *can't you see I'm trying?* Better still, sweep her off to somewhere fancy rather than let her walk away, looking like that, and leaving him here. But instead they say a civilised goodbye and kiss each other on the cheek.

He watches her go to the car and get in, and raises a hand in farewell but sun is reflecting on the windshield and he can't see if she or Donald reply. Every cell in his body is crying out for a drink. Surely they have brandy for emergencies? But no, Matron Oberführer is clear: no alcohol on the premises. Bobby isn't the only one there to dry out. He's noticed one or two others, and of course there's Bed Four, but he's a proper alcoholic, not someone who's just got into bad habits temporarily. Bobby checks his watch. Four o'clock. Six hours until lights out. At least on ship the routine was coupled with hard graft and the prospect of shore leave. He thinks of Thomas. Thomas knows this is a nonsense, that Rena is overreacting. He'd bring Bobby something, if he phoned. Or would he? Thomas has his own demons, Bobby would bet on that. And what if he told Rena? He walks past the public telephone and towards the ward, where Bert seems to be sleeping. Never mind. Tea time soon if the stench of boiling meat is anything to go by, and then chess later on. The wireless playing in the common room. Sleeping quarters are dry as a bone and clean as a whistle, and there are no torpedoes yet.

Worse things happen at sea. Worse things happen in dank single end flats. He's got through them all, and he can get through this. And when he does, it'll be him and Rena, side by side once more.

Rena, 1950

'I do love the smell of babies, don't you?' Aunt Margaret says to nobody in particular. 'Although you're getting to be a big girl now, aren't you Janet?'

'Well don't tire yourself out,' Rena says, more because she feels she should than because she's in a rush to take Janet back. The toddler is sitting on Margaret's lap in Min's sitting room at Balmaha (though with Min and Donald, every room is a showroom when it needs to be). Janet reaches up towards her great-aunt's face now and again with one tentative hand, but she's quiet as a mouse. Margaret catches her hand and blows a raspberry against it and Janet laughs and gurgles.

'This wee mite wouldn't...' Margaret begins but Min cuts her off: 'Give her to me. If we're going on this boat trip she'll need warmer clothes. And Rena, I'd take a scarf if I were you. It can get chilly on the water, even in August.'

Rena nods and goes to her room. Sharing with her mother once again, though they have a bed each this time. Her aunts have rallied round, whisking her away for a change of scene and fussing over things like draughts while setting her minor tasks to calm her idle hands. She spends her afternoons pottering, applying linseed oil and turps to tables, polishing brass jardinieres, restringing beads. Min professes that it's nice to have a full house again. Her children really flew the nest when they went: Hugh to Ontario (best place for him, according to Margaret) and then Belle falling for a friend of his and ending up in Vermont, where she manages to be as superior as she ever was but at least only by post. Rena looks out the fine shawl that Nell crocheted for her and arranges it over her shoulders. Jamie is staying with Thomas and helping in the shop, doing the deliveries that used to get Rena out of her bed at four in the morning. Here she's been sleeping in until eight thirty. Margaret's an early riser still and is happy to take Janet to the kitchen for breakfast, followed by her big ginger cat, which has also come to live with Min and Donald. At first Rena was afraid of her aunt falling over the cat, but together they seem to navigate Margaret's blindness. And Margaret is stoical, always has been: 'I nursed enough men who'd lost their sight,' she said, 'told them not to give up. What would I say to them now if I didn't get on with it as best I can?'

Rena should be missing Bobby more, she thinks, rather than agreeing to nice boat trips in the sunshine. Her husband and the father of her child. If people knew, they'd say she failed him as a wife, that it's her job to keep him upright and working. It's been a relief, if she's honest, to blame his weak chest and pass the problem to someone else while she sinks into the bosom of her family. Bobby's treatment is halfway through and they'll be going back to the flat soon enough.

Through the open window she hears the crunch of the motor on gravel and Min calling out, 'Look Janet, here's Uncle Donald bringing your Auntie Nellie!'

Donald stays to mind the shop and work on a campaign desk that needs some scratches and scrapes polished out before one of their good customers comes in, and the rest of them walk down to the pier and the Lady of the Loch. A large and rough-sounding Glaswegian family jostle in front of them, and they take care to find seats further away.

'We're in the shade here,' Hetty says, worried.

'It's all right. She'll turn clockwise round the loch and we'll be in the sun soon enough,' Min tells her.

Sure enough, by the time they pass the sandy beach at Port Bawn, where they're planning to take Janet bathing for the first time, Rena has to take off her shawl and spread it over the pram. Janet, lulled by the sound of the paddles and the gentle undulation of the water below, is sound asleep.

'If only I'd known,' Rena says. 'I could have had her on the boating pond in the park.'

A weak joke, but a sign she's feeling more like herself at least. Her aunts laugh and Min pats her on the shoulder. The water is blue and sparkling, and there's something about the scale of the loch, the glorious sweep of the green and brown hills that surround it, that makes Rena feel better than she has in ages.

They resort quickly to their picnic basket with its thermos of tea and assortment of biscuits. Janet rouses, and after a piece of shortbread is so lively that Hetty decides to walk her around while the others go to sit on the top deck and watch the sailing dinghies and rowing boats.

'It's like Sauchiehall Street out there,' Nell says, turning her face up towards the sky and shutting her eyes for a moment. 'Watch this sun on your skin, Irene. You don't want to get freckled.'

'Make you look healthy,' Margaret says.

'She doesn't want to look healthy,' Nell says. 'She wants to look pale and interesting.'

'The style's all changed since we were young, you know,' Min says, adjusting her wide-brimmed sunhat.

Rena lets her own eyes close for a moment, enjoying their gentle bickering and the heat that feels as if it's soaking through her eyelids. It makes her want to dip into the pristine water, and she can imagine teaching Janet to swim. The memory of being stuck in that hateful flat all day hardly troubles her.

'She's nothing to worry about there,' Nell is saying. 'She's kept her figure and she's still turning heads.'

'That's true. That chap on the gangway was falling over himself to help her step down onto the deck.'

'Lucky Irene,' Margaret says. 'And I'll bet that she's starting to blush right now, is she Min?'

'She is that.'

'It's just the sun,' Rena says, keeping her eyes firmly shut. She has no desire to turn heads, not in that way. That's the best thing about being married. No other men can come near you.

'You'll be looking forward to being back with Bobby, dear,' Margaret says.

Rena opens her eyes. 'Of course,' she says.

'It won't be too long.'

'No.'

'It can be hard on men, you know, when children come along.'

Nell tuts. 'And what on earth do you know about it,

Maggie? You've never had children.'

'Give me some credit, Nell. I would have liked children, you know that, if things had been different. If Alfred had come home.'

They sit in silence for a moment. As if to spite Margaret, one of the rough Glaswegian children comes tearing along the deck, yelling his head off about something and pursued by his older sister (or could it be his mother, Rena suddenly wonders), who is threatening to leather him.

'Hmmph,' Nell says. 'Well I don't have any regrets on that score. But I like being an auntie,' she adds, reaching up to pinch Rena's cheek. 'And a great auntie to wee Janet.'

'We all do,' Min says. 'And to Thomas's two as well, of course.'

'It's an age since we've seen them,' Margaret says. 'How are the twins, Rena?'

'Fine. Walking and talking, just about. You should see the way Evie has them dressed up to match. Drives Thomas mad to see how she has Malcolm turned out sometimes.'

'Has he a touch of his father's temper?' Margaret asks.

'Oh no,' Rena says. 'He can be sharp with Evie but that's just normal, isn't it?' She looks towards Min.

'Marriages change when there are children, and they change again when they've gone,' Min says.

Rena nods, and they all turn at the sound of a motor boat passing by. There's a man water-skiing behind it, letting go with one hand to wave at the children clustering along the railing of the Lady of the Loch to see.

'What a show off!' Min says, going over for a closer

look. 'Coo-ee, Janet! Hetty! We're up here.'

'Funny to think we've relations across the ocean, isn't it?' Margaret says, when her sister is out of earshot. 'Another niece and two nephews. And I'll never see how they've grown up now.'

She went with Min on the trip to visit Belle, and Hugh came along from Canada to meet them. The voyage of a lifetime, across the Atlantic Ocean. Rena envies them. She'd like to dine in a state room, or whatever they're called. Sit at the captain's table. Wear fancy jewellery. And yes, there would be Bobby too, charming, by her side.

'Maybe Bobby could go back to sea,' she says idly, unsure of what he might do other than wear a smart uniform with gold epaulettes. A chill creeps over her shoulders, but it's the memory that Bobby almost lost his life at sea. He wasn't idling on a calm loch in the sunshine: he was out there in the dark and the fog, with Germans all around.

'Well wouldn't you miss him even more then?' Margaret says. 'No, you'll find another business Rena. You're destined for better things.'

Rena is touched by Margaret's faith but she knows it's kindness rather than premonition. She's the substitute for the children Margaret and Nell never had, and the ones that have left Min and Donald for the glamour of a new world.

'You'd both been working your fingers to the bone,' Margaret goes on. 'A break will do you the world of good. And then – and I'm speaking as a nurse, Nell, and I may be blind as a bat but I know fine well when you're shaking your head at me – and then when Bobby comes home you'll be up to making a bit more of an effort again.'

'And so will he,' Nell mutters.

Margaret sighs. 'It's a woman's job to build up her man, Nell.'

Nell shakes her head and mutters something as she goes over to join Min at the railing. Rena doesn't feel so carefree, all of a sudden. She feels the familiar weight pushing down her shoulders again.

'Honestly,' Margaret says. 'Just because she's a confirmed spinster. We never did meet Nell's wartime sweetheart, you know.'

Nell wanders along the deck and Min comes back to sit in the shade.

'I was just saying to Irene, we never did meet Nell's wartime sweetheart.'

Min laughs. 'Oh Margaret, that's ancient history now. Nell's Nell, you know that.'

'What I was trying to say was,' Margaret pauses and takes a deep breath. 'Rena has a good man and a lovely healthy daughter. Everything will fall into place.'

Rena nods. The war is over and she has been lucky. Jamie was young enough to miss it, and Thomas came home with nothing worse than a gammy knee. So what if he gets a bit tetchy with Evie, after all he must have been through? She'll keep an eye on them. There won't be another divorce in the Jarvie family, she'll make sure of that. And she still has Bobby. She would never give him up.

Bobby, 1950

When Bobby gets his first piece of mail it's a postcard from Rena explaining that she can't visit that week as she and Janet are both under the weather with summer colds. The postcard shows a picture of him and Rena on the front at Largs, strolling along arm in arm. A day out to celebrate signing the lease on the tearoom. The tearoom that was taken from them, along with its fancy address. He looks at it closely. You'd guess the colour of Rena's hair from the way the light is hitting it, and the corners of her mouth are turning up, as though she's just spotted the photographer springing in front of them as they walk and is about to oblige him with a smile. It might have been the last time they were truly relaxed. They'd taken the photographer's chit and gone by the shop window to see the photograph and of course Bobby bought it for her. He would have whether it had been a good likeness or not but as it is, Rena looks beautiful, and he wishes she was coming to visit, to remind him what the fuck he's doing in this place.

'No visitors this week,' he tells his new friend Alberto

over limp toast and decent marmalade, a jar of which was thrust into his hand by Hetty when she visited. 'I'm joining you in solitary.'

'Aye well, I envy you that today, Bobby. It's visiting time for me.'

'Oh really?' Bobby says. 'Friend or family?'

'Friend or foe, more like.' Bert drains his tea.

'Ex-wife then?' Bobby grins, keeping it light.

'Let's walk,' Bert says, stuffing the last of his toast in his mouth. He's up to quite a speed on his crutches now, and Bobby doesn't have to take care to match his pace any more.

'Grand day again, Sister,' Bobby says as they pass one of the nurses – *strictly no alcohol, Mr Young* – and step down from the back verandah onto the grass. And indeed it is. The sky is a clear, deep blue and the red bricks of the back wall are shimmering in a heat haze. He imagines Rena striding along the loch-side, pushing the pram in front of her and smiling. If he only had money, it would all be a different story. She could dedicate her time to Janet, and shopping, and taking care of the house. But then he'd be bored, wouldn't he? Rena's more ambitious than that.

Bert waits until they reach the perimeter path, until their cigarettes are smoked halfway down, before he starts to speak. 'I got a telephone call yesterday. A kind of business associate, if you get my drift.'

Bobby nods. It's a funny kind of accident that leaves you with both legs broken at the knee, right enough, but if there's one thing he has learned in life – apart from never to cheat at cards on a ship – it's not to ask too many questions. People will tell you what they want to tell you, and there's not a lot you can do about it either way.

'Now, this fellow and me, as far as I'm concerned we're old pals.'

'And as far as he's concerned?'

Bert shrugs.

'Well, have the nurses say you're not up to visitors.'

'That won't do. If I don't see him, it might look as if I have something to hide. And I'm an open book, Bobby.'

'So you are,' Bobby says. The thing about crooks is that they need you to know that they're honest, and it's sounding very much as if Bert is a crook. They keep walking, until the red brick of the hospital laundry shows through the small copse of birch trees.

'We've rubbed along quite well here, haven't we, Bobby?'

'We have,' Bobby agrees. Turns out institutions only suit him when he's too preoccupied by missiles and his own mortality to let his thoughts wander. Bert has been a welcome distraction.

'So I'm going to need to have a private chat with this fellow,' Bert says. 'And what I'm thinking is that when you reach a spot like this you're out of sight.'

'In this place? Chance'd be a fine thing.'

'All I'm saying is that disagreements are less likely to happen if there's a witness.'

'Okay,' Bobby concedes. That's the other thing about crooks. They think everybody is out to get them.

'I'll show my gratitude however you want, Bobby. A wee present for the wife, a wee dram to pass the day better…'

'No need,' Bobby says. 'Not as if I've got anything better to do.'

As visiting time approaches Bobby is more preoccupied with Rena, her absence, than Bert's tendency to paranoia. He'd like to smell her cologne. None of the nurses smell of anything other than disinfectant, and those few that are under forty are kept well away in the geriatric ward. Lucky old buggers. They might not know their own names but you can bet they still recognise a tidy bust and a pert behind. Women are a civilising influence though, even when they're hatchet-faced. That YMCA was a hellhole of a different order.

Visitors arrive in dribs and drabs, and amongst them there's at least a couple worth a second glance. Bed Four (the nickname has stuck, even with some of the nurses, although he's been moved to bed nine) has given up screaming in the night but his skin is now as yellow as his sister's hair. She has nice big curves that you could sink right into for an hour or two. And one of the shrapnel-in-the-heid boys is having his hand clasped by a pretty-but-she-knows-it brunette who attracts Matron's disapproving glare. Rightly so, perhaps. Bobby wouldn't put money on this fiancée sticking around until the wedding, not when the poor sod who bought her that ring bursts into tears with no provocation and suffers from facial spasms.

It's a moment before Bobby realises that Bert has a visitor too, a thickset man in his thirties, wearing a brown suit and tweed trilby. His jacket is shiny at the elbows, Bobby notices, as the pair head towards the door out onto the verandah. Bert casts an anxious glance behind him and Bobby gets up and follows. Once out of the door he pauses and turns to shelter his lighter from the breeze. He'd hoped to catch their reflection in the window but that must be a trick from the movies, because all he can see is straight through to the ward, where everyone who is able has now gone to the lounge and the tea urn. He stands there smoking for a moment, but Bert and his companion don't look back. He notices Bert is using the crutches more than he needs to, playing it up. Bobby walks slowly on, giving them a head start. They're talking away, and the man in the hat is casual, his hands in his trouser pockets. You wouldn't do that in a decent suit. They turn to the left, the way to the copse and the laundry, and Bobby wonders why on earth Bert's heading that way if he's worried. For the love of God, he's got two broken legs, not a bit part in *The Lady from Shanghai*. Bobby shakes his head and thinks of Rena stiff beside him in the Alhambra, then dozing off halfway through the movie. It did her good to get out for a while, Hetty said, but it had been all Bobby could do to persuade her.

There's a clatter ahead and Bobby looks towards Bert, who's now on the ground, crutches beside him. Bobby casts his cigarette aside and shouts something indeterminate – *haw!* – as he starts sprinting. After that things happen quickly. Turns out there's a whole lot of anger pent up behind Bobby's fists, and it feels good to let it out. For a second it's MacPherson he's got down on the ground there, then Minto, then any other member of the Food Committee. It's only Bert whacking him on the shoulder with one of his crutches that stops him in the end. He picks up the man's hat and waits for him to get up, which takes a while, then throws it towards him. Nothing's said, nothing needs to be. The man turns tail and makes for the car park, wiping the blood from his nose as he goes. Bobby helps Bert up and back to the ward, where he explains that he saw him take a tumble when he was walking, managing to crack himself in the face with one of his crutches. The nurses are solicitous, and if they remember that Bert had a visitor at all nobody mentions it. Bobby feels elated, his heart still swooping with excitement in his chest. He'd give anything to go out on the town, to run into some folk and tell them the story, to raise the first cool glass to his lips. He was in a fight for Christ's sake, you're allowed a brandy to still your nerves. But it'll have to wait, because there isn't a snowflake's chance in Hell of a drink here, and he can't tell anyone about his wee adventure, even if he knew the whole story. Bert does him a favour straight away, saving his painkiller and sleeping tablet for Bobby. It takes that and his own allocation to get him to sleep, and when at last he feels greyness rising to smother the excitement of the day he thinks of Rena once more, and how proud she'll be of him.

When she does come to visit, for the last time before Bobby is due to come home, Min drives her and she brings Janet and Hetty as well. Not quite the wall of tweedy propriety that surrounded her on the day he saw her first, but close. A warning, perhaps, that he'd better have changed his tune. Min goes off to find a nurse Margaret knew and Bobby feels a moment of dread – there was a spy in their midst! – only to have it disappear blissfully when he realises that he has succeeded. He is sitting there clear-skinned and bright-eyed, and not a drop has passed his lips. Janet has changed over the past few weeks and seems quieter, more settled. The reddish tinge of her baby hair has given way to blonde but the shape of her face makes her the spit of Hetty, he realises, who is dandling her grandchild on her knee while Rena tells him about the boat trip they've been on and the lovely ivory gewgaws Min and Donald bought at auction and are selling on for thrice the price. She has brought him one as a present, a carved filigree ball with other filigree balls inside it. There aren't any joins and he doesn't know how anyone could have carved something so intricate. He lets Janet marvel over it too, and Hetty removes it from her hand just as it makes its way towards her mouth. Hetty must be used to children, after three of her own, so maybe it's her confidence that's calmed the wee one down. Bobby isn't sure if she doesn't know or has forgotten when she asks in all seriousness, 'And how's your chest, Bobby? Has that cough gone away?'

'Oh yes, Hetty, I'm fighting fit again now.'

'That's good. Sometimes a rest is what's needed, isn't it?'

'Let's take Janet outside,' he says on impulse. 'It's a nice day.'

'I'll stay here and finish my tea,' Hetty says, and she pushes Janet into his arms where she looks up at him with serious grey eyes, but doesn't utter a cry. He and Rena walk out onto the verandah and there's Bert sitting smoking, one of his legs propped up on a chair. Bobby realises he doesn't want Rena to have to shake his hand, but there's no avoiding it now.

'Bert, you remember my wife, Irene?'

'The one who gets him in check mate!' Rena says with a smile that looks like her old smile. 'Thank you for keeping my husband out of mischief while he's been here.'

'A pleasure, Mrs Young.'

'Oh no, don't get up,' Rena says, concerned, but Bert insists on balancing on one crutch and shaking her hand properly.

'Look, Janet,' Bobby says, pointing her towards the lawn. 'There's a wee bunny rabbit on the grass, do you see it?'

Janet makes a wordless trill that might be her approximation of *bunny rabbit*. Hetty says that Rena didn't speak properly until she was three, so they aren't worried about Janet being slow. When he shows her the trees by the side of the path she reaches out towards the rowan berries. Him with a child, a toddler, who'd have thought it?

'Careful, Bobby, we don't want her eating them.'

'I'm always careful.'

He has Janet balanced in one arm, propped up against him, so he can reach out and take Rena's hand in his. 'I'm sorry it had to come to this, Rena, but it's been good for me. Are you...'

'I'm fine. I just needed... a break. After Janet, and I really thought the tearoom was a beginning, you know?'

He nods, squeezes her hand harder. They don't talk about how he is because Rena knows. He's there, and she can see. 'We'll find another beginning, my love. I promise you.'

When she smiles at him he can believe that they will, that when he gets home the following week it will be a fresh start. He is going to sort something out, something that will support his family, and he isn't going to drink like he did before.

His final week in the convalescent home passes uneventfully. Fed three times a day, and no responsibilities? If it had a bar it would be perfect. Bobby can feel Bert's gratitude, and his new touch of respect. Bobby went over the score, he knows that, but come on: knocking a man off his crutches. And he felt better afterwards, he really did. They should install a boxing gym, that would help men like him. He and Bert still play chess though, and on Bobby's final night Bert thanks him again.

'Don't mention it.'

Bert makes his move and captures Bobby's second knight.

'Every time,' Bobby says.

'You risk them,' Bert laughs.

'I'm going to lose again, amn't I?'

'Never say never,' Bert says, and they play on for a while. At nine o'clock the tea trolley comes round for the last time, the auxiliary nurse murmuring 'lights out at ten' as she goes, although they all know that already.

'So what's the next move?' Bert asks.

'Can't tell you that,' Bobby says. 'Or you'll definitely beat me.'

'I mean when you're out.'

Bobby sighs. 'If we could find another business while we've still got the deposit from the tearoom to put down, that would be the thing. Can't say I liked being at sea, but being stuck in an office was even worse. Routine doesn't suit me. Makes me jittery.'

Bert nods, moves his pawn to no advantage that Bobby can see. 'I'm not cut out for it myself. Worked for my father in his café when I was a boy, but I was never up for inheriting the family business. When I was fifteen I went to Bantry to help my uncle on his fishing boat and then me and one of the other lads saw an advert for work on the railway. Paid much more and we finished up in Dublin, and it just went on from there.'

'And then you ended up back over here?'

Bert swirls his tea in his cup, as though he's about to read the leaves. 'Some fellows I knew were doing some jobs on the west coast. Got in with them and I was back nearer my old ma when my father died. Stalemate.'

For a second Bobby thinks that Bert's talking about

the jobs he got into but when he looks down at the board he sees that his king is cornered, able to step backwards and stop, forwards and stop.

'Good game,' he says, and shakes Bert's hand.

As Bert begins to replace the pieces in their wooden box he says, 'I've an uncle, well, more of a second cousin twice removed, who deals with a fellow in your neck of the woods. One of the good guys, Vittorio Caldera. I'll put the word out to bear you in mind if he knows of any opportunities.'

Bobby smiles. 'That's kind of you Bert, but I'm not sure I'd be cut out for it.'

'Away with you, Bobby. He runs a shop, imports from the old country. Pasta, olive oil. Cannae be doing with all that myself, but I hear he's good at getting hold of things. And that goes a long way if you're thinking of catering and hospitality.'

'You've already done me enough of a favour with the chess games,' Bobby says. 'Stopped me going doolally through boredom.'

As he brushes his teeth and splashes water on his face Bobby has every intention of not bothering with a tablet tonight. Start as he means to go on. But it's dark outside the high windows, and the ward is quiet, and if truth be told he's nervous. Bloody easy to get institutionalised, that's all it is. But he gets his cup of water and goes to the nurse's desk anyway, just in case.

Bobby, 1950

Under a month since he was released for good behaviour and Bobby Young, paragon of sobriety, has pulled it out of the bag. Sure, the premises are upstairs, but there are three fine windows over one of Kilmarnock's good streets and it's opposite the Alhambra Picture Palace. Best of all, it's cheap. A sublet from his new good friend Vittorio – 'call me Victor' – Caldera, who has a storeroom already in the basement and no desire to expand his shop into the upper floor. The entrance is separate, Bobby assures Rena, as they stride down the street together. She's keeping pace with him, walking tall in her double-breasted trouser suit, hatless to show off the shampoo and set that Min treated her to. Yes, she has her old spirit back. Margaret took him aside and told him that it happened to women sometimes, after a baby. That and losing the tearoom, well, it knocked her for six. As they pass the looming infirmary where she had Janet, Rena looks across the road, towards the spire of the High Kirk. As they walk past Weir's he points towards the cellophane-lined window and says, 'As soon as we're in the black we'll buy you a new frock from there.'

Rena smiles, 'I might have to mend my old ones a few times before then.'

Bobby makes a show of looking at his watch then links his arm in hers and pushes her ahead of him through the door of the shop.

'Can I help you?' The assistant looks stern, as if the presence of a man in a shop devoted to ladieswear is questionable. Or maybe she just has a broom handle up her arse. She's wearing a twin set and a tartan skirt that Rena wouldn't be seen dead in.

'Yes,' he says. 'My wife needs a… was it gloves, Irene? A silk scarf? Stockings?'

Rena blushes. Her pale skin gives her away every time. 'I'll have a look around,' she tells the assistant. She's using her posh voice, another good sign.

He watches as she fingers the scarves and the calfskin gloves. Her hand skims over a leather wallet patterned to look like crocodile skin, while the assistant trails her at a distance, pretending to be straightening already perfect rows of dresses and casting opprobrious glances at Rena's trousers. Rena is enjoying herself, he realises. She likes clothes, and furnishings, not for themselves but because she likes transformations. Because, like him, she likes the fantasy of becoming someone else. So easy to indulge, in the time it takes to slip on a new coat. Or slip down a strong drink, or slip alongside a new woman, not that Bobby's interested in that kind of thing these days. A drink to relax, sure, but he's a husband and father. A family man, and soon a man of business once more. He's not from here any more than Rena is, but he'll be a man of the town one day. She makes another circuit of the accessories before her hand comes to rest on the wallet again.

'This,' she says. 'How about this?' She drops her voice. 'But it's too extravagant, Bobby.'

'Done,' he says, taking it from her and beckoning the assistant. Rena goes outside to wait. The assistant turns out to be the proprietress, and he manages to find a flaw, a tiny score in the leather, and beat her down on the price. Still, it's the last note in his own wallet that he hands over.

When he goes outside again the wind is blowing harder and the sky is heavy. This time Rena reaches for him, slips her hand into the crook of his arm. 'Thanks,' she says. 'We can't afford it, but that was a nice thing to do.'

He shrugs. 'You deserve it. And I need to see you happy.'

They walk under the viaduct, past Campbell's the florist and the George Hotel, where, in the bar one evening he happened to get talking to Victor Caldera. Strategic drinking is an entirely different matter, even Rena sees that. They turn right into West George Street, where the picture palace is showing the new John Ford. 'Is this where you and Hetty came for the newsreels?' he asks, knowing the answer already.

'Yes,' she says. 'We had to come to the late show because we couldn't leave Jamie in the shop alone. And he wasn't going to miss it. Thought he'd see Thomas up there one day. Oh, thank heavens it's over. I don't know what I'd have done if…'

Her hand is still tucked under his arm. He squeezes her close. They've all been in jeopardy, he knows that, but it's onwards and upwards now.

'Mum would sit and knit all the way through,' Rena says. 'Click clack, click clack. Socks for soldiers. I've worn her socks and I'm not sure she was doing them a favour.'

'Well,' he says. 'Here we are. Look across the road. First floor.'

She looks where he indicates, but doesn't say anything.

'Of course the windows need that blacking taken off. Then we'll get gold lettering on them.'

'You're getting beyond yourself.'

'Aye,' he says. 'And who taught me how to do that, Irene Jarvie?'

She gives him a canny look, and he sees the corner of her mouth twitch upwards as she removes her arm from his. 'Let's go in then,' she says, pushing her shoulders back.

He takes her into Caldera's to get the key, introducing her to Victor, who is as charming as could be hoped. He knows, because Bobby has made it clear, that the deal depends on Rena. What Bobby hasn't told him is that they'll need to borrow money, yet again, from Thomas or her aunts or the whole lot of them. They'll have no luck with the bank manager, not with everyone knowing they lost Annanhill. Rena is walking around the shop, seemingly entranced by the sacks of rice, the dried sausage and ham hanging above the counter. Bobby feels his stomach rumble, decides it's the smell of salty cured meat rather than nerves.

'Is everything from Italy, Mr Caldera?' Rena asks.

'Call me Victor, please. Yes, everything you see. Pasta, rice for risotto, salami, grappa. A cure for homesickness, my brother – God rest his soul – used to say.'

'It must be very beautiful,' Rena says. 'Italy, I mean.'

'Yes,' says Victor, seriously. 'One day you must visit.'

'One day,' Rena smiles. Bobby knows she'll be taking in Victor's spotless shop apron, his gold watch, his perfectly barbered silver hair. He's well-to-do, no question about that.

'Where is my hospitality! Try an Amaretto,' Victor says, offering a shiny red tin of biscuits, all wrapped in coloured paper. Rena takes a green one. 'Hard, huh? Better to dip in our good Italian espresso. I have only just made some.' He hurries into the back shop and returns with a moka and small cups. 'A relief to have proper coffee, after so long,' he says, indicating the bright packets on the shelf behind him as he pours, adds sugar. It's to be part of the deal, that Victor will be their main supplier.

Rena thanks him, sipping her coffee appreciatively, but Bobby can feel her impatience. If it isn't a goer, she wants to know now. Victor hands him the key. 'Go on up, Bobby. I can't leave the shop.'

Bobby guides Rena back out into the street and unlocks the neighbouring door.

'So this would be open, of course, and we'd have a sign here.'

There's a connecting door to Victor's shop on the left as they go in. It's upstairs, yes, but the way there is not dingy. The steps are broad, and there's a big window with coloured glass at the half-landing.

'It could look smart enough,' he says, then stops. Better to let Rena take it in. You don't sell anything by sounding desperate. When they reach the top of the stairs, he unlocks the door on the left and ushers Rena in ahead of him. It's a decent size of room, he knows it. Just needs to be gussied up.

'Kitchen?' she says.

'Yes. And a toilet. They need a bit of work, but not nearly as bad as Annahill.'

'Aye,' Rena says. 'And someone else has the benefit of that now, don't they?'

Bobby can't stop the smirk that flickers over his lips.

'What?' she says.

'Ah well, they might not have found things working quite as well as they hoped.'

'What do you mean?'

'Me and Thomas. Spotted a few wee problems when we went in to do the final inventory.'

Created a few, he means, in a rare alliance with his brother-in-law. 'Nothing too obvious,' he says hastily. 'That leak we thought we'd fixed, oh dear, and the wiring was in a terrible state.'

Rena shakes her head and moves on. 'I don't understand why he isn't opening a café himself. Italians are famous for it.'

Bobby shrugs. 'Says he owned a share of a place in Troon but sold it last year to get the deposit for a house back home. He wants to retire, hand this over to his nephew. Us taking this on, it's free money for him until he goes.'

Rena stops at the window, intent on something. He goes closer to see what she's doing. Using her thumbnail to scrape a small square of blacking from the window. She puts her eye to the spyhole she's made. 'Look at the queue for the five o'clock showing,' she says. 'It's round the block.'

'Proper coffee,' he says. 'And nobody bakes like you and Hetty.'

'Ices,' she says, and turns to look at him. 'I saw a photograph in the *Picture Post*, a place down in England. It was so pretty. The waitresses all had uniforms. The Bantam Tea Rooms, it was called. What do you think of that for a name?'

'Hmm.' Bobby hesitates just long enough before saying, 'I can see it in gold in the windows.'

Rena nods, and takes both of his wrists in her hands, grips them. 'I want a lease that's watertight this time. We need long enough to make a go of this.'

Whatever they have to ask for from her family, whatever they need to do, it's going to be fine. Just as well: he bought a chap from the paper a skinful to make sure that a rumour will be started in the Cameo column on Friday. Something cheery, he specified. *Catering is about to take a step up in Kilmarnock, by the look of things!* No need to mention Victor's friends, or their favours. Even in the dim room Rena's green-grey eyes are alight, as if she's looking into the future and seeing all the notes and coins that will fall into her new mock-crocodile purse.

Rena, 1951

The air is heady with the smell of coffee. Most customers take it sweetened and with milk, but some are tempted by the look of the espresso, or rather the gleam and hiss of the machine. Victor got them a good deal on the rental for the Esportazione; a favour, he said, that would be more than repaid by their orders for his coffee. People with pretensions like it, men taking their girls to the cinema. Others prefer a big EPNS pot of the weaker filter stuff, and everyone likes the ice cream from the Venice. Turns out the owner there is a friend of Victor's as well, so another deal has been done on guaranteed orders paid in cash. Bobby sorted out the gold stencil in the windows, just like he said he would, and last week Rena was able to pay Min back the money she loaned them towards getting started. Alma hardly needed to be coaxed from the canteen at the shoe factory, although she did insist on a suitable new uniform to go with her raise. Better than that, better than all of that, they are just around the corner from the council offices and every day, Monday to Friday, that dreadful man MacPherson has to walk past their business and see that it is booming.

'That's me off,' she tells Alma, washing her hands at the kitchen sink. 'I want to take a walk down to Lauder's before it shuts.'

'Good,' Alma says. 'You need to take a wee bit time to yourself. That was some night last night, eh?'

Rena pauses to light a cigarette. 'Oh, it was, wasn't it? I didn't know it would be the Provost who'd come to present the trophy.'

The Howard Park Old Men's Cabin won the Ayrshire championships; Rena hadn't expected such a fuss over dominoes, but she's delighted that the Bantam was chosen to host.

'And the acts,' Alma says. 'They were fair away with it all.'

'They were.' A vote of thanks at the end, for her and Bobby, that brought a tear to her eye, as she stood there looking at her tearoom all set up as long tables for a change, packed with customers. She'd turned thirty that day, too busy to celebrate it, but Bobby had them all sing happy birthday and cheer her. 'Mr Young will come by to close up at eight.'

Alma's stuck with them for long enough for Rena to trust her, but otherwise she doesn't take her eye off the ball for a moment. She's still putting on a pinny and baking, taking orders, even clearing tables although rightly the staff take this as a rebuke. 'That's not your job, Mrs Young,' but Rena knows it sets the tone. Bobby gets the supplies in, and they both do the money. Through overestimating the amount needed for the house she manages to squirrel away a little each week in her own account. It's all going well, but you never know.

Alma nods, and they run through which cakes are

running low and how much sugar is left. Sugar's a hassle still, but they've enough sweetener and Evie's been useful when it comes to butter, Rena has to concede. She pulls on her gloves, checks herself in the mirror, and leaves. She does plan to go to Lauder's but she has set herself another task. She's going to find out what it is that happens on a Thursday evening after the Bantam Tea Rooms close. Bobby says he has a drink in the George with Victor and the boys, whoever they may be, and Rena tolerates this because he doesn't come home in a state and really, he's been a new man since the sanatorium. The source of her concern is not the George, which doesn't function beyond its bar anymore and is due to be closed down and, rumour has it, turned into a furniture showroom. Rena is more exercised by the hotel along to the left of the tearooms. The Ossington. Red sandstone, perched grandly on the corner, its coffee tavern announced in large gold letters on a sign painted on the stonework that's almost the size of Rena. Temperance, irreproachable, unlike the rooms of its upper storey and attic. Alma purses her lips talking about it, and her fingers twitch as if they're going to spring up and make the sign of the cross.

Rena walks quickly round the corner and on to John Finnie Street, as if immorality might be catching. The windows of the coffee tavern are grimy and it isn't even open; not that it would be any competition if it was, with its watery tea and burnt coffee. There's a suspicion in her mind, about Bobby, if what Alma says is true. The Ossington is almost next door to them. After Janet was born, well, Rena was hardly thinking of that kind of thing, and since they've been working again she's been too busy to bother. But men are different that way.

Walking around Lauder's soothes Rena. She likes looking at the displays and thinking of what she might have one day. Gloves like those, a suit like that. Unable to resist, she buys herself smart stockings, just to have something new that she'll be able to unwrap and wear pristine. Upstairs she looks at the furnishings, fingering curtains and upholstery fabrics until she has almost clean forgotten about her plans for the evening. *Just looking*, she says again and again, and then at last, *well actually, do you have these in the gold velvet?* There's a little rush of something that comes with handing over the money, with seeing her purchases carefully folded in tissue and packed. Rena is good at saving and at making do, but she loves buying things when she can. And then when she walks up the street it's clear that she has been shopping, that she is the kind of woman who can just pop into Lauder's. Even if it'll still take her forty minutes to walk home.

'Mrs Young? Irene?' Head down against the drizzle which is starting up, Rena startles at the voice calling out to her on Wellington Street. Councillor Gibson stops his car beside her, forcing other drivers to go around him. 'Can I offer you a lift?'

'Oh yes, thank you, Councillor, that's very kind.'

He gets out and hurries round to hold the door open for her, which is the kind of thing Rena appreciates. He's wearing a black suit and a black tie, but doesn't have the demeanour of someone who's been to a funeral. 'Shopping, I see. Good to see you looking so well again.'

'Just a couple of things for the house,' she says.

'Ah, I thought it would be a dress,' he says, waiting for a van to pass before pulling out. She catches a glimpse of the cufflink on his left wrist; blue enamel with gold Square and Compasses. 'I know what you ladies are like with your fashions.'

'Oh no, nothing like that,' Rena says, thinking of her stockings nestling at the bottom of the bag.

'Very restrained,' he says with approval. 'My wife never comes back without something new to clutter the wardrobe.' He clicks on the windscreen wipers and peers through the gap they clear at the wet street. 'And she doesn't have your figure.'

Rena doesn't reply. Is that drink she can smell in the fuggy warmth of the car? She wipes condensation off the side window. The shops at Dean Street are closed now, their signs blurry through the rain.

'The nights are drawing in.'

'Yes,' Rena says. 'Thank you for the lift.'

'And the new flat is an improvement, I take it?'

'Yes,' Rena says again. She'd like nothing more than to move to one of those great big detached houses up the Glasgow Road, just like Gibson's, or into the brand new houses they're building next to the park.

'I was very glad to help you, Irene, you know that don't you?'

And I wouldn't have been in that mess if your Corporation hadn't evicted me, Rena wants to say. 'I appreciate it,' she tells him instead.

'That's good,' he says, and horror of horrors, his hand reaches away from the gearstick and rests on her leg. He's looking at the road ahead but it's deliberate, of course.

'Mr Gibson,' she begins.

'Please Irene, we've known each other for a while now. Since you danced so prettily on VE day, as I remember. Call me Alec.'

The hand is clasping her thigh now. 'Mr Gibson,' she

says, louder now. 'Please.' She tries to prise it away with her own but feels at once that he is stronger than her. He puts his foot down and the car speeds up. 'Mr Gibson, Alec, my husband is expecting me home.'

'I've said it before, Bobby's a lucky man,' Gibson says, and there's something repellent in his tone, as if somehow he believes Bobby knows about this and is complicit. 'My wife is away at her sister's, as it happens.'

'Stop the car and let me out right now,' Rena says, keeping her voice as strong and steady as she can.

Gibson pulls in. Nobody is walking by, and she looks up towards the Mayfair Café, judging whether she should make a run for it. But her bag is on the back seat where Gibson put it, and she'll be damned if she's going without it. She turns and reaches for it, manages to clasp the handles and pull it towards her just as Gibson grabs her and kisses her moistly on the lips.

'You're an ungrateful woman, Mrs Young,' he says, sneering on the *missus*. 'After all I've done for you.'

Her heart flutters as she walks up the hill and she takes out her handkerchief and scrubs at her lips until every speck of lipstick is gone and the linen comes away clean. She looks around, wondering too late if anyone saw her get out of the car. It's a short walk home but long enough for the hem of her skirt to soak through, unprotected by her umbrella. Halfway there the paper of the shopping bag from Lauder's begins to dissolve and she just manages to clasp the contents to her chest in time.

When she gets there the flat is the same, small and drab. It could be worse, and she shudders to think back to that hell-hole in Riccarton that they were put after Annanhill. Gibson might have helped to get her out of there but she owes him nothing. Nothing. She puts her umbrella in the bath and splashes her face with cold water. Her cheeks look shiny and red in the bathroom mirror, her lips uncharacteristically pale.

'I got a new set of antimacassars in Lauder's,' she calls through to Hetty as she hangs up her coat. She needs to occupy her mind. 'Brighten the room up a bit.'

'That'll be nice, dear,' Hetty says.

'One day I'll get some new furniture too, something modern rather than rejects from Min.'

'Min's been very good to us,' Hetty says.

'I know that, Mum. Sorry. It was just a long walk in the rain. I felt a bit… fed up. I'm fine.'

'Well, you're just in time to have your tea with me and Janet.'

'All right. I'm starving.' Rena is surprised to find that she is, although only twenty minutes before she felt so queasy at Gibson's touch, his beery breath. 'Goodness, what have you done to her hair?'

'Curled it,' Hetty says. 'Didn't I, Janet?'

Janet smiles shyly.

'We'll need to take her to the photographer and get a picture of her like that,' Rena says. 'In her dress with the broderie anglaise would look nice. You could do that tomorrow, Mum. I'll leave you the money.'

'She's growing to be the spit of you,' Hetty says, and Janet beams. Her pork chop sits uneaten on her plate, although Hetty has trimmed the fat from it. Rena doesn't hold with fussy eating but she can't really blame her daughter. Hetty is an abysmal cook. Good with cakes, terrible with savouries. Not for the first time, Rena wonders how on earth to prepare Janet for the world, for life ahead. School next year, that'll be a start. Up the road at Rowallan. Hetty will need to walk her there, or Bobby drive her in the car, until she's old enough to go alone.

'Look at all these pictures she drew today,' Hetty says. Rena looks. Dog and dog after dog, or at least they have four legs and sometimes tails, executed in clumsy but determined crayon lines. Rena can't remember drawing when she was a child, but Evie gave Janet the crayons as a present, so the next time her sister-in-law comes round, pictures there will be. It's a funny thing, because Rena looked after Jamie so much when he was a baby. She fed him and dressed him and kept him quiet, but she doesn't remember many games beyond a hoop and a ball in the back garden. Life in the Lennox household was lived on tenterhooks.

'Do you like dogs then?' she asks her daughter now.

This time the answer is unequivocal: 'Yes!'

'Hmm. Well, maybe we'll need to think about getting you one, how about that? Once you've started school.'

After they've eaten Rena takes it upon herself to clean the grill and the cooker. Even as she's scouring away she knows that in spite – maybe because – of Gibson and his clammy hands she is going ahead with her plan. When she says she's going to meet Bobby at the tearoom at closing time and that they might see a late picture, Hetty says 'That's nice dear,' and that she's happy to stay late with Janet. Rena used to think that her mother was stupid – or, rather, that the wits had been beaten out of her – but now she wonders whether placid acceptance of all that you're told is an enviable quality. For the first time in years Rena thinks of how Min and Nell had sat and rehearsed Hetty for the divorce hearing: 'You knew he was committing adultery, and you were worried for the moral example he was setting the children. Say it again, Hetty. You knew…'

Rena is more determined than ever as she walks back into town. If Bobby is up to something, she'll make him wish he'd never been born. She doesn't usually go out alone in the dark, and is surprised to find that there is a tingle of excitement about it, or maybe it's still nerves that make her step away from the kerb whenever she hears a car coming up behind her. The rain has faded to a faint drizzle, and the light from the streetlights glistens in the puddles. It's only when she reaches the viaduct that she wonders where she'll place herself so as not to be seen. It is five minutes to eight, so Bobby will be inside, cashing up. Alma will be getting her coat and her hat and then walking down John Finnie Street to catch her bus. Rena passes the door of the George and sure enough, there's Alma hurrying up the street ahead of her. It'll take Bobby a few more minutes to set the float for the morning and lock up. If he comes out, she'll see him. The cinema queue has almost been drawn into the building. She checks what pictures are showing, although Hetty won't ask. One about the Resistance during the war, with the actress gazing up fearfully at a searchlight overhead, the Eiffel Tower silhouetted in the background. Rena goes into the foyer and buys cigarettes. Smiling at the kiosk girl feels like subterfuge. She stands outside and lights her cigarette; she could be waiting for a latecomer. Still no sign of Bobby.

By the time her feet begin to numb in the cold, Rena has realised she doesn't have the patience for espionage. She crosses the road and checks the downstairs door. It's locked. So if Bobby hasn't come out, has someone else gone in? The back door to the lane, Rena remembers. She tiptoes down the steps behind the Ossington, onto Strand Street, avoiding the puddles that have formed on the uneven treads. Now it's dark, in the shadow of the whisky bonds, and it feels less like subterfuge and more like danger. She peers round the corner to the left, to the lane. Yes, there's a figure walking up to the back door where Caldera takes in his stock. She had been imagining some tart from that disreputable hotel, but this is a well-dressed man.

Bobby, 1951

Thursday evening is a small but glittering jewel in Bobby's week. He bids Alma a cheery goodbye. She has Friday off; a family party coming up on the Saturday. Well, don't do anything I wouldn't, he tells her. And why doesn't she take some of the leftover pancakes while she's at it? They'll fry up just fine and he's sure she sends her husband to work on a full stomach. Her smile fades for a second at the mention of her husband and Bobby remembers that there's some rumour of him going on binges from time to time. Bobby doesn't blame the man one jot. If he had nine children he'd never be out the pub.

He locks the street door after her then returns to the tearoom to draw the blinds and move some of the small tables to make more space around the larger central one, which he clears of its settings and cloth. From the only place he can be sure Rena won't pry – the boiler cupboard above the door in the gentlemen's restroom – he retrieves his box of tricks. A cloth of green baize, which he smooths over the table. The crystal tumblers and the whisky, rum, vodka to go with them. He places ashtrays on the table and readies a dish of ice cubes, switches off the overhead lights so that the tearoom is illuminated only by the art deco wall lamps set into the dado. When they opened up, he thought the vitrolite and the wiring was an unnecessary expense but Rena and Min put their heads together and Donald came up trumps with some thirties relics that scrubbed up to look absolutely à la mode. It has to make Gardner's look old-fashioned, Rena said, after checking out the competition, and now he's glad of it. He makes a last check for gaps in the blinds that might reveal too much light, and goes downstairs again, right down to the basement. Leaning against the wall, he lights a cigarette and waits.

Victor is first, as usual. He slaps Bobby on the back and goes on upstairs. 'Help yourself to a drink,' Bobby calls and Victor draws a bottle from his overcoat, some Italian liquor. 'A taste of home,' he says. 'No slight on your hospitality.'

Bobby grins and remembers what they said in Naples. 'Salute.' He can feel the slink of cashmere in Victor's coat as he hangs it up.

Joe Fullarton is next, a sleekit item doing well from his lawyer's office. Alexander Buchanan the builder arrives hot on his heels, and then Iain Colquhoun the seed merchant bringing a new chap with him. Before they finalised the lease of the space above the shop, Victor mentioned that he had friends, or friends of friends, who liked a game of cards. A game for money. 'And why not?' Bobby said. 'Everyone needs a hobby.' 'It's not illegal,' Victor said. 'Or at least, Mr Ferguson likes to drop by when he's finished at the station.' 'Even better,' Bobby said. 'So why not make it a bit swish. Nice drinks, a bit of service. Sandwiches if the game goes on.' There's a tacit understanding that Bobby keeps an eye on things while Victor deals. Bobby has a good eye for cheating, funnily enough. Debts aren't an issue; Victor has other friends. 'Sounds like you've got a lot of friends,' Bobby said. 'Yes,' Victor said. 'Sometimes I wish I could lose some of the bastards.'

Todd the publican is late, and Ferguson the polis arrives last, straight from the station and with a good thirst on him. This is the time Bobby likes best. Before the game starts, the freshening of glasses and the idle chatter from which you can glean useful morsels if you keep your ears open. Most of all he likes the sense of playing his role in this illicit little enterprise, and the knowledge that nobody outside on the street knows what's going on up here. A parallel, night-time world. There's more preamble than usual tonight, on account of Colquhoun's pal. Victor vets him, subtly and deliberately, and shortly after takes Bobby aside. 'Inherited a house nearby, he says.' He whispers the name and Bobby blanks for a moment then laughs. It was one of the furthest stops on Rena's delivery run when she was a girl. He teased her about it: did she think she'd meet her prince at the castle?

'Landed gentry.' Victor repeats the unfamiliar phrase. 'Bene. I'll deal.'

Bobby guides the men to the table, offers further drinks, and retreats to his position, standing relaxed by the counter. He lights a cigarette, sips one of the two whiskies he allows himself (three, if time goes on, but he's enjoying not being in thrall to the stuff) and watches the game. Victor's shuffling is fast and thorough, without any fancy moves, and he deals in a steady rhythm. The sound of the cards soothes Bobby, now. This is a game he can't lose. Blair, the new man, is an enthusiastic player. The more he loses, the more he wants to win, and when at last he wins, he wants to play again. The atmosphere around the table heightens, and a few more drinks are taken, but in the end everyone is smiling. A square game, right enough, and nobody's lost his shirt. Victor takes a small percentage, of course, some of which he keeps, some of which goes to his other friends. There's always something left over for Bobby to fold into his own pocket at the end of the night, even after they have made the customary donation to the Police Benevolent Fund, care of Mr Ferguson.

'Thanks, Bobby,' Victor tells him as he leaves for the evening. 'Oh, and by the way. A couple of my friends need a place to meet on Saturday night. Late. Can they come here?'

'What kind of friends?' Bobby says.

'Ah, Bobby,' Victor says, with a sad shrug. 'What do you think I am?'

'I try not to think,' Bobby says. 'Thinking gives me a headache.'

Victor laughs, and then sighs. 'You know me. I'm an honest man. I'm not even a racketeer. I just buy from my friends to help them, and if their friends ask me for a favour, well, I help them too.' He makes an expansive gesture. 'It's my duty.'

'Why me? When you have so many other friends?'

Victor sighs. 'When Alberto mentioned you I thought two things. First thing, that I could return my favour to him by helping you out. Second thing, that you could help me. I want to be an old man in Italy, Bobby. I was born there and I want to die there, you understand?'

Bobby nods. Mediterranean types are given to emotion, he knows that. On leave from ship he saw all sorts: punches thrown, tears shed, grown men kissing each other.

'So when you pay me rent, Bobby, or buy my goods how do we say, under the counter, that's money that comes to me with no favours attached. Money that gets me closer to home, once my idiot nephew is old enough to run this place into the ground. Do you see?'

'I see. So do you want me to be here?'

Victor smiles. 'No, nothing like that. I have the key still. Maybe check round on Sunday, make sure everything is okay. It will be, of course, but you know…'

'Rena has eyes like a hawk.'

'Exactly.' Victor pats Bobby's arm, then peels one more note off the roll. 'For the inconvenience,' he says.

Bobby waves the money away. 'It's nothing,' he says. 'Nothing between friends.'

The first thing he does when they've all gone is pour himself a stiff one. He knocks it back in one. His cover story is the pub, after all. He pours another modest measure and sets about the clearing up, righting the tables, washing the glasses. He'd been worried someone would smoke cigars at first. Must have seen too many movies. He's polishing one of the tumblers when he hears the key turn in the door. He stops, slowly eases the glass down onto the draining board. A creak. The door, or just the night noises of the building? There's a tremor in his hand. Bobby turns to face the door of the kitchen, hears footsteps approaching.

'Rena,' he says, trying to read her face. It's raining outside and he can see where the drops have hit the shoulders of her jacket, but her expression is opaque. A different panic sets in. 'Has something happened? Janet?'

'Janet's the least of your concerns,' she says. 'Who were those men?'

What men, he wants to say. The kneejerk reaction. But if Rena is asking the question, it means that she has seen them.

'What were they doing here?' she persists.

He sighs. 'Where were you, Rena? Have you been waiting outside all this time?'

'I telephoned Thomas to bring the car. We've been watching the back door for the past two hours or more.'

Rena, Rena. Her determination will be her downfall one day. He pictures them sitting there in the shadows by the whisky bond, their cigarette tips kindling along with their tempers. 'Why did you have to bring Thomas in to it?' he says.

'He's my brother,' she snaps.

'And don't tell me you don't have secrets from him.'

Her face is colouring, and not in the pretty way it does when she is embarrassed. 'What did you expect, that I'd stand out there in the street all night on my own? You've no idea, Bobby Young, no idea.'

Her eyes tear up, and that isn't like Rena at all. He looks around. His cigarettes are there on the counter. He slips one from the pack, snaps open his silver lighter.

'Answer me, Bobby. Who were those men and what were they doing here?'

He has a sudden urge to blow a smoke ring, as a distraction, but doesn't. He exhales slowly and tells her exactly who the men were, starting with Ferguson and building up to Roderick Blair, the new Lord Rowallan. The blush starts to fade from Rena's cheeks as he talks, and he knows that she's conjuring a picture in her mind:

her husband in a room with businessmen, titled men, men of the town. He watches her eyes sweep over the tables, the counter, the floorboards, all pristine, and he wonders if he should just have let Rena in on Victor's nights in the first place. He could tell himself he was protecting her, or that Victor wouldn't like it, but really, he doesn't know why he kept it to himself. Well, there's no point in hiding the truth now and he doesn't need to. He has her.

'What will we do about Thomas?' he asks when he's finished.

'Leave Thomas to me,' she says. 'I'll deal with Thomas.'

Rena, 1951

There is nothing Rena is supposed to be doing, apart from this: sitting on a tartan blanket on the grass overlooking the beach. No baking, no bookkeeping, nothing. A pain throbs in her chest and a swell of dizziness overtakes her. She steadies herself with another hand on the blanket, feels the ground solid under her fingertips. She is on holiday, and her tablets are tucked away in the drawer of her bedside table. She screws her eyes shut for a moment against the glare, and then opens them again. Deep breath. Just because she has stopped for a moment doesn't mean everything is going to crash down around her. Evie is at the edge of the water, taking Janet's hand as they prepare to paddle, while the twins sit nearby, building castles from the shingly sand as though fortifying Lamlash against imminent attack from the Holy Isle. Where in God's name does the woman find those get-ups? Irritation sweeps the panic from Rena's breast. Today Evie's wearing a skirted two-piece in a loud floral print and what appears to be a turban. The turban doesn't match.

'Here you go, sis,' Thomas says, slumping down beside her and holding out a vanilla ice. 'This is the life, isn't it? Beats a day snatched at Girvan and back to work the next.'

'Mmm,' she says, taking the cone and catching the first melting dribble before it falls. Gulls are ha-ha-ing overheard and there's an occasional shriek as a bather realises that the water isn't as warm as expected, but otherwise it's as peaceful as Rena can remember being. 'Lovely. Where's Ma gone?'

'She's on a bench over by the pier. Chattering away to someone already. Is it tomorrow Min's coming down? I've only been away from the shop two days and I'm losing track of time.'

'Yes,' Rena says. 'They've taken two rooms in the Glenisle.' She stretches her arm towards the hotel's walled garden with its spiky palms. 'The doctor said a cruise would be the thing for Margaret, but dear God, the expense.'

'Weather couldn't be better than this. It reminds me of the Med.'

'Well, don't go rubbing yourself in olive oil to sunbathe this time.'

'Don't worry, I've learnt my lesson. Only caution I got in my entire military career and it was for sunburn.'

Rena laughs and kicks her shoes off, wiggling her toes in the light breeze. The terror of Thomas being away, of not knowing if he was all right, is so distant now. 'You were so handsome with your tan. Like Lawrence of Arabia.'

'You saying I'm not handsome now?' Thomas strikes a pose.

Rena shakes her head. 'Of course you are. You're my

brother, after all.'

'Conceited!'

'Oops, that was nearly Malcolm in the water. Evie just got to him in time.'

Thomas sighs. 'She babies that boy too much. He should be getting mucky and getting into scrapes.'

'Give it time,' Rena says. 'I'm sure he'll turn out as sporty as you were. Cricket, rugby, you were always at some match or other.'

'Best thing about school.'

'Games, ugh,' Rena says. 'This weather really is heavenly. We can get Margaret out on a boat, if she's up to it. She likes a boat.'

They sit in silence, eating their ice cream. She really ought to watch her weight but she gets so hungry, and if she didn't eat she'd never manage. Thomas finishes his cone, but Rena crumbles the end of hers and throws it on to the grass for the sparrows to squabble over.

'Thomas?'

'What?'

'There were times… so many times, when I didn't know if we'd make it. And here we are. In business. Married with children. And you and Evie in your new house.'

'Thank God we moved. I'd have gone loopy with the twins in that flat.' Thomas gets out his cigarettes, offers her one. There's a slight commotion just along the beach; a lurcher has snatched a small boy's fishing rod and is sprinting across the sand, gathering an entourage of other children and dogs as it goes. 'No, nothing was going to stand in your way, Rena. You got us out of that damned village and away from that sorry excuse for a father.'

Rena shrugs. 'I couldn't have done it without you.

Without Min and Nell, and Margaret.'

And now Margaret's had a relapse and isn't likely to see another year out. Neither of them say it, that this holiday is as much about seeing her as it is about doing what normal folk do at the Fair. Close their businesses and go to the seaside.

'Rena, I've been meaning to say to you. The plot next to ours in Edzell Place is going to come up. I spoke to Kennedy, the builder, and he'd give me first refusal.'

'Oh Thomas, really? I was just thinking how nice it is to be close to family.'

'Well, I know you're dying to get out of that flat.'

'Have I been going on about it?'

'Just a little. Look, talk to Bobby about it, see what you think.'

A toot from a car horn draws their eye to the road behind them, where Bobby's familiar Austin is crawling along. She waves back, then closes her eyes for a second, basking in the sunshine and thinking about Edzell Place, a new house all of her own with Thomas next door and Hetty and Jamie just five minutes away.

'Well, Bobby's survived then,' Thomas comments. Bobby is teaching their younger brother to drive, seeing as the roads are quieter than at home. 'About time Jamie grew up a bit.'

'You are hard on him, Thomas,' Rena says.

'Well, what do you make of it? His age and not a girl in sight.'

'There's no rush for him. There isn't a war on.'

'Doesn't know he's born.'

'Shh, here's Mum coming over.'

Thomas shades his eyes and looks down towards the beach, then hauls himself to his feet again. 'That bloody woman, always drawing attention to herself.'

Sure enough, Rena sees that a man is talking to Evie, who is gesturing towards the children. Janet is now playing alongside her cousins, and thank heavens there's a laundry room at the back of the house because her clothes will be all over sand. Thomas gets up and jumps from block to block down the sea barrier and onto the beach.

'I just met the nicest lady from round Whiting Bay,' Hetty says. 'Apparently they had royalty in the golf club. In the war, you know.'

'Really?' Rena says, watching as Thomas strides towards his wife. Evie has noticed him now and is pointing him out to the man by her side. 'Oh Mum, would you go and get Janet please? We'll need to get her tidied up if we're going to make an afternoon of it.'

'It's all right. She'd follow the twins off the side of a cliff. Look.' It's true, Janet has picked up her bucket and spade and is trailing after her cousins. 'If this weather holds we could take tea in the gardens, do you think?'

'Whatever you like,' Rena says. 'We're on holiday, after all.' She sees Thomas say something to Evie, his face close to hers. 'Mum?'

'Yes, dear?'

'Do you ever wonder if things are all right with Thomas and Evie?' She feels disloyal saying it, and when she sees the flicker of apprehension cross Hetty's face she wishes she'd kept her mouth shut. 'Oh, ignore me. I'm not used to having this much time to myself, that's all.'

'Well, they're together in the shop most of the time now the twins are at school…' Hetty trails off, as if the sunshine is strong enough to bleach out any hint of imperfection. Thomas is now walking Evie back towards them, her arm tight in his. Even at a distance Rena can see that she is smiling, not making a scene. Behind her, Malcolm's wail rises above the cries and laughter of the other children on the beach. He's dressed up in a little sailor outfit with pantaloons that Evie insisted on buying in Brodick. Maybe Hetty's right. She notices more than she lets on sometimes.

They have afternoon tea in the gardens at Lagg. Rena eats the sandwiches and has a scone with jam just to be sociable, but she doesn't touch the cake. It's almost as if rationing is long gone here. They've been munching on coconut ice since they got off the ferry – that sweetshop really is very good – and of course at the seaside with children, you do have ice cream every day. Hetty and Thomas work their way through everything that's put in front of them in true Jarvie fashion, Hetty's eyes widening with daring as she takes Rena's share of sponge as well. Evie nibbles modestly. Watching her figure as usual these days. Rena sighs. Her sister-in-law shifts herself, she'll say that for her. Working in the shop and even taking the odd evening in the tearoom if they're short.

'Jamie, you haven't even been in swimming yet!' Evie exclaims now, prodding her brother-in-law's arm. 'The water isn't that cold.'

'Too cold for him,' Thomas says, but Jamie doesn't seem to notice.

'He's been too busy being a terror on the roads, haven't you, son?' Bobby says, slapping him on the back. 'Took to it like a duck to water, I must say.'

Jamie grins. Bobby's been good for him, a father figure of a kind, and why shouldn't they indulge him a bit? He's the baby of the family, even if he's taller than any of them at five foot ten. And he is their brother. Rena remembers

Thomas after a drink or two, muttering about the age difference and their mother's naivety. She put an end to that. Jamie's a Jarvie, you can see it a mile off, though his temperament's more like Hetty's than that of his siblings.

'Well Jamie, you're coming in tomorrow with me,' Evie says. 'I won't take no for an answer!'

A flush creeps up Jamie's neck. He may not have Rena's colouring but he shares her propensity for blushing. She changes the subject before Thomas notices and teases him for it. 'Mum was talking about the golf club earlier. Might we go there one evening?' she says.

'It'll be members only,' Thomas says. 'These places always are.'

She looks towards Bobby. 'Leave it with me,' he says. 'They might allow visitors in holiday season.'

'That would be fun, wouldn't it?' Evie says. 'An excuse to get dressed up.'

'You don't need any excuse. You always look tip top,' Thomas says, and Rena is pleased to see her smile back at him.

Whether it's allowed or not, Bobby arranges for them to be signed into the golf club the very next evening. Once they have Hetty, Margaret and Nell ensconced in Rena and Bobby's cottage with the children, they go to the Glenisle to have a drink with Min and Donald. Jamie comes in to say hello for long enough for Donald to insist he'll take him fishing the next day, and then goes off to meet up with some lads he met the day before. Don't do anything I wouldn't, Bobby says, and Rena pretends not to see as he slips her brother some money. Let them be boys, why not? They're on holiday, after all. She's taken one of her tablets and feels just fine now. Thomas and Evie arrive shortly after them, Evie dressed to the nines in a cerise frock with gold bangles like a gypsy and her nails painted pillar box red. Rena can't fathom how she keeps them so long when she's working. They are arm in arm, and Thomas is all of a piece in his suit.

'Oh, you and Rena put me to shame,' Min says. 'You're like a pair of fashion plates.'

'That's my girl,' Thomas says, kissing his wife on the cheek. She strokes a fleck of dust from his sleeve.

'I think the sea air is a tonic for Margaret already,' Min says. 'That and seeing her nieces and nephew again. And we're glad to have a night out, aren't we, Donald?'

Donald nods enthusiastically, eyeing the whisky bottles lined up behind the bar as he stuffs his pipe full of tobacco. If Min feels frumpy, his holiday-wear makes up for it; the bright patterned tie against the checked shirt is enough to make Rena wish she'd kept her sunglasses with her.

'Now, what's your poison?' Bobby says. 'Donald, Min?'

'I'll take a gin and lemon,' Min says.

'For me too,' Evie says. 'What about you, Rena?'

'Just a lemonade,' Rena says, but Thomas cuts in, 'Come on, sis, let your hair down for once. You'll be back to work before you know it.'

'I'll go up to the bar and look,' Rena says. 'What should I have?' she asks Bobby.

'I know,' he says, after a moment's pause. 'Do you do a Pimm's?' he asks the barman. 'I mean a proper one?'

'Very good, sir,' the barman says, and Rena watches as he fills a tall glass with fruit and ice cubes.

'That dress is very sophisticated,' Bobby whispers

in her ear. 'A vision in green. Don't blush, it'll spoil the effect.'

'I can't help it.'

'No wonder that scoundrel Gibson tried it on with you.'

'Oh, don't talk about it, Bobby. I told you, it was horrible.' She hadn't told him the whole story, just the hand on the leg, but that was enough.

'You know I'll sort him out, Rena. I mean it. Just say the word.'

Rena waits until the barman has placed the gins on a tray and turned away again to say, 'You can't, Bobby. It could backfire on us, badly.'

'Well. He should watch his step. And you tell me if you see him again, all right?'

Rena slips her arm into Bobby's. 'Of course I will. Look, Bobby, Thomas said that he'd help us get the plot next to his on Edzell Place. Do you think we should go for it?'

Bobby takes her hand. 'I couldn't refuse you anything, Rena, not when you're looking as beautiful as you do tonight. Let's do it, while the going's good. No point in standing still.'

Bobby pays and carries the tray back over to their table. Everyone is laughing at some story of Thomas's, and Rena feels a rush of affection for him, for her family, for Bobby. She swirls the ice around her glass with her straw and takes a sip. It's delicious. Sophisticated, just like her dress.

'Do you see that above the fireplace?' Donald says, indicating a plaque.

'I can't read it from here,' Min mutters, getting her glasses out of her handbag.

'A temperance plaque! The barman told me this used to be a temperance hotel.'

Bobby and Thomas laugh, and Thomas raises his glass, 'A toast then, to intemperance!'

'A license to print money,' Donald says. 'Anywhere around here that sells drink.'

'Anywhere around anywhere,' Thomas says.

'Another toast,' Min says. 'To Rena and Bobby. Who've been through some hard times but are now settled.'

Bobby nods. 'Settled and solvent.'

'You can rest on your laurels now,' Donald says, raising his glass again.

'I don't know,' Rena says. 'I mean, look at this. High teas. If only the tearoom had a proper kitchen…'

'Oh come on, sis, don't get above yourself.'

'Let's not think about work tonight,' Bobby says. 'We're on holiday, with family around us. One more toast for luck, to family.'

'To family,' they all echo, and Rena touches her glass to Bobby's. Sometimes it's as if he can read her mind, after seven years of marriage. To family.

They walk up the hill to the golf club, and the views are stunning, Rena has to admit. The mainland is only just visible across the Firth and it looks exotic, somehow, like another country. Bobby rings the bell and asks for someone, John perhaps, who greets him with a slap on the back like an old friend, and signs them all in. There, framed on the wall above the visitor's book, is the evidence of Hetty's story. Scrawled signatures, a page apiece, from when they were in the Navy. Edward, well, enough said about that the better. But Albert. The King. The King has stood right there, a little before his coronation, but still. The thought comes back to her for the rest of the evening, popping into her head and cheering her even as she sees Bobby have another drink, and another. But that's all right, because they're toasting the fact that they are going to be neighbours with Thomas and Evie. There she is, Rena Jarvie Young, surrounded by her family and eating her dinner in the same room as King George.

Rena, 1952

The Youngs are moving up. Whatever Thomas says about being content with your lot (and really, it was all very well for him, stepping into the shop they all broke their backs in for years), whatever Bobby's failings are, nothing is going to drag her down. And Bobby wants this too, Rena can see the glint in his eye, the straightening of his shoulder as they view the function room. He's imagining himself mine host, surrounded by hail-fellow-well-mets and beery smiles. Once they get a license. Rena's heel catches in a worn patch of carpet and she rotates her ankle delicately to free it. The Ossington Temperance Hotel has seen better days. Bobby is chatting to the agent. Rena notices his reflection in the overmantle mirror, the skim of sweat on his upper lip. Breakfasts, lunches, high teas. The tables are scuffed and scattered. She imagines them in neat diagonal rows, dignified by starched cloths and teapots you can see your face in. And the evening functions; a procession of waitresses bearing *sole meunière* with sprigs of parsley, Bobby in a dinner suit pouring a champagne pyramid for a wedding. (She's never seen one of these in real life, but why not?) Give the customer what he didn't know he wanted until the suggestion was whispered in his ear, flashed in front of his eyes on a gilt embossed menu card. Wine, rather than crates of beer and bottles of Johnnie Walker. One step at a time though.

After that business with Annanhill it's a miracle they've got where they are, and if it's taught her one thing it's to trust nobody outside the family, not even Victor, for all that they've worked well together. And certainly not this Trust. Independent they may be, but they're still the ones who'll be holding the lease over Rena and Bobby. Formerly of Annanhill House, she had him write in the correspondence with them. They made that place what it is and people have short memories. One day nobody will be holding anything over them. Make a go of this and she'll furnish their half-empty house in Edzell Place. She pictures a cream carpet in the lounge. A sleek cigarette box on the coffee table.

The carpet here is covered in fag burns. It'll need to come up. Maybe there's parquet underneath; it's an old building after all, a presence in solid red sandstone, the peak of a solid red sandstone street. French Renaissance style, they've been told. Right at the centre of the town, the first building you see when you come out of the train station. Skirting boards can be varnished, brocade added to the shades on the wall lights. There's a tang of urine in the air, mice presumably, although again Rena's thoughts drift to just how bad it is upstairs. The things they say have been going on. Alma says her sister could take on the rough work, and they'll need someone, Rena can see. This is beyond family. Alma is excited by the prospect already. Glad to see the Youngs getting to where they should be. Moving up.

The agent has stepped aside, tactfully. Rena elbows Bobby.

'We're interested,' he says, with that laconic air that seems so confident, so attractive. 'More than interested.'

The agent adjusts his tie (crested, so Forces or Rugby Club, though he looks too skinny for either). 'And you understand, of course, the Trustees…'

'I have every sympathy with the Trustees,' Rena says, quickly. 'Disgust… distressing, that the reputation of a place gifted to the town…'

She sees Bobby gives the agent a sly wink. They're men of the world. Previous management ran half the rooms as a knocking shop, and six men were charged with breach of the peace after the Knights of St Columba saw in the new year in this very room. Rena lays her hand on Bobby's arm. He nods. 'We do appreciate that the wish of the Trustees is to continue in the spirit, if you'll pardon the expression… of the temperance movement.'

'And of course we'd keep the name,' Rena adds. 'Out of respect.'

'The Trustees won't trouble themselves over what you call it,' the agent says, drily. 'Just as long as the place is in the black and staying out the court reports.'

'The salary they offered though, that'll be negotiable,' Bobby says, smooth as a chancer at the shows. He looks at his watch, the good watch she bought him, and Rena smiles her good wife smile. The little woman, standing aside while the big boys talk. *A steady pair of hands at the helm*, that's what they've been told the Trust wants, and who could be steadier than Rena and Bobby?

'We'll want to refurbish,' Rena says. 'The cleaning I'll

have to do!'

The agent hesitates, then scribbles on a piece of a paper which he holds out to Bobby. Rena glances at it, turns a couple of sums in her head. Bobby thinks he's won already, she knows, he can taste the celebratory drink. But it's tight, it's still tight, because they're committed to Victor and the tearoom until October which will mean paying staff while they're here.

'And the percentage of the takings…' she murmurs.

'Is rather steep,' Bobby agrees, smoothing his lapel then smiling disarmingly. 'Quite the businesswoman, my wife, isn't she?'

'Quite the cook, you mean! I'll never be out that kitchen. Look, Mr Watson, can I be honest with you?'

'Please.'

'My husband and I,' she entwines her arm with Bobby's, 'This is precisely what we're looking for. We have the track record as you know.'

Watson nods. 'Let me be honest with you too, Mrs Young. The bottom line is that the Trust has enough funds remaining to run the place for three years. After that, it either pays for itself, and for you, or it'll be turned over to the Corporation.'

'But it's a ten-year lease,' Bobby says.

'I am being straight with you. You have three years to make it pay. And then as long as sufficient funds are coming in, the Trust is at liberty to extend the lease indefinitely. Accounts to be delivered quarterly.'

'That's fine,' Rena says, pushing Annanhill from her mind. 'But the only way we can afford to proceed, given what we'll need to do to get set up, is if I am paid a salary as well as my husband.'

Watson hesitates again. 'Well, Mrs Young, that's

rather… irregular.' He looks to Bobby, but her grasp on his arm is firm and he doesn't say a word, just looks straight back.

'I'll be working there too, day in, day out. It's no different from paying a cook or a housekeeper.'

'No more irregular than if two business partners took it on,' Bobby says. 'I'm quite happy with that, and you can be telephoning the Trustees with the good news this afternoon.'

'We'll accept the percentage of the takings that you suggest,' Rena says. 'Subject to revision in one year.'

'You have a daughter, don't you, Mrs Young?' the agent says.

'She's at school,' Rena says, airily. 'And believe me, Mr Watson, I am quite accustomed to working for my living.'

Bobby steps forward and says, 'There's only one problem that I can see.'

The agent looks at him. Rena looks at him as he waits a beat before adding, 'I'll get away with nothing working every day alongside my lady wife.'

And the hearty laughs all round seal it. Well done, Bobby, Rena thinks. After a firm handshake the agent says, 'I'll have the papers prepared, Mr Young.'

They step out from the mosaic-tiled entrance hall into the brisk March air and stand there for a moment, framed by the imposing main doorway of the hotel. Rena adjusts the fur collar on her coat, waits for Bobby to offer her a cigarette. He lights it for her, his eyes sparkling for a moment behind the flash of silver and flame. She glimpses the old Bobby, the one who pursued her along Sauchiehall Street that day, without a coat in the snow, and then drove her to the Grosvenor Restaurant in

Glasgow for dinner on their first date. God knows how he paid for it back then, but he did so to impress her. And sometimes he still does. But she can't rely on a man for everything, and if that's George Lennox's only legacy to her that's fine, God rot him. She'll draw her own salary, and pay it in to her own bank account, the one she set up to receive the bequest from her father's fancy woman.

'Well, Mrs Young, we've done it now.' Bobby smiles and takes her arm. Oh yes, Rena thinks, we've done it now. The darkened sandstone of the railway station reaches above them, and she hears the brakes hiss on a train as it slows across the viaduct. There's nothing but work ahead, hard work, but she throws her shoulders back as together they walk past their new business venture, the Ossington Hotel.

Rena, 1952

Rena's hand shoots out from under the covers and quells the rattling of the alarm clock by her bed. She pauses for a moment, runs her hands over the seersucker bed-linen sent mail order from Jenner's. The hotel that Min and Donald stayed in on Arran had it, and she decided it was just what she needed for the house. She's fed up with finding linen from the hotel in her airing cupboard. Bobby was up at the crack of dawn, as he has been every day this week, off helping Victor redistribute his remaining stock to relatives around the country. They've taken a bit off his hands too, and in return they've been released from the lease on the tearoom early. Rena sighs, swings her legs out of bed and stretches her hands up towards the ceiling. The sun must be shining because the yellow curtains are bright in the morning light. Her own house, at long last. Not a flat, and nothing to do with the Corporation. She has a second's panic as she thinks of Janet getting to school, and then she remembers that she's at the hotel with Hetty. They stayed over as the bridge club was in until late. Rena was doing their sandwiches at ten o'clock and it's too much of a fuss to bring Janet home with her at that time. Saves on the night porter too, having Hetty sleep there. Rena's stomach growls at the thought of the sandwiches and she rises, washes and dresses smartly, but not too smartly (cream blouse, checked skirt), as she'll be in the kitchen a good part of the day. Using the tail of her comb, she rearranges her curls under her hairnet. Powder, lipstick, and she walks out of the door and into Edzell Place just in time to step into the taxi that will take her to work.

The hotel has a service entrance in the lane at the back but Rena doesn't use it as a matter of principle. Instead, she pays the driver and stands for a moment at the top of John Finnie Street, looking at the town spreading out below her. Down to the council offices, the banks and the courthouse. Down to Tannahill's, where one day she'll buy brand new furniture, tables and chairs that haven't been gleaned from auctions and house clearances and repaired in Min's shed. And by then perhaps there will be a brass plaque on the door of the hotel, engraving their names, hers and Bobby's, on the fabric of this town.

The steps are scrubbed and the tiles of the vestibule gleam, she notices approvingly. Jeanette has done her work well. Jamie stands up behind the desk, bleary-eyed from the early breakfast service. She's had him helping out a bit, since he came back from his National Service. The devil makes work for idle hands.

'Did Mum and Janet get off all right?' she asks.

'Yes, about half an hour ago.'

'That's good. Thanks for helping out.'

Jamie yawns and rubs his face. 'No bother. But you ken it's Monday I start?'

'Yes, yes of course I do.' Jamie has an apprenticeship

at the printworks; a trade, at last. 'Jeanette's coming in to do tomorrow, so that's you finished. If you come round to Edzell Place on Sunday I'll give you your envelope.'

'Thanks Rena.' He hesitates. 'I'd have done it without being paid, to help.'

'I know.' He elbows awkwardly into his jacket and she straightens it up for him, patting his arms, then reaches to comb his hair back into place with her fingers. 'Now, go and get a coffee or get back to your bed, you look like a half-shut knife.'

Thomas is right, she thinks. Their brother is old to be living at home with his mother. Thomas tried to convince him to make a career in the Forces, but Jamie isn't cut out for that. Printing will suit him just fine, Rena is sure. And one day they'll be holding a wedding breakfast here for him.

When she gets to the kitchen the wireless is on, tea is in the pot, and Alma is just popping two slices of grilled bacon onto a buttered roll.

'Morning, Mrs Young. How are you today?'

'Ready for my breakfast, I can tell you.'

'My timing's not bad, eh?'

'Not bad at all.'

Rena takes the plate with the bacon roll and sits at the big marble-topped table; *French country kitchen*, Min had styled it on her list, but after a year unsold and taking up space she passed it on to Rena for Annanhill, and it's been just the job ever since. Rena runs her thumb along the bevelled edge. God willing this will be the last kitchen it'll be in. They've turned the place around, everyone says so. The Trustees have been gratified by the last two sets of accounts, to the point that a number of them are beginning to see the financial advantage of a license. She finishes her roll and pushes her teacup away.

'Breakfasts all done?'

'They are indeed. And Mr Jones has checked out. Says he'll be back next month as usual so I marked it in the book. And the hearing aid man is set up in the salon for his demonstrations. I gave him a coffee.'

'Good stuff,' Rena says. 'Did Mr Young leave the apples yesterday? I meant to check them.'

'In the pantry,' Alma says. 'Nobody'd ken they're windfall.'

Rena nods. Through the Honourable Roderick Blair, Bobby has gained access to the walled garden at Rowallan, which means gluts of apples and berries come their way. Blair's been up in London, and Walls the gardener isn't displeased to have someone benefit from his hard work. Bobby says Walls has a soft spot for Rena, but she doesn't believe him. A soft spot for the pies and cakes Bobby passes on to him, more like. Just because the man gave her grapes from the glasshouse. The card game keeps going, moved into the hotel now, and apparently even Mr Ferguson has intimated that it's a shame that they don't have a license now that the place has smartened up and is causing him less trouble. Rena should start going to church. Reverend MacQuarrie, the deputy chair of the board of Trustees, is still swithering and the Laigh Kirk is only round the corner.

'What's the soup the day?' Alma calls from the pantry.

'Cream of leek,' Rena calls back. 'But that new milk's rich enough I'd say. Save the cream.'

'Aye, that'll do fine,' Alma says, emerging with an armful of leeks and four onions balanced on the crook of her elbow.

'Soup,' Rena says, checking off the list in her diary.

'And apple tart, and for the main it's poached haddock.' It's Friday after all.

One day there will be a chef to do all this, but there's something nice about simply rubbing flour into butter with her cool fingers. Cold hands, warm heart, Alma jokes, happy to hand the task to Rena while she does the savouries. They lack the alchemy of combinations and textures that puddings have. Even whipping cream gives Rena a satisfaction. Or meringues. Elbow grease turning into something so light and delicate. She kneads the lump of pastry against the marble slab once, twice, and that's it. She wraps it up to rest in the cool larder and begins coring the apples.

'And where's Mr Young today?' Alma asks.

'Oh, I think it's Musselburgh.'

'That's an awfy long way.'

'Yes, he knows that when he's out in the motor I won't be finding things for him to do around here.'

'Men, eh?' Alma laughs, and to Rena's surprise, she finds herself joining in. 'Mind you, I've never seen one as quick at peeling tatties as your Mr Young.'

'Learned it at sea,' Rena says.

She likes these mornings in the kitchen, after the breakfast service has been cleared up and before the rush of lunch and high tea. Ingredients, oven temperature; she knows how it works, what the result will be. If it was down to the food and the décor and the ambiance, she could make this hotel the smartest place for miles around. Getting a license though, that's about making connections, greasing palms if need be. It's a man's game.

'One day we'll have a chef, Alma,' she says. 'And you won't be chopping onions and trimming chops all morning.'

'It's no skin off my nose, Mrs Young. I'd rather be doing it here than for that ungrateful bastard at home, if you'll pardon my French.'

Rena smiles, although Alma can still startle her, the way she speaks so openly. 'Never been so glad of anything in my life as when I had the change,' she said once. 'Good an excuse as any to put paid to his carry on.'

'You've been such a help to us over the years,' Rena says, unwilling to share any confidences of her own. You can't be friends with an employee, after all. 'Through thick and thin as well.'

'Aye well, that's life. The main thing is that you and Mr Young are on the up and up now.'

'Don't speak too soon,' Rena says. She isn't superstitious, not the way her aunts can be, but she doesn't want to count her chickens just yet. 'Now, will we have a cup of tea, seeing as we're ahead of ourselves this morning?'

Once they've been through the plans for the weekend – funeral purvey on Friday, the Kilmaurs WI followed by the RAFA concert on Saturday, a christening on Sunday – Alma regales her with stories of the misdemeanours of in-laws that Rena has never met, and Rena utters the right kind of shocked or sympathetic noises. Other people's troubles can be oddly relaxing. A niece has become pregnant out of wedlock and must be sent back to Ireland, and the resulting fisticuffs have resulted in the arrest of Alma's brother-in-law, who was only doing the decent thing.

'But you know what it's like,' Alma concludes. 'If he'd been a doctor rather than a machinist it would have been a different kettle of fish. Did you hear about that one Robertson from the surgery on Dundonald Road?'

'No,' Rena says, nudging the Rich Teas closer, in case

Alma needs the sustenance to complete her story.

'Well, it's no more than you'd expect, because his bedside manner leaves something to be desired, or so I've heard. Anyhow, he takes a drink – doctors often do, don't they? – and he was in an altercation, that's what they're crying it, with the barman of the King's.'

'Really?' Rena says. Dundonald Road interests her, with its large houses overlooking the park, its discreet surgeries and law offices.

'Oh yes. My Michael drinks in there from time to time, well, more of the time than not to be honest, and he saw the whole thing. The doctor went for him something awful, he said.'

'Your husband?'

'No, the barman. Bad enough that someone called a policeman, and there was no shortage of witnesses. The man's nose was broken. And what do you think happened?'

Rena shakes her head.

'Sod all, that's what. Polis drove him home and tucked him up in his bed.'

Rena nods. She knows that it's different for those and such as those. Knowing how the town works, that's the thing, and it isn't easy when you've no history in a place. She needs to charm MacQuarrie at the christening tea, get him on their side. He hasn't preached temperance to her knowledge, but others do, and people listen. The Youngs just need the right people to be listening to them.

Bobby, 1953

Bugger Rena, bugger the hotel, bugger Frank Gibson, bugger Frank Gibson's daughter, and bugger beef Wellington and pavlova for seventy. Bobby drops his speed before the schoolhouse. Doubtless Miss Kenyon is tucked up in her flannelette by now, but he doesn't want to take any chances. When he gets past Fenwick he kills the lights as well. It's a familiar enough route and the moon is out. He reaches for the glove compartment, swerving onto the other side of the road. Empty. Bugger Rena all over again. Wherever he planks a half-bottle, she finds it, and he's hoarse from telling her that he's better, that it'll never get out of hand again.

Getting Marjorie Gibson's wedding is a coup though, he has to admit; daughter of Frank, stalwart of the Rugby Club, niece of that councillor who made a pass at Rena. Bobby would still swing for him, but he can't argue with the man's taste and he's in with the bricks in the town. Rena aims high. Her campaign started a few months back by getting Jamie to go and watch the rugby matches, and Bobby has been gladhanding the man ever since. And now, here he is driving to Glasgow at midnight with a fistful of coupons and a wallet of cash, to see a spiv about beef fillet and icing sugar.

Bobby knows the city. Creeping up to it at night warms his blood and sends a tremor of threat down his spine. The tenement crush, the ninety-degree angles, temptation and retribution behind every door. He didn't run away to sea because the city was too small, but because it was too big. More chance of drowning there than in the Bay of Bengal. Thank the Lord he was saved by a vision. Rena, through the window of a furrier in Sauchiehall Street, trying on a musquash. A lily-white, red-haired beauty, surrounded by a gaggle of older women in tweeds and dark-rimmed spectacles. His cigarette burned down to his knuckles as he stood there and watched her turn this way, then that. To the mirror, not to her audience of widows and spinsters, as though there was another world through the glass. She looked a foot taller than them. He'd never seen anyone so self-possessed. That's when he knew she'd never get becalmed. He just wishes this bloody rationing would stop.

He turns on the headlamps again when he approaches Newton Mearns. The main road is the danger. The police sit with binoculars at the hill at Waterside, or at least that's how Archie Gemmell got done. So kill your lights, Rena said. She hasn't done too badly herself. Round the farms to sort out the eggs, butter and cream. Most of them minded her from when she was a girl, awfy bonny on her bicycle, delivering newspapers and bread rolls from a sack. Evie took the ones beyond Fenwick, and both of them are women people like to do a favour for, especially one paid in cash. Difference is, Rena still scarcely believes she's a looker. She hardly knew when he met her. Maybe that was the turning point, seeing herself as a woman in a fur coat.

At Jamaica Bridge Bobby's heart begins to pound. It isn't exactly the city that never sleeps but there are indications of wakefulness. Figures in doorways, lights in windows, cars hiccuping at traffic lights. He could turn left, go straight ahead, ditch the motor and walk along the lane on the right. There's a door. Ring the bell and when the grille opens say that Eva sent you. Up steep stairs, through another door. Candles and red plush. Neat'll be fine, just a drop of water in it. A brunette in the corner of your eye. Looks too good for a place like this but then there's theatre folk in, and all that comes with them. Buy her a drink, have another yourself. Chink every glass, fall for every line, right up until you're standing in front of the registrar hoping he won't come close enough to smell the whisky on your breath. Hoping he will. Anne wasn't ready to go straight, and Bobby was never the man to help her. Maybe that's why the city makes him uneasy. Even if it is where he first spotted Rena, his second wife, his saviour, with her milk white skin.

'I don't want to hear her name and I don't want anyone to know about her. They're not going to think I'm second best,' Rena told him once, and that is how it has been.

The only cures for thinking too much come out a bottle or between a woman's legs. Bobby would settle for the former. Ah Christ, that'd be the end though, wouldn't it. He turns right at the lights, heads towards Bell Street. Beef fillet and icing sugar it is. But he'll be damned if he's driving straight home afterwards.

'Silverside?' By the time Bobby finds the warehouse he is edgy and cocky. 'Come on, Lou.'

'Top quality. The best.' Luigi Zambardi had a tough time when he was interned, or so Victor Caldera says. He's emerged from it tougher still.

'I don't care if it's fucking gold-plated,' Bobby says. 'It isn't fillet.'

'There wasn't the quantity. You got your sugar.'

'And I paid you for it.' Bobby turns to leave. 'That'll have to do me.'

'Meat's been through the roof since it came off ration.'

'Aye well, it's not what I drove twenty miles in the dark for.'

'What am I meant to do with all this then?' Lou waves his arm over the table, fruit boxes stuffed with packages of blood-spotted newspaper.

'Lou Zambardi at a loss? I don't believe it. But you'd better get that lot in a refrigerator or you'll be lucky to sell it for dog meat. Sayonara.'

Bobby walks away, nodding to Lou's nephew, who is standing in the background. If he is there to provide muscle he doesn't look up to the job; he's as gangly as a teenager and there's scarcely more than bumfluff on his face. Bobby reaches in his pocket for his cigarettes, slips one from the pack.

'Hold on.'

Bobby stops, strikes a match. It fizzes into life and he touches it to the tip of his cigarette, inhales.

'I could do you a deal,' Lou says.

Bobby turns, palms open, all smiles. 'Why didn't you say so?'

It is another lane he finds himself in, leading to another after hours club. Immediate membership available, no card issued, strictly below board. Neat'll do fine love, just a drop of water in it. Bobby catches a glimpse of a woman with dark glossy hair, turns to look at her but it isn't Anne, how could it be? A pale shadow, powder gathering in the lines around her mouth, her crow's feet. Up closer, the hair is more than half hairpiece. She smiles at him, places a cigarette between her pinched lips, but he turns away, almost bumps into the blonde next to him at the bar, not that much younger than the brunette but her eyes are brighter and she looks as if her lines come from laughing.

'Buy you a drink?' Just one, he tells himself, just one more and he's off, with the boot of his car full of icing sugar, silverside, and a case of champagne. French champagne.

'Port and lemon'd do the job,' she says.

Bobby nods to the barmaid. 'And have one yourself, love.'

'I'm Jean,' the blonde woman says.

'Bobby.'

Before he knows it he's telling her about the wedding, asking if you can turn silverside into beef Wellington.

'Do I look like I learned cordon bleu?'

'You look like that actress, what's her name again…' He can't stop himself.

She laughs so that he can see a gold tooth flash at the back of her mouth. 'Oh yeah, I'm often told that.'

'I bet you are.' He downs his drink, hesitates. She pauses too, her glass halfway to her lips. Then her face breaks into that lovely smile again, except this time her eyes don't sparkle quite so much.

'Look love, I'm working. Either go back to your beef Wellington or…'

He thinks of Rena, a loose strawberry blonde curl falling over her forehead as she pored over the seating plan for the wedding. The linen is starched, the tables are set. Rena is smart. If Marjorie's wedding comes off it's just the beginning. Eleanor Anderson's engagement was in the paper last week, and the reports of Patricia Scott's twenty-first at the Foxbar are atrocious.

'One for the road?' he says. He hadn't guessed Jean was working. A woman alone, dressed up and drinking in an after-hours bar? Green, he supposes, but maybe he has always been. Look at Anne. But Anne was turning over a new leaf, wasn't she?

Jean glances around the room. It's busy, for two on a Tuesday morning, or so he supposes. 'You're wasting my time,' she says, fishing a compact out of her bag and checking her pink lipstick. 'Go home.' The old smile comes back, just for a split second. 'And take care.'

He nods. The banquettes here are green plush, and have seen better days, and the stairs lead up to the front door rather than down. He tips the doorman as he leaves, remembering his first date with Rena. She thought he was someone, the way he knew what to give the cloakroom boy at the Grosvenor before he slipped the musquash round her shoulders. And he thought she had money, not knowing about her mother's divorce. She's got sense though, the sense to leave the past behind, where it can't do you any mischief. And she's got class. You can't buy that. Beef Wellington; steak pie by any other name.

Cloud descends over the moor on the drive home. The moonlight struggles through until the mist congeals into dense fog, or is it just the darkness, he can't tell. More than once he hits the verge, has to shift back on track. The danger is enough to numb his thoughts. No lights until Fenwick, just like she said. So how far is Fenwick? He's been driving three quarters of an hour, more. The year before last, three walkers got caught in a snowstorm on the moor. They walked and they walked, not able to see a foot in front of them, not knowing they were going round in circles. They walked until they had to sit down and rest, with the soft snow still falling all around them. When they were found, they were in between the main road and the Covenanter's memorial, yards from the hope of discovery. No lights until Fenwick. Well, maybe he's at Fenwick, or maybe it isn't worth the risk. But he keeps going in the thick grey darkness, edging forward what feels like an inch at a time.

Bang.

His chest hits the steering wheel and he slams on the brake, too late. He's hit the buggering fence. Deep breath. And again. Nothing broken. Worse things happen at sea. He barks a laugh then pulls the gears into reverse, feels the wheels spin in mud.

'Come on.'

There's a sharp metallic whine. He gives it a rest, tries again.

'Come on.'

The Austin lurches and he pushes it further, waiting for the back wheels to hit tarmac and grip. He must be sideways on the road now, but the chances of anything coming up behind him are slim. Which way was he pointing? That way, must be that way. His hand hovers over the lights. As if there'd be polis out on a night like this. Don't take the chance. Keep going.

At last the fog begins to unravel into fine white threads. There's a light, up ahead and to the right. He leans on the brake. Slowly does it. Two lights, three. He is at snail's pace now. The lights resolve into a building. The farm at the Galston road end. Nearly there. By the time he reaches Fenwick the moon is almost full overhead, but he switches on the headlamps anyway.

He parks in the back lane by the whisky bond, opens the boot. Knock, double knock, knock on the kitchen door and there's Rena, wrapped in her coat, her face in shadows.

'Don't leave the boxes on the ground. There's rats.' He pauses, and she squeezes his arm. 'All right?'

He nods, and begins carrying the meat through to the big refrigerator.

'Leave it on the table,' Rena says. 'I'll put it away.'

He empties the boot, leaving the two wooden boxes of wine until last. Slinging one under each arm, he elbows the door open. Rena has opened one of the packages of meat.

'What do you call this?' she says.

'Silverside. It's all I could get.'

'Have you been drinking?'

'No.'

'If I'd wanted silverside I'd have got it from the butcher.'

'Not at this price you wouldn't. That's the whole point.'

'And you'll explain to Frank Gibson why his fancy dinner's tough as an old boot? That's if we don't poison him by undercooking it…'

'It'll be wrapped in blasted pastry and Gibson'll be three sheets to the wind by the time he eats it. Especially after we've warmed him up with this.'

He slams the boxes down on the table. The bottles chime against each other like church bells. A call to prayer. Rena tucks the newspaper back around the meat she's unwrapped and puts it away.

'Champagne,' Bobby says. 'Gratis. I made Lou throw it in to compensate for the meat. Look, it's French.'

She inspects the box. 'It's always French,' she says.

'Eh?'

'Champagne. It's always French.'

Rena, Rena. Bugger Frank Gibson, he wants to say, bugger staying up all night to make pastry, let's you and me crack one of these open and drink until we're giddy. He imagines her laughing, the way she laughed when he drove her back down the moor road after that first date. Hardly a drop of alcohol in wine, he told her, that's why they drink it all day over on the Continent. Tell me about Rome, she said, and he gave her a scrubbed-up version of Naples, added in the Coliseum and the Pope in a frock. Rena, let's drink champagne and run away to Rome. Would she have gone for it, ever? Ah well. That's why Rena has the edge, that's why she is his saviour.

Janet, 1954

Sliding down the banister is not permitted, but nor is wandering about the hotel at night, so when Janet reaches the last half-landing she cannot resist easing her tummy onto the rail. Pyjamas give the most satisfying glide. One, two, three and she boosts her feet up and casts off. She disembarks at the bottom with a thud that is less than surreptitious and waits, listening hard as befits the last Potawatomi scout. When she hears nothing she proceeds. Before she has even turned the corner a noise makes her freeze, but it's just the clatter of Ricky's claws on the stairs. She left him curled up in his basket when she snuck past her nana, who was slumped snoring over her knitting. Now Ricky can be the Lone Ranger to Janet's Tonto. Janet's nana always lets her stay up to watch the television, perhaps because Hetty loves it so much herself, although cowboys are not her favourite (they remind her of her smug niece, off in the States, she says, which makes it sound as though the niece has a very exciting time of it).

'Ssshh,' Janet tells Ricky, finger to lips, eyes wide. Obediently, he drops his sleek sausage body to the ground, his tail swooshing against the tiles of the hallway. She peers round to face the reception. A light is on in the office but there is nobody at the desk.

Janet tiptoes barefoot between patches of cover: the hallstand, the chairs by the fireplace with its large embroidered screen. The fire is only lit for very special winter functions, and Janet and her nana are not allowed downstairs on those evenings. The Lone Ranger's claws are a liability so she shoos him on to the rug. Stealth is all. Together they reach the office door to the left of the reception window. It is ajar, and from here Tonto sights the fugitive, shoes off and feet up on the lumpy night porter's couch, her splayed paperback rising and falling on her chest as she breathes. Tonto signals to the Lone Ranger and edges closer. On the cover of the book Staff Nurse Sally Malone's cape flaps as she hurries away from where Doctor stands glowering beside Matron. Janet recognises the heroine; Alma likes to relate the plots of her romances and this one has been on the go all week. Janet has heard her mother observe that it's odd that someone so fearful of doctors and hospitals should prefer a medical setting.

A rumbling groan in the pipes overhead puts Tonto on the alert again, but although Alma shifts she doesn't wake. Mr MacDonald probably, one of the permanents. He's up and down like a yoyo whereas the Misses Galbraith use a po rather than venture out into the corridors at night. The popping of trapped air settles, leaving only the small night noises of the building, the creaks and whispers of wood and stone. Janet isn't sure how the game should proceed, now she has succeeded in running down the quarry. A shift to highwaymen, perhaps.

Stand and deliver, Oddfellows or boilings. It's rare for a romance to be read without the accompaniment of a sooky sweet.

The Lone Ranger takes matters into his own paws, leaping up onto the couch and licking Alma's bunion-plagued toes through her nylons with his little pink tongue. She shrieks and sits upright.

'Holy Mother of God but you nearly ended me, Janet Young! What are you doing skulking around at this hour?' Alma glances towards the clock. 'It's past midnight.'

'Just playing. I couldn't sleep.'

'Acht well, no harm in that I suppose,' Alma says, although she's shaking her head. 'Is your nan asleep?'

Janet nods. 'But with her knitting, not in bed.'

'Well, how about this? I'll get you a glass of milk from the kitchen and take you back upstairs, but then you'll wake up your nan so she won't find herself all crooked in the morning.'

'Thank you very much, Alma,' Janet says. 'And I'm very sorry that Ricky licked your bunions.' She's certain that a trip to the kitchen will result in something to eat as well as a glass of milk and plans to leave her nana asleep in her chair so that she can see just how crooked she is in the morning. Perhaps as crooked as the man and his cat and its mouse, who all lived together in their little crooked house.

Alma laughs. 'You've got manners, I'll say that for you.'

Janet averts her eyes politely while Alma forces her feet back into her shoes. Just then, an urgent tapping sounds on the front door. Alma starts.

'God in Heaven, it's my night for scares, isn't it? There is a bell, you know,' she says to the unseen visitor. 'Janet pet, you'll have to run away upstairs now while I get that. Some bloody dawdler from the last train, too feart to go home to his wife. Though how it can take half an hour to cross that road I will never know.'

The tapping begins again and as Janet darts past the door, Ricky in front of her, she glimpses small white knuckles, distorted by the frosted glass. She turns and pauses, sees a pale face loom between the T and O of the gold lettering. Nobody she can recognise, at that distance, but Alma sighs.

'I might have known. Now off to bed, Janet, and mind and wake your nan.'

'Goodnight,' Janet whispers as Alma draws the bolt on the inner door, but instead of climbing up to the attic floor where she and her nana sleep she waits on the landing, holding Ricky's collar and rubbing his silky ears to keep him quiet as she eavesdrops. She feels the rush of cold air as the door opens, hears the rattle of dried leaves on the tiles.

'Not again,' Alma says.

'Oh Alma, I knew you were on tonight. Thank you.' A woman's voice, and there's a scraping, tapping noise.

'How did you get here?'

'Walked.'

'In those?' The noise must be shoes, Janet realises, straining to catch the conversation.

'My feet are gouping.' The voice is familiar.

'Does he know where you are?'

No reply that Janet can hear.

'What about the twins?' Alma says, in a stronger voice. It is Aunt Evie then. It takes half an hour to walk from Edzell Place. She and her granny do it sometimes. Her mother usually takes a taxi, if her father isn't there to drive her.

'They sleep through it. A few hours, that's all, and I'll be back before they wake up. Don't fret.'

Janet pictures Evelyn and Malcolm, also in their pyjamas, tucked up in bed. Their parents don't work so late, so they can sleep at home rather than somewhere else.

Alma sighs again. 'It's not me, Evie…'

'I know. But Hetty won't say a word and I'll be away before the breakfast shift. Promise.'

Janet creeps up another step, two more, and catches Alma saying, 'I need this job,' before she sprints up the rest of the stairs and back along the corridor.

'You wee besom,' Hetty says as Janet closes the Staff Only door behind her. 'Here's me wondering where you'd got to.'

'I'm sorry,' Janet replies. 'I couldn't sleep and then I wanted to play at being Tonto and now Aunt Evie's coming to visit.'

'Have you been sleepwalking again?' Hetty says, but then the fire door at the end of the corridor gives its familiar, homely squeak and she draws herself together. 'All right young lady, let's get you back into bed.'

'Can Ricky sleep in my room?' Janet asks.

Hetty sighs and stoops to pick up the wicker dog basket. 'Just this once. But he's not to jump up on the covers.'

'It's all right. His legs are too short.'

The blanket on her bed was tight earlier, when she was playing at being Houdini, but Hetty tucks it tighter now, as though her duty as grandmother and guardian is to prevent further escape.

'Sleep tight now, pet,' she says, and kisses Janet on the forehead.

'Don't let the bugs bite,' Janet says.

As soon as Hetty leaves the room, Ricky scrambles onto the blanket box and then the bed. He circles on Janet's legs until he finds just the right spot to curl up, and she feels his weight grow heavier as he shifts then settles. She wonders why she isn't sitting up to see Aunt Evie, who has come all this way in the dark. Dim threads of light trace the outline of the door that connects Janet's room to Hetty's. It is hot under the covers, but Janet is beginning to feel sleepy and comfortable now. Ricky is already snuffling, chasing rabbits in his dreams although she was told that dachshunds went after badgers originally. She can't imagine Ricky going after a badger, but then he is a miniature. She can hear voices, low and confidential, and it reminds her of the times when her mother finishes work after a late function and has her nana bundle Janet up in her blanket to be driven back to the house with them. Sometimes the journey doesn't wake her at all, so she never quite knows where she'll be when she opens her eyes in the morning. The kettle shrills and rattles on Hetty's hot plate and then is stifled so that Janet can hear more clearly. A low sobbing, accompanied by the tinkle of bracelets.

'What can't be cured must be endured,' Hetty says. The words are muffled but Janet has little difficulty recognising the phrase. It's applied to anything from lumpy porridge to starting school to moving house to sleeping here in the hotel rather than in her room at home. She likes the hotel though. There's always someone to talk to. And there's always something to eat in the kitchen, which is not always the case at home. If Evie says anything in return, her answer is unintelligible. Janet struggles free of the blanket and raises her head from the down-filled pillow. Ricky snuffles.

'Tomorrow's a new day,' Hetty is saying. 'He'll be sorry, you'll see, that's the way it always goes.'

Evie's voice rises, clear and urgent. 'Don't tell Rena.'

Janet's nana agrees to this, it seems, because not long after the light snaps off and the bed is swathed in darkness once more. As Janet drifts off she remembers, once, being in the house in Edzell Place and allowed to stay up late. Hogmanay perhaps, an occasion at any rate: devilled eggs and vol au vents, faces gleaming with sweat and whisky, the air thickened by cigarette smoke. After Auntie Evie and Uncle Thomas went next door, back to their own house, Janet's mother began washing glasses and handing them to Janet to dry; never put off until tomorrow what you can do today. After a while Evie returned, battering on the kitchen door, reaching one manicured hand up to the window above the sink, as she begged 'please, Rena, please let me in, I can't stand it, please.' 'When will she learn,' Janet's mother said, as she sent Janet up to her bed. *Sticks and stones.*

Rena, 1954

Everything is in order for the evening, a function that has been relocated to the hotel by Lodge St Marnock while the Halls on London Road get a new damp course. In spite of her father's involvement Rena finds herself intrigued by the idle talk of regalia and rituals. Bobby says there's no need, and that he doesn't have the time, but would it make a difference, bind them up with the town? Surely to God they must be bound up by now, with all that they've achieved. Perhaps Thomas should think of it as well, now he has the Post Office, but Thomas will remember their father, as she does, coming in drunk from the Lodge. He takes after George Lennox, she's loathe to admit it, and she knows he hates it in himself. He and Evie are at each other's throats too much and she needs to have a word with him before they do it in public. She plans on entertaining, now she's getting the house more to her taste, and she wants everything to be perfect. As do the Masons tonight. They need privacy and another room for the wives to wait in while the men conduct their business before the meal. The old coffee salon is done up as a lounge bar now, with new upholstery on the chair seats, even if they don't have a proper license to go with it. Thank goodness Nell got the curtains done in time.

'Alma?'

'Yes, Mrs Young?'

'Nobody must enter the function room, and I mean nobody, until I say so. Understood?'

Alma grins and says, 'Don't you worry, Mrs Young. The girls have been warned within an inch of their lives and I'm in no hurry to get in there myself.'

'Good.' Rena allows herself a smile in return. 'There will be a tip tonight. Tell the girls that.'

Even if she has to pay it herself. Everyone needs an incentive, and money is a good one. Corkage is a start but it doesn't add up to much, even with the amount the Masons have laid in. Nothing compared to what a bar would take. She has a cupboard full of beer, wine, whisky, and the wives have to be given sherry or gin while they're waiting. 'Not too much of it,' Worshipful Master McTaggart said with a wink. 'You know women when they get together.' She laughed as if delighted by the perspicacity of this insight, and promised to rustle up some canapés, just to keep them going. Stuffed tomatoes, mackerel pate on toast, that kind of thing. Men are easily kept happy – and who knows how long they'll go on, rolling up their trouser legs and whatnot – but women notice the details and it's them that'll choose the venue for the next engagement party or funeral tea.

'All right,' she says, looking around the kitchen one last time. 'All set, Ugo?' A cook at last, introduced as a parting gift from Victor before he went back to Lucca. The staff all call him Shug, but Rena enjoys telling customers that they have a new continental chef, even if she can't help wishing he was French. Well, he worked in Monaco once, or so he says, and at least he's not the type to turn the waitresses' heads.

'All set, Mrs Young. It will be a banquet.' He pinches his thumb and forefinger together, kisses the air. He has big hands, with hair on the knuckles, but his spun sugar is the most intricate Rena has ever seen.

'That's what they're paying for,' she says, although really they're only paying for cream of tomato soup and a bread roll, escalope of veal (Ugo wanted to call it Schnitzel Wiener Art but Rena soon put the kibosh on that), coffee and petit fours. They've been over the margins three times. All silver service, naturally.

'Telephone for you, Mrs Young.' Alma hurries in from the reception desk. She lowers her voice when Rena approaches. 'It's the police.'

Her first thought is Bobby, driving too fast in that damn car. Then Janet, but when she checks her watch she sees that school will still be in.

'Hello,' she says, waving Alma away. 'Yes, this is Mrs Young speaking.'

She has to ask the constable to repeat it while she stretches the cord and shoos Alma from the lounge where, right enough, she's hovering within earshot. 'I don't understand. Has there been an accident at the printers?' No, but if she comes to the station the man's superior will give her all the information. 'You do mean James Andrew Jarvie?' Rena says. 'Of the ground floor flat at number seven Beansburn?'

There's no mistake. It's Jamie he's talking about. 'My husband and I will be there directly,' she assures him, and as soon as she has replaced the receiver she yells, 'Where is Mr Young?'

Alma's head pops round the lounge door. 'He went to pick up the floral centrepieces.'

'When? How long ago?'

'Not more than ten minutes.'

Rena considers telephoning Thomas at work, dismisses the idea. The last thing she needs is bluster, and with the way things are between him and Jamie there would be bluster, and it won't be Jamie's fault, whatever this is. Needing to curse something she finds herself cursing Hetty, for the fact that Jamie is still living in the flat with her, at his age. Rena leaves Alma in charge and storms round the corner to Campbell's, where she finds Bobby is loading the top table centrepiece into the boot of the car.

'That policeman,' she says. 'The one who plays cards.'

Bobby dislodges a carnation and picks it up, holding it at arm's length as if it's come from outer space. 'Ferguson?'

'Will he be in the station now?' She takes the flower and wedges it back in to its oasis.

'I don't know.'

'Phone him,' Rena says, waving towards the telephone box across the street. She rummages in her handbag for her small address book.

'Rena, what's going on?'

She flicks through to P and sees the station number, thrusts it towards Bobby. 'It's Jamie. He's been arrested.' Her voice rises to a shout as a train thunders over the viaduct above them.

'Jamie? What in Christ's name did he do?'

Rena drops her voice again. 'Nothing. He hasn't done anything. It's a mistake. So get Ferguson on the phone and tell him to meet us there immediately.'

At least Bobby moves fast when there's need, she thinks, lighting a cigarette and watching him dial the number. His expression is serious for the initial polite inquiry and after a few moments turns expansive. He must have got hold of Ferguson. The card game is still going and her understanding is that Bobby joins in occasionally, as a member of the group as well as provider of the venue. She does not approve of gambling but allows that a small investment may yield returns; Ferguson has indicated he'll support the Trust's application for a license publicly, for instance. Seeing Bobby replace the receiver and wait to cross the road, she flicks away her cigarette and gets in the passenger seat. There's a sickly smell and she turns to look behind her. The small table posies are on the back seat. She ordered them for the lounge as well as the function room. Could Jamie not have picked a better day to mess up?

They drive back past the hotel and down John Finnie Street towards the police station. Rena has been kept calm by action, by taking charge, but soon she'll have to step back and let Bobby take the lead. She feels the moisture prickle under her arms as he stalls the car at the lights by the court house.

When they get there they are taken to Ferguson's office. Tea is provided, on a tray with biscuits, she notes, and the Inspector joins them within a few minutes. He moves quickly, as if there are plenty of draws on his time.

'Nice to see you again, Mrs Young,' he says. 'Even under the, em, circumstances. And it'll be twice in one day, I believe?'

'You should see what Rena's got planned for you this evening,' Bobby says. 'I have to hand it to her, she knows how to put on a do.'

He and Bobby shake hands and slap each other on the back. Imagine if Bobby had the right handshake, she thinks. How much easier would things be then?

'Yes, well, I've made some enquiries about your brother, Mrs Young, and I'm sure we can sort matters out.'

'I knew it would be a misunderstanding,' she says.

Ferguson doesn't reply. Bobby offers him a cigarette, which he accepts. After the business of lighting up, he says, 'It must be a busy day for you, with our lot coming in tonight.' His tone is sympathetic, but he is looking at the door rather than meeting her eye.

He and Bobby seem to be following the same script, one that she hasn't had sight of, because Bobby says, 'Yes, not a bad idea to get a rest while you can,' and then Ferguson is on the phone arranging a car to take her home for the afternoon.

'Ssh, Rena, it's all right. Alma can manage this afternoon, and I'll drop off the flowers then come and collect you in plenty of time.' Rena notices that there's a bit of fern leaf stuck to his sleeve. She wants to brush it away but he's looking to Ferguson. 'Marvellous work ethic, my wife.'

'Aye, that's the way to be,' the policeman agrees.

Rena understands that she can't tell them to wait a minute. She has to leave them to it, men together, to sort out whatever it is that needs sorting out.

'But...' she begins. Bobby and Ferguson turn to look at her. There's a coldness to them, somehow, as though she's facing the icy surface of a mountain, something she has no hope of scaling.

'Is,' she softens her voice. 'Is my brother all right?'

Ferguson nods again. A woman's question, quite

acceptable. 'I can vouch for that, Mrs Young. In the cells, certainly, but enjoying the very same tea and biscuits as us.'

Rena hasn't touched her tea, never mind a biscuit. A young constable comes to the door and she is led away.

'Hold on,' she says, as they reach the reception area. 'I don't want to be driven to my door in a police car.'

'No, of course not,' he says, all solicitous. Rena realises that he is younger than her. Not much older than Jamie. 'DCI Ferguson gave me the keys to his own vehicle. I'll be on duty tonight as well, you see.' He smiles and leads her through the car park.

When she's home she telephones the hotel to make sure everything is all right, and is reassured by Alma and then by Ugo. Illness in the family does fine as an excuse. When Hetty turns up with Janet, Rena smiles, views the marks for the Primary Two arithmetic and dictation test, and in reward gives them money for ices and the end of a loaf for the ducks in the Kay Park. It's a nice day and Ricky could do with a decent walk. Hetty mustn't know about Jamie. Alone again, Rena paces around the living room, smoking and looking out of the window for Bobby's car, then at the clock on the mantel, then out of the window again. When the clock reaches five she realises she'll have to get ready, maybe take a taxi to the hotel. She reaches for the telephone, lets her hand fall. What would she say, if she phoned the station? Of all of them Jamie's the one who has fitted in, made friends, picked up the accent and kept his aspirations modest.

Rena goes to her bedroom and begins to look through the wardrobe. The same bloody wardrobe they've been carting around since she came to this town and it was hardly heirloom quality then. Masons, she thinks.

Policemen. Black is too stern, too funereal. Blue perhaps, although she suits green better. It looks softer with her colouring. She runs through the hangers. Nothing is right. She needs new clothes. Then she sees a shawl collar dress with a full skirt, in burgundy. Evening wear, definitely, but modest. Appropriate. She changes her foundation garment and puts on fresh stockings, tries the dress on, adds a string of pearls. Her wedding ring sticks at the knuckle. She used to be so proud of how slim and pale her hands were but now they seem wider, the veins more prominent. Working hands. She smooths on some Pond's and the ring goes on fine, but when she looks in the mirror the outfit is all wrong. It looks defiant. It makes her look like one of the guests. As if she's trying to upstage the guests. She tears it off again, leaves it crumpled on the bed. A navy dress instead, fitted, a crossover skirt with a detail on one hip. Yes, that's the one. That, with the pearls, and her navy courts with the buckle. She tucks a handkerchief carefully into the neckline and powders her nose. A touch of rouge, a dusting of eyeshadow, the slightest whisper of mascara. Nothing that looks like makeup, really, until the final, precise painting in of her lips.

As if on cue, she hears a screech of brakes, a car door slamming. Bobby's in the door before she's down the stairs.

'Rena,' he says, looking at her standing there, one hand on the bannister. 'You look… perfect.'

'Tell me,' she says. 'While you're getting your suit on, tell me.'

He comes to the bedroom with a whisky in his hand, a brandy for her. She waves it away but he says, 'Take it, Rena. Just the one.'

She holds the glass while he speaks. There's a chip in it. They need more crystal for the house, that's a priority if they're ever to entertain. The brandy burns her throat when she sips it, and her lipstick leaves a print on the edge of the glass. She makes Bobby go through it again. Jamie, her little brother Jamie, arrested for indecency, for exposing himself in a public place.

'No,' she says. 'Someone's lying. You told Ferguson it was a mistake.'

Bobby looks at her, and it takes her a moment to realise that what is in his eyes is pity. 'Rena. I saw him. I spoke to him. To Jamie.'

'Where?' Rena asks. 'Where was it?'

'Kay Park,' he says. Where she sent Hetty and Janet, she thinks. They'll be on their way back now, after feeding the ducks or eating ice cream from the van that parks there. 'A mother and child. No, no,' he adds, seeing Rena's face. 'He didn't see the child until it was too late. No harm done and nothing the woman hadn't seen before.'

'Who are they?'

He shrugs. 'They came in from Crosshouse on the bus. They don't know anybody.'

'Well, how did the police know it was Jamie?'

Bobby recites: 'Beanpole of a lad in an overall with printer's ink all down it.' He sighs. 'Besides, one of the parkies chased him and knocked him to the ground. He's got some shiner.'

'So what happens now? Where is he?'

'Ferguson says they'll have to keep him in overnight but he'll make sure it's swept under the carpet the morra. We'd better give him a good time tonight.'

Rena sips the brandy again, feels it bringing a flush to

her cheeks.

'That's good,' Bobby says. 'You need to go in there as if you don't have a care in the world.'

'So what's wrong with him,' she says. 'With Jamie? Is he sick in the head?'

Bobby sighs. 'He's just young. Stupid. But we need to make sure it doesn't happen again.'

'Of course it won't bloody happen again,' Rena says.

'Ferguson says he should find a girlfriend.'

'He should get married,' Rena says. 'He's twenty-one, for Christ's sake. We need to get him settled down.' She looks at Bobby, checking the time and straightening his tie. 'Ferguson will keep quiet, won't he?'

'Oh yes. Quid pro quo, as it were. With the emphasis on quid.'

'We can't afford for anything to get out, not when we're getting somewhere.' Will scandal always be at her coat tails, she wonders?

'It won't get out, Rena,' Bobby says, touching her lightly on the arm. 'I can promise you that.'

'All right,' she says. 'Well. You deal with it. You find Jamie a girl.'

The function comes off fine. Everyone stays out of the room while the ceremony occurs, the wives pick off the canapés like gulls after a fishing boat. Drinks flow, and by the time the main is cleared Rena begins to relax. She walks by the top table to check that everything is in order, tall and proud past Councillor Gibson, who is right up there whispering in the ear of the Worshipful Master. He doesn't look at her, not until the Worshipful Master turns away from him to tell her that he's delighted. Everyone is delighted, and Ferguson is red-faced and beaming. She thinks about the young constable who drove her home, who'll be waiting outside for his boss right now, dozing over the steering wheel in the dark street. He was engaged to be married, he said. She told him to come in with his fiancée, that she'd give them coffee while they considered their options for the wedding breakfast.

Bobby joins her by the service door, trim in his dinner suit. Together they're hitting exactly the right pose.

'Did you see? Harvey from the Trust is here,' Bobby says. 'He said his mind was turning to the benefits of a license.'

Rena nods, watching the sweets go out. Alma has five extra girls in to help her, serving a table apiece.

'And he isn't taking that bloody church in the old operetta house seriously,' Bobby adds. 'With their preaching and petitioning.'

'We can't underestimate them, Bobby. They've got people talking about it, which is precisely what we didn't want.'

Bobby nods. The last wave of peach Melba sweeps across the function room. There was parquet underneath that manky old carpet, and it's gleaming.

'What about these girls?' Rena says. 'Can you get Jamie to ask one of them out?'

Bobby's had a drink too, she can tell, but it's all right. He knows he can't go too far, not tonight. 'A waitress, for your brother?' he says.

She won't stoop to say what she's thinking. Anyone, and the cheaper the better. A bit more normality, was the way Bobby had paraphrased Ferguson. So they think Jamie needs sex, that must be the problem. Isn't that always the problem, with men? Wasn't that what that bloody doctor was getting at, all those years ago, when Bobby was at his worst? She watches closely, tries to isolate whether there is one of the girls that the men are more effusive towards, one that they follow with their eyes. 'What about the blonde one?' she says, spotting Wylie the bank manager's wife elbow him in the ribs at some cheeky comment made to the girl while accepting his pudding.

'Oh, Rena,' Bobby laughs, 'you never fail to surprise me.'

'My younger brother spending the night in a police cell is no laughing matter,' she says. 'I don't give a damn who it is. Just sort something out.'

She goes to check that Ugo and the kitchen team have put doilies on the plates for the petit fours. When she returns, she sees Bobby going along the top table with the Black Label they decided to offer Ferguson and his cronies on the house.

Bobby, 1954

When Bobby sees the waitress closer up, he isn't so sure about Rena's skills as a matchmaker. The girl must have a couple of years on Jamie and she's more firmly upholstered than she appeared darting around her table in her neat little heels at the function last week. She breezes in and out of the kitchen with a no-nonsense solidity offloading armfuls of plates and filling teapots from the urn. Her blonde updo doesn't even quiver as she moves, which puts Bobby off. You need a bit of softness, the possibility of yielding.

'What's that girl's name?' he asks Alma.

'Frances,' she says.

'Uh huh.' He realises that she's looking at him with suspicion. 'Rena told me she's a good wee worker,' he adds. 'We were wondering about offering her something more permanent.'

'First I've heard of it,' Alma says. 'But Mrs Young telt me to bring her in for more shifts and I can't say I'm complaining about the help.'

When Frances finishes with the high teas he contrives

to be outside, so that he can offer her a lift home.

'Bus stops right over there,' she says, and he realises from her tone that she is sharper than Rena might have assumed from the dyed hair.

'It's no trouble at all,' he says. 'But if you'd rather not.' He unlocks the driver's door of the Austin. She keeps walking. Spots of rain start to fall, quickly gathering pace. He sees her stop and fuss with her handbag.

'Forgotten my brolly,' she calls.

'Come on then. No point in getting soaked.' He strides round to open the passenger door and she hurries towards him, pulling her scarf over her hair. 'So where are we off to then?'

'Glebe Road,' she says, and he eases the car into a U-turn.

Fifteen minutes, tops. He'll have to work fast. He leans into his pocket and brings out his cigarette case, flicks it open one-handed. She helps herself and the car veers in towards the kerb as he lights it for her.

'Try to get me there in one piece,' she says. Her manner is tart without being flirtatious.

He perseveres: 'So are you enjoying your work with us, Frances?'

She shrugs. 'Pin money. I'm doing a secretarial course.'

'Very good,' he says, imagining her as a secretary. Efficient, with the illusion of glamour under a thick cardigan and support stockings. She'd guard her boss well though and keep the typing pool in check.

'Look,' he says. 'There's a reason why I gave you a lift today.'

'Oh aye? And here's me thinking it was to save my shoe leather.'

Don't worry, he's tempted to say, you're not my type. Her cheek might have its charms for some, but he prefers his women to be spirited in a different way. Rena or Anne. Toss a coin. Neither of them worldly, despite appearances, both of them reaching for the stars. Rena through the business, the house, that diamond engagement ring she insisted on after the fact; and Anne, well, she was trying to go somewhere with her bottles of gin and all those pretty little coloured pills. Frances doesn't strike him as the imaginative kind, though she's thinking the worst of him right now, he'd put money on that.

'I have a friend who'd like to speak to you, but he's a little bit shy around ladies.'

'Does he have a name, this friend of yours?' She winds down her window, to let the smoke escape.

'James.'

'And who's James when he's at home?'

Bobby smiles. 'The boss's brother.'

That stops her. Not for long though. 'Are you not the boss then?'

He laughs, stubs out his cigarette in the ashtray. 'As I'm sure you can guess, my lovely wife is the brains.'

'Where does that leave you then?'

She's irritating him now, but he holds it in. He's good at holding it in these days, most of the time at least. 'James is Mrs Young's younger brother.'

'I don't think I'm familiar with him. What age is he?' Is he imagining it, or is she speaking more properly now?

'Nearer your age than mine.'

'Well that's something.'

'And he's just finished an apprenticeship at Wilson's the printers. He's to be kept on.'

'Uh huh.'

He's turning off London Road now. 'Where would you go, if someone was taking you out for the evening? Dinner? Dancing?'

She sighs. 'Don't go down Glebe Road. I need to run an errand to the dairy first.'

She doesn't want to be seen in a car with a man, and especially not her boss's husband. Even if James does take her out he'll be on a hiding to nothing. But she might have friends with looser morals. Flashing at a woman in a park, for God's sake. Bobby believes that Jamie didn't see the child. His horror at that was genuine, but there's something he's not saying. The stories Bobby had to spin Ferguson, stories that would make Rena livid. Loss of his father at an early age, a bit of a mummy's boy, oh yes, Jamie was your full headshrinker's case study.

Bobby pulls in, leaving the engine running. She waits for him to get out and open her door, which he does.

'So if you don't mind me asking, why's this James not asking me out himself?'

Bobby laughs. 'I told you. He's the shy one in the family. Begged me to do it for him.'

He hopes she won't ask when Jamie has seen her, but she's flattered, Bobby can tell. Has a high enough opinion of her looks to believe it.

'Friday night then,' she says at last. 'I was planning to go to the dance in the Laigh Kirk hall. I'm at number fourteen. He can call in for me at seven. Meet my mother.'

Either Rena has picked a winner or she's bitten off more than she can chew.

The scene when Bobby gets home is all a bit *and when did you last see your father?* Rena standing by the mantelpiece, Bobby taking his place behind the settee as if to block any attempts at escape. And Jamie sitting there in the brocade Parker Knoll by the fire, hangdog, out of custody and awaiting the real sentencing. His black eye isn't bloodshot anymore but the bruising is still purple and yellow. It has the effect of making him look older and tougher than he is, though his expression is contrite. Rena kicks off with 'What the Hell did you think you were playing at?' – and Bobby steps in to give manly advice. That's a laugh. Just as well he didn't have a son. He wouldn't have known what to tell him.

'Do you have any idea how hard we've worked to make a life here?' Rena says. 'And now this stupidity.' Her neck is flushed, not her usual blush but the mottling of sheer rage. 'Explain yourself right now, James, because I don't understand.'

Bobby can see Jamie's face darkening too, his hands clenching and unclenching by his sides. 'Come on, son,' he says. 'Tell us the whole story. Because I don't think this is you, Jamie. I don't think it's you at all.'

In stumbling phrases, it all comes out. Most of the staff at the printers are let go early on a Friday as they come in on Sunday to begin Monday's typesetting. Jamie and the apprentice compositor decided to buy some beer and go to the park, and too much drink was taken. Dares ensued, and under the influence, Jamie performed his.

'I didn't see them,' he says. 'I swear to God, I didn't see the wee boy. I know I shouldn't have done it.'

'Thomas is right,' Rena says in disgust. 'You are too easily led. I'd have thought your service would have sorted you out.'

An expression of abject horror crosses Jamie's face. 'Don't tell Thomas. Please.'

Rena goes to the cigarette box on the coffee table. Bobby reaches for his lighter but she picks up the heavy onyx one instead. Jamie's lucky she doesn't throw it at him, Bobby thinks.

'Well,' she exhales slowly, the flush retreating from her neck. 'Why on earth didn't you tell the police that it wasn't your fault? That you were put up to it?'

'I didnae want…'

'Speak properly, for Christ's sake.'

'Nobody wants to be a clype,' Bobby says. 'That's normal.'

'You have a very strange idea of normality,' Rena says, angry enough to catch him in the crossfire. Normality. He wishes that had held some sway at sea. *It's a war, Seaman. These people are different from us. Normal rules don't apply.* He's sick and fed up with this family drama and is anticipating his early run to see Luigi. Above board this time, bona fide all the way. Except maybe a couple of under the counter bits and bobs. Foolish not to.

'If it wasn't for us you'd be in that jail tonight, and you'd be being fired from that bloody apprenticeship tomorrow,' Rena says. 'Blood is thicker than water, Jamie, just you remember that.'

Bobby rouses himself and picks up the good cop role again.

'We've got to move on from this, Jamie. So, I've fixed up a date for you on Friday. A nice girl. Take her out, have a good time.'

'What?' Jamie says.

The poor sod looks the way Bobby must have when he got off the *Bluebell* in Greenock that time. He takes out his wallet, sorts out a few notes. 'I'll lend you the car so that you can pick her up, and here's some money. Don't let her pay for anything.'

Rena tuts. 'For Christ's sake, Jamie, you're going out with a girl, not being sent to the salt mines.'

Bobby wishes Jamie would say something. Shout at them. Anything but start crying, and it looks as if that's on the cards.

'Her name's Frances. Fourteen Glebe Road.'

Rena says, 'Frances? What is she, a Catholic?'

'I didn't ask. But they're going to the dance in the Laigh hall.'

'That's all right then.'

Rena is contradictory; she maintains that you can't trust Catholics but says she couldn't hope for a better worker than Alma, believes they're daft to be in thrall to the Pope and at the same time sullied by an excess of sex.

'I don't want to,' Jamie blurts.

Rena fixes him with a glare. 'Well, you're going to. You need to be seen to be normal.'

Bobby watches Jamie closely. Is the Jarvie temper going to break out at last? Not likely. 'She's a good-looking girl, Jamie. And she knows her mind. You don't have anything to worry about.'

'And you can thank your lucky stars that I haven't told Thomas anything about this,' Rena says. 'You're not too old for him to beat some sense into you.'

'Look, son,' Bobby says. 'You take Frances out on Friday, and we'll forget about this. All of it. All right?'

'All right.' Jamie takes the money from Bobby and puts it in his pocket. Frances will eat him alive. But he's used to being bullied by Thomas and bossed by Rena, so maybe it'll go just fine.

'One more thing,' Rena says. 'Your friend. We need to know who he is.'

Trust Rena to think of everything. *What's the point in getting Jamie off if there's some boy somewhere who could drop him in it?* This isn't the man he wants to be, Bobby realises, even as he's scaring the life out of a silly lad in a lane behind a Corporation terrace that evening. Doing a deal with Luigi is one thing, holding this boy by the neck against a brick wall is another. But Rena is right, they're still interlopers, they're still vulnerable.

'Not one word. Because if you do, I will come and find you. Do you understand?'

Something splashes on his new brown Oxford wing-tips and he realises the boy has wet himself. He lets him go.

After that he's glad to be on the road to Glasgow. Lights on this time, and a story prepared about going to see his sister. That'll be right. It goes well with Luigi. He makes a delivery for a friend of Victor's, gets something for himself by return. Not booze – he's explained he can't sell it – but enough tea and coffee to keep them going for a week. Good stuff as well. And then, and God knows he's earned it, Bobby gets drunk. Drunker than he's been for a while.

By midnight he's in the kitchen of a woman as far gone as him, sliding his hand up her skirt and fumbling for a way beyond her undergarments. What the Hell's wrong with Jamie, that he isn't striving for this? There's a twang of elastic and both of them laugh, and then he watches her face. The way her eyes widen, the way her lips part and her breathing coarsens. As if something animal has taken over. Surely there's a purity to this too? A clarity of focus, at least. She's pulling him closer, dragging him towards the box bed in the corner. Her husband, where is he? Dead or in jail, Bobby hopes, although when he looks up he can see trousers and work overalls on the pulley. That and the stench of bone broth reminds him of his childhood, but he can forget that again too, with a little effort. She tries to take her dress off but he doesn't care about that, pulls at her knickers instead. She wriggles out of the tight elastane, kicks off her shoes. It's weakness, this loss of control, nothing pure about it. That's why he has never seen it in Rena, that's why he never will. But here he is again, giving in.

JANET, 1956

Janet passes her hands over the figurine and gently turns it over. *Fine bone china.* What kind of bones, she wonders. Once at Balmaha she watched her Aunt Min set a blackbird's broken wing. And it's just the same for people, she said, prompting Janet to imagine a future of injuries in need of tending. There's a mark on the underside of the figurine like a little crown, and what looks like a signature, but Janet can't read it. She had wondered if there would be a name, and if that name would be *Irene*, because the figure looks so like her mother. She replaces it carefully on the sideboard. Her father gave it to Rena for their wedding anniversary last week, along with a horseshoe from the blacksmith's because it's their steel anniversary. Janet wore her velvet dress when the family came around, and her nana took her to see *The King and I* at the pictures while her parents went for dinner with Thomas and Evie, and Jamie and his *fiancée* (odd word, especially as she isn't as fancy as either Janet's mother or her Aunt Evie, and certainly not any of the ladies that the king was married to in the picture). When Janet's mother opened the box she smiled and smiled, and kissed her father, who took Janet to the drinks cabinet to help pour another round of whiskies and soda and sweet sherries to celebrate. She was allowed a lemonade turned pink with two sticky cherries from the jar. Just like her mother (and indeed Deborah Kerr, her nana's favourite) the figurine has pale skin, and strawberry blonde hair (not red, Janet knows you mustn't call it that). She is smiling and reaching out one long, pale arm. She should have a cigarette between her fingers really, but perhaps that would be too difficult to make out of fine bone china. Janet strokes her middle fingertip down the ornament's smooth arm.

'Do be careful,' her mother says behind her.

'Maybe you could get a dress like this one,' Janet says. It's off the shoulder with a huge full skirt of purples sweeping into pink.

'It's a funeral we need clothes for, not a ball. Now, get your coat. Your father's going to take us in the car.'

'Can I bring Ricky?'

'No. Run next door with him. Malcolm and Evelyn can take him today.'

Janet gets her coat and Ricky's lead. He jumps around her ankles in excitement, and she feels guilty that she isn't taking him into the park. Aunt Evie's in the front garden next door, wearing a headscarf and capri pants and pushing a lawnmower across the grass.

'Hello pet,' she calls. 'That's a shame about your Aunt Margaret, isn't it?'

'Yes,' Janet says. She doesn't remember her aunt very well, to be honest, but she can tell that her nana is upset. 'We're going to get me a black dress for the funeral and Mum wondered if Malcolm and Evelyn could look after Ricky for the day?'

'Malcolm's helping his dad in the shop today and Evelyn's at her music lesson, but you just leave him with me. He can keep me company while I do the garden. And I'll take him for a good walk later, how about that?'

'Thanks, Aunt Evie,' Janet says, and runs back out into the street, where the car engine is running. She jumps into the back seat beside her nana, who slips a barley sugar into her hand straight away. Janet pops it in her mouth and waves to Aunt Evie as they drive off. Janet hasn't been in the car to Glasgow very often but she checks off the landmarks as they pass them. Her school on the right-hand side past the creamery, of course, and then the horses. The dappled grey that Janet loves is wearing a rug, and its friend the Shetland pony pokes its head through the gate to eat grass from the verge.

As they leave the town behind them Janet watches the trees in the distance to the right closely, and yes, a gap between them gives a second's glimpse of Craufurdland Castle. They once had venison for a dinner in the hotel that came from there. Janet liked it until she overheard that somebody her father knew had been helping with the deer cull. That didn't sound so nice. The moor isn't very interesting until the Covenanter's memorial that her father pointed out (*and the moral is, sometimes discretion is the better part of valour*), and then the Red House where they once stopped for coffee that was, according to her mother, undrinkable. When they reach the city there's plenty to look at, tall buildings and people everywhere, but Janet thinks she prefers the countryside. You couldn't keep a horse in the city. She still likes to see the cowboy movies, where they ride across vast open plains, although she's slowly coming to the conclusion that the Indians might be the good guys (Tonto being a case in point).

As they drive along Sauchiehall Street her father says, 'I met your mother right here, Janet. Do you remember, Hetty? You were there. Love at first sight, it was. I followed her along the street and invited you all to tea, you and Margaret, and Min and Nell.'

'I do remember,' Hetty says. 'You were persistent, we said that for you.'

'I was bowled over, that's what I was. By Irene on her twenty-first birthday, in her new fur coat.'

Rena tuts. 'It wasn't my actual birthday, you know.'

'Never let the facts get in the way of a good story,' Bobby says.

He drops them at the store and Rena makes an arrangement for him to come and collect them later on, so that they won't have to take the train home with their bags. Min and Nell are already waiting in the café. Like Hetty, they're taking mourning seriously already; Nell's in black tweed slacks and Min's wearing a black dress with a beige slit down one side. They embrace their sister, then Rena, then Janet herself, and order another pot of tea.

'Well, I knew as soon as I came down the stairs in the morning,' Min says, dropping a second cube into her cup. She stirs her tea and replaces the spoon neatly on her saucer. 'Because I'd put a bowl of roses on the big table, just cut from the garden the day before, and do you know, all the petals had turned black. And then the telephone rang and it was Nell, asking if I'd been in to check on Margaret yet.'

'And you said no,' Nell picks up, 'but that you'd do it while I was on the line. I'd woken at four, you see, because I'd dreamed that she was in my room, but she told me not to worry, to go back to sleep. And sure enough, when

Min came back on the line she said that was her gone.'

'In her sleep at least,' Hetty says. 'That's a blessing.' She sips her tea and a flash of distress passes across her face. 'Can you believe it, that there's just the three of us now? Out of that big family.'

'Don't you emigrate, Janet,' Min says, and Janet can't tell if she's serious or not. 'There's few enough Jarvies left in this country.'

They sit in silence for a moment, and then Nell says, 'She was ready to go though, wasn't she? She'd been ill for such a while.'

Min nods. 'It was her time. The last couple of weeks I'd caught her talking to William and Douglas more than once, and poor Andrew.'

'That's your great uncles,' Janet's mother says. Janet was waiting for her to say it's all nonsense, this talk of flowers changing colour and speaking to the dead, but Rena doesn't. She is superstitious about some things, Janet has noticed. Hats on beds, spilled salt, nails on a Sunday. This must be another.

'Yes, they died in the Great War, poor boys,' Hetty adds, although Janet knows this already. Her nana has shown her the photograph of them that's inside her gold locket. 'Andrew was just seventeen. Thank heavens Jamie was too young last time.'

'Amen to that,' Rena says. 'I was worried enough about Thomas and Bobby.'

'And what's this about him getting engaged?' Min says.

'Frances, her name is,' Rena says. 'They're not having a party, thank goodness. I don't know what the mother would do for it.'

'It seems a pity not to celebrate,' Hetty says. 'With the

hotel...'

'If they want it quiet we should just let them get on with it,' Rena says, gesturing to the waitress with her menu. 'Now, shall we order some sandwiches? I could do with something before we go round the shop.'

'Oh yes, let's,' Min says. 'My stomach thinks my throat's been cut.'

'Maybe we should think of getting Janet something she can wear for a wedding as well,' Hetty muses. 'That'll make it a brighter day, to think of something cheerful ahead.'

'Well, let's wait and see,' Rena says. 'We don't want to tempt fate, do we?'

Once they've eaten – not just sandwiches, but shortbread biscuits as well – they go from floor to floor of the shop, splitting up for a while so that Nell and Min can go to haberdashery. Janet doesn't usually spend a great deal of time with her mother, except when they're on holiday on Arran or if she's enlisted to help with housework or be present at a social occasion. Being the focus of Rena's attention makes her glow, even if she does feel a bit like her cardboard dress-up doll, in and out of outfits until her arms and legs are limp and bendy.

'What do you think?' Rena says to Hetty, straightening the white lace collar on the dress she has given Janet to put on. 'That collar's not right, is it?'

'A bit old-fashioned,' Hetty agrees.

'Try this coat with the grosgrain trim, Janet, and we'll see how that looks.'

Janet puts the coat on and fumbles as she pushes the little buttons through their tight fabric loops.

'Oh now that's nice, don't you think?'

Janet realises that her opinion is unnecessary to proceedings, and she is getting too sleepy to care. The coat fits neatly at the waist and flares out, a bit like the jackets she's seen in pictures of ladies riding side saddle. Soon they've accumulated a plain black dress for her to wear under it. 'And a wee string of jet beads would just set it off,' Rena says, tucking a loose strand of hair behind her Janet's ear. 'Min has ropes of the stuff in the shop, she can make one up.'

'Will you get something too, Rena?' Hetty asks. 'You can't go in what you wear for the funerals in the hotel.'

Choosing a dress for Janet's mother is even more of a production, in which Janet has her own role doing up zips and hook and eye fastenings, replacing discarded garments on hangers. Her aunts gather on a couch in the ladies' dressing room on the first floor, which is bigger and fancier than the one in the children's department. With an assistant fluttering around, Rena tries on dress after dress, her feet slipped into a pair of black high heels that have been found to help her make a decision. One black frock looks much like another, apart from a silk one that Min urges Rena to try just for fun although it's clearly inappropriate, with its dropped back. Janet thinks again of the bone china figurine. It's fragile, with its slender arms and delicate feet poking out from under its ballgown, whereas her mother stands straight and composed.

'That's a good fit,' Nell says, checking the shoulders and waist of a neatly fitting wool crepe with a slash neck.

'I almost forgot,' Min says, rummaging in her handbag. 'I brought Margaret's jade brooch, the one you always liked, Rena. It'll go perfectly on that. Here Janet, can you open the clasp on this, please? I don't have my glasses.'

Janet unhooks the fastening on the small leather box and hands it to her mother, who takes out a brooch and turns back to the mirror to hold it against her shoulder.

'She wanted you to have it,' Min says. 'And it's eighteen carat, by the way.'

Hetty makes a noise, a rapid exhalation of air. 'Oh. Oh dear,' she says, and pulls out her handkerchief. Nell puts her arm around her. 'We'll all miss her, Het. Our older sister. Always said she was wiser as well.'

'And that was the truth,' Min says, with a sigh.

'She helped me a lot over the years,' Rena says. 'I don't know what I'd have done without her. Without all of you.'

'You can manage on your own, Rena,' Nell says. 'You've proved that.'

When she turns to face them, Janet is surprised to see tears rolling down her mother's cheeks.

Rena, 1958

The paper sits open in front of Rena: *Temperance Hotel to Plea for Drink Permit to Prevent Closure.* Embarrassing, yes, but the Trustees have agreed it's the best strategy and what else can they do? Nobody knows or needs to know how well Rena and Bobby are doing, nor about the money that will make its way back into the pockets of the Trust, or indeed the Trustees, at the end of the financial year. Pleading poverty it is. Rena looks at her watch.

'Would you please get some coffee ready to take through to the lounge when Mr Watson arrives, Alma?'

'Yes, Mrs Young,' Alma calls back from the front desk. 'Biscuits?'

'The home-made ones.'

Rena stands up and smooths her skirt. She's wearing a taupe underdress and jacket, and a modest string of pearls. Responsible, sober. Except her new shoes are threatening to pinch her feet; at least there isn't far to walk. The front door swings open, the gold etching that says Ossington Hotel flashing in the late spring sunshine.

'You will not credit it,' Bobby says, scuffing his feet

against the mat and taking off his hat. He's been at the barber and thankfully has left his grey hairs alone this time. The touch of silver makes him look serious, and that's what they need today.

'What?' she asks.

'They're actually going to demonstrate outside the court.'

'Oh for heaven's sake,' Rena says. 'Do I look all right?'

Bobby looks her up and down, taking his time. 'Perfect as always. I'm glad you didn't go for the trouser suit.'

Rena shakes her head. 'Honestly. That hasn't been the style for years. Besides, I'm not sure I'd carry it off these days.'

'Of course you would,' Bobby says. 'Legs like yours.'

'It's my middle that's the problem,' Rena says. 'Watson should be here any minute.'

Bobby reaches for her arm, lays his hand on it. 'It'll be fine,' he says. 'The licensing court will see sense. There's no earthly reason why not.'

Rena sighs. 'Apart from seven hundred signatures from God-fearing churchgoers on that bloody petition.'

'Aye, MacLeod's a pain.' Bobby squeezes her arm. 'We can only do our best.'

'Well, it needs to be good enough,' Rena says. 'That school's holding a place for Janet for August and it isn't cheap.'

She and Bobby don't have a qualification between them and she wants Janet to be educated, enough to mix with the right sort of people at any rate. Rena's all right, she can hold her own, but that's because she has to. It's part of her position as proprietress of the hotel. She wants Janet to be on the same level as the daughters of the doctors and the lawyers, the men who own the factories rather than the ones who work in them. It's part of hauling herself and Bobby up in the eyes of those that run the town. Bobby sees that and besides, they're both agreed that a girls' school would be preferable.

When Watson arrives Rena rings down to the kitchen and Alma enters a moment or two later with the silver coffee pot and some lovely little almond biscuits from a recipe of Ugo's.

'Mmm, these really are quite delicious,' Mr Watson says, brushing non-existent crumbs from his moustache as he helps himself to another. 'Melt in the mouth.'

'Very moreish,' Bobby says. 'My wife is too modest to say she made them herself.'

'Oh well, I have to keep my hand in. I'm pleased you like them, Mr Watson.'

They're good at this routine now. The Trust was so suspicious at first of paying Rena a separate salary, and these feminine touches reassure them. Not as much as accounts that are in the black, but it all helps.

'So,' Watson says, laying some papers in front of them. 'This is our main worry.'

Rena glances at the top sheet, sees straight away the Sun Inn, the Foxbar, the George. The three other hotels in town, all of which are licensed. 'Ah,' she says.

'Indeed,' Watson continues. 'And when you add to that forty-eight public houses and thirty-eight licensed grocers, it begins to look as if the town is awash with booze.'

'For heaven's sake,' Bobby says. Rena wonders how many of these establishments he has frequented during their marriage. Not least of the considerations of having a license is that it'd make him more likely to drink in the hotel itself. His own bar, a dream come true. She supposes she'd always have an eye there to make sure he didn't end up in a bad way again.

'It's one licensed premises for every six hundred and forty-seven residents of the town,' Watson says. 'Even taking into account that half of that number will be of the fairer sex, that doesn't seem too bad to me either, Mr Young. Whether the members of the burgh licensing court will see it that way is another matter.'

'Would you like some more coffee?' Rena says, holding up the pot. She can't help but wonder what difference one more license would make to the town's moral probity.

Bobby smiles. 'Well, we can't offer you anything stronger, can we?' he says.

Watson gestures towards his cup, and Rena pours. 'In the first instance, we are simply applying for a license to sell drink at social functions,' he says.

'And a social function is…' Bobby says.

'Open to interpretation,' Watson says. 'Rest assured, the Trust is behind you on this, Mr Young. In confidence, it is not its dream to be responsible for this hotel forever. A license might be the first step towards an amicable and mutually beneficial separation, if I may put it like that. Let nothing stand in the way of progress.'

'I'd drink to that,' Bobby says.

Rena imagines a day when there will be no leases to renew, no landlords holding anything over them. To think they had to put on their support for temperance when they viewed the place. Watson thanks them for the coffee and goes ahead to the court, and then Rena and Bobby walk down together. When they turn the corner into St Marnock Street Rena sees what Bobby was talking about. Men and women with placards, a dozen of them at least. She slips her arm into Bobby's. 'Who are they?'

He nods towards an embroidered banner strung along the courthouse railings. 'The Hurlford Tent of the Rechabites,' he says. 'We'll need to walk past them, I'm afraid, but with any luck they won't have a clue who we are.'

He takes her arm and leads her on. 'Bit rich, isn't it?' he says to one man holding a placard saying *Shame, shame, horror!*

'*Ye shall drink no wine, neither ye, nor your sons for ever,*' the man intones, through a missing front tooth. He's wearing a pretty embroidered sash around his neck, Rena notices, with gold fringe and a tassel.

'Aye well, each to his own,' Bobby says, and they go up the steps to the courthouse. An usher holds open the door for them and takes their names.

'Lively out there,' Bobby says.

'It is that.'

The tiled floor inside the courthouse is slippery under Rena's leather soles, and she wishes she hadn't worn her new shoes. They're really pinching now, after walking no more than the length of John Finnie Street. She holds the banister as they climb the marble stairs up to the small courtroom in which the meeting is to take place. 'Will they come in too?' she whispers to Bobby, who nods down the stairs to where the usher and another man are blocking the doorway. 'Only a limited number of interested parties allowed, and they won't want the disruption, I suppose.'

Sometimes – more often than she used to – Rena thinks back to the emergencies of her youth, to all those frantic sweeps she would make around the house to try and anticipate what might arouse her father's rage, to all her efforts to keep Thomas out of the way and Jamie quiet, or to stem her mother's tears. And when she does it's odd, because she doesn't remember panic. Her heart must have been pounding in her chest, but if it was, it was all anger. Rena can work with anger, she can use it to propel her to winkle Bobby out of a pub, or turn up on Gibson's doorstep. This is different. Maybe it's being in a courtroom again, for the first time since the divorce, but still, her breath feels short and her throat tight. Part of their future will be decided here, and there's nothing she can do but leave it to Watson to act as a lawyer, on behalf of the Trustees. She and Bobby take a seat together on the benches. She'd been imagining a proper court, with a judge in a wig, but of course it's nothing like that. Councillor Stoddart from the other end of the town is chairing, flanked by men in suits and men in dog collars, and a secretary taking notes. The secretary isn't the only one; there's a man with a reporter's notebook just along from Rena and Bobby. Please God he'll be writing up their success rather than another story about the Trust's financial straits.

When Watson is invited to lay out the reasons for the Trust's application, he explains that the hotel was established in 1885 with a total sum of £3000. 1885, Rena thinks, doesn't that cement us to this town? Less than half of that sum is left to the Trustees now, and money has to be found.

'The liquid assets of the hotel are low,' Watson says. 'If this license is not granted Kilmarnock will lose a hotel. The Trustees will not be able to carry on.'

The figures he showed Rena and Bobby are mentioned, all of those other public houses and grocers, the three licensed hotels (none of them a patch on the Ossington).

'And is there evidence of alcohol having been consumed on the premises historically?' That's Ferguson, the polis, who sits on the committee too. Rena feels Bobby sit forward slightly. A leading question. Ferguson has been at such functions himself, has he not? His face certainly has the florid aspect of a man who likes a whisky.

'To my knowledge,' Watson says, 'drink has been consumed at functions for the past fifty years. Indeed on some occasions, guests have taken too much drink.'

This gets a laugh. Everyone remembers the Knights of St Columba.

'In all seriousness,' he goes on, 'a license will allow greater control over consumption. The law is strict, as the Superintendent knows. Those who are inebriated cannot be served. Responsibility for that lies with Mr and Mrs Young, who so ably run the Ossington.'

Rena rubs her fingernails against the smooth leather of her handbag. She wishes they could speak.

'That's as may be,' says Reverend MacQuarrie. 'But we must take into account the public feeling represented by the petition we have in front of us, courtesy of my colleague Reverend MacLeod. If this license is granted, there will be no temperance hotel left in the town. Where will those who do not wish to associate with alcohol go?'

Watson turns to him. 'That is not the case, Reverend. The Ossington will still be under the auspices of a temperance trust. But it is vital to note that what we are talking about here is temperance. Not teetotalism, nor prohibition – heaven forbid – but temperance. Moderation, in other words. Moderation closely overseen by Mr and Mrs Young.'

Rena can't help it. She reaches for Bobby's hand. He

squeezes hers in return. Surely this is it? You can't argue with common sense and decency. The room is cleared while the court discusses the application. When they come out into the corridor Rena hears rain battering against the lantern light above them. The sky is a thick grey through the glass. She'd wanted some fresh air, in spite of the people with their placards, but instead she and Bobby sit on a bench in the entrance hall. He offers her a cigarette from the silver case she bought him.

'Where's Watson?' she says, leaning in towards Bobby's lighter.

'I don't know,' Bobby says. 'I think they have a special room up there,' he jabs his cigarette towards the stairs.

'I'm glad you never lost this,' Rena says, taking the lighter from him and tracing the engraving with her finger. *IJ & RY*. 'We've come a long way, haven't we?'

'And we've more in us yet.'

The usher calls them back to the room where, to Rena's dismay, Councillor Stoddart announces that the licensing court will take a fortnight adjournment to consider their decision.

Watson offers them a lift back to the hotel in his car. The rain is flowing down the gutters and a huge puddle has formed at the junction of Portland Road. Rena is glad not to be walking. These bloody shoes were a mistake. They go back into the lounge and sit down. She can hear the clink of plates and a low babble of conversation from the high tea service. Bobby pops into the office and comes back with a bottle of whisky. He pours them each a tot, and although Rena won't touch hers – nasty stuff and she hates the smell – she appreciates the sentiment when he raises his glass to the health and good sense of the licensing court. The lounge was to be a bar, that was the plan. She wanted to do it up in a modern style.

'So what now?' she asks. 'What does this mean?'

'Well, the picture isn't bleak, not by any account,' Mr Watson says, looking towards the door. Bobby jumps up and closes it, calling through to Alma that they've not to be disturbed.

'I managed to get a word with Chairman Stoddart in the recess. And I think you'll find that the court might be minded to be amenable, after the adjournment.'

'Well they might have been a bit more bloody amenable today,' Bobby says.

Watson swirls the whisky in his glass and takes a deep sniff. 'Black Label, am I right?' Bobby nods. 'Well, Stoddart is not unsympathetic, shall we say. Perhaps if spoken to personally. Informally, as it were.'

Bobby pours another tot of whisky in Watson's glass. 'And would that be a conversation better had by you, as representing the interests of the Trust?' he asks. Rena holds her hand over her glass, then pretends to sip at it when the men do. Typical, really. They've done everything above board, more or less, and now it comes down to the same thing as ever.

Watson shakes his head. 'Oh no, Mr Young. Keep the Trust in blissful ignorance. Better you make your own overtures.'

The 1960s

Janet, 1960

There is something birdlike about Auntie Evie, Janet thinks. Her Aunt Frances's feet are heavier on the ground, as she brings in the tea tray and returns a moment or two later with the Victoria sponge. She carries it as though it's made of lead, and Janet is sure her mother notices and will pass remark later if the cake is anything other than featherweight. Rena is fond of passing remarks about Aunt Frances. Evie darts around, pouring and handing out cups, as if she might fly away at any moment.

'Anyone for anything stronger?' Uncle James says, his hand on the door of the liquor cabinet.

Janet's father glances towards her mother, shakes his head, but Uncle Thomas, for whom perhaps the question is intended, says, 'I'll take a dram, Jamie, that's the boy.'

The sitting room of the Corporation villa stretches from the front to the back of the house, so that dining room and living room are combined. Nonetheless, Thomas seems cramped in it. The array of small ornaments clustered on the built-in fireplace and shelves leads

Janet to imagine a bull in a china shop. Crystal bells and baskets of pastel flowers stomped underfoot, milkmaids and little Dutch boys rendered limbless. James takes a modest whisky himself, hands a slightly larger one to his brother, and retrieves his cigarettes from the mantelpiece. He lights one and as an afterthought, offers the packet to Evie, who is leaning over the coffee table next to him, dropping sugar lumps in her tea. Splish, splash, splosh. Evie's sweet tooth drives her to walk for miles a day – into town, round the shops, up to Fenwick to visit her sister. On the couple of occasions that Janet has joined her aunt on these rambles her feet have been aching by the end, and once she had to pick Ricky up and take him back on the bus. 'His poor wee legs,' Evie said, sympathetically, handing over money for the fare before walking back herself. She shakes her head at James.

'Och, sorry Evie, I forgot,' James says, withdrawing the packet.

'Have you tongs?' Janet's mother asks, indicating the sugar bowl.

'No,' says Frances.

'She's never been a smoker,' Thomas says to James. There is an edge to his voice, as though this is a failing in his wife. Mind you, there is often an edge to Uncle Thomas's voice. Janet recalls her father saying that Thomas believes himself the only sane man in a world full of idiots.

'Oh well, remember those cocktail cigarettes,' Evie says to nobody in particular. 'They were awful pretty.'

Thomas snorts. 'Hardly proper fags though.'

Before long Evie is the only person in the room who isn't smoking, Janet aside of course. Janet can't imagine ever smoking. She hates the thick fug that marks every family visit, but then she doesn't really like the family visits either. She feels cheated, on this occasion, having expected her cousins to have been dragged along as well. Evelyn is attending a friend's birthday party, and Malcolm is at the cricket club, which sounds unlikely as he was always hopeless at Donkey. Frances's Labrador is sleeping in the kitchen, and perhaps if he wakes up Janet will be allowed to get Ricky out of the car and take both of the dogs for a walk on her own. Four-legged get out of jail free cards. Frances opens the window pointedly, although she is smoking too.

'So how are you getting on at school then?' Evie says, perching beside Janet on the couch. 'Evelyn and Malcolm say there's a sports day coming up. I like to see the races up in the big field. Lovely if you get the weather for it.'

Janet nods and tells Evie about her good marks for spelling, then emphasises her problems with sums just in case anyone thinks she's boasting.

'And you'll be off to the big school after the summer, won't you? They'll sort out your sums for you. All the way to Ayr too. Aren't you smart?'

Janet nods. She'd have liked to have gone to the same school as her cousins, but secretly hopes that her school will be like St Clare's in Enid Blyton. Although she's glad she'll come home to her nana every day rather than staying there at night.

'What we were going to tell you,' Rena says to Uncle James, 'is that they're going to release the last plot in Edzell Place. Isn't that right, Thomas?'

Thomas stirs himself. 'Same arrangement as before, if we get in now.'

'You wouldn't be next to us or Thomas, though,'

Rena says. 'It's at the main road end.'

'They need a quick sale.' Thomas has finished his whisky and is looking into his glass.

'So we can go up front between us, and you can pay us back,' Rena says.

Frances is standing behind James, her hand on his shoulder. Janet isn't sure how she'd feel about having her aunt as a neighbour, although she would be happy enough with the Labrador.

'Rena,' Uncle James says. 'We've settled where we are.'

Frances withdraws her hand and pulls her shoulders back. The gesture makes her bust look enormous and threatening under its orange sweater. 'My sister's just round the corner here, with her kids.'

'Well, that's what cars are for,' Rena says. 'It would hardly take you longer to drive to them.'

'You don't have to remind us that you loaned us the money for the motor.'

Now James turns to put his hand on his wife's arm. 'I don't think that's what Rena's saying, love.'

Frances folds her arms. 'That's exactly what she's saying.'

James sighs. 'Look Rena, it's a kind offer, it really is, but we don't want to move.' He pauses. 'Thank you though, for thinking about us. It's very generous.'

Frances glares at her husband. Janet's father has been standing at the window, leading Janet to hope that he might suddenly remember an errand and whisk her away. He's good at recognising itchy feet, and a too-fast drive somewhere followed by waiting in the car for him outside a shop or warehouse would be preferable to a family row. 'Just when we're talking about cars,' he says, 'how's that motor of yours running?'

James begins talking about engines and miles to the gallon and Evie asks Janet about her ballet lessons. Janet admits that she's given them up.

'No point,' Rena says, taking a cup of tea but rejecting a further slice of sponge when Frances offers it. 'They said she'll turn out too tall to make anything of it.'

'Do you know what would be good for you, Janet?' Evie says. 'Horse riding. I bet you'd like that, eh? You always used to love to see the milk float horse.'

'We'll see,' Rena says, with an ominous look.

'Och, even your Auntie Evie had a go on the cuddies. Imagine me perched way up on top of my father's Clydesdale.' Evie looks wistful, for a moment.

Janet knows that the farm was sold when Evie's father died. 'Like a lady in the circus?' she asks, to show an interest (which is a tricky balance, sometimes, with speaking when you're spoken to).

'Did I ever tell you that I could have gone on the stage?' Evie brightens up, and Janet nods in encouragement. She likes this story, and it is still easy to imagine Auntie Evie singing or dancing. She did so at new year, waltzing round the front room with Janet's father.

'Me and my girlfriend Isobel Jones saw the advertisement one day in the *Gazette*, and Izzy was such a good tap dancer, honestly, a regular wee Ginger Rogers. And I said to her that she should go for it, I'd come with her. And she said that she'd go for it if I entered as well.'

'And what did you say?' Janet asks, knowing the answer already.

'I said, what would I do? What would my talent be? And Izzy said that I should sing, and she'd teach me a wee dance routine, and besides, hadn't I just bought a new two-piece swimming costume? Thought I was the height of fashion, so I did.'

Where is Izzy now, Janet wants to ask. She likes the idea of the friendship, the conspiratorial giggling, and the girlishness that comes over Auntie Evie when she remembers it. Thomas watches his wife as she speaks. As Evie goes over the familiar story – the shoes she borrowed from her sister without asking, Izzy's permanent wave that made her look like Shirley Temple – Janet notices his cheeks turning ruddy. He is like a gouty uncle in a storybook, the unwilling recipient of orphaned relatives, who when provoked suffers apoplexy (whatever that means). In Janet's books these fictional uncles often reveal their long-suppressed pleasant side. Thomas stubs his cigarette out as though he is trying to annihilate it.

'Don't be so bloody stupid,' he says.

Evie stops speaking. Everyone stops speaking. Janet wishes she wasn't on the settee next to her aunt, and feels guilty for thinking this. Her father is over by the window with James. They don't move. The only person who moves is Rena, who finishes lighting her cigarette, as though she is watching a play on the television. Or a Christian being thrown to the lions, Janet thinks, recalling an illustration in her Bible Stories for Children.

Thomas harrumphs, although nobody had said anything to him. 'I'm just fed up with this bloody fairy tale,' he says. 'Audition my arse. Do you think they were really going to take anyone? Do you? From the open-air baths in bloody Prestwick?'

It's warm in the room, stuffy even, but Evie shivers as she takes a deep breath and says, 'Well, it was ENSA, and they advertised for people to audition…'

Thomas cuts her off with a sound that's halfway between a cough and a laugh. 'It was a morale boost. So folk could come and jeer at poofs making a show of themselves and silly tarts walking about in their swimming costumes. And there you were, first in bloody line.'

Each word seems to hit Evie like a slap, but she keeps going. 'It was an audition. They gave me their card. Call anytime, they said.'

Thomas laughs again, an ugly sound. 'Aye, I'll bet they did.'

'Thomas,' Rena's father says, but her mother makes a shushing noise. Frances stands up and says brightly, 'Evie, come and see the garden, before the rain comes on.'

'Yes, let's do that,' Evie says. She looks dazed. 'Is your sweet William out yet? It's my favourite.'

'James,' Rena snaps.

'What?'

'Why don't you go out and see the garden too, Janet?' her father says, sitting on the arm of the settee beside her. Now it's like a chess game, Janet thinks, although she hasn't yet mastered what knights and kings can do. Partly because her father doesn't have the patience for it. He played enough chess to last a lifetime when he was younger, he told her, and she has learned that he is a much safer bet at gin rummy and knockout whist.

As they walk through the kitchen and out the back door Frances puts her arm around Evie. The garden is grey and damp but Janet likes the way it is partitioned up, a communal drying green and a rectangle for each of the villas. It looks cosy, somehow, compared to the lawn at Edzell Place and the fence beyond which lies the vastness of the park. Evie and Frances lean over the waterlogged border of bedding plants.

'I came second in the bathing beauty contest,' Evie says, her voice stronger now she's outdoors. 'I've still got the card. They were from ENSA.'

Frances notices Janet and calls over, 'Such cheery flowers, aren't they, Janet?' It sounds like an accusation.

'Yes,' Janet says.

'I don't know when we'll get enough sun for your Livingston daisies to come out.' Evie runs her hands through her hair and smiles. 'And speaking of bright things, did I ever show you my old dresses, Janet? You might be old enough to fit into them now, for some dressing up. What do you think, Frances?'

Frances appraises Janet. 'You were always petite, Evie. She's filling out at some rate.'

Evie's waist might be the same size as one of Frances's thighs, it's hard to tell. How many Evies could you fit inside one Frances?

'Oh well, we'd better get back inside,' Evie says.

The atmosphere in the living room has changed. Rena has her coat on.

'Hurry up, Evie,' she says. 'We'll give you a lift.'

Evie blinks and Uncle James speaks more gently. 'Evie, Robert Fullarton rang me from down by the playing fields, looking for you or Thomas.'

Janet glances at her uncle, who is still sitting in the chair, whisky glass in hand. He's been topped up. When she looks back to her Aunt Evie she sees that all façade of cheer is gone. Evie's face is naked, vulnerable.

'Malcolm's fine, Evie, but he got hit on the head with a cricket ball. Knocked himself out and you've to get him checked for concussion.'

'I've rung the surgery, they're expecting us.' Rena

stands in front of the window, appearing bigger for a second with the light behind her. 'Meikle says we've to jump the queue.'

'Time he learned to take a bloody knock without greeting to his mother about it,' Thomas mutters, but nobody pays him any mind except Rena, who leans over and hisses, 'Pull yourself together.'

On the way to the doctor, Janet sits in the back of the car with Malcolm and Evie. It is hard now to imagine Evie on the stage, as she strokes her son's head and gives him a fresh handkerchief to press to his bloody nose, all the while murmuring at him not to worry. If Thomas is the apoplectic uncle from a storybook, she is the perfectly kind mother.

'I hate cricket, Mum.'

'That's all right, darling, you don't have to play it again.'

Malcolm sniffs. He is a bit of a cry-baby, especially as he's two years above her at school. Although she'd have liked to hear her own mother say the same about hockey. 'What about Dad?' he says.

'Just because your dad played it doesn't mean you have to.'

Malcolm lays his head on his mum's shoulder and closes his eyes. Evie turns to the window and Janet follows her gaze. They drive past the park where the aviaries are, past the rhododendrons that hide the cholera grave from long, long ago, and then past the big houses of Dundonald Road. Her mother is looking out the window now too.

'That's where Dalgleish the surgeon lives,' she says, pointing to a large detached house with steps up to the front door and crow-stepped gables. 'Mind we did the funeral tea for his mother?'

'Mmm.' Janet's father keeps his eyes on the road.

'Had to be watercress for the sandwiches. I mean, really.'

Janet had been lurking in the hotel kitchen that day, alternating between making herself useful and keeping out of the way of those who were working, according to her mother's whims. Sophisticated, that had been Rena's word for the sandwiches then. Vile, Alma said. Leaves in a sandwich indeed, what's wrong with fish paste? she'd asked Janet, who quite liked the bitter leaves, or at least the thick layer of salty butter that went with them.

They pass the manse and the English church and then Bobby twists round to check on Evie and Malcolm.

'Nearly there,' he says. 'Looks like you're going to have a couple of war wounds Malky, eh?'

The funny thing is, Janet can remember Thomas boasting: my Evie could have gone on the stage, she could've travelled the world. But she stayed with me, she stayed for love. That is the proper end of the story, after all, the answer to the inevitable question: why didn't you go and entertain the troops, Aunt Evie? Janet would never pass up the opportunity to travel the world. She spins the globe in the lounge and imagines all the places she could go one day. By the time of Evie's audition she had been out with Thomas three times while he was on leave. They'd gone to the dancing, and she'd been impressed by his tales of the Mediterranean and his fancy footwork. The next time he came back they got married. It was a real wartime romance.

Bobby, 1963

Rena's in a fishtail frock that sways lightly from side to side, caught in the current as she moves from lounge to kitchen and back again. He zipped it up for her earlier, in the bedroom she's had done out in cream and café au lait. Brown, it looks like, but who is he to argue? David Murphy must have been rubbing his hands together in glee when Rena walked through the doors of his furniture shop. Not that Bobby is complaining, about any of it. Standing here in a cashmere jumper, sipping Black Label from a crystal tumbler, his lovely wife smiling and laughing with their guests? The bedroom suite is cream melamine. He watched Rena sitting at the dressing table, powdering her pale skin and painting in her lips. It takes a little longer these days, but the effect is still there; marvellous how money counteracts the years.

Every inch the perfect hostess, she clicks open the silver cigarette box and offers it to Councillor Stoddart, now deputy head of the town planning committee. Bobby sees the man glance towards Rena's milky white décolletage, marvels that she can be so unknowing. What would be blatant in another woman is, just, Rena. Or is he the only one that knows the secret? It isn't a come on, because she couldn't care less. Stoddart leans over to light her cigarette. Bobby remembers bribing him for the license for the hotel. 'A donation for the Shortlees Boys' Club? How very kind,' Stoddart said as he peered into the brown envelope. 'And generous too.' Well, they'll have to stay in with him now that Rena's heart's set on them buying the hotel from the Trust.

'You take it from me, Mrs Young,' the councillor is saying. 'With these new developments there will be a lot of money to be made in this town. A lot.'

Shame that bastard Gibson's on the planning committee as well, Bobby thinks, as he saunters towards the hallway, wondering if he's imagining Rena's eyes sharp in his back. He pauses to smile at Tom Lauder, brushes past Evie, who doesn't quite realise how strong her drinks are. Her dress is tight brocade, a real headturner. She clasps his arm and whispers something; he sidesteps graciously. A compliment to Mrs Stoddart, and he's clear. A moment alone in the kitchen, looking out the window towards the shadowy mass of the park beyond. And oh, his hand has found the cool curve of the whisky bottle.

'Aye,' says Freddie MacConnechie behind him, by way of friendly greeting. Bobby smiles, reaches for the black rum instead.

'Coke, was it?'

'Aye,' says Freddie again. It must be a while since Freddie had to get his hands dirty – these days he concentrates on selling cars rather than fixing them – but he still has the slightly awkward aspect of a man more used to physical work than chit-chat and fine crystal. 'Grand wee night, Bobby. Grand wee night.'

Bobby smiles, splashes Coke into the rum. 'It's all

Rena's doing. I wouldn't know a canapé if it bit me on the arse.'

Freddie guffaws. 'Women, eh?'

'Aye.'

The small kitchen window is winking darkly at them. Freddie stares out. 'Handy to be so near the park.'

'Mmm,' Bobby says, following Freddie's gaze only to find it's turned towards him. Freddie's eyes are blue and there's a tiny twitch at the corner of one of them.

'Right there, eh?' he says, keeping his eyes on Bobby's and letting his hand gesture loosely back to the window.

Bobby gets it at last. 'Janet takes the dog round every day,' he says, in gentle deflection. 'I tell her to be careful, you never know what you'll come across in a park,' he adds, just to show he's a man of the world and that sort of thing doesn't bother him. When he was at sea, well, different storms, different ports. But that chapter of his life is closed.

When Freddie has gone Bobby's hand returns to the whisky bottle. There's a new ice bucket. He lifts it above his head to check it isn't bloody silver as well. They aren't made of money, not yet. Eschewing the tongs he dips his fingers in to retrieve a few slippery cubes before freshening his glass. On the rocks. Time to ring the changes. Freddie MacConnechie, well well. He'd tell Rena, but she'll only send him there to get his next motor and if things keep up, Bobby has his eye on a Jag. They need a license first though. As if on cue, he hears Rena's laugh tinkling above all the others in the lounge. If she doesn't care about sex, truly, he wishes sometimes she'd just… but no, Rena would never, and he loves her for that. And she's not daft. She knows you'll string someone along for longer on a promise.

There's a delicate hiccup. He sees Evie's reflection in the dark window, teetering towards him. He slugs his whisky, checks his smile is intact before turning. Rena would go mad, heels like those on the new linoleum.

'Evie,' he says, and for want of something better takes the empty glass from her hand. 'Another?' he offers, although he can hear Rena's voice in his head, telling him Evie's had enough.

'Yes please,' Evie says. She should have gone on the road with the ENSA boys and girls when she had the chance. That smile, those hips. A tiny wee thing, but she'd have brightened the troops no end. He remembers when they all went to Arran, not long after she married Thomas. A ruffled bikini at Lamlash. That, and the sunglasses; she looked like a movie star. Bobby supposes his brother-in-law must be behaving himself these days because Evie doesn't look cowed, far from it. Her eyes are outlined in turquoise, and her eyelashes are thick and black. A forest from one of those fairy tales Hetty used to read to Janet. Don't go in, he warns himself.

'Lovely party,' she says, with a slight slur. Glug, glug, glug, goes the liquor in her glass. He tops it up with lots of lemonade. 'Can I have a cherry?' she asks, pointing to the jar of maraschinos.

'Sure.' He spears one with a cocktail stick and drops it into her drink.

She fishes it out and catches a drip with her tongue. 'Oh Bobby, I think I'm a little tight,' she says.

'It's a party. We insist on it.'

She grins and pops the maraschino in her mouth, her lips pursing together as she chews.

'D'you remember, Bobby, that time in Arran?' she says, shyly.

He'd been thinking about the ruffled bikini, but there was more, wasn't there? Rena had to talk to Thomas and Jamie about family stuff, Margaret's will perhaps, and Frances was pregnant, napping every afternoon. So he and Evie were the spare wheels. Let's go for a spin, he said, with Rena's blessing. They went up the west coast of the island, stopped at a hotel for a drink, it was such a scorcher. Evie took a soda and lime, Bobby thought her innocence charming. Guessed what Thomas saw in her; pure as his mother and just as eager to please. They drove on to the next beach and looked at the waves, and the next thing Bobby knew she was saying let's go in. I don't have a costume, he said, coy in spite of the double he'd knocked back.

She'd been like something wild and weightless, running barefoot across the sand. He followed, of course he did, splashing in after her, ungainly until the water caught and carried him. They laughed and swam until the salt stung his lips and he felt freer than he had since his first voyage out, except he couldn't swim back then. Bad luck at sea. Nothing happened, nothing like that, but still he stopped the car in a passing place on the way back, combed his hair and gave Evie time to reapply her lipstick. There had been something final in the way she scrutinised herself in the mirror and snapped the sunshield back up, her face composed again. No need for either of them to say it. Don't tell Rena or Thomas. He'd have sorted Thomas out, put a stop to the beating, if Rena had let him. What kind of man hits his wife? As if in answer, Anne drifts through Bobby's mind on a wave of acrid breath and *Vol De Nuit*. If both parties are drunk is it a level playing field?

'Oh, we had fun back then, didn't we?' Evie says.

'Yes,' he says. 'I remember that time at Arran.'

Her makeup is heavier than it was that summer, that's the style now, and Evie has always liked to keep up with the style, but there's a slight blur to her edges. He looks down at his glass, at the bottle beside it. How much has he drunk, since that first whisky he laid down on the glass surface of the dressing table so he could pull the fabric of Rena's dress taut and do up her zip?

'Sometimes I wish,' Evie says, then smiles again. Neat white teeth, the tiniest gap between the front two. 'There's nothing wrong with fun, is there Bobby?'

'That depends,' he says, but it doesn't come out as he intended, with a hint of sternness.

'I adore these maraschinos,' she says. He's left the lid off the jar. She selects another one and her mouth forms a perfect O to receive it. The brocade of her dress is gold on blue. He can see where the hemline sits close against her legs, imagines his hand sandwiched between the rough of the brocade and the smooth of her nylon-clad thigh.

'I like what Rena's done with the kitchen,' she says, trailing her finger along the edge of the worktop. 'Funny to think we grew up with pantries and coal-fired ranges. On the farm, at least. I don't know how it was in the city.'

Miserable, he thinks, we'd have been glad of a bloody pantry. 'I forgot you grew up on a farm.'

She laughs. 'Can you imagine a more unlikely farmer's wife?'

'Did you go to the dances?'

'Oh aye. The Young Farmers were looking for something a bit broader of beam though.'

'And what were you looking for?' No, he thinks, no: she's married to Thomas, and so that's what she was looking for, that and their twins and their house next door. Just like he was looking for Rena, even when he was married to Anne.

'A wee bit more glamour,' she says, giving her eyelashes an exaggerated flutter. Her eyes pick up the blue from her dress and for a second it looks as if the irises have gold in them too.

He's been following her round the room as she glances at the cooker and the fridge, the food mixer and the twin tub. She stops at the sink, leans over to see better out of the window. What's out there tonight, he wonders? It's as if everyone's caught in the swell of something beyond the house, beyond the glass. He doesn't look though, because of the way that gold-on-blue brocade is stretching over her body, because of the way her eyes meet his in their mirror image in the darkened window. He moves closer, lets his hand drift towards her hip. Reflected in the glass, he could be half the age he is now.

'Oh for God's sake,' says Rena. Dread washes over him, chilling his skin like the cold sea off Arran. Not like this, he thinks. Don't let it happen like this, when I haven't even done anything. But no, it's as if he and Rena are in cahoots, working undercover towards the same end.

'Get her home, will you?'

All of a sudden he realises what it looks like: that Evie is feeling poorly, and he's standing by concerned.

'Yes,' he says firmly. 'I think that's for the best, eh Evie?'

Evie has dipped her head closer to the sink. He can see the nape of her neck. Her curls are looser at the back, and they're trembling with what might be laughter.

Rena sighs and begins to remove glass after glass of syllabub from the fridge. 'Come on. That's a new sink you know.'

Evie straightens up. 'My handbag,' she says, looking around and then teetering back out into the hall. Is she acting it up, now? She could have gone on the stage, she said.

'She's plastered,' he whispers in Rena's ear. 'Look, I'll walk her round the park. Sober her up before Thomas gets home.'

'Don't be ridiculous,' Rena says, sifting through the cutlery drawer and fishing out the small spoons. 'What if one of the neighbours saw?'

He nods, as if conceding the point. Yet Edzell Place is a cul-de-sac, their house and Thomas's at the end, the gate to the park between them. The neighbours would have to be standing in the middle of the road with flashlights to see him slipping into the darkness with Evie. Rena does it unconsciously, saving him from himself.

'Get her in the house and get a black coffee down her. I'll keep Thomas here. I'm not having him shouting the odds while we've got guests.'

'What about the twins?'

'Upstairs with Janet. They'll be fine.'

Is Rena a double agent, he wonders, and as she bustles out, her fishtail swaying behind her. How long has it been since he could take her by the hand, spin her round and into his arms? He grabs the Johnnie Walker and takes a mouthful straight from the bottle. Rena's back in a moment, herding Evie in front of her, her hand on her sister-in-law's arm. Evie's nails are painted powder pink, Rena's gleam from the chamois buffer. Is Evie exaggerating, or not? He'll know soon enough. Rena thrusts Evie's beaded clutch bag towards him and picks up the first tray of syllabub. Evie's come without a coat, being just next door. Chivalrous, he lays an arm across her shoulders as they walk up her driveway and round the back. She doesn't fumble at all as she turns the key in the back door. He wonders if the view from her kitchen window is the same, all dark.

Janet, 1963

Having done their turn at the party – handing round canapés, looking well brought up – the three cousins retreat to Janet's room. She catches sight of herself in the mirror of her dressing table. Her hair has been set just like her mother's, in large curls, though hers are light brown. She's wearing an ivory satin dress that she can't help feeling makes her look washed out now that her summer tan has faded. She looks ages with Malcolm and Evelyn. Older, given that Evelyn's just been to Morgenthaler's, where she saw Jean Shrimpton on the cover of a magazine. Her hair is now swingy, and she has a fringe. (Janet's mother disapproves of fringes.) Malcolm's hair has also been a source of banter, some of it good natured and some not, for the half-inch that's just beginning to curl towards his nape. His mother is his biggest ally, even against Uncle Thomas. It's the fashion now, she tells everyone. And you have to keep up with what's in, especially when you're young and handsome. This last comment accompanied by a chuck at Malcolm's cheek, if he's close enough.

Janet appraises Malcolm. She isn't sure if he is handsome. He's her cousin. She's seen him snivelling with a broken nose after being hit by a cricket ball, and wailing when expected to pee at the roadside on one of the holidays in Arran. Evelyn on the other hand is definitely pretty. She can do eyeliner (and is allowed to wear it), never gets spots, and has a natural kind of ease in the way she moves that makes the shift dress run up by Aunt Nell from a Simplicity pattern look like a fashion plate. They aren't very alike, for twins, which is probably a relief to both of them.

'Ugh,' Evelyn says, kicking off her sandals and sitting on the floor with her legs curled under her. 'I got stuck with Mr Sutherland earlier. He gives me the creeps. Does he you, Janet?'

'Yes. When I was about twelve we went to Peebles Hydro with him and his wife, and I spent the whole weekend trying to avoid him. He kept trying to get me to sit on his knee.'

'Ghastly,' Evelyn says. 'He looks exactly that type. And he brings his face so close when he speaks to you that you can smell his breath.'

The girls laugh. Malcolm opens up Janet's Dansette and leafs through a box of records he's brought with him.

'Well, I got stuck with Mr MacConnechie,' he says. 'He was nicer than that but desperate for me to come to his garage one Sunday so that he could show me how to take an engine apart. I said I wasn't that into cars and then your dad rescued me and put me to work making drinks.'

He pulls out an orange paper sleeve and holds it up to them. 'I bought it today,' he says. Janet just has time to catch a picture of three girls with big hair below the title 'Be My Baby' before he slips the disc from its sleeve.

'Mum asked me to play something modern earlier,' he says. 'I didn't.'

Evelyn smiles. 'I think Mum's been at the Cointreau and lemonade.'

'Aha,' Malcolm says. 'Look what I've got.'

Janet hadn't quite noticed that he'd brought a bottle of something from downstairs.

'Are you allowed, Janet?' Evelyn asks.

'Of course she is,' Malcolm says. 'She's fifteen.'

When I was your age I was up at four every morning... One of her mother's refrains. Evelyn produces three glasses from behind her back. Janet feels shy of her cousins sometimes, despite all the family holidays and dens and hiding away from rows together. Not because they're almost eighteen, but because they're twins and wrapped up in one another. Malcolm pours and Evelyn hands her a glass. There's a scratching at the door and Janet jumps up to let Ricky in. He isn't usually allowed in the bedroom but she was warned to take him away if he started getting under people's feet.

'Hey,' Evelyn says, rubbing behind his ears. He wags his little tail so enthusiastically that his whole body follows it, then rolls over to have his tummy tickled. 'Have you had enough as well, Ricky? You're a good old boy, aren't you?'

The needle catches and the music starts. Malcolm turns the volume down. It feels more illicit like that. Sometimes Janet has to lean close to catch the words.

'Can I tell you a secret?' Malcolm says.

Janet nods. She feels older, sipping at her drink (whatever it is tastes sweet, and warm). Or perhaps they all seem younger, now that they've escaped the party and their best behaviour and are sitting on the carpet together.

'I'm going to go to the art school. In October.'

Evelyn smooths the sleeve of his shirt, an oddly maternal gesture. 'It's very hard to get in.'

He nods. 'Mr Patterson helped me with my portfolio. I worked on it every day after school.'

'That's great,' Janet says. 'It'll be… another world.'

He nods, serious. 'Yes. That's it exactly.' He looks down at the carpet, traces a pale squiggle amid the blotchy brown design with his index finger.

'I can't wait to leave school. I hate it.'

'Hasn't it got any better?' Evelyn says.

Janet shrugs. 'You met them, didn't you, at that awful birthday party Mum made me have, just so that she could meet some of their parents.'

'They were dreadful,' Evelyn says. 'Although I felt a bit sorry for some of them. That girl from Burma, was it? And the one whose parents were in South America.'

'Oh, they're all right,' Janet says. 'They even got left there for Christmas last year, along with Margie Dodd, and her parents are just in England.' A thought strikes and comes out of her mouth before she can suppress it. 'What does Uncle Thomas say, about the art school?'

Malcolm and Evelyn exchange glances. 'We're not going to tell him,' she says.

'Mum knows,' Malcolm explains. 'Well, I've mentioned it to her. As a kind of outside possibility.'

'She'd be happy whatever you did,' Evelyn says, smiling. 'You're her golden boy.'

'And something's different, about Dad. He isn't as cross. Maybe it'll be okay.'

It's true. Uncle Thomas has the same temper as always, but he doesn't show it as much. He doesn't take it out on Evie any more. He bottles it up and cuts hedges in the garden until he's red in the face and sweating or, like tonight, he slumps into a glass of whisky. Janet wonders if it is because Malcolm is older, and bigger. Closer to being a man himself. Or could her mum have something to do with it? Everything is meant to be perfect now, with the hotel, and the house, and the smart people who have come to the party tonight. Marital discord is not perfect. *Let me in, Rena, I can't stand it. Please let me in.* Janet isn't sure if she dreamt it now, Evie coming to the kitchen door that time.

'Not tell him ever? But…'

'Oh no,' Evelyn says. 'We will tell him, just not yet.'

'Not until I've started,' Malcolm says. 'Matriculated and been to my first classes. Then it'll be too late.'

'Too embarrassing to make a scene,' Evelyn says. Janet doesn't want to mention that for all her family care about what people think, very little seems to stop them making a scene.

'Oh God, we're going to have to take him home later, aren't we?' Malcolm says.

'Both of them,' Evelyn sighs. 'Can you stand it?' she asks her brother. 'If he has a go at you, I mean.'

'Hmm,' Malcolm says. 'Is your mum on any pills, Janet?'

'What do you mean?'

'Let's go and have a look.'

Janet follows him to the bathroom where they look in the cabinet above the sink. Malcolm shifts the codeine linctus and milk of magnesia, checking behind them.

'What are you looking for?' Janet asks.

'Oh, just leave it Malcolm,' Evelyn says. 'It'll be okay. I'll take him and we'll say you're helping clear up or something.'

'I suppose so. Unless…' he leaves the bathroom and goes to the door of Rena's bedroom. Even Janet doesn't go in there that often, although sometimes she watches her mother get ready for functions at the hotel, if Rena needs a hand with her zip or buttoning her gloves. She likes these times together, when the focus is elsewhere, on the evening ahead. When her mother reminds her of a movie star. Some people look awkward in their finery, walk differently in their higher heels. Janet's mother hits her stride.

'Malcolm,' Janet says. 'What if someone comes?'

They can hear laughter rising above the babble of talk, and underneath it all a tinkle of music, Frank Sinatra maybe. Her father loves that kind of music, although of course he doesn't admit it. He buys the records as gifts for Rena, who couldn't care less. Men are allowed to sing Burns on the 25th of January, or mumble hymns in church, but that's about it. Apart from Malcolm, but he's younger.

'Okay,' Malcolm says, after they've stood frozen at the top of the stairs for a moment. 'You and Lynnie go back and wait on me. I'll only be a mo.'

'What's he looking for?' Janet asks Evelyn, when they're back in the bedroom. Her mother does take tablets, she knows. Sometimes Janet fetches them for her. To help her sleep, usually, or sometimes in the morning or before a function at the hotel.

'Oh, Janet,' Evelyn says, reaching out and clasping Janet's hands in her own. 'I'm so pleased for him and I'm going to miss him so much.'

'But he'll be at home, won't he? I mean, I know there'll be evening things, but not every night. And weekends.'

Evelyn tops up their glasses. 'That's the thing though. That's what he hasn't told Mum. He wants to go into digs there. He wants to leave home.'

Ricky runs up to the door just before Malcolm opens it. 'Bingo,' he says, holding out his hand. Several white and blue tablets are nestling in his palm. 'Only a couple of each,' he says. 'She'll never notice.'

Don't be so sure, Janet thinks. Her mother notices everything. But they have a houseful of people, and there will be some way around it if she does. Malcolm swallows two of the blue tablets and tucks the rest in his pocket. 'There,' he says. 'That'll make it easier later on. I won't rise to any bait tonight, Lynnie.'

Evelyn sighs. 'Honestly, I don't know why they give women these things when it's their husbands that cause the problems.'

'Ha,' Malcolm says. 'You're right. We should grind them up and slip them in Dad's tea.'

'What will you do at art school?' Janet asks. It's a vague kind of concept to her. Rows of young men with hair like Malcolm's sitting in front of rows of green glass bottles with flowers in, and Mrs Nimmo the art mistress from school, with her frizzy hair, walking around and pointing at their still life watercolours with her stick. Malcolm tells her about life drawing and the famous teachers and the studios in a strange building at the top of a hill.

'Oh, and dances of course, and film screenings, and happenings. All of that.'

'Are there girls? Woman artists, I mean,' Janet says, feeling a blush start at her ears and spread forward over her cheeks.

'Yes of course, it's mixed. Teachers and students. Any kind of girl you could want, if that's your bag.'

Malcolm has been trying out more slang. It doesn't always sound right, but Janet supposes it's a prerequisite for his flight to the city, to new people with new ways of speaking.

'You look glum, Lynnie,' he says.

Evelyn sits up and shakes herself. 'It's only up the road really, isn't it? Not the other side of the Atlantic.'

Malcolm laughs and takes her hand. 'And you're the only girl for me,' he says.

Evelyn smiles and says, 'Let's have another record before we have to go and do our duty. How about Bob Dylan, Malcolm? A nice sad song for the end of the evening.'

Malcolm finds his Bob Dylan records and Evelyn selects one song then another. Ricky is a useful early warning system, springing to his feet and cocking an ear so that glasses and bottle can be hidden before Janet's mother arrives to tell Malcolm to get his father home. Rena wouldn't knock, not in her own house. Nor any of her family's.

Janet looks out of her bedroom window and sees Evelyn spring ahead, the flash of house keys in her hand. Malcolm walks behind and to the side of Thomas, as if he's herding a large and unpredictable animal. At one point he takes his father's arm but Thomas shoves him away. Janet can't hear what he says, but she sees the way Malcolm's posture changes, as though something heavy has been thrust onto his back. Evelyn comes over and coaxes Thomas along. Where's Aunt Evie, she wonders? Janet has never really admitted that she dislikes her uncle; you're not allowed to dislike family, or perhaps liking doesn't count for much given that *blood is thicker than water*. She thinks of the photograph of Thomas that sits in the lounge, under the lamp made from a porcelain vase. Sitting in uniform, gazing into the distance beyond the frame, hat at an angle that belies gravity. He is young, not far from the age Malcolm is now, hair and moustache as dark as can be, eyes bright and kind.

Bobby, 1964

Here he is, new suit, new tie. Strolling into a bar, no change there, but what's the difference tonight? It's his bar. He is the publican. His name is on the license, Robert Young (alongside Rena's, of course). The Trust has signed the hotel over to them in its entirety, money has changed hands, and tomorrow he will be nipping round to Lauder's to collect the brass plaque they're having engraved for the door. And given the hotel is no longer owned by a temperance trust, non-residents are welcome in its bar up until ten o'clock. And after that, as guests of those who are residents. Nothing crazy, nothing like those dives he used to frequent – well, how could it be? The place has class. The polis pop in when they come off shift, sometimes before. It's a cocktail bar, according to Rena, who is entirely responsible for the peach-swagged pelmets and the wall-lights, the zig-zag inlaid veneer.

'Can I get you anything, Uncle Robert?' Evelyn is behind the bar, washing glasses and wearing a high-necked shift dress that matches the silky blue wallpaper. Keep it in the family when you can, that's fair enough.

Helps that she has turned into a looker, if a bit on the skinny side, and that she keeps it spotless. No beer slops on the counter, no dust on the shelves, and she's wiped the tables already. He looks at his watch and savours the feeling of having a choice. He could step away, and it wouldn't be a problem.

'Just a small one then,' he agrees, and sighs. Who's he fooling? Evelyn has seen him at parties over the years, like that one at the house after which he walked her mother home. Nothing's been said, and Evie has been just the same as ever with him. He wonders if it's possible he could have dreamt it, hallucinated even. Wishes that was the case, because what was he thinking? In his own backyard. The risk of it makes him feel sick to his stomach.

Evelyn places a paper napkin in front of him, sits his glass of whisky on top of it and nudges the water jug closer. Johnnie Walker branded, of course. The ashtrays and the jugs, all pale blue with the man himself striding across them. Bobby drops in two ice cubes instead, lights a cigarette. He's down to twenty a day, give or take, on account of shortness of breath, even though Meikle is sceptical about the report linking smoking to cancer. The tightness is just another legacy of those damp years at sea. There are a couple of residents in the bar. A travelling salesman drinking alone at a table, reading his newspaper. Regular enough customer, through every month or two. And the husband from a couple breaking their journey back to Inverness from Carlisle. Bobby avoids his eye. Don't talk to strangers, that's what they tell Janet, and he doesn't want to get caught up. The door springs open and he hears Evelyn say, 'I'm sorry, sir, it's residents only after ten.'

There's a familiar cast to the man's walk that Bobby

catches in the mirror, and when he turns to look he sees that the latecomer is the slouching figure of Roderick Blair. He's been absent from the card game for a while; other fish to fry with his titled pals, Bobby assumed. Blair's had a drink already, Bobby can tell, but he's clearly in the mood to be discreet.

'It's all right, Evelyn. Mr Blair is my guest. Serve him what he wants.'

Blair indicates that he'll have the same as Bobby, helps himself to ice cubes from the bucket. The husband from Inverness recognises that three will be a crowd, drains his beer and says goodnight.

'I hope you and your wife have a good journey tomorrow,' Evelyn says.

She does add a bit of charm to the place, Bobby has to admit. 'Evelyn, that's you finished up for tonight,' he says. She nods gently towards the travelling salesman. 'Don't worry,' he tells her. 'I'll mind the bar and lock up. Or do you need a lift up the road?'

Blair is swirling the unmelted cubes around his now drained glass, cowlick of light hair twisting over his forehead. Bobby can feel his agitation.

'No, it's okay. Thanks, Uncle Robert,' Evelyn says. 'Malcolm's coming by to get me. He's probably outside already.'

'All right then love, safe home.'

She leaves, and the travelling salesman stays engrossed in his paper. Blair edges closer to Bobby.

'Long time no see,' Bobby says, noncommittally.

'Wouldn't mind a word with you, actually,' Blair says, and Bobby nods, slipping behind the bar to pour another half pint for the salesman. Blair takes another whisky.

'We were up at your place last week, as it happens,'

Bobby says. 'Old Sid let Rena and Janet go round and pick rasps. The garden's looking good.'

Blair's expression suggests that he doesn't give a toss about gardens, whether he's due to inherit acres of them or not. 'Looks as if I'll be spending more time there. Thanks to my father.'

'It's a beautiful spot.'

'Ha. No fool like an old fool, isn't that what they say? Daresay it'll be in the rags soon enough.'

There are rumours about Roderick Blair's father. Par for the course when a titled man marries a very untitled Vogue model. Bobby couldn't say, neither of those are circles he's ever moved in, but even he has overheard a tall tale or two. Eventually the salesman drinks up and retires, and Bobby freshens their glasses and says, 'So what's on your mind then?' He won't call him Mr Blair, certainly not the Honourable, but somehow he thinks using Roderick's Christian name isn't quite the done thing.

'Find myself in a bit of a tight spot,' Blair says, gazing morosely into his glass. 'Owe a couple of fellows some money and my plan for paying them back has been… disrupted.'

Bobby takes a sip of his drink, and wishes that he hadn't had another, and that Blair wasn't telling him this. Three questions run through his mind. He starts with the obvious:

'What kind of fellows, and how much money?'

Blair hesitates and then blurts. 'Got into another card game, you see. Not with Caldera and Ferguson. In the city.'

'I see,' Bobby says. When he used to play cards with the Yanks he or one of the boys would ask *are you in?* or *stick?* and they'd answer *Geez, that's the $64,000 question.* And now Blair has got into trouble and the question that will either win or lose the money is the obvious one. 'Can I ask why you're telling me this?'

It turns out that Bobby is the only person Blair knows who might be on his side, who might know people able to help him, might know of a game where he can win enough to…

'Hold it right there,' Bobby says. 'Card games got you into this, and I'd be lying if I told you that there's a snowflake's chance in Hell that they'll get you out of it.'

Advice is better requested than volunteered, so Bobby shuts up after that and lets Blair brood over his drink for a while. The salesman nods goodnight and slopes off to his room, and Bobby clicks off the switch for the wall lights so that only the bar itself is left illuminated.

'You're right, Young, I know you are. I'm going to have to sell off some land, and there's little enough in my name just now.'

It's hard to feel sorry for the man but Bobby has been in some tight spots himself. Everyone has their limits, even if he can't imagine there's much of a choice between flogging off a few fields and having your knees broken. And if Blair owes some city boys over cards, he'll be lucky if they stop at the knees.

'Well, that sounds like a plan,' he says. Blair's glass is almost empty, and Bobby'll be damned if he's giving him another drink on the house. No point in making enemies though, so he pats him on the back and says, 'Let me know how it works out, eh? Let me know if there's anything I can do.'

Bobby doesn't feel like drinking after Blair has gone. He locks the front door of the hotel then goes back into the bar to wash their glasses and put them away. He throws the salesman's newspaper in the bin and wipes over the counter so that it will be perfect for Evelyn the next day. His own bar. He and Rena have the hotel and the hotel has a liquor license. They have everything they've worked for or else it's as good as in the bag. If Roderick Blair has money worries, it isn't Bobby's problem.

Two days later a similar scenario plays out. They've had a meeting in the function room, the Rotary, and Bobby always likes to be around for that. A talk about hypnosis, of all things, but there's no harm in a bit of backslapping; Rena has had wedding brochures printed up that she wants distributing. Their name on the front: *Proprietors R & I Young. Phone Kil. 21400. All arrangements can be made here regarding bridescake, refreshments, band and photographer. We give advice regarding menus and generally undertake all arrangements to ensure that everything goes smoothly on such an important day.* Bobby finds it droll, that he's the man handing the brochure to anyone whose daughter might be of age. His own wedding days have not been a success, although Anne has grown distant recently, and isn't that as it should be? She was part of a previous life. A life in which he didn't use a silver cigarette case, a life in which he wasn't the proprietor of anything. Thank the Lord Rena has stuck with him even when he's come close to fucking it up.

He singles out Tulloch from the carpet factory first. His daughter is only seventeen but she's pretty and has a reputation for running around town; he's seen her out with Thomas's kids and wondered if she might sway towards Malcolm, but she strikes him as a bit too worldly for that. Malcolm is going to need someone more inexperienced. Someone who'll save herself for marriage before receiving the unlooked-for wedding present that her duties will be modest. Thomas doesn't know about Malcolm, or if he does he isn't saying. Maybe it's just a phase, like the long hair, but either way, Malcolm himself is the soul of discretion. Just as well, given Rena's obsession with appearances, and keeping them up. Just in case, she's tasked Bobby with checking out every coffee bar that their nephew and niece might take Janet to. He has an eye for undesirables, that's true enough.

'Ah no,' Tulloch says. 'Our wee Brenda is still too young to be thinking of courting. She's only just moved from horses to folk music.'

You can't be too careful, Bobby wants to say. Don't you remember yourself at their age? Simm the veterinarian takes a brochure though; his wife's niece is engaged, and Bobby offloads a couple more.

'My wife is wedding daft,' he explains. 'Honestly, I'm getting worried she might divorce me just so that she can do it all over again!'

It's true, Rena loves it. It's as if she's in the starring role rather than the betrothed, sitting with the mother of the bride, explaining toasts and planning centrepieces. He can't tell if it's down to a romantic nature or the fact that the price they can charge for everything goes up when it's a wedding. If there's one quality Rena has in common with Anne, God forbid, it's that her taste is more for gifts that will last until a rainy day than fripperies like flowers and chocolates. But there were lots of rainy days for Anne – he'll never forget the shame of getting her wedding ring from the pawn – and Rena hasn't taken off the eternity ring he bought from Min to celebrate them taking over the hotel from the Trust. Bobby rather likes having his wife wear diamonds, he's discovered, so everybody's happy.

Except for Roderick Blair, turning up in the bar again. Some of the Rotary members are still there, having a nightcap. Tulloch corners Blair to explain that they'll be seeking donations for the blind for their Christmas drive. Bobby could have told him not to bother, but Blair nods and says they should be in touch, he and his wife would be delighted. The Rotary men are in no hurry to go so he excuses himself, says he was just popping in for a nightcap on his way back from visiting a friend outside Ayr. Bobby holds the door open for him, giving Blair a chance to whisper, 'I need to talk to you.'

Bobby indicates the bar, the men gathered there. They're not leaving any time soon and so he can't either. For a second the desperation he saw in Blair earlier in the week flashes back.

'All right. Kitchen door in the lane, five minutes,' Bobby says, then louder, 'Goodnight.'

What's he thinking, Bobby wonders, when he hurries down to the back door of the hotel on pretence of changing a keg. It opens onto the lane where Rena sat in the car with Thomas that night, thinking he was having an affair. Well, she needn't worry about that. The last thing he's ever wanted is another relationship. Anything he's done with another woman has meant less than nothing. Evie was a mistake, a reminder not to get too cocky. Not to seek out excitement just for the sake of it. Just because things are going well doesn't mean he's invincible. Which he should remind himself of now, casting his eye down the lane to see if Blair is waiting for him or if he has sensibly gone home and forgotten all about whatever it is he wants to talk to Bobby about.

There's a sheen of ice on the cobbles and the air is chill and misty, clear apart from a tang of fresh cigarette smoke. The muffled sound of remonstration on the main road drifts down the steps and along the lane towards Bobby. A punter unwilling to leave the Fifty Waistcoats, perhaps. He steps down into the lane and Blair draws away from the wall and pulls his coat tight around himself.

'I did it. Sold the land.'

'That was fast.'

Blair makes a harrumphing noise. 'Well, the Dean estate manager's been at our heels for years. Always ready to take a few acres off our hands.'

Bobby nods. There's something going on there, but it's not something he can understand, having been born in a damp and overcrowded tenement and working his arse off to get where he is now. 'So you're sorted out.'

'That's the thing. It bought me some time but it isn't enough.'

'I can imagine,' Bobby says, drily. 'The interest.'

'But listen, because I can sort it out. I've the title deeds to some of the land in the town, and with a bit of ready cash, I could be up to my oxters in the development.'

Bobby nods. He's heard murmurings from councillors about new roads, and some of the Rotarians have been talking about the slums in Boyd Lane and Soulis Street, how they could be improved. Blair has fallen silent but is looking at him intently. Bobby nods back towards the hotel, the light puddling onto the steps from the kitchen. 'I need to get back inside.'

'This isn't a game of cards, Bobby, this is a sure thing.'

'I've heard that before.'

'You'd be buying into an investment. Your money would come back double, I can promise you. I'm going to know in advance who'll get the tenders, so all I need to do is make sure I've the right shares in the right places.'

'Things are going well for me. They're going smoothly.' And you've told me you're skint, Bobby thinks, and I know you can't stay away from the poker table.

'They can always go better, you know that. You're an ambitious man.'

'The deeds. Can't you invest the proceeds?'

'It's the timing of the thing.'

Bobby's getting impatient now. He wants to leave this dank street and go home to his house and his wife. 'Well. Just sell the land and get your money that way.'

Blair waves his hand dismissively. 'Might make more sense to lease it. Play the long game.'

Bloody typical, Bobby thinks. That's precisely how the rich get richer. He looks at his watch. 'I'm sorry...'

'Look, Bobby,' Blair catches his arm. 'The estate manager was telling me, de Walden's bringing his family for a house party for the September race weekend. They've started sprucing the place up already.'

'So?'

'So I know de Walden. I like the horses, my father used to run a couple. Beat his Derby winner once, as it happens. They're going to make a splash. Entertainments for all the tenants, a big dinner. It's going to be quite a show.'

A circus then, to remind everyone who owns the farms and cottages, the quarry where so many people work, what side the bread is buttered on. But Bobby's mind is working. Circuses need tents, don't they, and someone has to provide the bread.

'His commissioner is coming up next week to see caterers and venues. They're thinking of the Grand Hall, maybe bringing someone in from Ayr. But why would they, when there's a hotel right here?'

Bobby thinks of Rena, what she'd say if he let this slip through the net.

'All it needs is for someone to put a word in. Let me do that for you, Bobby, eh?'

It's late and it's cold, and what can Bobby do but nod? As he locks up he thinks about Victor Caldera, about his friends and his favours, and where he is now. Happy as Larry (or maybe they say Luigi over there). Knowing that time passes, and it's up to you to get where you want to be.

Rena, 1965

The hotel has never looked so glorious. Nothing in this town has ever looked so glorious, or at least Rena has never seen anything to match it in her life. The tables blaze with the light from silver candelabra, specially sent from His Lordship's London house. The tenantry was entertained last week in the Grand Hall, and Rena and Bobby catered high tea for all three hundred guests, plus a late service of cake and ice cream. Janet was allowed to come in and help at the buffet so that she could see the magic show by Davallen (though Bobby was the one who was captivated, right at the front and marvelling at every sleight of hand), and everyone cheered and clapped when his Lordship's daughter – the Honourable Hazel Scott Ellis – was duly presented with two silver entrée dishes by the estate manager on account of her coming-of-age. There hadn't been such a party since 1907, apparently. And as far as she knows, there's never been a dinner like this. And the Ossington chosen to host it, proof positive that they're the best hotel in town. She stands at the back of the function room – and yes, tonight, bedecked in flowers, it can surely be called a banqueting hall – and looks at the guests, the guests who are right now being photographed for the newspaper. The newspaper that Rena used to cycle to deliver to the castle where Lord Howard de Walden is now in residence with his family, because he has horses running at Ayr. And wasn't Bobby clever, thinking to get the menus and the flowers done in apricot and gold to match his silks; already that's raised a smile and made her swell with pride.

Rena folds her hands across her stomach for a second and steadies her breathing. She's the caterer, in her own version of black and whites – black silk velvet and a double string of pearls – but she is in the same room as those people whose tradesman's door she stood at every week, waiting to be paid. Flash, and the first photo is taken: His Lordship and the Provost. Flash: the Sheriff and his magistrates. Flash: the Chief Constable and the town clerk. Flash: the chairman of the football club and the group captain from the airport. Everybody is here, everybody who is anybody in this town, all under her roof. This, surely, is what she has hoped for.

She nods towards Bobby to make sure the champagne is poured, and goes to check on Ugo and his team. The girls are lined up in the corridor, waiting for the signal to take the starters out. Two per table; it's worth the extra investment to make sure that nobody is left waiting for their melon glacé, and when she looks in on the kitchen Ugo is checking that every serving is garnished with a sprig of mint and ready to go. She looks at her watch. His Lordship isn't known for standing too much on ceremony but the Provost might go on. Provosts do. Ugo doesn't risk a smile just yet but he gives her the thumbs up. They spent a few happy hours in the kitchen together, drinking coffee and planning this menu. He might be Italian but he speaks French, and Rena has learned enough about food to know that if there are silver candlesticks then it ought to be cordon bleu all the way. He translated from his *Larousse Gastronomique* and she figured out what would strike the right balance between sophisticated and good plain food. 'That will be eminently suitable,' wrote His Lordship's commissioner, noting that wine would be sent from the castle's cellar but any champagne could be served on arrival providing it was non-vintage. Rena insisted on coming to the wine merchant with Bobby for that.

'Pray silence for grace by the Reverend Arthur Howie,' says the toastmaster, and for a second Rena recalls the reverend florid and bellowing the Selkirk Grace at the Burns Supper earlier that year. But no, he pitches it perfectly and even manages to modulate his accent for the benefit of the guests from England and Her Ladyship's foreign ears.

The meal is like a ballet. No plates clattered or glasses smashed, no collisions between staff. Starter plates are removed from all tables before the fish comes out, fish plates vanish before the *filets de boeuf Maître d'Hôtel* is laid down. Some of the council folk will never have had a meal like this in their lives, and all by the munificence of His Lordship and the Ossington Hotel. Side dishes fly by; *chou fleur a la Milanaise, carottes Vichy*, jellied beetroot, and two kinds of potato. And still the candles burn and the silver sparkles and Rena couldn't feel fuller if she was eating it herself. Her Ladyship has finished both fish and meat, in spite of her slimness, and His Lordship has waved a girl over to spoon more *pommes purée* onto his plate.

Alma, entrusted with the top table, stops to whisper delightedly to Rena that the leader of the council's wife has been flummoxed by the French and is asking what *betterave* is. Alma who didn't have a word of French herself until she saw this menu but is now almost as proud as Rena of what they've accomplished (and almost as scathing of the leader of the council's wife, with her put-on airs and graces). Nobody tonight is going to mutter that the Youngs have got above themselves.

After *Ossington Suprême*, an invention of Ugo's involving ice cream and meringue, there's cheese and fruit, and then the coffee is poured (*café noir*, Rena put on the menu, but there are jugs of cream for those who want it) and the petit fours presented and the toastmaster calls out 'Pray silence' again. The staff has been primed but several of the senior officials have enthusiastically drained their whiskies and Rena only just manages to grab a bottle from one of the girls and swoop by in time for His Lordship getting to his feet and raising his glass.

'The Queen.'

'The Queen!' echoes round the room and Rena wonders if she and Bobby should have taken the toast too. On the other side of the room he's pouring drinks for the newspaper reporter and photographer, who've been given supper in the bar. She'll need to make sure they get menus to take away, they'll never remember all the details without it written down.

The speeches go well, with His Lordship praising the town and its industry and the Provost being gracious but making a joke about His Lordship's lack of luck at the races, before saying how well the estates are managed, how much their cooperation is valued. *Long may it continue in the interest of the future development of the town.* The Provost ends by congratulating Hazel on her coming-of-age and yet another toast is insisted upon before the Dean house party gather themselves to leave. *Wha's like us? Gey few and they're a' deid.* They are followed closely by the rest of the top table. It said carriages at ten thirty on the invitation, and it's twenty-five past on the dot.

'A tremendous evening, thank you for your hospitality,' His Lordship says to her in the hallway, as coats and furs are brought from the cloakroom. She tells him it's been an honour, and their pleasure, and plucks up the courage – and she knows it's gauche but she must – to ask the party to sign one of the menu cards. They take turns to do so in pencil, pen and ink. She stands in the doorway and watches the chauffeurs leap out to hold open doors and settle blankets over knees, waves goodnight as they round the corner and head back to the castle that's fifteen minutes' walk from the flat that she and Hetty and the boys squashed themselves into when they came here.

When she and Bobby are done standing on the doorstep shaking hands and saying farewells, and all the guests have gone, full and radiant with wine, they go back into the hall and check that the tables have been cleared. Alma has sent the girls home already, no gratuities from the guests of course, as they've been treated themselves, but Rena added ten percent to the bill as she would for a wedding and there was no complaint, so they'll have extra in their envelopes at the end of the week. As will Ugo and the kitchen staff, who are clattering away downstairs. Rena and Bobby walk around the room extinguishing all the candles so that His Lordship's man can come and collect the silver the next day. The flowers are to go to the infirmary, and God knows the wards there need some brightening, but she gives one setting to Alma and plans to take another herself as a souvenir.

'Not that one,' she finds herself calling to Bobby, who has reached the top table. 'Not yet. Let's just leave it, for a moment.'

He smiles at her and he looks so debonair, in his dinner suit. So polished, and sober. She walks over and sits on one of the chairs. They're a little jumbled now, so it might have been where His Lordship's wife sat, or his daughter, or the wife of the Provost. Bobby hands her a cigarette from his case and puts his hand out to stop her lighting it from one of the candles.

'Bad luck,' he says. 'We used to say that every time someone does that a sailor dies.'

He flicks his lighter open, the one she gave him all those years ago. *IJ & RY.* 'Look, Rena, there's champagne unopened. It isn't to be accounted for. Will you have a drink with me?'

She nods, because she wants to taste a little of what her guests did, and because although her feet and legs are aching she still feels excitement bubbling up inside. On the table in front of her she has one of the apricot-coloured menu cards, and on the cover of that, all around the gold crest of the estate and its family, are the names of her top table guests.

'What's that?' Bobby says, handing her a glass. She pushes it towards him but first he looks her in the eye. 'The Queen,' he says. 'The Queen then Irene Young. Irene Young then the Queen.'

'That's probably treason,' she says. 'Oh Bobby, we pulled it off, didn't we?'

'Couldn't have been better,' he says. 'The newspaper man was fair away with it all. It'll be in Friday's paper, he said. We're a great team, you and I.'

'We are,' she says, and leans in against him so that he can put his arm around her and hold her close. 'What do you think they're doing now, at the castle?'

'I imagine they're talking about what a swell evening that was,' Bobby says.

'Yes,' Rena says. 'Yes, that's exactly what they're doing. Let's drink another toast, Bobby. To us. To our success.'

The sound of their glasses chiming together rings out through the banqueting room, as loud to Rena as if the bells of the town are finally ringing in their honour.

Rena, 1966

When Rena sweeps into the kitchen at Edzell Place, one eye on her watch because her taxi will nearly be there, she sees Janet hunched over the kitchen table, in danger of dipping her school tie in her toast and marmalade as she scribbles a final bit of homework.

'Do sit up straight, Janet,' Rena says. 'Or you'll end up with a dowager's hump like your nana.'

'All right, Jenny,' Bobby calls, 'Are you ready to go?'

'I'll just get my blazer,' Janet says, closing her jotter and stuffing a final piece of toast into her mouth.

'Are you going to get her to school on time?' Rena asks.

Bobby winks. 'If I get a good clear road I will.'

Rena shakes her head. 'Well, don't drive too fast. And remember to check that they've monogrammed the napkins, will you?'

'Of course. Anything else we need? I might hang around and bring her home again this afternoon.'

'Good idea.' Now that their daughter is in her last year at school Rena is more and more concerned about where she is and who she's with. 'You could see if they've new Empire tatties in any of the farms,' Rena tells Bobby. 'They're always popular on the menu. And while you're at it, find out what they're doing for a bar lunch in that hotel by the racecourse. I keep hearing about it.'

Bobby sidles up and slips his arm around her. 'Why don't you come with me? We haven't had a day together in ages.'

'I've got to get the wages done for Thursday and the suppliers paid,' Rena says. 'Next week though, let's go somewhere nice next week. Troon, maybe.' There's a dress shop in Troon that she's fond of, and a good one for shoes as well. A horn honks outside. 'That'll be my taxi. What've you to remember?'

'Napkins.'

'And?'

'Not to drive too fast.'

'And?'

'Tatties and bar lunch.'

'Good.'

The sun is shining when Rena steps out of her taxi outside the hotel, and she pauses to whip out her handkerchief and rub it over the brass plaque that says *Ossington Hotel, Proprietors Mr & Mrs Young* until she's satisfied that it's gleaming. The shop, Annanhill, the Bantam Tearooms, and now this. It's funny how time concertinas. It's yesterday and a lifetime ago that she and Thomas were weighing tea and slicing bacon, stocktaking tins and balancing books, kids playing at shops until, by force of will, they made it work for their family. And yet here she is, with a daughter of seventeen and her name on a brass plaque outside the smartest hotel in town.

'Any post?' she calls to Malcolm, who's just getting

ready to go home. He's been night-portering for them during the long Easter break from that art school of his. Well, they can't exactly let him near the customers with that hair, can they?

'Here you go, Auntie Irene,' he says, then, 'I like your dress. Very groovy.'

'Thank you, Malcolm,' she says, smoothing the fabric. 'One of the new Paris fashions from Hourston's.'

'The colours really set off your hair,' he says, which is exactly why she chose the swirling pattern of green, gold and red. The lengths of current styles might not always be to her taste, but she does like the bright colours. Trust Malcolm to notice. Bobby picked up on it first, their nephew being a queer, but at least that means there won't be any unwanted pregnancies. Evie won't hear of it, of course, nothing perverted about her son, but Thomas can tell, Rena's sure. That's why they don't get along. That and the hair, of course, though he's stopped at shoulder length and does keeps it clean.

'You're a real flatterer,' she says, picking up the diary from the desk before heading down to the kitchen for her breakfast as usual. The run of bookings that came after the de Walden dinner is still going. *Betterave gelée* is all the rage, now. At least Malcolm's studies are an excuse for him not going with girls. Though on reflection, Rena finds it hard to be disgusted by the idea of a man who doesn't bother women about sex all the time. All he has to do is make sure he doesn't get arrested. Once he's finished with this art school nonsense he can marry a decent girl and nobody will be any the wiser.

'Smells good, Ugo,' she says, reaching for her cereal. She'd rather a bacon roll any day, but this dress from Paris is a size up from her usual. Maybe she should go back to Meikle, see if he can give her something. The weight fairly dropped off her when she was taking his pep pills, and her current prescription seems to have the opposite effect.

'Vichysoisse,' Ugo says, handing her a spoon.

'Mmm, delicious.' She dips into the simmering soup, making sure she gets plenty of potato. She could eat a bowlful right now, but will resist until lunchtime at least.

'We could ice it, in this weather,' Ugo suggests.

'Oh good God no. We'll only have folk sending it back,' she says. 'And it's only Easter. Even in a heatwave I'm not sure you can serve cold soup before June.' She looks questioningly at Ugo, but he's in a bit of a huff. She strikes on a compromise of sorts. 'How about some small butter croutons? They were so elegant when you did them for the *Potage Crécy*.'

Ugo sighs and nods. His head has swollen since the success of the dinner. She's raised his wages, but has to keep an eye on him. They almost got into hot water over the sweetbreads on the high tea menu. Honestly. Rena loves her food and she'll try anything once, but sometimes a cold tongue salad is as far as it needs to go. When she's finished her bowl of husky, tasteless cereal she goes to the office, trying not to think about the soup with croutons she might have for lunch. With just the smallest swirl of cream.

At the top of the bundle of mail there's a postcard from Min and Donald, who are on their annual trip around the Highlands looking for bargains that can be cleaned up and quadrupled in price. *Holiday Time in Fort William*, it says, but it looks a bit bleak to Rena. After the weekend they all spent in London together, she feels like spreading her wings further. They took Janet to see the changing of the guard, and Donald agreed to Harrods if Min didn't buy anything, but then she insisted on going into Liberty's as well. Those inlaid sideboards. Maybe one day. And now that Bobby has driven to London, she's coaxed him into promising to drive to Italy as well. She doesn't like the idea of flying and, surprisingly, neither does he. Rome, the sights and all the people in cafés on the pavements, all their stylish clothes. After the postcard she opens a letter expressing *sincere gratitude for all your efforts to ensure our daughter's wedding was a memorable day*. She checks the name. Ah yes, it could have been memorable for quite the wrong reasons. She recalls the mother of the groom's insistence that her elder son was 'just having a wee lie down' when in fact he was flat out on the pavement outside as if he had every intention of losing them their hard-won license. Bobby had to get the best man to take his feet and help carry him up to an empty bedroom. And that with a cash bar as well.

Bills, bills, bills. She files them in the in-tray to go through with Bobby the next day. For all they're making money, it's expensive to do things properly and there's a limit to what people will pay here. The final letter comes with the Corporation's stamp on the envelope. Rena imagines for a moment a Provost's dinner, then realises it's probably more to do with the work that's beginning in the town centre. You can hardly walk down the street without there being a man there measuring or photographing something. She knew they were going to remodel the slums, but they're all over the Cross and Duke Street too.

When she opens the letter she shuffles the two pages again, and again, unable to take in the words or the sense of it. Inside her that feeling of spinning, being out of control. Her heart, her chest, her breath coming fast and tight. Her handbag is beside her, her tablets right there. 'One for a normal episode, two in extremis,' Meikle told her. 'It's symptomatic of your age, Mrs Young.' She fumbles with the lid and swills one tablet back with her tea. Closes her eyes until she can take a deep breath. Not steady, not at all, but at least the oxygen is getting in. Then she gets up, almost knocking her chair over, and clutching the letter, she hurries outside and around the corner.

Pursuant to the licensing act of the previous year, the Fifty Waistcoats is permitted to serve alcohol from eight until ten on account of the night shifts at the whisky bonds. When Rena walks through the door and sees a handful of men standing at the bar, half pints in their hands, she has a horrid surge of recollection of that day she took Janet in her pram and went looking for Bobby. But she's a different woman now, and she stands up straight and says to the glum-looking man behind the counter, 'Good morning. I need to see Mr MacWhinnie, please.'

'Went to the shop twenty minutes ago and hasnae come back,' the man says, pointing to his right. 'Can I tell him who's looking for him?'

'Mrs Young from the Ossington,' Rena says. 'But it's all right. I'll go and find him myself.'

Victor Caldera's nephew proved a dilettante, and his cousin Giorgio now runs the shop and rents what was the tearoom to another cousin, who runs a dance school there. Rena goes to him still to buy coffee, and Giorgio's wife even persuaded her to have a go with spaghetti but really, she can't shake the memory of Hetty's vile macaroni boiled in milk. Ugo did promise to make it for her with a meat sauce at some point, but in his current mood who knows when that'll be. Outside she catches a glimpse of the headline written on one of the boards: *Lord Rowallan Divorce Scandal!*

Sure enough, inside the shop MacWhinnie the publican is holding a letter just like Rena's. 'My grandfather was the license-holder when it was the Railway Tavern,' he's saying. 'It's been in the family for near on a hundred year.'

Giorgio has his arm around his wife, who is holding a handkerchief to her face. 'Oh, Mrs Young, our shop!' she cries, when she sees Rena.

'What's the meaning of this?' Rena says. 'Compulsory purchase order?'

'I never thought they'd touch the hotel,' MacWhinnie says to Giorgio. 'And all for a bloody one-way system. Essential modernisation works my arse.' He looks at his feet and mutters, 'It's not right, I tell you.'

Although Rena finds MacWhinnie a bit coarse, she can't help but agree with his assessment. It's not right. She looks more closely at the letter. *A drawing of the new street layout may be viewed in the council offices.* It's signed on behalf of the development committee – and there are their names, Minto and Gibson and all the others – by Mr MacPherson, head of the planning department.

'That bloody man,' Rena says. 'I should have known.'

'What can we do?' says Giorgio.

MacWhinnie sighs. 'They're not asking for opinions, or objections, are they? It's compulsory. A done deal.'

'Nothing's a done deal,' Rena says, exasperated at the way people here just accept things as if there are those that know better. MacWhinnie might be pushing sixty, but if his family has been there a hundred years why isn't he spoiling for a fight? Her tablets are working now, and she knows that she needs to find Bobby. They need to do something before all that they've worked for falls through their fingers.

Bobby, 1966

Bobby knows he's a man capable of many things, but there have been times when he has reached his limit. This isn't one of them. Right now, he would kill to sort this out. If only it was as easy as sticking a knife between a man's ribs or shooting him dead. It's half past one in the afternoon and Rena has taken to her bed. Bobby has never been so frightened, it seems to him now. His heart isn't sitting right in his chest, and as soon as one cigarette burns down he lights another. Day was, he could have drunk this feeling all away. Day was, he had nothing to lose.

On the kitchen table in front of him lies a clipping from the newspaper. Left carelessly, within half an inch of a coffee ring, when usually Rena keeps it pressed safe in her photo album. A description of de Walden's visit, of the tenantry entertained. *Mr and Mrs Young, the manager and his wife, put their best foot foremost to make the tables most attractive… the silver candelabra, specially sent from London, and the floral decorations gave the Ossington a magnificence seldom seen in Kilmarnock.* No photo of the hotel, which disappointed

Rena, but a candid shot of the Hon. Hazel receiving her silverware from her subjects. Good-looking but horsey, as those types always are, in a fancy brocade frock. And Christ, there he is thinking of Evie again. For someone who has fucked up so much, and got away with it, how could he have fucked up so badly this time?

'Can't you buy us out of this?' Rena said, when she showed him the letter. 'There must be a way.' But Bobby can't think of a way, can't think of anything except what he's found out by asking around. *It's Bobby here, Bobby Young. Talk to me.* Folk talked, in the end, enough for him to piece it together. Roderick Blair has invested in Buchanan the builder's business, and Buchanan the builder has gone into roads, just in the nick of time for the Corporation's development contract to land on his doorstep. A contract proposed by Minto, Gibson and the rest, with that cunt MacPherson at the helm, that will steer its course through the town centre, the Cross and all round about, smashing everything in its path including the Ossington Hotel. Christ, Bobby thinks, he dealt cards for these men, poured them whisky and made donations to their so-called charities.

'Bribe them some more,' Rena said. 'If they're crooked, that's the only language they understand.'

Oh Rena, Rena. Of course they're crooked, every last widow's son of them. He lent Blair the money, high on the success of the de Walden dinner, greedy on the promise of greater things to come. Well, they've come all right, but not the way he expected. Did Blair even look at the plans? Perhaps not; the man has no eye for detail, that's why he loses so badly at cards. Bobby knows Blair is sly but he can't believe he'd stiff him like this. Either way, he'd better watch his back.

'It's too big for that, Rena my love,' he told her, although she knew it already, he could tell. She'd gone to the office and looked at the plans. Six of them on the committee and every one of them will be due a kickback when the new buildings go up. The parade of shops and the bus station, the car park and the pedestrian mall.

'I don't understand,' she said. 'How can they do it? Why would they rip the heart out of the town?'

Bobby has an answer to that, and the answer is greed. He's no stranger to it himself, why else would he have lent Blair the money? And neither is Rena. Would she ever forgive him, if she knew? He crushes both his hands into fists, wishes he could stop the thoughts that are threatening to burst out of his head. Of falling overboard, of drowning. He steps softly, although the carpet in the hallway is thick and plush, and goes through to the bedroom. If Rena is awake, maybe they can pull together and tackle this.

The curtains are half-closed but the afternoon light is still strong enough to make Rena's hair blaze against the white seersucker pillowcase. Her face is pale, and over her lies a dark fur jacket, one arm stretched down over her legs. It has been remodelled to a shorter style, but it is unmistakeably the musquash he saw her in that February in Sauchiehall Street, when he hadn't even a coat on his back. She is still the woman he married. Still the only person on God's earth that can save him. There's a glass of water by the bed and a small bottle of tablets from Dr Meikle. His heart gives an almighty lurch and he stoops to check her breath. In, out, in, out. As peaceful as anything. Not like that day with Anne, way back, when all he could do was pray that she wasn't still breathing. The worst thing he's ever seen, and he's seen a lot.

The sleek fur is tucked under Rena's chin and her eyelids are closed so firmly, not even a flutter beneath them, that it takes him a moment to picture the brightness in her grey-blue eyes. His chest is sore for the love of her, and his body feels heavy with the weight of all his memories of their times together, everything they've overcome. It's been worth every struggle, every lonely warehouse meet and every night time drive, every envelope of cash and every hour of hard bloody graft. There's no way to appeal. The recompense they'll get is less than they paid the Trustees, and wasn't that conveniently timed? Even so, can't they pick themselves up once again? That's why Bobby is scared though. Because Rena has always been a fighter, and now she's lying there quiet and still in the middle of the day, and he doesn't know what to do.

Janet, 1966

Janet is wearing a teal knit dress from Young Jaeger. Sleeveless, and a bit smart for working in the hotel bar, but it's a birthday present from her mother, who insisted Janet put it on for her first shift. *What's the point in saving things for good?* Rena's the kind of shopper who leaves the store wearing the shoes she's just bought, and she likes it when others share her enthusiasm, Janet has found. Rena herself is in sharp green tailoring, softened by a warm waft that's half Chanel No. 5 and half Benson & Hedges. Her strawberry blonde curls are newly set and her diamond rings are sparkling. Something's going on, but Janet doesn't know what it is. She's used to the infectious buzz of her mother's adrenaline, the rush and bustle that surrounds an important function. Instead, Rena is gliding along as though she's insulated from the world around her. As Janet hurries up the kitchen stairs with more sliced lemons her mother sails past as if the tray laden with silver coffee pots she has in her hands weighs nothing. When Janet goes into the lounge she sees that her father has stepped behind the bar to cover for her. He plunges his own empty glass into the sink as soon as he spots her.

'Look at you,' he says, and she can hear the alcohol in his voice. 'Tell me about the haircut again.'

'It's Vidal Sassoon,' Janet says. 'Well, inspired by. Evelyn took me to Morgenthaler's.'

'The son does these modern styles, doesn't he?' he says. 'But some things don't change. It'll be the fur coat next, eh?'

'When I'm twenty-one, Mum says.' Janet thinks of the silkiness of her cousin's silver mink jacket. It's soft and cold, but a little ghastly to touch as well, when you think about it. Not that anything looks ghastly on Evelyn.

'Your mother knows what's what,' Bobby says, vaguely. His suit is pressed, and he's clean-shaven as always, but he seems distracted. He runs his hands over his hair and she notices that his skin has a grey tinge to it too. But then he puts his arm around her and squeezes her close, smiles. 'She's got class. And so do you. Like mother, like daughter.' He looks at his watch. 'You'll be staying here tonight?'

'Yes,' Janet says, stepping forward to pour another half pint for Mr Murphy from the furniture shop. 'I'd rather that than wait up until you've both finished.'

'Take one for yourself,' Murphy says, and she thanks him and counts enough change for a gin and bitter lemon into the jar. Always go for a dear one, her father told her, if it looks like you can get away with it. If not, the price of a half of shandy's better than a poke in the eye with a burnt stick.

'Yes, it'll be a late one through there,' Bobby says, lighting a cigarette. 'Silver wedding. You'll be better off upstairs.'

However her father phrases it, Janet knows that the truth is that she isn't allowed to be alone in the house at night, not even now that she's turned eighteen. One day soon she'll get away from the stifling propriety of this too-small town, but tonight she doesn't mind. She's slept in the hotel so often over the years that the small room in the attic sometimes feels more homely than her room at Edzell Place. Much cosier to have breakfast in the hotel kitchen with Alma and whoever is working the early shift.

Bobby looks at his watch again and sighs. 'Pop off now, if you like. I'll call time.' He rings the bell on the bar, and a couple of people get up to order a last drink before closing. 'Oh, and could you take two more bottles of Red Label through to your mother before you go? There's a few with a thirst on.'

Janet nods and takes two bottles down from the gantry. 'Goodnight,' she calls, and goes through to reception. The after-dinner speeches must be over, as the noise from the function room has risen. She slips along the corridor and through the swing door, delivering the whisky to the small bar in the corner of the room. It's full of smoke and chatter, and the tables have been moved and the carpet rolled back to reveal the dancefloor. The three-piece band are taking to the stage.

'Ah, there you are, Janet.' Her mother rests a hand on her shoulder and Janet turns. 'This is my daughter,' Rena says to the man beside her.

'A pleasure,' he says. His face is blooming with alcohol, and for a horrid moment Janet thinks he's going to lean in for a kiss but no, it's just that he's swayed forward more than he intended. He leans back.

'This is Mr Douglas from the Rotary,' Rena says. 'One of our oldest and dearest customers.'

'It's a crying shame, if you ask me,' he says, clasping Rena's hand before setting a course for the bar.

Janet doesn't ask what he's talking about. She can guess, and besides, drunk men witter on. Serving behind the bar will hold few surprises on that score, she thinks. Her mother stands there, gazing around the room. The empties are starting to accumulate on the table nearest to them, and Janet knows that her mother can never bear to see work left undone.

'Shall I help with the clearing?' she asks.

Rena pats her hair gently, although it's perfect already. 'You should have seen this place when we first moved in,' she says. 'The state of it.'

'Was it awful?' Janet asks, although she knows that it was. She's heard about it before.

'Mice.' Rena lowers her voice and turns to look at her. Is that the glint of a tear in her eye? Janet can't tell. 'It was overrun. How Hetty screamed, when we brought her in to see it and one ran over her foot. That, and the dirt, and the light fittings hanging from the wall. And the carpet. You wouldn't believe the state of the carpet.'

They stand for a moment, watching as the first couples take to the dancefloor. It sounds as if the band is attempting Gene Pitney, but Janet can't be sure.

'Dad's rung time in the lounge,' Janet says.

'Has he?'

Janet nods. 'Are you sure you don't need a hand with anything through here?'

'Did you see what they wrote in the newspaper?' Rena says. 'After the big party?'

'Um…' Janet curses her reflex to hesitate, to um and ah. Her mother usually picks up on it, but not now, not tonight.

'We left the candelabra on the last table lit, after everyone had gone home. A magnificence seldom seen in the town, that's what they said.'

'It was beautiful,' Janet says. She and Hetty had come in to see the banqueting hall all set up, and her mother had directed her as she took photograph after photograph. They haven't been developed yet.

'It was,' Rena says. 'Are you sleeping here tonight?'

'Yes.'

'We'll be here until the wee small hours getting this cleared, I should think, and there's only four rooms in. Did you say that your father had rung time?'

'Yes.'

Rena nods. 'I wish…'

Whatever her mother wishes Janet will never know, as a man has tripped on a chair leg and upset a tray of drinks and there's glass all over the floor. Alma hurries out from behind the bar with the dustpan and brush.

'Oh for Heaven's sake,' Rena says. 'Is it too much to ask that there not be a mishap? Open the doors again to get the air circulating, will you? The perspiration's dripping off me.'

Janet does as she's told, pushing the heavy doors back against their hinges until they catch and stick open. She thinks again of the thickening in her father's voice, her mother's shade of melancholy. Is this really the last function they will hold in the hotel? It's hard to imagine. Who are her parents when they aren't dressed for the evening? Before her father adjusts the lapel of his dinner suit, or her mother slips her feet into her high-heeled court shoes? All the rest is rehearsal.

Janet is climbing the stairs to the attic rooms when she feels her stomach rumbling. It always does when she's anxious, and besides, she realises that it's hours since she's eaten. And it was lamb tonight. There are bound to be cold slices put aside for tomorrow's high tea, and Ugo won't grudge her just a couple with a good sprinkling of salt for her supper. She turns and goes back down, running her hand along the smooth wooden banister of the main staircase. Her mother had brass studs put in it, to stop any children sliding down as she did when she was younger. As she turns on the landing she hears a noise, something soft and heavy slumping onto the parquet below. Not wanting to have to deal with any of the party guests, especially those who are blotto, she hunches down and peers through the spindles into the lobby. The first thing she sees is a bottle of Johnnie Walker resting on its side on the floor. Black Label, her father's favourite. The noise from the function seems to fade and Janet can feel the blood pulsing in her ears as she moves down two steps and looks beyond the bottle to where she can now see her father, lying in the middle of the polished parquet floor.

Just then her mother sweeps out of the function room, her professional smile wide across her face. Everything staggers into slow motion. Rena doesn't falter. Like an actress returning for her curtain call she turns back towards the function room and Janet sees her incline her head towards a group of guests, and them raise their glasses to her in return. Rena gives a jolly wave before she snaps the heavy doors closed.

The band's music distorts. Janet finds that she has come down the last few stairs and is standing in the hall. She stoops and picks up the bottle of Black Label, tucks it behind the brass pot of the aspidistra. When she looks up again her mother's face has changed. The delicate powder is still there, the blush on her pale cheeks, but the smile has gone, and with it a mask has fallen away. Janet slows down, as if the floor is coated in treacle, as if she shouldn't be here, seeing this. Rena sinks to her knees and reaches towards Bobby's face, his wrist. He's lying on his side, and Janet can't see if his eyes are open. A strange keening noise breaks from her mother's throat, and Janet hears her say her father's name.

'Bobby…'

Janet walks past, towards the reception desk, even though there's a great mass aching inside her chest, her stomach, her head. Actions speak louder than words, that's what Rena always says, and Janet knows what to do. She will telephone for an ambulance, and then for her two uncles. The family. She will run and catch Ugo before he goes home, and he will help move her father into the office. Janet doesn't know if he's breathing, she realises. She has to force herself to exhale and draw air into her own lungs. Once the calls are made, she will stand up straight, and go back into the function room. Nobody will be any the wiser. Nobody's evening will be disturbed. Janet doesn't know how to comfort her mother, there hasn't been a chance for her to find out, but for once she knows for certain what Rena would want. If this is the last party that will send laughter and music into the rafters of the Ossington Hotel, the last time whisky and tears will soak into its floorboards, then it will come off beautifully.

Rena, 1966

Here they are, just the two of them. Rena can still hear the band but they seem distant, too distant to make out what song they're attempting. Voices raise in a cheer, laughter mingles with the music. She can see Ugo's back through the reception hatch. He's still in his whites, ready to deflect any wandering guests, waiting to usher the ambulancemen through to the office. Next to Rena, Bobby is lying on the night porter's couch, tie removed, shirt loosened. Her knees are aching, and she shifts to sit down on the rug, legs folded awkwardly to one side. Why didn't they ever replace it, she wonders, poking her fingers under some exposed weft threads. It's done, really. With the other hand she holds Bobby's wrist lightly. The pulse is hard to feel but his chest is rising and falling weakly. She takes his silk pocket square and dabs the sweat from his brow, stroking his hair back into place afterwards.

'The ambulance is coming,' she says. 'It's going to be fine.'

Her voice sounds unfamiliar, as if she's merely moving her mouth while a ventriloquist is speaking. She puts her hand on Bobby's chest, tentatively, and his eyes jerk open and then close again. He moves his lips.

'Ugo,' she hisses. 'Fetch water, will you?'

Ugo can't hear her so she has to call louder. Bobby stirs again. 'Bobby, it's me, I'm here,' she says.

For a split second, there's an answering pressure in her hand, but it fades so quickly that she isn't sure if she imagined it. Bobby is moving his lips again.

'What is it?' She leans closer.

'Money,' he says.

She shakes her head. If he's confused, if he doesn't remember that it's too late for favours, or special arrangements, she won't tell him now. There's a magazine under the couch, she notices. On the back is an advertisement for Red Label. *The luck of the Scotch.* She slides it out of sight.

Ugo opens the door and hands her a glass of water. 'Where is that bloody ambulance?' she says.

'I'll look out on the street,' he says. 'It must be here soon.'

The hospital is ten minutes' walk away, but Bobby can't walk. He can't even speak, although he seems to be trying. She dips her finger in the water, moistens his lips.

'Air,' he says, and she looks around helplessly. There's no window in the room, and she can feel only a whisper of cool from Ugo going out the front door. She unbuttons Bobby's shirt a little further, retrieves the magazine and starts fanning him with it. The man in the advert looks as if he's raising his glass of whisky to his lips again and again.

'Blair,' Bobby says.

'Ssh,' she says, 'Don't try to speak.'

He opens his eyes again, looks at her urgently. 'Blair.'

His eyelids quiver as if it's an effort to keep them open.

There's something, she realises. She doesn't understand, but there's something he's trying to say. Something he needs to tell her.

'Blair?' she repeats.

'Money,' he says again and then closes his eyes. His breath is coming in ragged gasps now. Whatever it is, a gambling debt, a kickback for the dinner, it doesn't matter now. She tries to tell Bobby that but he's agitated, his free hand is fluttering. She leans right in until she feels his breath on her ear, and he whispers it clear as day: 'He… owes… us.'

The front door crashes open and a gust of cold air swirls around them. Thomas bursts in, followed by Ugo. 'Get up, Rena, we'll get him in the back of my car.'

She grabs her handbag and hurries after them. Janet is standing in the foyer, holding open Rena's musquash as though she is a departing guest. Rena slips her arms into its cold silk lining and waves a hand helplessly towards the function room doors.

'It's fine,' Janet says. 'Ugo will stay. It'll all be fine.'

Rena clutches her daughter's arm then runs on, clattering out onto the pavement, towards the passenger side of Thomas's car. Up on Langland's Brae, the railway station clock glows implacable on its tower. She turns her back on it and stands for a second in the darkness while her brother settles Bobby on the back seat of the car. John Finnie Street stretches downhill ahead of her, in the distance the Post Office and the Linen Bank, then the Co-operative and the Oddfellows Hall, the Laigh Mission and the Kilmarnock Club, right up to the Operetta House and the Ossington Hotel. All the lights of the town glitter below her.

AUTHOR'S NOTE

The Ossington Hotel and the Bantam Tea Rooms were real places. Annanhill House and the Bungalow Stores still exist, though in very different incarnations than they appear here. My characters are fictional but several of them have their roots in real people, and much of their story is drawn from fact. Every detail of the de Walden dinner menu is correct, but Roderick Blair is entirely made up. Nevertheless, by the mid-1960s plans were proposed to redevelop Kilmarnock's town centre to accommodate more cars, and in the early 1970s many of its historic streets were demolished. John Finnie Street, and the building that was once the Ossington Coffee Tavern and then the Ossington Hotel, escaped.

This is one of a few small liberties I've taken with history, dates, or geography. The British Newspaper Archive was particularly useful for unpicking the intricacies of licensing applications and the hospitality industry in Kilmarnock. Quotes and figures relating to these are as reported at the time. Various useful details came from the websites of the Mitchell Library, Future Museum, the Imperial War Museum and the BBC WW2 People's War. I had access to private photographs, clippings and papers, and recollections of many stories I heard or half-heard growing up, tantalisingly incomplete.

I owe thanks to several organisations and individuals for their support during the writing of this book. I worked on sections while on a Fellowship at the International Writing Program of the University of Iowa, during a wonderful residency at Cove Park, and on a Scottish Writer's Fellowship organised by the University of Otago and hosted at the Pah Homestead. I am very grateful for these opportunities. My colleagues at the Creative Writing Programme at University of Glasgow are the best that I could hope for, and I am also indebted to Kirsteen McCue, Alan Riach, Wayne Price, and Jane McKie. David Miller was not just an agent but a dear friend, and his enthusiasm for an earlier draft was more important than he could know. I miss him and appreciate all the help Sam Copeland has given me. My role as Patron of the Imprint Festival in East Ayrshire keeps me close to the Dick Institute, which wasn't my first library (I think that was Longpark) but was certainly the most inspirational and formative. Everyone at Blackwater Press has been fantastic, but special thanks to John Reid for a truly engaged and enjoyable edit! Minnie the cat's support takes the shape of inveterate and unrepentant sitting-on of manuscripts, while my partner Louise Welsh is my first reader, my best friend and my love, always.

Printed in Dunstable, United Kingdom